SPOTSYLVANIA COUNTY

A Civil War Romance

NIKKI STODDARD SCHOFIELD

authorHOUSE®

AuthorHouse™
1663 Liberty Drive
Bloomington, IN 47403
www.authorhouse.com
Phone: 833-262-8899

Published by AuthorHouse 08/30/2021

ISBN: 978-1-6655-3656-1 (sc)
ISBN: 978-1-6655-3657-8 (hc)
ISBN: 978-1-6655-3658-5 (e)

Library of Congress Control Number: 2021917527

Print information available on the last page.

Any people depicted in stock imagery provided by Getty Images are models, and such images are being used for illustrative purposes only. Certain stock imagery © Getty Images.

This book is printed on acid-free paper.

Because of the dynamic nature of the Internet, any web addresses or links contained in this book may have changed since publication and may no longer be valid. The views expressed in this work are solely those of the author and do not necessarily reflect the views of the publisher, and the publisher hereby disclaims any responsibility for them.

Scripture quotations marked KJV are from the Holy Bible, King James Version (Authorized Version). First published in 1611. Quoted from the KJV Classic Reference Bible, Copyright © 1983 by The Zondervan Corporation.

Set your minds on things that are above,
not on things that are on earth.
-- Colossians 3:2
(New Revised Standard Version)

Dedicated to
Rev. Mark McClintock
Pastor of
Speedway Baptist Church,
2986 Moller Road
Indianapolis, Indiana 46224.
He advises and inspires me
to use my gift of writing;
And to
Mary Donahue
(1945- 2020)
She not only proofread an early draft
of this novel, but often inquired
about my progress in revising,
thus encouraging me to
continue this work of writing.

CONTENTS

HISTORIC NOVELS

By Nikki Stoddard Schofield

Alas, Richmond (2011)
A recent widow rents a room to a Union spy in the capital of the Confederacy and they fall in love as the city falls.

Treason Afoot (2013)
The Indianapolis Treason Trials take place while a bookstore owner suffers battle fatigue and provides shelter for a schoolteacher from Danville, Indiana.

Savannah Bound (2014)
An English woman and an escapee from Andersonville Prison share a mansion in Savannah, Georgia, as the Union Army blazes a trail toward the city.

Confederates in Canada (2016)
When Confederates set fire to a hotel in New York City, the heroine rescues the hero, and they take two orphans to their grandparents in Guelph, Canada.

Washington City Citadel (2017)
A Union doctor from Edinburgh, Scotland, marries a nurse from Alexandria, Virginia, and shares his boardinghouse in Washington City during the final year of the war.

CAST OF CHARACTERS BY CHAPTER

Characters are listed in the order in which they speak. Historic characters have an asterisk before their names. Ranks of soldiers are given as they were at the time of this story. If a person was still alive in 1864, his or her year of death is not given. Only those people who have speaking parts are listed below.

CHAPTER ONE: SOLDIER AT THE CLOTHESLINE
Bradby Tucker, born 1839, reporter for the *New York Times*

Paxton Faulconer, hero, born 1840 in Gordonsville, Orange County, Virginia, Confederate Captain, Company C, 13ᵗʰ Virginia, Scout for the Army of Northern Virginia

Albany Anne Trubridge, alias Albert Cook, heroine, born 1844 in Spotsylvania County, Virginia, daughter of Shedrick and Luciana Trubridge

Susa Pinkney, born about 1841, slave of the Trubridge family

Audine Cook Trubridge, born 1799, grandmother of Albany, mother of Shedrick

Greenup Fortier, born 1841, reporter for the *Richmond Examiner*

*Robert Edward Lee, born 1807, Confederate General in command of the Army of Northern Virginia

Coffer Dunn, born about 1832, slave of the Trubridge family

Gerow Gately, born 1838, wounded Union Lieutenant with the Topographical Engineers, Third Ohio

CHAPTER TWO: IN THE GUISE OF A MAN
Luciana Trubridge, born 1820, wife of Shedrick, mother of Albany

Shedrick Trubridge, born 1818, husband of Luciana, father of Albany

CHAPTER THREE: A BLIND CONFEDERATE

*Bill, birth year unknown, runaway slave, servant to General Grant

*Adam Badeau, born 1831, Lieutenant Colonel, Aide-de-Camp to General Grant

*Horace Porter, born 1837, Lieutenant Colonel, Aide-de-Camp to General Grant

*Ulysses S. Grant, born 1822, Commander-in-Chief of the Armies of the United States

*Peter Couse, resident of Spotsylvania County

*Henry Heth, born 1825, Confederate General

*Cadmus Marcellus Wilcox, born 1824, Confederate General

*Ambrose Powell Hill, born 1825, Lieutenant General in command of the Third Corps, Army of Northern Virginia

CHAPTER FOUR: IT'S LONGSTREET

*James Ewell Brown "J.E.B." Stuart, born 1833, Confederate General and cavalry leader

Grandon Faulconer, born 1848, brother of Paxton, wagon driver for the C.S.A.

Ainsley Bracken, private, wagon driver, partner of Grandon Faulconer

*James Longstreet, born 1821, Lieutenant General of the First Corps, Army of Northern Virginia

*Gilbert Moxley Sorrel, born 1838, Confederate Lieutenant Colonel, First Corps

Thornton Faulconer, born 1838, brother of Paxton, private, Company C, 13th Virginia

*Micah Jenkins, born 1835, Brigadier General in the Confederate Army; fatally shot on May 6, 1864, in the Wilderness

CHAPTER FIVE: THE BLACKENED CLEARING

CHAPTER SIX: A WILDERNESS OF WOE

CHAPTER SEVEN: GETTYSBURG REVERSED

*Martin Thomas McMahon, born 1838, Union Lieutenant Colonel

*John Sedgwick, 1813-1864, Union Major General, commander of the VI Corps

Eliza Edgerton, nurse at Chimborazo Hospital and friend of Luciana Trubridge

CHAPTER EIGHT: EMORY UPTON'S BOLD PLAN

*Emory Upton, born 1839, Union General

Statesman Prather, birth year unknown, slave of Myers Chesterton, husband of Liney

Liney Prather, birth year unknown, slave of Myers Chesterton, wife of Statesman

Florence Chesterton, born 1851, daughter of Myers and Madelyn

Forrester Chesterton, born 1848, son of Myers and Madelyn

Blake Chesterton, born 1853, twin, son of Myers and Madelyn

Drake Chesterton, born 1853, twin, son of Myers and Madelyn

CHAPTER NINE: THE SEVERED HEAD

Melora Faulconer, born 1816, wife of Evandon, mother of five children

Evandon Faulconer, born 1814, printer, husband of Melora, father of five children

CHAPTER TEN: THE BLOODY ANGLE

Angus Mintzer, doctor from Philadelphia working at the Trubridge house

*Edward "Alleghany" Johnson, born 1816, Confederate General

*Winfield Scott Hancock, born 1824, Union General

*George Hume Steuart, born 1828, Confederate General

CHAPTER ELEVEN: IMPRISOMENT IN THE TOWER

*Edward Ferrero, born 1831, Brigadier General in the Union Army, commander of a Negro division in the Ninth Corps

Wilfred Davies, private in Negro division in the Ninth Corps

CHAPTER TWELVE: ALL THE HOSTS OF HELL

Eleutheros Supplee, born about 1839, slave and preacher

Oliver Frankinberry, companion of Thornton Faulconer

Biglor Bibb, typesetter at *Gordonsville Gazette*

Eunice Faulconer, born 1846, daughter of Melora and Evandon, nurse

* * *

CHRONOLOGY OF HISTORIC EVENTS IN 1864

May 3 --   Advance forces of the Union Army of the Potomac left winter quarters

May 4 --   Army of the Potomac crossed the Rapidan River thus beginning the Overland Campaign

May 4-5 --   Confederate First Corps marched all night to reach the battlefield

May 5-6 --   Battle of the Wilderness

May 5 --   Battle in Saunders Field

May 6 --   Confederate Brigadier-General Gilbert Moxley Sorrel's flank attack

May 6 --   Confederates accidentally shot two of their own commanders, Generals Jenkins and Longstreet

May 7-8 --   During the night, hundreds of men suffocated or burned to death

May 8 --   Battle of Spotsylvania Court House began

May 7-8 --   Cavalry battle at Todd's Tavern

May 8 --   Battle of Laurel Hill

May 8 --   Inadvertent creation of the salient at the Bloody Angle

May 8 --   Generals Phil Sheridan and George Meade had a bitter argument

May 9 --   Union General John Sedgwick killed

May 10 --   Breakthrough at the Mule Shoe by Union Colonel Emory Upton

May 11-12 -- Night of heavy rains

May 11 --   Battle of Yellow Tavern; James Ewell Brown Stuart mortally wounded

May 11 --   General Grant wired General Halleck that he planned "to fight it out on this line if it takes all summer"

May 11 --   General Lee had artillery removed from the Mule Shoe

May 12 --   Battle at the Mule Shoe called Bloody Angle

May 12 --   Confederate General James Ewell Brown Stuart died at 7:38 p.m. in Richmond, Virginia

May 13 --   General Grant recommended George Meade and William Sherman for promotion to the ranks of major-generals

May 13 --   General Lee moved his men out of the Mule Shoe

May 14-17 -- Relatively quiet on the battlefield

May 15 --   United States Colored Troops confronted the Army of Northern Virginia in battle for the first time

May 17 --   Sun shone after five and a half days of rain

May 18 --   Final assault on Spotsylvania Court House

May 19 --   Battle of Harris' Farm fought

May 21 --   Battle of Spotsylvania Court House ended

May 22 --   General Grant issued the order to move south

* * *

CHAPTER ONE

SOLDIER AT THE CLOTHESLINE

Wednesday, May 4, 1864

Well before dawn on Wednesday morning, May 4th, 1864, recently-appointed Commander-in-Chief of all Union armies, Lieutenant General Ulysses S. Grant, directed the Army of the Potomac to cross the Rapidan River, a major tributary of the Rappahannock, in central Virginia. His plan was to swing around the Confederate Army and place his Union troops between General Robert E. Lee and the capital of the Confederacy, Richmond, Virginia.

Following the armies were war correspondents. Most were real reporters but today, among Grant's men, lurked a spy, Paxton Faulconer. A handsome, clean-shaven young man with brown eyes, side-parted brown hair, and a muscular build, Paxton easily fit the role of journalist for the *Washington Chronicle*. He was studious, pleasant, quick-witted, and observant, the perfect traits for a writer and also for a spy.

Paxton was saddling his horse when he felt a tap on his shoulder and jerked in surprise.

"It's just me, old boy," said Bradby Tucker, a reporter for the *New York Times*. "I didn't mean to startle you."

Paxton smiled at the slender young man with whom he had become friendly in the two days he had been in the Union camp. "I didn't think you were up." Paxton returned to buckling the saddle strap.

"Where are you going?" asked Bradby, pushing up the nose of his wire-rim glasses.

1

"We're all going. Look around you."

As the New York journalist turned his head, he exclaimed, "Something's afire!"

"They're burning their huts," said Paxton. "They have no plans to return."

"So it's finally come." Bradby stared at the smoke rising from the burning shanties.

"Grant is on his way to do battle with Lee."

I must get the news to Lee. Our signal corps has probably already seen the fires. They'll know Grant is moving.

"Did you hear which route they're taking?" Bradby asked. "Who is the lead unit?"

"The Third Indiana Cavalry crossed the Germanna Ford about three o'clock."

No harm in telling him. He could find out from others easily enough.

Paxton went to the horse's head and attached the halter.

"Three o'clock -- the middle of the night." Bradby searched his pockets for his notepad before realizing it was still in his tent. "What route? Are they all going over Germanna?"

"No, it looks like Grant is dividing his men. Some are crossing by Ely's Ford."

This will make it easier for us to attack. We can take them by halves instead of the entire army together.

Paxton flipped the reins over the horse's head.

"How are they getting across? Wading?" Bradby was close beside Paxton. "What about the wagons? How are they crossing?"

"Engineers laid down pontoon bridges." Paxton put his foot in the stirrup and mounted.

"Over a hundred thousand Union soldiers," said the real reporter looking up at the fake reporter. "How many do you suppose the Rebels have, Paxton?"

"Battle victories don't depend on numbers, Bradby. Don't you know that by now?"

"What do victories depend on?"

"The commanders," answered Paxton, tipping his hat.

"See you in camp tonight," said Bradby as Paxton rode away.

"Maybe." Paxton waved as he rode away.

Not likely, Bradby, unless I'm caught and brought to camp as a prisoner. I plan to be at General Lee's headquarters tonight, if all goes well.

* * *

All was not going well for Albany Trubridge and her slave Susa Pinkney, struggling to haul a heavy, dusty rug out of the Big House on the Trubridge Plantation, a few miles outside the village of Spotsylvania Court House, Virginia. As they dragged the fringed rug through the grand hall, it snagged the leg of the narrow table.

"Oh, dear!" exclaimed Albany as the table toppled.

Susa caught the glass candlestick before it landed. Albany went down on her knees to grab the silver calling card tray inches away from hitting the tile floor.

Both young women eyed each other and giggled.

"I hope the rest of our day goes better," said Albany.

"It's a lovely, sunny day," said Susa. "Just to be outdoors will be nice."

Albany appreciated her companion's cheerfulness. Although Susa was a slave, the Trubridge family had always treated her as a companion to Albany, since the day she was purchased by Shedrick Trubridge at the Fredericksburg slave market.

Albany, a pretty woman, wore a pale pink dress and matching ribbon at the back of her neck to confine her long, curly brown hair. She was the only daughter of Luciana and Shedrick Trubridge, currently in Richmond. Susa, the family slave for the last eight years, since Albany was twelve, was caramel-colored and stood several inches taller than her young mistress. Susa, in a green print dress, wore her hair braided and twirled like a crown on her head.

"Look at all this dirt we're leaving in our wake," said Albany, dragging the rug into the kitchen. "We will have to mop the floors when we're done with the rugs."

"I'd rather beat rugs outdoors than mop floors indoors," said Susa, smiling.

"Mother will be pleased with our spring house cleaning when she gets home."

The women continued chatting as they went into the back yard where

3

Coffer, the only other slave on the plantation, had strung a clothesline. The yard was spacious, as was the Trubridge's Big House, one of the largest in the area. The two-story brick structure was a showplace. Double windows on each side of the large front door matched the second floor windows, where a small balcony extended over the main entrance. Albany had one of the front corner bedrooms. Her parents had the other one. Chimneys book-ended the sides of the house with two more chimneys evenly spaced on the roof.

"Come and hold this end on the rope," said Albany. "I will move along and put the rest of the rug up."

"No," said Susa. "You hold the end there and I'll put the rest up. I'm stronger than you are."

"All right," said Albany, doing as her slave suggested.

I'm so glad Susa and Coffer are here and didn't run off when the other slaves did. She's more of a friend than Mimoria was.

Mimoria, Albany's nanny since infancy, died of pneumonia a week before Shedrick went to Fredericksburg and bid on Susa Pinkney, paying more than he had planned.

With the rug over the clothesline, the women picked up wooden clubs Coffer had cut from branches for them and began beating the rug. In the barn, Coffer, the Trubridge's slave since 1858, heard the blows on the rug from the barn where he was working. In his early thirties, Coffer did not know his exact age but did know that he had an Indian ancestor. His skin was slightly darker than Susa's. He had high cheekbones, black eyes, a narrow mouth, and slender physique.

The only other person on the Trubridge Plantation was Albany's grandmother, Audine Cook Trubridge, who now came to the back door and called, "Where is my hankie? I can't find my hankie."

"I'll get it for her," said Susa, dropping her stick on the ground and going indoors.

As Albany beat the rug, she let her imagination have free rein.

That's for the stupid men who started this war!

Dust flew in her face.

And that one is for Jeff Davis who keeps up the slaughter!

This time, she stepped back as dust puffed toward her.

Here's one for all the slave owners who do that to their servants!

4

Albany struck the rug as hard as she could.

This is for the stupid Confederate Congress!

Suddenly, the clothesline collapsed. Gerow Gately, a Union soldier, fell against the rug, knocking Albany onto her back. His body fell atop her.

* * *

The Army of Northern Virginia, led by General Robert E. Lee, had gained few additional soldiers during the winter just passed. The Confederates, numbering 66,000, were scantily supplied with both clothing and food. Nevertheless, their morale was good. They were well equipped with weapons and knew how to use most of them.

Greenup Fortier, a correspondent for the *Richmond Examiner*, held his pencil over his notepad ready to write as a courier dismounted at the Confederate headquarters camp.

"The enemy is on the move." The messenger doffed his hat.

"Where?" asked the white-haired, distinguished-looking commander of the Army of Northern Virginia.

Catching his breath, the young soldier said, "Signal men on Clark's Mountain saw fires. They're burning their camp buildings and crossing the Rapidan."

"Could you tell how many?" asked Greenup.

"Looks like all of them."

"Captain Faulconer is with them," said General Lee. "I'd like to hear from him. He's one of my best scouts. I hope he arrives soon."

* * *

But Paxton did not arrive at General Lee's camp because he was caught between the two marching lines of Union soldiers, some crossing the Rapidan at Germanna Ford and others at Ely's Ford. Paxton crossed downstream from his enemies, out of their sight, although his civilian attire would not have called attention to him. Paxton just wanted to be away from the Yankees. Two days had been enough contact with the blue-clad soldiers for the loyal Confederate.

Crossing the Rapidan – reminds me of a history lesson about Julius Caesar crossing the Rubicon River in 49 B.C. The schoolmaster told us that was

Caesar's declaration of war. Now Grant has declared war in the same way, but crossing a different river.

Paxton, fascinated with the history of the Roman Empire, let his mind wander.

If Caesar had remained in Gaul, he would have forfeited his power against those enemies back in Rome. Instead, he crossed the river into Italy and thus chose war.

Paxton, too, had chosen war. In Gordonsville, he was just beginning to make a name for himself as an attorney when John Brown raided Harpers Ferry in 1859. Friends and neighbors formed the Gordonsville Grays which Paxton joined.

At the end of June 1861, President Lincoln designated Gordonsville a mobilization center for troops to defend the Union. On July 1, 1861, the Gordonsville Grays ignored that directive, mustered into service as Company C of the 13th Virginia, and left town in the middle of the night. They elected Paxton captain of their company, but last fall, General Lee, acting on recommendations from several sources, called Paxton to his headquarters and offered him the dangerous job of scouting. Paxton knew that meant spying. Without hesitation, he accepted.

* * *

Coffer Dunn heard his mistress scream. He dropped the bucket of oats and ran from the barn. Two bodies struggled amid a tangled rug.

What's on top of me? I can't breathe.

Coffer yanked the rug away. Albany gasped. Gerow Gately, dressed in a blue uniform, rolled onto his back and remained motionless. Susa banged the back door open. Audine shuffled across the kitchen.

"Albany!" Susa jumped down the steps.

Coffer dropped the rug and knelt beside the stranger.

"Forever more!" exclaimed Audine at the back door. "Did the clothesline break? Who is that?"

Coffer said, "He's wounded."

Albany, kicking her feet to untangle her long skirt, took Susa's extended hand and managed to stand.

Susa looked beyond her mistress to the stranger and exclaimed, "A Yankee!"

"He is indeed!" said Albany.

"He's bleeding." Coffer lifted the flap of Gerow's blood-stained jacket to reveal the red stain on the white shirt.

"Get him inside," said Albany. "Quick, before anyone sees."

Gerow moaned as Coffer lifted him. With his strong arms around the soldier's waist, the slave helped him toward the house.

"My horse," murmured Gerow.

Coffer looked around, saw a horse standing near the corral where Joab, Albany's horse, was whinnying and nuzzling the weary newcomer. Albany, too, saw the horse and said, "Coffer will tend to him as soon as we take care of you."

Albany and Susa rushed ahead of the men into the house, with Susa holding the door.

"Land sakes," said Audine, moving back for the men to enter. "Who is this man? Did we invite him?"

"No, Grandma, but he is here and needs our help."

A Yankee in the Trubridge house – land sakes indeed. What would Father say?

Audine exclaimed, "He's wearing a gun. Is he going to shoot us?"

"Grandma, he's wounded. He can't hurt us." Albany opened the door to the small sick room off the kitchen. "Bring him in here, Coffer."

"Wounded how?" Audine twisted her hankie and scowled.

* * *

Didn't know a bullet felt like this. Hurts so bad.

But Gerow did not speak. He pressed his lips tightly to suppress his moans.

Albany turned the bedding down, draping the quilt and sheet over the brass foot rail. Coffer lowered Gerow to sit on the bed. As he did so, the black man felt the soldier's back. Holding up his hand to reveal blood, he said, "His back is bleeding."

"Don't lay him on the clean sheet," said Susa.

"Here. Use this." Albany handed Susa the towel from the washstand rod.

"The bullet went straight through him," said Coffer.

Audine, in the doorway, said, "Yankees will murder us in our beds."

7

"Grandma, you wait in the parlor." Albany ushered the old woman out the door.

"I can't find my spectacles," she muttered, walking away.

While Albany dealt with her grandmother, Coffer gently placed Gerow on the feather mattress.

Finally -- rest.

Gerow closed his eyes. He felt his shoes coming off. Opening his eyes, he saw Susa drop the shoes on the floor.

The map is safe.

"Get water, Susa. Coffer, take his jacket and shirt off," said Albany. "I'll find something for bandaging."

Thank you, Lord, for kind people.

* * *

Wondering what news his best scout would bring him soon, General Lee gave orders for his officers to be ready but remain where they were. Greenup Fortier approached the Confederate commander and asked, "Excuse me, sir, but can you tell me why you are delaying?"

The correspondent held his pencil at the ready above his pad of paper.

"I hope to hear from my scout, Captain Faulconer, who has been among those people," said General Lee. "He always brings me good news."

"What about the Black Horse Cavalry or those companies of the Virginia Cavalry?" Greenup touched his pencil point to the paper. "Have you heard from them?"

Shaking his head, the general said, "No, I haven't, Mr. Fortier."

"When will the First Corps get here?"

"I've sent two messengers to Gordonsville and ordered General Longstreet to join us immediately."

Scribbling the words *Old Pete on his way*, Greenup asked, "Are you worried about fighting in this wilderness? The thick woods make it hard to see the enemy."

"We fought here last year. In fact, it was almost exactly one year ago."

"Your great victory at the Battle of Chancellorsville," murmured Greenup as he wrote: *Chancellorsville, May '63.*

"I am familiar with this terrain," said General Lee. "Grant is not. That should play to our advantage."

"Then you expect another victory." Greenup wrinkled his brow.

"Quite so, young man."

* * *

Albany returned to the sick room while tearing an old sheet and saying, "This should do for bandaging."

The small room had a minimum of furniture, a single bed, washstand with ceramic bowl and pitcher, and a cushioned platform rocker. Two pegs for hanging clothes and a print of Jesus holding a lamb were on the walls. The single closed window was bracketed by a white lace curtain.

Susa came with a kettle of warm water and poured it into the ceramic bowl. "Hold him up, Coffer, so I can wash his back. You wash his front."

Seems appropriate, Lady Susa, thought Coffer. *You should have been a nurse.*

Coffer did as Susa directed while Albany concentrated on tearing the sheet and avoided looking at the half-dressed man. The servants silently worked washing the soldier.

Bleeding's stopped. That's good.

"What's your name?" Albany looked up from the torn sheet.

"Lieutenant Gerow Gately." With narrowed eyes, he watched Coffer take the bandage Albany handed him. "Are you going to report me?"

"Report you to whom?" Albany scowled.

"The Rebs."

"Certainly not," she said emphatically. "We're loyal Unionists, all three of us. My name is Albany Trubridge. This is Susa Pinkney and Coffer Dunn."

The slaves nodded to Gerow as Albany said their names and proceeded to wrap the bandage around his chest and over his shoulder. The couple worked well together in silence.

"Can you tell us what happened?" asked Albany. "Who shot you?"

"Didn't get the sharpshooter's name."

Coffer smiled at him. Gerow responded with a weak smile.

"Where do you come from?"

"Ohio." Gerow shifted his gaze from the bandage going around him to meet her eyes. "Cincinnati."

"Should we notify your family?" Albany asked.

Susa said, "You can't, Albany; mails aren't going north."

"I forgot." Albany nodded. "What were you doing out here by yourself?"

Gerow clamped his mouth tightly closed.

He doesn't want to tell us his business.

Leaning toward Gerow, Coffer asked, "Could you use some whiskey?"

The soldier nodded. Coffer looked at Albany. "Can I give him some of the master's whiskey?"

"Yes, of course. Do that, Coffer."

As Coffer went to the study where Shedrick kept his whiskey in a cabinet, Susa cleaned up the wash cloths and basin of bloody water. Coffer quickly returned with the bottle. As soon as Gerow drank the whiskey, he asked, "Will you tend to my horse, please?"

Leaving the house, Coffer went to the corral.

When he's well enough to travel, I can go with him.

Coffer took the horse's halter and led the animal into the barn.

The blue-coat soldiers give freedom to slaves.

He removed the saddle and heaved it over the stall partition.

Would Susa go with me? How could I ask her? I have a wife, but where?

Coffer brushed the horse while the animal ate.

I do love Susa. If I ran away, I might never see her again.

* * *

In the little sick room, Susa said, "If you don't get a fever, Mr. Gately, you should be all right."

It's the fever that kills, Susa said to herself.

She pulled the sheet up to Gerow's neck.

Albany said, "I've read Florence Nightingale's book, <u>Notes on Nursing</u>, but she doesn't make a single mention of how to treat bullet wounds. It's mostly about keeping things clean and admitting fresh air into the patients' rooms. Oh, I'll open the window."

But when she tried, the window was stuck. Coming to Albany's side, Susa opened the window and said, "You're lucky the bullet wasn't inside you."

I never tended a bullet wound, just whip lash wounds.

"We would have had a terrible time if it was," said Albany.

"I am grateful," murmured Gerow.

10

Susa picked up the bloody shirt and jacket from the floor and hung them on the wall pegs.

Look at this blood. It's the same red color that black folks have. The white man's blood is no different.

* * *

Coffer returned from the barn and entered the sick room, where Susa was tucking back the lace curtain from the open window and Albany was expounding on the local Unionists in the neighborhood.

"Peter Couse and his widowed mother and sisters at Laurel Hill are from New Jersey." Albany held up fingers for each family she mentioned. "The Supplee family, George and Mary, comes from northern states, somewhere. Isaac White is from Delaware."

What is she talking about?

Gerow tried to focus on Albany's chatter.

"And there is old man Isaac Silver with his nice, big farm. That's all I can think of right now." Albany took a step closer to the bed. "We all admire President Lincoln and what he is doing to hold this country together."

Coffer came to the foot of the bed and said, "What's your mission?"

"We want to help you if we can," said Albany. "Just tell us what we can do for you."

I have to trust them. There's no choice.

"My shoe," Gerow said.

* * *

As Gerow Gately revealed his hidden map at the Trubridge plantation, Captain Paxton Faulconer trotted his horse down a narrow road lined by thick woods. Hearing laughter from behind a log house, he rode to the back where he saw two people. A boy about thirteen or fourteen was digging a hole while a woman holding a wooden box watched him.

That's not a baby's grave or they wouldn't be laughing.

Paxton reined in his horse. The mother and son glared at the intruder.

"Are you here to warn us?" asked the woman.

"We know they're coming," said the boy. "We got word."

She said, "Those thieving Yankees won't find our silver."

So they're burying silverware.

Paxton dismounted and held the bridle strap toward the boy. "If you water my horse, I'll do the digging."

Without hesitation, the boy traded his shovel for the reins. As Paxton dug, the woman babbled about rumors of the oncoming Union Army and her plans to get her family away. When the box was buried, Paxton drank from the tin cup she offered, thanked them, and mounted.

"How much time do we have before the fighting starts?" the woman asked.

"I cannot rightly say, ma'am." Paxton tipped his hat. "I'm not a general. They're the ones who decide the times of battle."

He rode away from the mother and son with their well-concealed treasure.

* * *

Coffer grabbed up one of Gerow Gately's shoes. Susa took the other one. "The heel," said the soldier.

Susa pulled the heel loose, retrieved a paper, and gave it to Albany.

"Good hiding place, the heel of your shoe," said Albany. "The Rebels would not be likely to find … Oh, it's a map." Unfolding the single sheet, Albany spread the hand-drawn map on the bed. "I thought it would be a message."

"No message," Gerow said. "I'm with the United States Topographical Engineers. That map is for General Grant."

"If the only map General Grant has is that Tourist's Pocket Map of Virginia, printed in Philadelphia, he's at a decided disadvantage." Albany leaned over the bed to see the map more closely.

"Why?" asked Susa.

"That map is incomplete and out-of-date, especially for our area." Albany pointed to markings on Gerow's map. "Even this one isn't very good. Look, here's Spotsylvania Court House, so we're about here, but look how he's drawn the Brock Road and the Plank Road." Albany looked over at Gerow. "I'm sorry to be critical, but…"

"No. Don't apologize. If it's wrong, I want it corrected."

"Susa, bring me a pencil," said Albany. "I can fix this."

As Susa hurried out of the room, Albany said to Gerow, "I'll make the necessary changes. We don't want General Grant mislead by a faulty map."

"Does it matter?" murmured Gerow, "I can't deliver it anyway."

Surprising everyone in the room, Albany said, "I can."

* * *

CHAPTER TWO

IN THE GUISE OF A MAN

Wednesday, May 4, 1864

Both slaves were astounded by Albany's declaration that she could deliver Gerow Gately's map, now including corrections and additions they made. Susa and Coffer knew that their mistress was extremely shy. They attributed her fear of strangers to her isolation on the plantation and being an only child. However, she was trying to overcome her unreasonable fear. Since her mother left for Richmond to care for her father in Chimborazo Hospital, Albany had become more the mistress, taking charge as head of the house.

Not knowing any of this history but unwilling to trust a woman, Gerow looked at Coffer. "Can't you take it?"

"Oh, no," said Albany. "Coffer would be arrested for going anywhere without a pass."

"You can write him a pass," said Gerow.

"I cannot. He doesn't belong to me. Only his master, my father, can do that, and Father's in the hospital in Richmond." Albany twisted the pencil in both hands. "The slaves won't belong to me until I inherit them, at which time I plan to manumit them, set them free, you know."

Turning from the man in bed to her servants beside her, Albany asked, "Is there anything more I need to add to this map?"

"The unfinished railroad cut." Coffer pointed to the spot.

"Ah, yes, that might make a good hiding place for soldiers." Albany marked the location as she talked. "You know Claudius Ptolemy, in the second century after Christ, made the first realistic maps, and for the strangest reason. Ptolemy was an astrologer who wanted to place everyone's birth town on a map so he could tell accurate horoscopes. Isn't that silly? Horoscopes are such nonsense."

Having completed her drawing, Albany folded the map, faced the servants, and said, "Now to get ready. What should I wear?"

"Wear my uniform," said the wounded soldier.

* * *

Paxton crossed Ely's Ford behind a supply wagon carrying fodder for the horses.

They're moving too slow. I need to get to Lee as quick as I can.

As soon as his horse climbed up the slope from the river, Paxton turned off into the woods. He quickly realized his mistake.

This mass of scrub oak and pine trees makes it almost impossible to move.

Dismounting, he led the animal through the tangle of brush until he gained the road again. None of the wagon drivers questioned a man in civilian dress riding beside them. Those who noticed Paxton just assumed he was a sutler, plying his trade of selling to the soldiers.

I better not stay in one spot too long. Someone might question me. I'll ride ahead.

But changing his location on the long line of the wagon train did not hurry Paxton to his destination. The slow-moving wagons were a hindrance to his goal of reaching Lee and reporting what he knew.

* * *

Albany knew she had to make adjustments to Lieutenant Gately's uniform before she could wear it.

"We need to sew up the bullet holes. Susa, get his shoes." She took the shirt and jacket off the wall peg. "Coffer, you dress Mr. Gately in one of father's nightshirts and bring his pants to my room." Heading out of the sick room, she asked, "Where did we leave the sewing basket?"

Susa followed Albany chattering her way up the narrow back stairs.

"I was just reading about Deborah Samson in the Revolution. She was a self-educated indentured servant who dressed as a man and scouted for General Washington."

"Joan of Arc dressed as a man," said Susa.

"That's right." Albany reached the second floor hallway. "Joan of Arc wore armor and fought amid her army. That was a good book we read about her, wasn't it, Susa?"

Answering only with a nod, Susa said, "At least, you're not joining the army and fighting."

Pushing open her bedroom door, Albany said, "I'll just deliver Mr. Gately's map and come straight home."

The women entered the spacious corner bedroom decorated in green and purple flowered curtains and bedspread. The Queen Anne style furniture and abundance of books spoke of wealth and wisdom. This was Albany's haven from the world and her favorite place to be.

"I left the sewing basket in your wardrobe." Susa dropped the shoes by the door, went to the mahogany wardrobe, retrieved the basket, sat down at the table by the window, and began to thread a needle.

Albany, joining her, asked, "What should we do about the blood stains?"

"Nothing can be done." Susa took the blue jacket from Albany and felt the wool. "It's still wet."

"So is this." Albany tapped lightly at the red blotch on the shirt.

"It won't matter," said Susa as she proceeded to sew. "You can wear binding underneath, so you won't feel the dampness."

"Binding for what?" Albany retrieved a needle.

"To disguise your female parts, Albany. You're going as a man, remember."

Albany giggled and Susa joined her. Coffer found them sewing and chatting as they often did when he tapped on the open door and entered. *Is she really going to do this? I shouldn't let her.*

"Let me do this, Miss Albany." Coffer draped the blue pants over the arm of Susa's chair. "I can wear the soldier's uniform and take the map to the general. You know about the United States Colored Troops. I can say I'm one of them, so no one would suspect."

"But, Coffer, you know those USCT men are not likely to be out alone. The Yankees don't have that much faith in them. They wouldn't send them on special assignments like map making." She looked up from her sewing. "Thank you for offering, but I really want to do this. Besides, I need you to guard the place."

"The soldiers might come here." Susa's eyes widened as she imagined being alone with old Mrs. Trubridge when hoards of white soldiers descended on the plantation.

Albany reached over and patted Susa's knee. "Don't worry. Coffer is staying."

Of course, I will protect you, Susa. I just wish I could do both.

"I won't be gone long," said Albany, returning to her sewing. "Joab is a fast horse. Oh, Coffer, will you saddle Joab, please?"

"And pack food and water for her," said Susa as Coffer left the room.

As Coffer left the house, he pondered on his lost opportunity.

If I delivered the map, I could just stay with the Yankee soldiers. But, no, I cannot desert Susa. Oh, my Lord, what am I going to do about this problem of loving two women?

* * *

Albany hurried behind the screen painted with brightly colored flowers. Susa brought the binding, a second old sheet torn into strips.

"I'll wrap it atop your camisole," the servant said.

"I can tuck the map between the two."

"You mean between the binding and the camisole." Susa giggled.

"What else could I mean?" In an instant, Albany realized why Susa was amused, pushed her shoulder gently, and smiled.

"Do you think I'll get away with it?" Albany asked as Susa wound the white fabric around and around her mistress.

"We'll pin up your hair. You'll have to wear a hat. Keep your head down. Try not to talk much."

With the binding fabric in place, Susa helped Albany into the blood-stained, white shirt with stitched-up bullet holes and said, "It's fortunate you're not so big at the top. This disguise will work."

Albany was dressed in Gerow's uniform. Her hair was pinned up but she wore no hat over the thick tresses. Susa, kneeling, was cutting off the pants cuffs when Coffer returned.

"Here's Mr. Gately's hat." Coffer put the black slouch hat on the table.

"Joab is waiting at the back door. I put an apple, a chunk of cheese, and two slices of bread in the soldier's bag. His canteen is full. The straps are hanging over Joab's pommel."

"Thank you, Coffer, but I shouldn't be gone long enough to need that much food," said Albany.

Standing up, Susa said, "Now show us how you walk."

Albany walked across the bedroom to the front window and back. She laughed and said, "I don't have to lift up my cumbersome long skirt."

Susa looked at Coffer and asked, "Does that look like the way a man walks?"

"Not quite," said Coffer. "Try to stay on your horse."

Albany crammed the hat over her head, tugging the brim low on her forehead. "How's this?"

Both Susa and Coffer nodded their approval.

* * *

But when Albany rode out of the Trubridge's back yard, Susa lost her courage and broke into tears.

"She's g-gone."

Coffer took Susa in his arms and let her cry on his broad chest.

"She will be all right," he said soothingly. "Don't cry. Miss Albany will come home safe."

With the initial shock dispelled, Susa stepped back, wiped her wet cheeks with her fingertips, and thudded her fists against Coffer's chest as she said, "You should have gone."

* * *

Albany unbuttoned the top buttons of her shirt and reached between the binding and camisole to push down the map which poked at her throat.

Mustn't lose this or my trip is wasted. Maybe it's wasted already. I can't find the Union soldiers.

She saw a Negro man carrying a sack over his shoulder and reined in Joab.

"Do you know where the Yankees are?" Albany called.

The man stared at her.

He's not going to answer me. Does he know what I'm asking?

"The soldiers in blue uniforms," said Albany. "Have you seen them?"

"Dah ones dat come to set us free?"

"Yes, those soldiers. Do you know where I can find them?"

The man pointed up the road. Albany thanked him and rode in that direction.

* * *

Unlike Albany, Paxton did not ask directions but tried to avoid contact with the marching federal soldiers with whom he had been living for two days and from whom he had been gaining information.

My information is worthless if I don't get to Lee soon.

Because the woods were too thick for his horse to get through, Paxton turned the animal toward the road. His horse was trotting along beside a line of marching Union soldiers when commotion ahead caused the men to halt.

"What is it?"

"Have they seen the Rebs?"

"Are we getting into line already?"

Paxton urged his horse forward and soon reached the sight of the bottleneck.

"I just went to pee," wailed a man sitting on the ground with his pants leg rolled up and several men watching him rub his bare calf. "The snake dropped out of a tree. I didn't see it until it bit me. Am I going to die?"

"Was it poisonous?"

"I don't know. How should I know? We don't have snakes in Chicago. Will I die?"

"Maybe, maybe not."

"The doc should put a poultice on it."

"A medical wagon is not far ahead."

"But I can't walk."

"Hey, Mister, can you give him a ride on your horse?"

Dismounting, Paxton helped the man onto his saddle. As he led the horse toward the medical wagon, Paxton had no idea that the very next day someone would come to his aid when he was injured.

* * *

At Chimborazo Hospital, a sprawling complex of buildings on the eastern hills where Broad Street in Richmond ended, stewards started to serve the evening meal to the patients. In the ward for men suffering with diarrhea and dysentery, Shedrick Trubridge, Albany's father, was feeling restless.

How much longer will I be here? Why doesn't this darned flux clear up? What makes it so common among the men? The doctor said it was common.

With his mind on his illness, Shedrick, a big man with thick white hair and full beard, was surprised to see his wife coming toward him. Luciana, a pretty, well-dressed woman, approached his bed.

"Shedrick, my darling." She bent over to kiss her husband.

"Luciana, you shouldn't have come."

"I couldn't stay away." Tears welled in her eyes. She searched for a hankie in her reticule, dabbed at her tears, took his hand, and sat on the chair beside his bed.

Shedrick held her hand in both of his and murmured loving words to her until her happy weeping ceased.

My dear wife, she's really here.

"I've been so worried about you since we got word you were here."

Shedrick raised Luciana's hand to his lips and kissed the back of her hand. Tucking her hand under his chin, he said, "I'm receiving good care. You should not have made such a trip in these dangerous times. Did you have any trouble getting here?"

"It seemed to take forever," said Luciana. "Everyone is in turmoil about the nearness of the Yankees and wondering when they will come."

"You didn't see any."

"No," she said, "of course not. I got to Fredericksburg with no problems. The train to Richmond was crowded. It seems everyone was talking about that new general, Grant. But let's avoid discussing the war. Tell me how you are. What are they doing for you?"

"My recovery is entirely too slow, but I'm fortunate this illness has not killed me."

"Will you get a medical discharge?"

"Yes, the doctor said so. I hate to leave the Quartermaster's Department – they're short staffed -- but I can't function like this. The doctor said as soon as I can travel, I should go home to recover completely."

Luciana gave a deep sigh. "Oh, I'm so grateful. We need you at home."

"Tell me how things are there."

* * *

Albany's parents talked about the Trubridge Plantation at the same time she thought about the place.

Has Grandma missed me? What has Susa told her? Is Coffer tending Mr. Gately? I wonder what they're having for supper.

She moved her legs, taking her feet out of the stirrups and wiggling them.

These shoes are too big. Doesn't matter, I won't have to wear them much longer. But I do like wearing these pants. I wish I could ride in trousers all the time. It's so much better than a bulky skirt around my legs. I wonder if ladies will ever be allowed to ride in pants.

She looked up to the darkling sky, a stripe of gray between the leafy overhanging trees, making this part of the road like a tunnel.

Will that Yankee soldier get well or die? If he dies, Coffer will bury him. It's a good thing there is no tell-tale uniform in the house. No one will ever know a Union man entered our door. Father would be so angry if he knew.

Albany thought of her parents. Although Shedrick maintained strong prejudices against the northern invaders, Luciana said little about the conflict. Albany's mother knew that her daughter disliked slavery and thought it should end, but, wanting to keep peace between husband and daughter, encouraged Albany to keep her opinions private, especially in the presence of Shedrick. An obedient child, Albany honored her mother's wishes.

Father must never know. What would he say to me? Surely, he would not disown me. I'm his only child. I'll have to be sure Mr. Gately is gone before Father comes home. Is Mother in Richmond by now? She should be. Maybe he can travel with Mother's help. But they can't get home too soon. Would Coffer have enough advance notice to move Mr. Gately to one of the slave cabins? How would the servants explain Mr. Gately's presence if my parents arrive without warning? Oh, I hope Father doesn't punish them when this has all been my idea.

Joab whinnied, startling Albany out of her musings.

"Do you hear someone?" Albany leaned over the animal's neck and petted his mane.

I have to have an excuse for being out. What story can I tell if asked? Lord, be with me.

Albany leaped down and led Joab off the road.

Will it be anyone I know? What if it's a neighbor? Would they recognize me in my disguise?

Albany heard the rattle of musketry as the marching soldiers neared the spot on the road where she had just exited. Standing motionless behind a tree, she petted her horse's nose and whispered, "Sh-h-h."

Confederate soldiers marched down the road. Albany tried not to breath.

Will I be captured? Would they search me? Molest me? No! I mustn't think such thoughts. I would have to scream. They would know I'm a woman.

Her grip tightened on the two leather straps leading to the horse's halter.

I am a coward. If I were brave, I would not be so frightened. Oh, I never should have embarked on this mission. How foolish of me.

The line of soldiers seemed to go on for hours. Albany's hand hurt from holding the reins in such a tight grip.

My back aches. It's getting dark. I have to get away from them.

Leading Joab as quietly as she could, Albany went deeper into the woods. Dusk descended. After a long walk, Albany no longer heard the marching soldiers. Only the sounds of woodland creatures scampering away from her approach penetrated the quiet forest.

When they reached a creek, Albany stepped into the ankle-deep water before seeing it. Joab lowered his head and drank.

"I'm afraid we have to sleep outdoors, Joab." Albany shivered and hugged herself, dropping the reins in the process.

"Maybe I'll have to go home without delivering this map." She patted the horse's neck. "We'll be home tomorrow, Joab. I'll find our way out of the wilderness when the sun comes up and I can see where we are. The road can't be far. Do you know the way home?"

She unhitched the saddle girth as the horse continued to drink.

"I know Coffer says you can see in the dark but that's no help to me." She looked to her right and left. "I don't know which way to lead you."

She lifted the heavy saddle off and dropped it on the ground.

"Deliver a map and go home. That's what I planned to do. I must be crazy. Why didn't my servants stop me? What a foolish notion."

Taking the saddle blanket, Albany wrapped it around herself and stifled the urge to scream.

"I suppose I should eat."

Taking the haversack, Albany knelt, retrieved an apple with brown spots, and began eating. She gave the core to her horse.

When she wrapped herself, completely exhausted, in the blanket, she prayed as was her habit before going to sleep. Her eyes were closed for only a minute before she opened them and said, "Oh, Joab, I forgot to braid my hair. It's going to be a mess in the morning."

But Albany did not sit up and braid her hair. She was too tired. For the first few hours, she slept soundly from sheer exhaustion but then awoke and could not get comfortable to fall asleep again. She rolled and wiggled. Thoughts of yesterday swirled in her mind. Her sleep was intermittent.

* * *

At the Trubridge house, Audine Trubridge went to bed after an hour of fussing over Albany's absence. When Coffer and Susa finally pacified her, telling the old woman that Albany went to Fredericksburg to care for her aunt and uncle, they met on the back porch steps. This was their favorite place after the day's work was done.

Susa scooted closer to Coffer so their upper arms touched and asked, "Do you think she will come home in the night?"

"I doubt it," Coffer said. "She would be smarter to wait until daylight."

"Maybe she will be gone until she finds the Yankees."

"They won't be that hard to find. There are thousands of them."

"How do you know?"

"We talk. We know things."

"You want to go with them, don't you?"

Coffer faced her, smoothed a wisp of hair away from her cheek, and said, "You know I do."

Susa tipped her head down to rest on his shoulder.

"Do you think the battles will be as bad as in 1862?" she asked him.

"Worse, I expect," said Coffer, crossing his long legs. "The Yankees have General Grant now. He's a whole lot better than that McClellan fellow they had in '62."

"How can one general be better than another?"

"By winning battles," he said. "This Grant fellow won a lot of battles in the western part of the country before coming here."

After a brief silence, Susa asked, "Do you expect to be digging more soldier graves like you did in '62?"

"No telling, but I'd rather be doctoring soldiers than burying them."

Thinking of tending soldiers, she asked, "Do you think Mr. Gately will recover?"

"Hope so. Both his wounds look clean."

"We just have to pray he doesn't get a killing fever," said Susa.

After another comfortable silence, Coffer said, "I wonder what they'll call this battle."

"How do battles get their names?"

"They pick out the town or river or some landmark nearby," he answered.

"Like Chancellorsville, the little town."

"Yes. But I heard that the two armies sometimes give the battles different names.

"That must be confusing."

Coffer said, "It's a good thing their mighty Stonewall Jackson is gone so the Union has a better chance of winning."

"I heard he was a good Christian man," said Susa.

"I wonder if he owned slaves," said Coffer.

Rain began to sprinkle upon them. Coffer leaped up, took Susa's upheld hand, and pulled her to her feet. They hurried indoors.

* * *

On that night, as General Robert E. Lee made plans for attacking in the morning, Greenup Fortier listened to the officers gathered around the headquarters tent.

"This reminds me of a year ago when Stonewall Jackson was here."

"Sure was a different time, wasn't it?"

"Jackson and Lee took an incredible gamble."

Greenup asked, "What made them so formidable?"

"They were willing to take risks."

"I'll say. Dividing our army was a risky tactic."

"The future of the Confederacy lay in the outcome."

"Secrecy and speed won the day for us."

"But we lost General Jackson at Chancellorsville and haven't been the same since."

Greenup pondered a possible story he could write.

Can I compare a battle in 1863 to now? How would I title it? Wilderness Again But Without Stonewall. No, the focus should be positive. Another Victory in the Wilderness. That sounds better. I'll make an outline before I go to sleep.

* * *

Not many miles from the camp of the Confederate commander and the *Richmond Enquirer* journalist, Paxton Faulconer, having failed to reach General Lee, dismounted and made his bed on the forest floor, using his saddle for a pillow and his hat to cover his eyes.

* * *

CHAPTER THREE

A BLIND CONFEDERATE

Thursday, May 5, 1864

The Battle of the Wilderness began on Thursday, May 5th, with an attack in a small clearing called Saunders Field. The Wilderness was six miles deep and twelve miles in length, bordering the southern bank of the Rappahannock River. A young forest grew where once huge stands of timber had been. Settlers in the early 1700s had cut that lumber to burn in their iron furnaces smelting and processing ore, a valuable export. The furnace owners cut as much as 750 acres of timber every year. Now, a second growth of scrubby pines, saplings, honeysuckle, and thorn bushes replaced the magnificent trees and made travel difficult.

The fighting was as forbidding and grim as the thick wilderness surrounding the warriors. Although the landscape was usually silent, it was now alive with battle noise. Both Albany and Paxton awoke to the sound of gunfire.

"Hear that, Joab?" Leaping up, Albany tossed her blanket over the horse's back. "Stay still. I've got to go into the bushes for a minute."

As soon as she returned, Albany saddled Joab, prancing nervously.

"We must get home today. Grandma will be worried about us. If we don't see any soldiers in blue, we will just go home without accomplishing our mission."

I hate to say that but it's true. I don't want to be out here when bullets are flying.

Her fingers moved rapidly as she buckled the saddle strap. Her unbound hair, with only a few hairpins remaining, kept getting in front of her eyes. Before attaching the halter, Albany fixed her hair, searching the ground for missing hairpins and tugging her felt hat down tightly to contain her thick hair.

"Should we go near the sound of those guns?" Albany put the halter on Joab. "I'm sure we would find federal soldiers but…"

Albany did not complete her sentence. The gunfire sounded close. She mounted and flipped the reins. Joab proceeded to walk, not being able to go any faster in the tangled thickets. The tree branches filtered the morning sunshine as Albany rode slowly in shadows.

The soldiers of both sides broke into small fragments as they battled. Officers had to guess at the progress of the fight based on the noise from musketry. Brigades and regiments became mixed.

Albany knew nothing of the difficulties amid the various battlefields. When she heard gunfire, she avoided the area and searched for a road. Without much thought because she was so focused on staying out of danger, Albany ate one of the biscuits from Gerow's haversack and drank a few swallows of water from the canteen.

"Halt, Joab." She leaned over the horse's neck. "Let's see who those marching men are."

In the next minute, she sat us straight, smiled, and said, "It's Yankees."

Albany rode out of the woods onto the narrow lane. The soldiers moved aside to make room for her horse. Albany galloped to the head of the column.

"Sir, oh, sir, can you help me?" she called to the cavalry officer in the lead.

"Yes, what is it?" He turned his head and faced her.

Will he recognize I'm a woman? Am I safe?

"Can you direct me to General Grant's headquarters?"

He pointed down the road. She thanked him, turned her horse in the direction, and did her best to avoid the marching men.

I will accomplish my mission after all. I'll be home before dark and sleep in my comfortable feather bed. No more hard ground for me.

When she reached an old tavern and saw a flag flying above the tents, she urged her horse up the knoll toward the busy campsite. Horsemen were coming and going, trampling down the weeds. Men were drinking coffee, milling about, and talking in small groups.

What a lot of strangers. Can I do this? I feel sick.

Albany murmured, "Lord, protect me."

As Joab changed from a trot to a walk, Albany stiffened.

Will they ask my name? I have to come up with one. Albert Cook. Albert sounds enough like Albany. Cook for Grandma's maiden name.

Taking a deep breath, Albany rode toward the tent where the flag was posted. She passed a man sitting on a tree stump, an unlighted cigar in his mouth, whittling a stick with a penknife. Because she had never seen a picture of Ulysses S. Grant, Albany had no way of knowing this was the General-in-Chief.

How lazy. He should be doing something worthwhile.

A black man approached. Albany balled her hands into fists around the reins.

"What's your business?" asked Bill, a runaway slave who served General Grant.

I'm going to vomit.

"I have a map for the general."

Coming to Bill's side, Lieutenant Colonel Adam Badeau, wearing a straw hat, repeated, "A map?"

I didn't know soldiers wore straw hats.

"Where did you get it?" Adam grabbed Joab's halter. "Let's see the map."

Albany reached into the front of her jacket.

Can they tell? Is my binding concealing me enough?

Pulling the paper out, she handed it to the officer.

"Climb down. I'm Adam Badeau." He unfolded the map. "Who are you?"

"Private Albert Cook." She dismounted.

Bill took hold of the halter so Adam could study the map.

I feel dizzy. I might faint.

Albany reached up and gripped the pommel of her saddle to steady herself.

"Porter, come see this!" called Adam, holding up the map.

Horace Porter, another member of Grant's staff, joined his fellow officer, gazed briefly at the map, looked at Albany, and asked, "Who are you with?"

"Mackenzie's t-topographical engineers," Albany muttered.

Do I sound like a girl? Is that why they're staring?

"The engineers?" Colonel Porter's thick moustache twitched slightly. "I thought they were taking up the pontoons. When did they have time to make a map?"

"I was asked to because I'm from here."

Should I have said ordered instead of asked? I feel salvia rising.

Albany gulped. Rifle fire startled her. She jerked. Bill eyed her but the two officers focused on the map and did not seem to notice.

"Looks authentic."

"Roads are well marked."

"We can sure use this."

Albany snatched Joab's reins.

Can't vomit now.

Albany mounted. As she flicked the reins, she saw the man whittling with a pen knife rise and walk toward her.

Must not faint.

Joab bounded forward.

"Hey, come back here!"

"Where are you going?"

General Grant reached the three men and asked, "Who was that?"

At the edge of the camp, Albany leaned over and spit up stomach bile.

Escape. I've got to escape.

Wiping her mouth with her sleeve, she raced down the road.

* * *

In the Trubridge house, Audine wandered through the house calling to her granddaughter. Susa came indoors from the barn where she had been talking to Coffer. After looking downstairs, the slave went to the second floor and located the old woman on the balcony overlooking the front yard.

"Albany, time to come home!" Audine called in her quavering voice.

"Albany is not here, ma'am. Remember, I told you." Susa took the old woman's arm and guided her inside.

"She missed supper last night."

"Yes, we know." Susa led Audine down the hall to her bedroom. "Albany is all right. She will be home soon."

Please, Lord, let it be so.

"Is that man still in the sick room?" Audine sat in her comfortable rocker. "Did he die yet?"

"He's still alive, getting better." Susa adjusted the small pillow at the old woman's back. "Remember, that's your grandson, Joram and Sarah's boy, from Fredericksburg."

"What's he doing at our house? Why isn't he fighting those infernal Yankees?"

"He's been wounded. We're caring for him until he gets well. Then he will go back in the army and fight the Yankees."

"But where is Albany?"

Susa took a deep breath before saying, "Albany went to Fredericksburg to care for your son Joram and his wife. They've taken ill."

Lord, forgive me for all these lies I'm telling.

Coffer came to the open bedroom door and said, "Someone's coming."

* * *

Paxton mounted the nervous horse, recently purchased by the Confederate Army and unaccustomed to the sound of guns. He patted the animal's neck.

"Calm down there, boy. It's only cannon fire. They're not aiming at us."

I'll have to hold tight to these reins if we get in a real scrape.

Reaching a small clearing, Paxton saw a Union artillerist standing beside a cannon yank on the lanyard. A spout of flame ten feet long erupted from the mouth of the Napoleon. A deadly projectile and puff of smoke invaded the air. Paxton's horse reared. A riderless horse raced toward them.

Albany, on the edge of the clearing, saw the two horses. The man on the rearing horse tried to get his mount under control. The riderless horse barely missed the flying hooves of the other animal.

Shells burst overhead. Muskets popped, popped, popped at the edge of the field. Sulphurous smoke obscured the landscape. Albany coughed and closed her eyes. The riderless horse raced past her. Opening her eyes, she saw the other horse rearing in panic. Blood streamed from the big animal's side. The horse fell backwards, pinning the rider.

Can't breathe. Trapped. Gotta get out.

Paxton struggled to free himself.

* * *

That man is trapped. I must help him.

Albany, leaning against Joab's neck, raced him across the clearing. The dying horse thrashed wildly atop Paxton. On his back, Paxton opened his eyes wide in alarm. The artillery kept up its loud duel. A shell burst overhead. The bright flame blinded Paxton. Albany had closed her eyes so was unharmed. Joab stopped beside the trapped man. Albany opened her eyes, leaped down, and barely missed the horse's dying kick.

"I'll help you." She shoved her hands under Paxton's armpits and pulled.

"Ugh," groaned Paxton, pushing with his right foot against the dead animal.

A cannon blast rent the air. Albany tugged with all her strength. Paxton rammed as hard as he could against the carcass. Suddenly, his left foot came free. Albany fell backwards. Paxton landed on top of her.

* * *

At the Trubridge Plantation, the visitor Coffer announced at Audine's bedroom door was Peter Couse, a neighbor, waiting on his horse at the front portico. When Audine, with Susa holding her arm, came onto the balcony to greet him, he removed his hat.

"Stopped by to see how everyone is doing," said the middle-aged farmer.

Peter was the oldest child and the sole provider of his widowed mother and five sisters. He knew Mrs. Luciana Trubridge had gone to Richmond so only the old woman and young Albany were home alone with their servants.

"We're doing fair to middling," Audine said. "How are Katherine and the girls?" Without waiting for his reply, she asked, "Have you seen Albany?"

"No, ma'am, I haven't," said Peter. "Where did Miss Albany go?"

"She went to Fredericksburg to tend her aunt and uncle," said Susa. "They took sick. Mrs. Trubridge forgot."

Mr. Couse nodded.

"What do you hear of the soldiers?" asked Coffer, who had gone back downstairs and stepped off the front porch.

"There was a battle the other day around the Plank Road," the neighbor said. "Soldiers are still hereabouts. It doesn't appear they're done fighting yet."

"Do you know who won yesterday?" Coffer lowered his eyebrows.

"Couldn't rightly say." Peter shook his head. "Might be even the generals don't know the answer to that question."

Audine said, "My boy Joram and his wife live in Fredericksburg. Is there fighting in Fredericksburg like there was last year?"

"It wasn't last year," murmured Peter before raising his voice to say, "No, ma'am, all the fighting is around these parts."

"We got a man in the sick room," said Audine.

Susa quickly said, "Joram and Sarah's boy."

"He's been wounded," said Coffer. "But he's getting better. He couldn't stay home with his folks being sick."

Peter nodded his head.

"Oh, I do wish Albany was home." Audine twisted her hands. "She's been gone for quite a long spell."

"Are we safe here, Mr. Couse?" Susa patted Audine's arm.

"Safe as anywhere, I expect, just stay indoors and away from the windows."

"We'll do that," said Coffer. "Thank you for stopping by."

"Maybe we should flee," said Audine.

"No, Mrs. Trubridge," Coffer called up to her. "You know your nephew isn't fit to travel."

Ignoring Coffer's statement, the old woman asked, "What's wrong with the windows, Mr. Couse?"

"Bullets, ma'am."

"What about bullets?" the old woman mumbled as Susa led her into the hall.

Again, Coffer said, "Thanks for coming, Mr. Couse."

Peter nodded to Coffer and rode down the lane.

* * *

Paxton Faulconer was stunned. He struggled to lift himself off the small body beneath him.

Who is this? What's happened?

When he opened his eyes and saw only darkness, he instantly closed them again. The sting of his eyes made him winch. His left leg throbbed with pain.

I'm blind. Leg hurts. Gotta get up. Get out of here.

Albany rolled Paxton off her.

"I can't see," he said.

She gasped for air. Paxton got to his hands and knees. Another cannon ball zoomed overhead, landed, and exploded.

"Don't stand up." Albany grabbed Paxton's jacket and pulled him down.

Joab neighed and nuzzled Albany.

"Get on my horse." Albany took Paxton's hand and shoved his palm against Joab's leg.

Paxton knocked against Albany's shoulder as he felt for the saddle.

"Who are you?"

If it's a Yankee, I'm a prisoner.

Gulping, Albany did not answer. She placed his hand on the stirrup. Paxton, blinking continuously, mounted.

"We've got to hurry," said Albany, plopping onto the horse's rump and reaching around Paxton to grab the reins.

Two cannon shots exploded almost simultaneously. The ground trembled. Albany pushed Paxton forward, leaned against his back, and shouted, "Go, Joab." The horse sped toward the trees. The sounds of cannon fire trailed them. Not until they heard only woodland noise did Albany sit up straight and sigh deeply.

He's a small fellow.

Paxton reached for the reins, covering her hands with his.

He has soft hands.

"Who are you?" he asked again.

* * *

Beside the gun carriage, Union soldiers, their cheeks and hands smudged black with gunpowder, busily loaded their weapon.

"Did you see that?"

"I couldn't see with all the smoke. What happened?"

"The man under the dead horse got rescued by a little Yankee."

"Was it one of our men?"

"The fellow under the horse was in civilian garb."

"Where'd they go?"

"I don't see them."

The cannoneers said no more about the event. One yanked the lanyard. They watched the cannon ball fly.

* * *

Albany shoved Paxton's hands away from hers and let the reins go limp. The horse changed from a trot to a walk, finding the underbrush too thick to move faster.

Did he recognize my hands are a woman's?

Paxton rubbed his eyes. They hurt. His ankle hurt. His back hurt.

"Do you have a canteen?" Paxton felt around as he asked the question. "I want to put water on my eyes."

"We'll stop," said Albany. "I think we're far enough away."

"Do you see anything?"

"Just trees." She dismounted and removed the canteen strap from the pommel.

Paxton slid out of the saddle, being careful to put all his weight on his right foot.

"I am Captain Paxton Faulconer, Company C, 13th Virginia."

"Albert Cook." Albany watched him limp away from the horse.

"Is your leg injured?" she asked.

"Ankle hurts." He sat on the ground, pulled up his pants leg, and felt for blood. "It's not bleeding but it feels tender."

Kneeling beside him, Albany unscrewed the canteen lid and asked, "Is it swollen?"

"Perhaps a little."

"Well, there is nothing I can do about that, but I can pour the water into your eyes. You can't see to do it." Raising the canteen, she said, "Tip your head back."

Obeying her, Paxton asked, "Who are you with?"

"Topographical Engineers." She dripped water into one eye.

"What's an engineer doing out here alone?"

"Mapping."

"Mapping what?"

"The terrain, of course."

What nice eyes he has. I hope his blindness is only temporary. It would be such a shame if...

She did not finish her thought because water trickled down his cheeks and she hastily wiped away the moisture with her fingertips.

His whiskers are prickly.

"Were you out alone?" Paxton asked.

"Yes. I was drawing a map, I said." She switched the dripping canteen to the other eye.

Does he believe me?

"They wouldn't have sent you by yourself. Where are the other engineers?"

"We got separated."

That seems logical to me. Does it to him?

"What's your unit?"

I don't know what to say.

"I told you. I'm with the Topographical Engineers."

"Confederate or Union?"

"Well, Confederate, of course."

Lord, forgive me for lying. You know I must.

* * *

Should I believe him? There's something not right here. If only I could see him.

35

"How are your eyes? Does that feel better?" Albany withdrew the canteen, resting it in her lap.

"Still hurt a little." He blinked. "But I can't see a thing."

"Maybe it just takes some time. Close your eyes again. Let them rest awhile."

She looked around. Her horse munched grass.

"Joab needs a rest, too."

"Joab?"

"My horse."

"That's the name of King David's army commander."

"I know," Albany said. "I named him after that brave man."

Paxton chuckled.

"I don't even know the name of my horse. This morning was the first time I rode him."

"Why aren't you in uniform?" she asked.

"I'm on special assignment."

I should not say more until I can get a good look at him. Determining a man's character depends a lot on his appearance, his facial expressions, and his whole demeanor. I can't tell that when I can't see him.

* * *

They traveled in silence with Albany walking, knocking branches away and finding the best path for Joab. When the woods thinned enough for the animal to make his own way, Albany remounted behind Paxton again.

Unknown to the couple because of their distance from the Catharpin Road, Confederate troops attacked Union forces there at five o'clock and prevailed.

Into Albany's mind came the scene of cannons firing. She broke their silence by asking, "Why didn't they shoot us?"

"What?" Paxton released the reins and rubbed his left leg. His ankle hurt worse than his eyes. The leg pain seemed to throb whereas the sting in his eyes had abated.

"Those men firing the cannons must have had rifles."Albany frowned. "They could have shot us. Why didn't they?"

"We made a good show."

"A show?"

Turning his head slightly toward her, he said, "Once when my company was in line for battle, a rabbit ran across in front of us. All the firing stopped as we watched the fuzzy little creature. It was better to look at that rabbit than the death and destruction we were creating."

"So we were like that rabbit."

"Either that or they didn't want to waste their ammunition on just two men."

Two men – so he believes my disguise. Why shouldn't he? He can't see me.

Noticing his hand rubbing his leg, Albany asked, "Would your ankle feel better if it was wrapped?"

"Do you have bandage material?"

What should I say? No sense in lying.

"Yes, I do." She felt of her midriff and the binding beneath her shirt.

I cannot withhold aid when his pain could be relieved.

"I'll get it." She halted Joab, reached around him for the strap of the haversack, and dismounted.

Let him think I have the fabric in this bag. He need not know it came from around me.

"I will be right back." She disappeared into the woods.

* * *

Where did he go? Did he desert me? He left the horse.

Paxton dismounted, petting Joab's nose, and awaited Albany's return.

"Do you have some secret stash?" he called. "Where are you?"

"I'll be right there. I haven't gone far."

He's gone to pee.

Paxton unbuttoned his pants, turned his back on the horse, and peed into the bushes. As Albany returned, she heard the sound and guessed what it was. She waited until the noise ceased.

"I have the bandage for your ankle," Albany said louder than she needed to.

Paxton buttoned his pants and sat down, extending his sore leg toward the sound of her voice. He pulled up his pants leg. Albany knelt and put the torn old sheet in his hands.

"Here. Use this."

Taking the material, Paxton wondered at the weight.

How could all of this material been in the haversack?

"Do you need help?" she asked.

"No, I can do it." Paxton dropped the fabric on his leg, turned down his sock, and proceeded to wrap his ankle.

This cloth is warm. Could the heat from the horse have gotten through the leather haversack?

For the second time since meeting Albany, Paxton thought: *something's not right.*

"Is there any food in your haversack?" Paxton asked as he finished tying the ends of the old sheet and pulling up his sock.

"Some cheese," she said. "I ate the biscuit and apple."

"Can we share?"

As Albany broke off pieces of cheese and handed it to Paxton, they ate in silence.

I'm exhausted. I wish I could tell if Albert is tired. What time of day is it? I don't even know if it's night.

Suddenly, Albany grabbed his wrist. "Sh-h-h. I see lights."

"Campfires?" he whispered.

She said nothing. He listened but heard only night noises. Releasing his wrist, Albany said, "It's only fireflies."

"Then it's dark."

"Yes," she said.

"Why didn't you say so?"

"I was hoping to get…" Albany almost said *home.*

"Back to your men?"

"Yes, that's right. I slept on the ground last night and did not want to do that again."

"Where do mapmakers sleep – in hotels?"

Albany did not answer his question. Instead, she said, "Joab needs water. We could go back to that little creek we passed."

"Yes. We can camp there for the night," Paxton said. "I'm completely worn out."

* * *

They did not go far before coming to the creek where Joab lowered his head to drink. Paxton swung his leg over the saddle and dismounted carefully.

"This binding sure makes it feel better," said Paxton.

I feel better, too, without that around me. It's been hot.

"An ankle isn't serious," he said. "It's my eyes that really concern me."

"Your vision might return in the morning."

Hopefully, I can be gone before you can see again. You'll never know my secret.

Paxton lay flat on his back and stretched his long legs out.

Where should I lie down?

Animal sounds punctuated the peaceful night. Joab, having finished drinking, began munching grass.

What should I do? He's not moving. Can I just sleep as far away from him as possible?

As she pondered where to lie, he thought of something else.

"How old are you, Albert?"

"I'll be twenty next birthday."

"Really?"

"Yes, I am nineteen."

I am not lying about my age just about my gender.

"Is there any water in the canteen?"

"No. I'll fill it."

She went to the creek, removed the canteen lid, and waited for it to fill.

Why is he asking about my age? Is he beginning to doubt me? I need to watch my step. I don't want him to take me prisoner. I must continue the ruse and sleep with him.

Carrying the full canteen back to Paxton, Albany realized what her most recent thought meant.

Am I really going to spend the night with this man? No one must ever know. There seems to be no option.

Paxton heard her return and asked, "Don't you topographical engineers sleep in tents like the rest of us?"

"Well, not if we can help it."

What should I say? He's being too inquisitive. Does that mean he doubts my truthfulness?

"I'll unsaddle Joab and bring the blanket," she said as she set the canteen in his hand.

Paxton dripped water in his eyes while Albany unsaddled her horse.

Goodness sakes, one blanket for the two of us. What excuse can I give for not sharing it with him? Do men share blankets?

Paxton asked, "Are you a light sleeper?"

"Why?"

"If I hear something, I'll have to waken you. I won't be able to see anything. Is the moon bright?"

Albany dropped the saddle near his head and said, "Not very. The tree branches obscure most of the moonlight. I can't see any stars."

Paxton moved the saddle under his head for a pillow.

"Here's the blanket." Albany dropped the covering on his arm.

"Hold up there." He started to spread out the blanket. "You're sleeping right beside me."

"Must I?"

I should not have said that.

"I told you," said Paxton, "I will awaken you if I hear something. You must sleep beside me."

Oh, dear me.

* * *

Paxton had no worrisome thoughts about sleeping with a stranger as Albany had.

Will I find General Lee in the morning? Is my information still valuable? How soon before my eyesight returns?

"What are you doing?" Paxton removed his belt and holster, placing the Colt revolver near the saddle.

Hesitantly, Albany said, "I'm not tired yet. I'll sit up awhile."

In a gruff voice, Paxton said, "Get over here."

Surprised by his order, Albany got up and cautiously took a few steps. Dead leaves crunched under her feet. Paxton lifted the blanket and waited.

What's wrong with him? Why doesn't he come and lie down?

Albany crept toward the outstretched man, appearing as a dark mound at the base of a large tree.

"What's the matter?" Paxton turned his head, listened, and heard only nighttime creatures.

At his side, Albany said, "I always say prayers before going to sleep."

"So do I," Paxton said. "Do you want to start?"

"You start," said Albany.

"Dear Lord, thank you for preserving our lives this afternoon. You know our dilemma now. I'm blind and have a sprained ankle." Paxton paused before adding: "My companion distrusts me."

Albany gasped.

I am right about that. Must be the reason he didn't want to sleep near me.

Although Paxton heard her slight intake of breath from surprise, he continued. "You know my heart, Lord. I mean no harm to Albert Cook. He has been a great help to me, so I ask your blessings upon him."

Paxton reached toward Albany but she was too far for him to touch her.

"Give us a good night's rest and aid us tomorrow," he prayed. "You know our needs. We rely on you, Lord, to supply them."

Paxton was silent. Albany said nothing. After a long moment, he said, "Now it's your turn."

Albany simply said, "Amen."

Paxton spread the blanket over them both, rolled onto his side so his back was toward Albany, and relaxed.

"Do you want the saddle for a pillow?" he asked.

"No, you keep it."

Unlike the previous night when she wiggled and turned in an attempt to get comfortable, tonight Albany remained stiff as a board, not wanting to disturb Paxton. Although she thought sleep would be impossible next to a man, Albany soon drifted into a tranquil sleep, warm and sheltered by Paxton's body.

* * *

As Albany and Paxton slept, Lieutenant General A.P. Hill met with his two division commanders. Generals Henry Heth and Cadmus M. Wilcox complained that their troops, after heavy fighting during the day, were scattered in disarray along the Orange Plank Road, leaving them vulnerable to attack.

"The troops need to be reorganized."

"They must be ready for battle in the morning."

General Hill, feeling sick, said, "The men are all right where they are. I don't want to disturb them."

I'm too ill to issue the necessary orders. I just want to lie down.

"I will hear no more about it." General Hill turned his back on Generals Wilcox and Heth.

As soon as the two generals departed, General Hill lay on his cot, not knowing what calamity would result from his decision in the morning.

* * *

CHAPTER FOUR

IT'S LONGSTREET

Friday, May 6, 1864

At midnight, General James Longstreet's First Corps started marching toward the battlefield in the wilderness. Their guide James Robinson, the former county sheriff, knew the way. Among the gray-clad troops was Paxton's youngest brother, Grandon Faulconer, excited for this opportunity to defend his homeland, driving a supply wagon.

* * *

Albany, feeling warm and comfortable, awoke slowly. She was reluctant to stir. Having slept poorly the previous night, she was grateful for the thick carpet of dry leaves beneath her, almost as soft as her feather bed at home. But something else added to her cozy feeling.

Why do I feel so peaceful?

She felt movement behind her. Paxton's arm flopped over her shoulders.

It's him! Goodness me. I forgot.

Carefully lifting his arm, Albany inched away. She felt her hair against her face.

Oh, my hair has come down. My disguise...

Albany sat up slowly and felt the ground where her head had laid.

I must find my hair pins.

The dead leaves, good for a mattress, were also good for concealing tiny hair pins. Albany brushed her hand back and forth on the layer of pine needles and leaves. She found her hat, tucked it between her knees, and continued to feel for the pins. When she had six hair pins, she quietly stood up.

This will have to do.

Albany held her hat in one hand and the hair pins in the other. Although she took long steps, she could not keep silent. The crunching leaves beneath her feet seemed loud to her.

He must not wake up. If he sees me with my hair down, he will certainly know. But maybe he's still blind today.

Albany reached her horse. Joab neighed in greeting.

"Sh-h-h. Don't wake him."

Stepping behind the big animal, she used him as a screen while fixing her hair.

I can't believe I slept next to a man last night. No one must ever know.

Because the pins could not hold all her thick hair, she re-pinned until most of her hair was up. Tugging on her hat, she still had to tuck loose strands underneath. With that task accomplished, she went twenty paces away, searching her surroundings with each step. Unbuttoning her pants, she crouched to pee.

* * *

Unlike Albany's slow awakening, Paxton woke up suddenly. He swept his hands on the ground around him.

Where is my Good Samaritan?

Blinking, he looked up but saw only black trees and dark gray sky.

I can see a little. Everything is not total darkness. My eyes don't hurt. Thank you, Lord. I will regain my sight.

Paxton heard the foliage crunch.

I hope that's little Albert and not a Yankee.

Paxton felt around for his holster, found it, and slipped out the gun. Aiming in the direction of the sound, he listened.

Seeing the gun pointed at her, Albany halted. "It's just me. It's Albert."

"I thought you had deserted me." Paxton returned the gun to its leather holder.

"I was looking for a cane for you," she said.

"Did you find something?"

"I found this sturdy branch." Albany came forward and touched the wood to his hand. "Is it too thick?"

Bracing himself on the branch, Paxton stood up. He pounded the cane against the ground, smiled, and said, "This will be most helpful. Thank you very much, Albert."

"There's still some cheese in the bag," she said. "Are you hungry?"

"I'd love a cup of coffee but cheese will have to do."

They were sitting and eating when Paxton asked, "Did you sleep well?"

"Yes, better than last night."

"We need to find a road," he said.

"I agree. These woods are too dense for Joab."

"Too dense for any horse." He swallowed the last of his cheese.

"If I could just see something familiar, some landmark, I'd know where we are and which direction to go," she said.

"You will tell me if you see Yankees, won't you?"

"So your eyesight is no better than yesterday?"

Not sure I should tell you the truth.

"No, it's no better."

Albany finished her cheese and said, "Yes, I'll warn you if I see Yankees, but what should we do. You can't shoot them."

"Don't you know how to shoot a gun?"

"Of course I do."

"Well, feel free to grab my Colt from the holster and take out one or two," said Paxton as he wiped his mouth with the back of his hand.

Albany gave a nod of consent, remembered he could not see her nod, and said, "Yes, all right." She put the cheese wrapping paper into the haversack. "How is your ankle today?"

"Better. The binding needs re-doing. It's loose." He proceeded to pull up his pants leg, push down his sock, and unwind the fabric around his leg.

Watching him, she said, "We should get back to our own men today. They can't be far, don't you think?"

I am not sure who your men are, Albert. I doubt you are an engineer. There's just something fishy about your story. I can't put my finger on it. Maybe I need to interrogate you. That's how spies learn the facts.

"You know the Dahlgren-Kilpatrick Raiders came through this area recently," said Paxton. "When was that, February, March?"

"Yes, that's right."

"What did you think of their mission?"

"I am glad they did not succeed." Albany's words came hesitantly.

"Do you believe Ulric Dahlgren's orders found on his body were authentic?"

"Do you?"

"They might have been forged," Paxton said.

"Yes, they might have been."

Well, that was a waste of breath. I didn't learn anything except Albert is wary. Does he distrust me as much as I distrust him?

* * *

As Albany and Paxton listened to small animals scamper among the leaves and birds call overhead, soldiers pitched into battle.

Because the Confederate lines were not rearranged, as Generals Heth and Wilcox urged General Hill to order the previous evening, Union General Winfield Scott Hancock's Second Corps struck a blow that not only injured the Rebels physically but also morally. The Union attack began at dawn. General Hill's veterans, exhausted and poorly entrenched, faced an overwhelming blue-clad force. Lieutenant Colonel William T. Poague's artillery, stationed at Widow Tapp's farm, endeavored to halt the onslaught of Yankees erupting from the woods.

Bradby Tucker guided his horse behind the protection of a tree, withdrew his notepad, and feverishly scribbled notes. *Army of Northern Va. defeat at dawn.*

"What's that?" asked a soldier near the reporter.

"Where?"

"Over that way. See the flag."

The *New York Times* correspondent snatched his binoculars off his pommel, looked through the glasses, and listened to the Union troops around him.

"They're getting re-enforcements."

"Who is it? Can you tell?"

"It's Longstreet."

"I see the First Corps banner."

"Are you sure it's them?"

"Certain sure."

An idea came to Bradby. He shoved his binoculars back in their case, took his pencil, and wrote: *Sept. 17, 1862, Antietam, Longstreet's wing collapsing when Hill arrived and saved the day. Today, Hill's front giving way; Longstreet arrives.*

The Yankees cocked their guns and listened to their enemy cheering across the field as they welcomed the weary veterans who had trudged forty-two miles to reach the Orange Plank Road.

General James Longstreet led his gray-clad soldiers like a Roman warrior. The Confederates counterattacked, unraveling the Union's well-laid plans. General Grant quickly suspended his movement south and endeavored to hold the strategic crossroads of the Brock and Plank roads.

* * *

Grandon Faulconer, Paxton's younger brother, held the reins of the two-mule team wagon beside the other driver, Ainsley Bracken, a gray-haired man with arthritic hands who was grateful for his eager young partner.

Wonder if I'll see fighting. Grandon flicked the reins. *Whatever I see, it will be something to tell my children one day. Thornton and Paxton won't be the only ones sharing their war stories.*

Instead of seeing a battle, Grandon saw the wagon stopped dead ahead in the road. Infantrymen were marching around the disabled vehicle.

Supply wagons choked the narrow, rutted road. Each wagon had a number painted on the canvas indicating the brigade, followed by words: artillery ammunition, infantry ammunition, hay, bread, meat, grain, coffee, or medical. Grandon and Ainsley's wagon said *Hay.* The disabled vehicle said *Beef.*

The third wagon in front of Grandon and Ainsley had lost a wheel and careened sideways. As Grandon and Ainsley walked up the road to see the problem, they heard angry infantrymen shout.

"If your wagons didn't block our way, we could make a proper fight!"

"Get your broken-down wagon out of here!"

Are they going to start a fist fight?

An officer with an auburn beard and stern expression galloped up. The long feather in his hat waved as he halted his horse. "March around the wagon, men!" the officer ordered.

As the men marched, Grandon came closer to the disabled vehicle.

"The bolt is broken," said Grandon."

"Needs a blacksmith," Ainsley said.

The mounted officer ordered, "Push it off the road."

Grandon shoved the wheel onto the axle and held it there as the men began pushing.

This hurts but I can't let go.

Grandon's palms were scraped and his left hand sustained a cut by the time the wagon careened off the road.

"Thanks, kid," the officer said to Grandon. "Who are you with?"

"No one, sir," answered Grandon. "I'm not a soldier. Not eighteen yet."

"Well, we're glad to have you." He tipped his feathered hat and rode away.

Grandon smiled at the departing officer, spit on his sore hands, and rubbed the saliva and blood onto his pants legs.

"I never expected praise from an officer," Grandon said to Ainsley. "Who was that?"

"J.E.B. Stuart," Ainsley replied.

* * *

Albany intended to ride on Joab's rump as she had yesterday but Paxton had another idea.

"You ride in the saddle today," he said.

Albany put her foot in the stirrup. "No, you should."

She felt his hand on her bottom. Paxton pushed her up. A rush of blood reddened her face. She banged down hard in the saddle.

Sakes alive. He put his hand...

She refused to finish her thought. Instead, she rubbed her hot cheeks. Paxton swung up behind her, reached around her, and took the reins. Joab plodded over the ankle-deep leaves. They made slow time winding their way around tree trunks and shrubs.

Why did he ask me about the Dahlgren-Kilpatrick Raid? What should I have said? What was the purpose of that raid? They intended to release the federal prisoners in Richmond. If Colonel Dahlgren's papers found on his dead body were authentic, they also planned to assassinate Jefferson Davis. Should I have an opinion about that? Was he trying to trap me? Does he suspect I'm a Northern sympathizer?

Startled out of her musings by a sound ahead, Albany pulled on the reins.

"You hear it, too," Paxton whispered close to her ear.

"I'll investigate." She slipped off the horse.

Paxton, too, dismounted. Joab whinnied and stomped in place.

"What do you see?" Paxton put his hand on her back and slid it to her shoulder.

"Nothing yet." Scanning her surroundings, Albany walked toward the thicket where the sound was.

"Take my gun." He held the weapon in front of her.

I will take it but not shoot it.

Holding the gun, she realized the noise was not human. She pushed aside branches of a scrub and laughed. A sow and her large litter of squealing piglets, startled by the intruders, set up a loud racket. Paxton joined Albany in laughing as the frightened animals wiggled and ran.

"How many pigs are there?" Paxton asked.

"Too many to count." Albany touched the Colt revolver to Paxton's chest and added, "Take this."

Paxton replaced the weapon in his holster and said, "There must be a farm nearby."

With a brief search, they located the small farm. No people were in sight.

Maybe they are hiding and will jump out with guns.

"Where's the water trough?" Paxton kept his hand on Albany's shoulder. "Joab needs a drink."

While the horse drank at the trough, Paxton took the canteen and, feeling his way, filled the canteen, pouring water on his eyes and filling it again. Albany turned her head and searched for the farmer's family or soldiers.

"You'll tell me if you see anyone." Paxton capped the canteen and reached toward her.

"I don't see a soul." Albany felt his firm grip on her shoulder again.

I don't mind your hand there. It makes me feel safe. How is that possible?

"Let's go inside and get some food," he said.

"Steal from these people, you mean?"

"We're hungry. If they were home, I'm sure they would offer us food."

* * *

They were riding again, along the lane leading from the small farm to the main road. She was in the saddle; he was on the horse's rump.

I wish we had found something more to eat in that deserted house. I wonder why Albert had such an aversion to invading the place. He's not been in the army long is probably why. Surely, he's as hungry at I am. At least, I persuaded him to eat a little something. But we need to find more food.

Albany jerked the reins. Joab halted.

"What is it?" Paxton tensed.

Starting the horse in a walk, Albany said, "Just a squirrel. It startled me."

"If I could see, I'd shoot it and have a good meal."

She shivered at the thought. He felt her movement.

"Don't you like squirrel meat?"

"I don't like killing God's creatures," Albany answered.

"Well, keep an eye out for the movement of those creatures because they might be cavalry horses or cattle coming along with the supply wagons." He brushed hair off his forehead. "My hearing is good, but I feel imprisoned by this temporary blindness."

Reaching the road, Albany halted Joab.

"I'm reluctant to travel on this road." Albany looked in turn at both ends of the empty roadway. "I don't see anyone but soldiers could appear at any minute."

"Stay along the edge so you can duck into the trees quickly."

Albany started the horse along the side of the road.

"What should I say if we're caught?" she asked.

"If they're our men, just say you're giving me a ride to the nearest medical wagon. I'm injured. That's true."

"And what if they are not our men?"

"Make a run for it."

With that instruction, Albany kept Joab close to the road's edge. They had not gone far when the road came to an open area. On the hill in the distance, Albany saw a flash of fire. She jerked.

"What is it?" Paxton gripped her waist.

They heard several loud reports.

"Cannons." Paxton answered his own question.

Albany turned Joab toward the trees. Once concealed, she dismounted and said, "The woods are too thick here. I'll lead Joab."

"Keep the road in mind so we can get back," he said.

They went only a hundred yards before coming to a small clearing. Albany stopped.

"What's there?" Paxton leaned forward.

"Bags on the ground," Albany said.

"Haversacks you mean?"

"Yes, haversacks." She walked among the pouches strewn around. "Why are they here?"

Dismounting, Paxton said, "The men have gone to fight. They'll be back. Let's see what food they have." He pulled his cane from beneath the pommel and used it to poke the ground.

"Are you going to steal from them?"

"I am." He reached for her. "Show me where they are."

Taking his wrist, Albany guided him to the nearest haversack and knelt. Paxton went to his knees, reached out, felt for one of the canvas bags, opened it, and said, "Lord, we thank you for this nourishment. Forgive our thievery. You know our needs. I pray in the name of Jesus. Amen."

"Does that prayer justify our stealing?" she asked.

"Don't talk. Eat. We must hurry."

Albany found saltine crackers, ate one, and continued searching.

Paxton bit off a piece of hardtack. When Albany found hardtack and tried to bite it, she could not.

"This is hard as a brick." She shoved the stick back into the haversack.

"That's why it's called hardtack." Paxton chuckled and chewed. "You engineers must eat better than the rest of us."

Albany found a pickle and munched on the brine-preserved cucumber.

"Stuff your pockets," he said. "We'll eat while we ride."

Albany hurriedly put crackers, a moldy piece of cheese, and several biscuits in her pockets. Paxton, too, filled his jacket pockets.

Gunfire shattered the peaceful air.

"They'll be coming back." Paxton stood up. "Where's the horse?"

Albany made a clicking sound with her tongue and Joab came. Quickly, they mounted. By the time the warriors returned to their belongings on the ground, the couple was out of sight.

* * *

They stayed on the road only a short distance. The cannon fire grew louder. Albany said, "I should lead Joab in the woods."

She lifted one leg over the pommel, intending to dismount, when a bullet zinged by her head.

Paxton pushed her against Joab's neck. The pommel jammed into her stomach. Her raised leg was crushed. She struggled against his weight and dropped to the ground. Another bullet zoomed a foot away. Paxton slid from the horse's rump, landing almost on top of her. Albany shoved against him. Paxton drew his gun. A third bullet whizzed through the air. Albany grabbed his Colt and fired. The bullet went high in the air.

"Did you aim?" he asked.

"No, I don't see anyone."

Paxton reached for his weapon. His hand brushed her breast. Albany quickly backed away.

"Help me aim," he said.

Albany, still in shock over his brief touch, took his hand and pointed the gun in the direction of the gunfire.

"Do you see the shooter?"

"No. He must be behind a tree."

"I don't want to shoot one of our own men," Paxton said.

"I see a uniform," Albany said. "It's blue."

Paxton pulled back the trigger. "Aim it."

When she did, he fired.

"Did we get him?" he asked.

"I hope not," she replied.

"What?"

Albany did not answer. The gunshots became loud from both directions. Crawling away from him, Albany made her way to Joab's dangling reins. Using the horse as a shield, she called to Paxton. He crawled toward her. Feeling the horse's back leg, Paxton reached out to find if Albany was there.

"I'll mount," she said when his fingers touched her shoe.

As soon as she was mounted, Paxton stood, put his foot in the stirrup, and climbed on the horse's big rump. Gunfire continued as they disappeared into the wilderness.

* * *

Unbeknownst to Albany and Paxton, at the same time, Generals Robert E. Lee, A. P. Hill, and J.E.B. Stuart, along with staff officers, rode into a field belonging to a widow, Catharine Tapp. They could see long lines of Federal soldiers in the open valley of Wilderness Run. Engrossed in the sight, the Confederates were surprised when enemy skirmishers came from the pine thickets and advanced within pistol shot.

"Hold up there," the Union officer in the lead admonished his men.

Not recognizing the three Confederate commanders, he ordered, "Right about!"

The federal soldiers disappeared back into the woods. The Confederate commanders were as surprised by the sudden appearance of the enemy as the body of blue-coats had been.

* * *

As Albany and Paxton rode, he could not get his companion's remark out of his mind.

Why would Albert say that? Is he a pacifist? If so, he should be working in a hospital.

"Why did you say you hoped we didn't hit the gunman?" Paxton asked.

"I don't like killing," she replied.

Is that all? Is there more to it than that? I hope Albert isn't a coward. My life depends on him spotting danger. I'm almost completely dependent on him. I don't like that. I want my sight back.

Albany kept her eyes in motion, searching for soldiers aiming guns toward her. She had to dismount when they reached thick foliage. Guiding Joab by his halter, she walked cautiously, having no idea that Lieutenant-General Longstreet, not far away, was giving instruction to his Chief- of-Staff, Lieutenant-Colonel Gilbert Moxley Sorrel.

* * *

With pencil in hand, Greenup Fortier, *Richmond Examiner* correspondent, scribbled notes as the two Confederates conversed.

Sorrel, bank clerk, Savannah before war. Greenup wrote in his own shorthand. *No military experience.*

General Longstreet said, "Colonel, there is a fine chance of a great attack by our right. If you will quickly get into those woods, some brigades will be found much scattered from the fight. Collect them and take charge."

Longstreet order Sorrel to command, Greenup wrote.

"Form a good line and then move your right pushed forward," continued the general as the journalist wrote. "Turn as much as possible to the left. Hit hard when you start."

"What time should that be?" asked Lieutenant Colonel Moxley Sorrel, putting on his gloves.

"Start when you have everything ready," said his commander.

Moxley took his horse's reins and mounted.

General Longstreet said, "I shall be waiting for your gunfire and be on hand with fresh troops."

Moxley departed. Greenup added: *Sorrel leading four brigades.*

Heading north, Moxley led the Confederates unseen along the railroad cut, the one that Coffer had told Albany to add to the map for General Grant. They burst from the brambles, and, screaming the Rebel yell, attacked General David Bell Birney's exposed flank. The Federals tried to make a stand by their reserve line but were swept off their feet in the mad rush of Southerners. The Northerners retreated in disorder.

Lieutenant Colonel Sorrel, riding his horse amid the tangled growth, kept in conspicuous sight of his troops. After the battle, the men in gray told Greenup Fortier about their young commander's bravery.

* * *

Albany stepped in a knee-high mud hole. Gripping the reins by which she was leading Joab, she kept from falling.

"What's wrong?" Paxton called.

"A swamp." Albany struggled to find solid ground. "It's deep."

Paxton dismounted. "I'll help you. Give me your hand."

He extended his hand toward her.

"Over this way." She waved her hand until their fingers touched.

"Got you."

His strong arm gave her the support needed to climb out of the bog. She sat down, breathed deeply, and said, "I need to rest a minute."

Paxton sat beside her as Albany brushed the mud off her pants legs.

"Didn't you see that marsh?"

"No. I was looking ahead not down," she said.

"I'm not sure I'm safe with you," he said. "How good a shot are you?"

"Why?"

""I'm good with a pistol at sixty yards. What about you?"

"Do you expect me to shoot someone?"

"I expect you to defend us since I cannot," he said. "Back there, when you said you hoped you didn't hit the gunman, it was stupid not to aim at him."

"We got away, didn't we?"

"You can't even watch where you're going."

"Would you prefer we part company?" Albany glared at him.

"I want to get out of this wilderness." He gave a heavy sigh. "I can't do it alone."

"That's the best I can do with getting the mud off." She stood up. "Let's go."

Riding again, they were on the edge of a narrow lane when suddenly a cannon ball landed thirty feet in front of them. It ricocheted and bounded toward them. Albany jerked the reins. The ball went by with an angry whiz. They were among the trees when it exploded.

* * *

In the afternoon, on a small rise, Albany saw movement and yanked on the reins.

"There's someone," she whispered.

Joab halted.

"Can you see who?"

"No, they're across the clearing ahead." She leaned forward. "It's two soldiers."

Shots rang out.

"They shot each other." Albany gasped.

One of the men fell. The other man approached and fired a second shot.

"He's killed him." She clutched the pommel. "He was just wounded and the other man killed him point blank."

Paxton tugged the reins to turn the horse.

"Did he see us?"

"I don't think so." She lowered her head. "They looked at each other not at us."

When they were out of sight of the two gunmen, Albany said, "He might have just been wounded. The other man could have taken him prisoner."

Paxton said, "A wounded prisoner is a lot of trouble."

* * *

The 13th Virginia obeyed their commander and lined the Plank Road where Paxton's older brother, Thornton Faulconer, joined them. His unit had become discombobulated in the morning fight.

Seeing men riding toward them, Thornton asked the soldier next to him, "Who is that general; the one beside Longstreet?"

"Jenkins," said the Virginian. "Why do you ask?"

"He reminds me of my brother. He's handsome like Paxton."

They heard Brigadier General Micah Jenkins say, "Colonel Sorrel, it was splendid; we shall smash them now."

The young officer rode from Moxley Sorrel's side to Longstreet's and said, "I have felt despair for some months but am relieved now. I feel assured that we will send the enemy back across the Rapidan before night."

Micah's mouth was open as he intended to say more when a bullet struck him in the head. He dropped from his saddle, mortally wounded.

Another Minie ball pierced General Longstreet's throat and lodged in his right shoulder.

Seeing that the gunmen wore gray uniforms, Thornton shouted, "Stop firing! Friends! They're friends!" He ran forward, waving his arms.

Major General Joseph Kershaw, running, yelled the same words as Paxton's brother. The bullets ceased flying. Confederates looked in horrified astonishment at their fallen officers. Besides the generals being hit, two staff members were killed.

Thornton, gripping his rifle barrel close to his chest, scanned the trees for the enemy. He heard General Longstreet give orders to his staff as a bloody foam bubbled from his mouth. He was almost choking with blood. Dr. John Syng Dorsey Cullen, the First Corps's medical director, was quickly summoned and stopped the bleeding.

Thornton helped lift the wounded general onto a stretcher.

"Tell General Field to go straight on," the commander said.

"Yes, General."

"Sorrel, hasten to General Lee. Report. Urge him to continue the attack."

"I will, sir," said Moxley.

As Thornton and three other soldiers carried "Old Pete", as his men called the big man, toward the nearest ambulance, gray-clad soldiers along the route watched.

"Is he dead?" a man asked.

"Looks like it."

"His hat's over his face."

Hearing the remark, General Longstreet lifted his hat with his left hand and waved it to assure his men that he was alive.

Other voices murmured as they saw the General carried past.

"Just like Stonewall."

"Shot by our own men."

"Almost the same place as last year."

"And just when we were winning."

Thornton sat next to the driver as they drove to the field hospital near Parker's Store. Dr. Joseph Haskell tended General Longstreet's wounds. When the decision was made to send General Longstreet to Lynchburg to recover, Thornton was assigned to follow as a guard.

* * *

Albany's mind was in a whirl.

Morning and missing hair pins – pigs in the woods – eating stolen food – firing a gun and intentionally aiming high – a mud hole – and everywhere, everywhere, the sound of guns. What next?

"Are you all right?"

Albany jerked at the sound of his voice.

I forgot about you. You're the most disturbing of all.

"Yes. Why wouldn't I be?" she asked.

Having felt her sudden movement, Paxton spread his fingers more firmly around her waist and said, "These detours we've had to make, due to the guns, is unnerving."

"Aren't you veterans accustomed to this?" She wanted conversation to get her mind off the stress. "When did you join?"

"In '61, and the answer is no." He scowled. "I'll never become accustomed to men shooting other men." He paused before asking, "When did you join the army?"

"Recently."

"Your first battle?"

Albany nodded, turned her head slightly toward him, and said, "Tell me about your life before the war."

Thus, they engaged in a conversation about earlier days. After listening to his story of growing up in Gordonsville and becoming a lawyer, she, without hesitation, told him about plantation life.

* * *

While their daughter rode horseback with a Confederate spy, Shedrick and Luciana discussed going home.

"You should be at home, dear," Shedrick said. "Chimborazo is no place for your delicate sensibilities."

"I am not leaving here until you are fit to travel and we go together," Luciana said as she glanced around at the row of beds lining the wall.

"Of course you must have an escort."

"I traveled here without an escort. Another lady on the train was doing the same." Luciana focused on her husband's face, thinner than she remembered. "Besides, I like the lovely room I've rented at Mrs. Verity Stuart's mansion. She's a widow experiencing hard times and forced to take in boarders. Did I tell you that?"

"Yes, you told me. How did you find the place?"

"One of the nurses here, Eliza Edgerton, told me that she boards her children there and sees them on the weekends. It is a beautiful big house on a nice shaded street."

"A mansion must be more expensive than a hotel," her husband said.

"Not at all, it's very reasonable, and the other boarders are pleasant people. I especially enjoy the Edgerton children. Tilly is knitting with me. Mason writes poetry."

"Owned by Mrs. Stuart, you say." When Luciana nodded, Shedrick asked, "Is she related to J.E.B. Stuart?"

"I don't know," said Luciana. "I'll ask her when I see her this evening."

As Albany's mother tended to her father, they were unaware that the Battle of the Wilderness had entered its second day and that their only child was amid the battle.

* * *

Distant fires halted Paxton and Albany's ride. She saw the flames clearly through the trees. He could see spots of light come and go.

"What is it?" he asked. "What do you see?"

"Fire," she said in low tone. "It looks like the forest is aflame. Would the soldiers do that? Are they trying to burn out the enemy?"

"If so, it's not a normal battle tactic." Paxton flipped the reins. "We had better get away from it."

They made camp a good distance away with a marsh between them and the fires. Grateful for an end to the long day, Albany almost collapsed when she dismounted.

"I'll unsaddle Joab," said Paxton.

Albany crawled to the nearby tree, pulled her hat tight, curled into a fetal position, and was sound asleep when he finished tending to the horse. Paxton discarded his cane when he brought the saddle for a pillow. His ankle no longer hurt. Realizing his companion was asleep, he removed the binding on his ankle, stuffed the fabric in the haversack, set his holster close to the saddle, and lay his weary head on the hard headrest. While in the midst of his bedtime prayer, Paxton fell into a grateful slumber.

* * *

CHAPTER FIVE

THE BLACKENED CLEARING

Saturday, May 7, 1864

Unbeknownst to Albany, Paxton's sight returned. When he opened his eyes on the final day of the Battle of the Wilderness, he smiled at the birds fluttering overhead and scanned the landscape.

Trees, bushes, leaves covering the ground, the horse over there. I can see!

His smile broadened, showing his straight white teeth.

But where is Albert?

Paxton sat up, looked around, and listened.

No cannon fire, no rattle of musketry. Are the men still sleeping?

Standing up, he stepped to the nearest bush, unbuttoned his pants, and peed.

Albany, coming from the far side of the little clearing where they had slept, heard the faint noise. She halted. Seeing his back and hearing the faint sound, she knew what he was doing. Her face flushed. When he turned around, she had no idea that he saw her. Walking toward him, she could feel the warmth in her face slowly recede.

Who is that? Am a dreaming?

Stooping, Paxton grabbed his gun from its holster atop the dry leaves.

"Stop where you are?" He aimed the barrel toward her.

"It's m-me," Albany said in a trembling voice.

"Albert?"

"Yes." She pressed her fists under her chin. "Don't shoot."

He lowered the gun and growled, "You're a Yankee."

60

There's no mistaking that uniform.

"My sentiments are, that's true." She put her arms down. "You won't kill me."

I don't believe this!

"Why did you deceive me?" he shouted.

"I never did."

"You led me to believe we were on the same side."

"I thought we would separate before you could see again."

"Well, we didn't separate," he snarled and stomped toward her.

Albany backed away. In one swift motion, he lunged and grabbed her upper arm. "You're my prisoner."

White ashes wafted toward them, dusting their faces. Maintaining a firm grip on her arm, Paxton used his other hand to brush the flakes away.

"What is this?" He looked around as more ashes filled the air.

"Is there a fire?" Albany asked.

"We'll see." He pulled her behind him, heading toward Joab.

* * *

Joab stopped at the edge of the black devastation, neighed, and pranced in place. The ground was hot. Paxton had to release his hold on Albany in order to calm the horse. Patches of flames blazed up in various spots. The air was filled with smoke.

"What is that?" Albany wandered onto the blackened ground.

Does he know what those mounds are? He can see those lumps?

Albany repeated her question but Paxton did not answer.

"Don't go out there." Paxton tied Joab's reins to a tree branch.

They both coughed. Clouds of smoke wafted toward them.

I can't breathe. It's so hot. What's that smell?

Albany stepped on a body, so black and blended into the burned earth that she did not recognize this was the remains of a human being. Bones crunched under her shoe. She stumbled and fell, landing atop another burned body. The palms of her hands touched the hot ground. She yelped, withdrew her hands, and scrambled to her feet. Her hat became precarious atop her head.

"It's … it's people." Albany stood stunned, motionless, staring.

Paxton called, "Come quickly. We have to get away. We're a target here."

Albany bent over and vomited. Since they had no breakfast, she only spit up stomach bile. But the vomiting with her head down caused her hat to fall off. Her long hair, having few pins to hold it in place, swirled around her shoulders.

* * *

Paxton halted in his tracks. The heated atmosphere was stifling, making it hard to breathe. Nothing like this had ever existed in Spotsylvania County or on any other Civil War battlefield. Paxton estimated over a hundred bodies lay in the clearing. His mind was reeling.

Who is that? Am I dreaming? Is that a vision?

Coughing, Paxton went toward Albany. He could not keep from stepping on dead men. Brittle bones broke under his feet.

It's a woman! That's no vision. It's Albert – a woman.

He snatched up her hat as it blew along the ground.

Albany, unaware that her hat was gone and that Paxton now knew her second secret, gazed at the gruesome sight surrounding her. She covered her nose to avoid the putrid smell. Two large black birds descended to feed on the unburned flesh.

Paxton's anger dissolved with each step.

No woman should see this.

When he was near enough to touch her, she lifted her eyes from the burned corpses and locked eyes with him.

"Some evil giant burned his rag dolls and flung them into grotesque ..." Albany clamped her lips tightly together. Her chin trembled.

What can I do for her?

Paxton reached for her hand. When he touched her, she jerked her hand away.

"Ow," she whimpered.

She burned her hands when she fell.

"I'm sorry." He took her wrist. "We must go."

Paxton stepped, felt something hard, looked down, and saw a rifle barrel fused to a dead man's hand. He shivered in revulsion.

Your gun is no help now.

Albany trod on a man's rib cage, smashing the bones into pieces.

We can't walk without stepping on them.

A gunshot blast shattered the eerie stillness. Paxton dropped to his knees, yanking her down with him. Looking around for a gunman but seeing no one standing, Paxton rose. Albany, too, stood up and looked for the shooter.

"There." Paxton pointed. "He shot himself."

Albany saw where he was pointing. A partially-burned soldier had a pistol barrel in his mouth. No birds chirped. No forest animals made a sound. The stillness was eerie.

If only I could have remained blind another day.

Paxton continued leading Albany off the burned area. Suddenly, she stooped down.

"What are you doing?"

"It's a daguerreotype," answered Albany, staring at the tin-encased portrait melted into a soldier's palm.

Paxton glanced at the picture of two blonde children in white dresses.

"They're orphans," she said softly as tears trickled down her cheeks.

Pop! Pop! Pop! Pop!

Gunfire came from a cartridge box where the bullets exploded from the heat. Paxton jerked her up and ran, unmindful of the corpses. When they reached the horse, she did not extend her hands to the saddle but held her hands out and stared at the reddened skin.

"I'll wrap bandages around them." Paxton retrieved the fabric from the haversack, tore it in two strips, and quickly wrapped one hand.

"What happened here?" asked Albany, watching him work.

"They must have been wounded and couldn't get away from the fire."

"How did a fire start?"

"These woods are like a tinder box." He started bandaging the other hand. "When cartridge papers land…"

"Cartridge papers?" Albany scowled.

"The paper used as wadding in the musket barrels." He tucked in the end of the fabric. "When the paper lands on the ground, it can catch the grass on fire. Cannon shots start fires, too. If they could have crawled away, they would have. These men must have been too badly wounded."

Paxton helped her onto the saddle, being careful to place his hand on her waist not her bottom.

She's a woman. Remember she's a woman.

From behind her, Paxton reached around and took the reins. "My grandmother always said bad things come in three. First, I learn you're a Yankee. Second, I find out you're a woman. What's going to be number three?"

Albany did not reply. She tipped her head back against his shoulder and closed her eyes. Her slightly burned hands felt better with the cloth around them. Her mouth was dry. Her eyes stung from the smoke. She felt overwhelmed with emotion.

Still trying to comprehend this new turn of events, Paxton was unprepared for Albany's fountain of tears. Her small body shook with sobs. Without a second thought, Paxton wrapped his arms around her and held her close.

"Sh-h-h. Don't cry. You're all right. Hush, now."

I can't say Albert. What's her name?

"Please, don't cry now. Sh-h."

Paxton flicked the reins and Joab moved away from the blackened clearing. As soon as they were in the woods, at a grassy spot, he halted the horse and dismounted, pulling Albany with him. Albany's legs gave way. She sank to the ground. Paxton fell to his knees with her. Her sobbing intensified. Joab nuzzled her shoulder. Paxton reached up and patted the horse's nose.

"I'll take care of her, boy," he said to the animal.

The horse moved away but not far. Albany cried and cried. Paxton rubbed her back with one hand while holding her close around the waist with his other hand. Amid her sobs, Albany heard Paxton say, "Why, Lord?"

* * *

Will the Lord answer him? Albany wondered as her crying lessened. With a few last shivering sobs, she lay still against Paxton's chest. His legs were stretched out. Her bent legs were tucked against his thigh.

"Why didn't you tell me you're a woman?" He stopped rubbing her back.

What's he asking?

Without waiting for her reply, he said, "Tell me your real name."

Albany released a deep sigh before saying, "Albany."

"Albany what? What's your last name?"

"Trubridge."

"Not Cook?"

"No. That's my grandmother's maiden name."

Grandma, I wish I was home with you now. What am I doing with this man? Why am I here in this wilderness?

"I can't take you to the Provost Marshal as I'd planned," he said. "That's where prisoners go, you know. But now that you've revealed your true identity, albeit unintentionally, I need to get you home, or at least set on your way home."

Is he talking to himself or to me?

Tipping her face up with his fingers under her chin, Paxton met her eyes and asked, "Do you feel better?"

She said nothing but struggled to stand. He helped her. The horse came to them. Before long, they were riding again. They had gone only for a short way when bullets whizzed through the air.

"Put your head down." Paxton pushed Albany against the horse's neck and covered her body with his own.

Joab plodded ahead until the tempo of gunfire diminished. Paxton sat up and eased Albany to a sitting position. Moaning, she covered her stomach with both hands.

"Are you shot?" Paxton pulled her hands away. "Let me see."

He pulled her shirt out of its waistband.

"The pommel," Albany said.

Leaning around her, he saw the red mark on her bare stomach.

"Oh, forgive me," said Paxton, yanking her shirt down.

Forgive him for what?

Paxton guided the horse through the thick chaparral.

"Why didn't you tell me?" His soft voice was inches from her ear.

Tell him?

Albany's mind was in a muddle. Her surroundings seemed foreign. Bodies and bullets, smells and sounds, nothing was familiar. Paxton's embrace provided the only stability. When a lock of hair blew across her face, Paxton reach up and tucked the tangle behind her ear.

"Why did you deceive me?" he whispered.

What should I say?

After a long moment, Albany said, "I had the map."

"Where did you get a map?"

She turned her head. Their eyes met.

"From a wounded Union soldier who came to our house."

"Did he ask you to deliver it?"

"No. He wanted Coffer to go. But Coffer had no pass. I offered."

"Why?"

"I've always been shy. I want to be brave."

Almost choking on his words, Paxton said, "You've been brave, my dear."

The horse halted. Paxton shifted his gaze from her eyes to the hazel thorn bushes blocking their way. Dismounting, Paxton did his best to lead the horse around the briers.

Before long, they came to a small stream. Joab lowered his head to drink. Paxton dropped the reins, went to her, reached up, and pulled her from the saddle. As she slipped to the ground, he drew her close, only for a moment.

"The water might make your hands feel better." He spoke while undoing the bandages.

Albany soaked her hands in the creek while he filled the canteen. He gave her a drink from the canteen before taking one himself.

"We need to pray," said Paxton, capping the canteen.

Yes, prayer, we need prayer.

Side by side on their knees, Albany and Paxton closed their eyes. Their arms touched. Joab grazed.

"Dear Heavenly Father, Loving God, Living Lord, I pray for peace." He paused to take a deep breath. "We offer our prayers for those men who recently departed this life. We pray for their souls."

Albany, with her hands palm up on her lap, murmured, "I pray for their families."

What if one of those men was part of my family?

"Yes, Lord, we pray for their families who will grieve for them."

In an anguished voice, Albany asked, "Why did they have to die?"

Paxton looked over at her. Her eyes were closed.

"We do not know your plans for us, Lord." Paxton closed his eyes again. "But we believe you have spared us for a reason. Show us your way, the way you want us to go."

"Amen," she said.

Paxton repeated the expression of faith. Taking her wrists, he looked into her eyes and said, "I don't know why they had to die, Albany." This was the first time he used her real name. "But I know that we are alive for a reason. I must get you home. Come."

With that, Paxton stood and helped her to mount Joab. Riding again, Albany was first to speak.

"I can't get the sight out of my head. There were so many of them. I never saw so many dead men."

"I know what you mean," Paxton said. "I remember the first time I saw the dead on a battlefield."

"When?"

"It was after the Battle of First Manassas, the first battle. The 13th Virginia was held in reserve, but my tent mate and I saw it afterwards." Paxton paused before saying, "The landscape was a horrible sight. It really affected my tentmate, Searcy Ryals. He had a delicate soul."

"Tell me about him."

Paxton narrated the tragedy of his companion at the beginning of the war.

"Searcy had been a cheerful fellow, talking a lot, friendly with everyone, but after that day, he changed, had gloomy spells, especially after fighting battles."

"Is he still in the army?"

"No, he's not."

"Why? Was he killed?"

"He was sent to an insane asylum," said Paxton. "The final straw was one day, during a skirmish, Searcy started shooting at the sky."

I can still see that image. I wish I could forget it.

"Why would he do that?"

"To kill God -- that's what he said."

"Why did he say that?"

"Because his reason had departed from his mind," answered Paxton. "He blamed God for all the killing."

"God is not to blame," she said. "We are suffering this war for disobeying God, for enslaving people God created to be free."

"Is that what you think?"

"Yes," said Albany.

They rode in silence. Paxton recalled the good times he had spent with Searcy. Memories of the bad times intruded into his thoughts. He recalled what the regimental doctor had told him about soldiers who went insane.

Get them to talk. That's the only thing that seems to help.

"You're too quiet, Albany. Tell me why you wanted the Federals to have that map instead of the Confederates."

I need to get her mind off that blackened clearing.

"General Lee doesn't need a map," she said. "He knows the area. He fought here last year."

"But why do you give aid to the enemy?"

"I believe in keeping our country together."

"And ending slavery?"

"That's right," she murmured.

Joab had stopped, unable to see a path. Paxton dismounted. Albany did the same. Holding the halter, Paxton led the horse as Albany walked close to him though the dense woods.

"I recognize the wrongs done to some black people in Confederate States," he said, "and agree that slavery should end one day, when they are able to care for themselves."

"They can do that now."

"Can they?" he asked. "They cannot read or write. Decisions are made for them. They are unaccustomed to handling their own affairs. We need to train them how to live on their own before we turn them loose."

Albany said, "You talk about these people as though they are wild animals."

"I don't mean to," said Paxton. "I just think we need a system to prepare them for freedom."

"Then you don't believe in sending them to Africa?"

"That's not working very well, I admit," said Paxton. "They don't seem to like the scheme promulgated by the Colonization Society."

I'm engaging her in debate. That's good.

"I would not want to be sent away to live in a foreign country," said Paxton. "Would you?"

Albany murmured, "I just want to go home."

"I'll do my best to see that ..."

Paxton did not finish his sentence because suddenly two men appeared. Their faces were powder-grimed, their lips black from biting cartridges, and their blue uniforms dirty. Stopping in their tracks, they breathed heavily from running.

"Who are you?" snapped one of the soldiers.

"What are you doing?" snarled the other man.

Paxton stepped in front of Albany but too late.

"That's' a woman!"

"Give me a drink." The Union soldier snatched the canteen from the pommel, uncapped it, and guzzled water.

"We're lost," said the soldier who was not drinking.

"Us, too," said Paxton.

"We're with the Sixth Vermont." He grabbed the canteen away from his companion and guzzled the water.

"What are you doing with that woman?"

"Escorting her home," Paxton answered.

"Why's she wearing a Union uniform?"

How do I explain that?

"I found her wandering," said Paxton. *Think fast.* "Her dress was torn. Some Rebels attacked her. I took that uniform off a dead man. She needed something to cover her."

"Damn Rebs, abusing a helpless woman."

"They're not chivalrous as they claim to be."

Nodding, Paxton said, "They are not gentlemen -- that is certain. She's experienced an ordeal."

Although Paxton was making reference to his imaginary explanation of Confederates molesting a female, Albany thought of burned corpses.

"The men were all burned," she said.

"We saw some of those ourselves."

"Fires sprang up everywhere in this wilderness."

Albany covered her face with her hands, trying to block out the memory, and emitted a soft cry.

"Ma'am, are you all right?"

"Has he harmed you?"

Paxton stepped close and gently took Albany's hands away from her face.

"Have I harmed you?" he whispered as the Vermont men watched intently.

"N-no."

"That's all we need to hear. We've got to get back, Joe."

"I'm with you."

"Good luck to you, mister."

"Ma'am, you, too."

The men from the Sixth Vermont disappeared into the forest.

* * *

When the two soldiers were out of sight, Paxton released Albany's hands and went to Joab's halter, intending to continue guiding the horse. Albany took a step. A wave of dizziness overwhelmed her. Paxton heard her low moan.

I'm going to fall.

"What's the matter?" Paxton turned toward her.

"I'm dizzy." She swayed. Her hat fell off.

"It's not surprising." He caught her around the waist. "You haven't eaten. We need to find food."

Food? I can't eat.

"Those men will never eat again." She touched her forehead against his shoulder.

"They are feasting at the banquet in heaven," said Paxton, embracing her.

He's holding me. I won't fall.

Albany brought her hands up and pressed her palms against his chest.

"You must get your mind off those men." He tipped his head so his chin rested atop her silky hair. "It does you no good to dwell on that awful sight."

"How can I forget?"

"Think about getting home." Paxton said.

Home. When will I be home?

"Tell me about who will be waiting for you there." He picked up her hat and put it on her. "What is your house like?"

* * *

The rattle of musketry penetrated the trees. Paxton turned the horse in the opposite direction from the sound.

Grandma Faulconer's prediction of bad things happening in threes could mean all kinds of possibilities for the third one.

Rain began to fall. Because of the thick branches, Albany and Paxton were not immediately aware of the rain. Before long, however, they were soaked.

We've got to get out of this rain. We need to find dry clothes. I must not think of her in wet clothing or changing clothes. I should think of Albany as I would my sisters. What if this was Lorella or Eunice? How would I want a gentleman to treat them? That is how I must behave toward Albany Trubridge.

Before long, Paxton dismounted under a large oak tree. It was dusk. Using the saddle blanket, he covered Albany and crawled under the blanket beside her. The horse sheltered beneath a nearby tree. Paxton wrapped his arms around Albany and drew her close with her back against his chest. She made no protest. They were both exhausted. Before Paxton finished his whispered prayer, he fell asleep. Albany slept peacefully in his embrace.

* * *

Because of rain, the armies did not fight. Instead, soldiers tended the wounded, removed the dead, and made battle plans. Cooks prepared meals despite rain dousing the fires. Bradby Tucker and Greenup Fortier wrote articles, although they could not be sent. No telegraph lines were set up yet.

Bradby wrote that men used corpses as fortifications, piling dirt over the dead and hiding behind them. He added: *this has never been done before.*

Greenup wrote that soldiers fought by sound not sight, that the thick woods hampered visibility, and that the continuous cannonading and gunfire wreaked havoc on men's nerves.

Bradby wrote: *Battle of the Wilderness is bushwhacking on a grand scale. All formation of troops is lost.*

Greenup wrote: *No consistent line of battle is possible. The two armies are simply howling mobs.*

The journalists expected retreat and recovery, the usual procedure after a big battle. But this was Grant versus Lee so nothing was as usual.

* * *

CHAPTER SIX

A WILDERNESS OF WOE

Sunday, May 8, 1864

Spotsylvania Court House, the county seat, got its name from colonial Governor Alexander Spotswood, who was a Lieutenant-Colonel in the British Army. He and his wife, Anne Butler Brayne, lived in Williamsburg when he served as Lieutenant General of Virginia. Governor Spotswood explored beyond the Blue Ridge Mountains and was the first to establish colonial iron works. In private life, he enjoyed his 80,000 acres, his three iron furnaces, and his four children. The town named for him had a general merchandise store, the Sanford Hotel which Joseph and Agness Sanford built, a blacksmith shop, a one-room school for white children only, a small shoe shop, a jail with exterior walls two feet thick, a few scattered houses, and the courthouse with four stately pillars. This town was now the goal of two mighty armies.

* * *

When Paxton awoke, he was momentarily disoriented. Albany stirred beside him.

Who is this? Oh, it's her.

Paxton tucked the blanket under her chin as he sat up. Smoke from nearby camp fires wafted through the trees. Looking around, he saw the horse munching grass but could not see any soldiers' camps. He cautiously entered a thick clump of bushes to relieve himself, turning his head and searching the landscape the entire time.

"Good boy." Paxton patted the horse as he returned to Albany.

"Time to get up." He slipped the blanket off her. "We must go. I need breakfast."

Albany woke up slowly. While she sat rubbing her eyes, Paxton saddled the horse.

"Is the war still going on?" She came to his side.

With a quick grin, Paxton said, "As far as I know." He buckled the saddle girth. "If the war is over, we'll no doubt hear about it soon enough."

Albany said, "Excuse me," before going into the bushes.

This morning, Albany rode in the saddle and Paxton on the horse's rump. Joab plodded slowly through the dense woods.

Wanting to think of something besides his empty stomach, Paxton asked her, "Why did you choose the name Albany? Is your family from Albany, New York?"

"No, I was named after the Treaty of Albany."

"That's very strange." He slipped his hand more firmly around her midriff. "Did your ancestors have something to do with that treaty?"

As though reciting a class lesson, Albany stated: "Governor Spotswood, for whom our county and town are named, negotiated the Treaty of Albany with the Iroquois Nations in New York in 1721."

"Tell me more." He spoke close to her ear. "Was your ancestor at that negotiation with the Indians?"

"Horatio Trubridge was there."

"Why did you choose Albert for your false name?"

"It sounds like Albany."

"Smart. You would answer to a name that sounded similar."

* * *

Just as Paxton was learning about Albany's name, General Lee was puzzling about the name of his replacement for James Longstreet, now recovering from his wound by friendly fire from the day before. To aid him in this quest, the commander summoned Moxley Sorrel.

Greenup Fortier poised his pencil over his note pad to record the conversation as the two men conversed under a tree.

"I must speak to you, Colonel, about the command of the First Corps," said General Lee. "I need to assign a new commander and have three in mind." After naming the three officers, he said, "You have been with the corps since it started as a brigade and should be able to help me. I solicit your opinion."

The readers will be glad to know Lee seeks advice, wrote the journalist.

"Thank you, General Lee, for your confidence," said Moxley. "Probably Jubal Early would be the ablest, but I'm afraid he would be unpopular with the men. He has an irritable disposition."

Early irritable

Robert Lee nodded and asked, "What do you think, Colonel, about my friend Ed Johnson? He is a splendid fellow."

"All say so, General, but he is quite unknown to the corps."

Johnson unknown

"Who then?" asked General Lee.

"General Richard Anderson, sir," said Colonel Sorrel. "We know him and would be satisfied to have him lead us."

Sorrel says Anderson.

"Thank you, Colonel," said the older man. "I have been interested in your ideas, but Early would make a fine corps commander."

Who is he appointing?

As Moxley Sorrel left the shelter of the tree, the *Richmond Examiner* correspondent assumed the new leader of the First Corps would be General Early. Much to his surprise, Richard Heron Anderson replaced James Longstreet to command the First Corps.

* * *

The *New York Times* correspondent, Bradby Tucker, observed General Grant and wrote in his small notebook: *USG appears deep in thought, says little. Keeps a cigar in his mouth from morning 'til night.*

Walking among the blue-clad soldiers, Bradby continued his entry: *Men getting all the rest they can. Must wonder what next move will be. Hear frequent mention of Chancellorsville, battle fought last year. Men speak of eerie exactitude. Veterans expect another retreat.*

The journalist did not know that General Grant was pondering the special qualifications of his corps commanders. Bradby thought if George

Gordon Meade needed replacing, Grant would select Gouverneur Kemble Warren, an able military man.

Not far away, General Meade was in his well-known snapping-turtle mood. Angry at Sedgwick's slowness, Warren's caution, and Sheridan's cavalry command, General Meade exhibited his annoyance on whoever came into his sphere.

* * *

By mid-morning, with the hot sun raising the temperature into the nineties, Albany showed her annoyance with the wool uniform she wore. She had unbuttoned the jacket and struggled to remove it. Paxton stopped his rambling narrative of his boyhood to help take it off her. The Union jacket was tucked in a roll between them. Now, she was scratching her legs from her knees to her ankles.

"What's wrong?" Paxton asked.

"These wool pants are so hot and itchy."

"Well, you can't take them off. There's nothing else for you to wear."

Into his mind flashed an image of Albany wrapped only in the white bandages stored in the haversack.

For shame -- forget that.

"Don't your pants itch?" she asked.

"Mine aren't wool like yours. They're twilled cotton – much more comfortable in hot weather."

"I wish I had a skirt to wear."

"Hopefully, we will find some civilization soon."

There isn't anything I can do for her. I just need to keep her mind off the scenes of yesterday.

Paxton resumed his commentary on his life in Gordonsville, going from his childhood to his time as a lawyer.

"I'll tell you a funny courtroom story that happened shortly before I enlisted."

Albany stopped scratching, clutched the pommel, and leaned her head back against his shoulder. Paxton let the reins go loose.

"I was giving my closing argument, trying to persuade the jury that my client had not stolen his neighbor's cow, because he was home minding his own affairs. Unfortunately, there was no witness as to my client's whereabouts, but neither was there any concrete evidence of his being the thief of the vanished cow."

"Why was he accused?" she asked.

"There was animosity between the two men; had been for years."

"What happened?"

"Just as I was concluding, Mrs. Client entered the courtroom with a cow on the end of her rope."

"The missing cow?"

"That's right." Paxton smiled. "Old Bessie had gone to the field of another neighbor, farther away, to visit Old Bossie, her gentleman friend." Remembering the scene, Paxton chuckled. "That case ended in a lot of back slapping and joking."

Albany bent over to scratch her legs. When she straightened again, she asked, "Why weren't we there?"

"Where?"

I think I know what she's asking.

"Where they burned up?"

She's still thinking about that.

"If we had been in those woods when it caught fire, Albany, we could have gotten away. We are not wounded. Even with my sore ankle and your itchy legs, we could have escaped the flames."

"I wish they had escaped."

"So do I," he murmured as he rubbed his cheek against her hair.

Not twenty minutes later, Paxton exclaimed, "Look -- shelter!"

Finally, a safe haven – at least I hope it is.

Paxton directed the horse toward the narrow porch with sloping roof.

"Pray the owners are hospitable." Paxton slid down from the horse's rump and reached up to help Albany.

She lifted her leg over the saddle, put her hands on his shoulders, and came into his arms. He held her close for only a moment.

Pounding on the door, Paxton called, "Anyone home?"

They might not be friendly.

Drawing his gun, he opened the door. "Hello. Is anyone here?"

He kept his gun aimed and ushered Albany into the room with his hand on the small of her back.

"Hello," he called again.

Keeping his gun in front of them, Paxton took Albany's hand.

Could someone be hiding?

"We'll look in the rooms before I tend to Joab."

Albany stayed close as he searched the rooms, only three – the main room they entered, a kitchen to the left and a bedroom on the right. Both side rooms had sloping ceilings. In the kitchen, the last room they entered, he holstered his gun.

There's nobody.

Seeing a trap door, Paxton lifted it by the metal ring and saw a ladder leading to a dark hole.

A root cellar – make a good hiding place if we need it.

"If we can't find food in the cupboards, I'll look down there." He dropped the trap door. "See if you can find ladies' clothes to change into while I'm in the barn."

Albany went toward the bedroom as Paxton left the house.

In the barn, which was nothing more than a large shed, Paxton scanned the two stalls. "Well, what a nice place for you, old boy." He proceeded to unsaddle the horse. "There's hay and oats, Joab, and that rain barrel is full. You have plenty to drink." After taking the saddle and bridle off, Paxton began brushing the big animal, already munching on hay. "What good fortune. Someone must have had a horse to enjoy these comfortable quarters. I wonder where that owner has gone."

With the horse eating contentedly, Paxton returned to the house.

"I'm back, Albany." He hooked the straps of the canteen and haversack, as well as his gun belt, on pegs by the door. Scanning the room, which he had given only a quick glance on arrival, he saw a small couch, a rocking chair, a table, a three-shelf bookcase, a tall bureau, a bench, and a cold fireplace.

We need a fire. I want some hot food. Coffee. I hope they have coffee. Where's Albany?

Paxton went into the kitchen. Albany was not there. Going into the bedroom, he found her standing beside the double bed, still wearing her Union uniform and staring down at the colorful quilt.

"Albany, why haven't you changed?" He came to her side. "Did you look for something to put on?"

"See this yarn?" She plucked at several strands of cream-colored yarn used to tie the quilt.

"I see. It's a lovely quilt." Paxton went to the trunk against the wall, lifted the lid, and began searching the contents.

"I feel like this yarn, all in tiny bits, mingled amid a patchwork maze, not in a safe and secure ball any longer." She spoke in a monotone while continuing to gaze at the various patterns of the bed covering.

"We are safe now. We're out of the woods. I don't hear any guns. There will be a lane leading from here. We can find a road and get you home." He held up a peach-colored cotton dress with buttons down the back. "Here. Can you wear this?"

"You don't understand." Albany glanced at the dress Paxton draped over the iron foot rail. "My life feels all unraveled like a ball of yarn tossed about, like those bodies appeared to be."

"Albany, you must stop thinking about those men." He pulled out more garments and placed them on the bed rail. "These underclothes should fit you. Get out of that uniform."

"I can't stop thinking." She sat on the end of the bed and scratched her pants legs below her knees. "The memory is vivid."

Standing in front of her, Paxton took her hands in his. "Stop scratching. You'll just make it worse. Change into those things."

Albany yanked her hands free, turned, and collapsed on the bed, drawing her legs up into a fetal position. Tears gushed from her eyes as she sobbed.

What should I do? She's so miserable. I must help her.

Paxton sat on the bed and began to take off Albany's shoes and socks.

She's got to get out of those itchy pants.

He dropped the footwear on the floor.

I cannot remove her clothing. She must do that.

"Albany, sit up." He leaned over to pull her to a sitting position. She gripped the quilt in her fists and continued crying. With a strong pull, Paxton yanked her up.

"Take off these pants or I'll do it."

"Don't touch me." She gave him a push but he did not budge. "I don't want to be here."

"Neither do I but we have things to do, such as tending to your legs."

79

Paxton pushed up the pants cuffs and saw her reddened skin.

"It's not just the wool. You've got bug bites." Reaching for her waist, he began unbuttoning the pants. "Come on, get these off. I'll look in the kitchen for some lotion or something to put on."

Paxton went to the door, stopped, faced her, and said, "Get out of those pants before I come back or I'm going to get you out of them."

He marched across the living room. In the kitchen, he searched the wall cabinets and the pie safe. Finding a ceramic crock, he peered in.

Bacon grease - this will have to do.

Back in the bedroom, he found Albany sitting on the bed. The wool pants were on the floor. She wore the soldier's shirt and the petticoat he had set out.

"Put this on your legs." He held out the crock.

Because Albany made no move to obey, Paxton went down on one knee. "All right, I'll do it." He lifted the hem of the petticoat to her lap. "Hold that up." Scooping his fingers into the crock, Paxton used both hands to smear the grease on her legs, starting just below her knees and moving down to her ankles.

"Does that feel better, Albany?"

There was no answer. She gazed at the wall. He continued applying the bacon grease.

I can't believe I'm doing this. I've never touched a woman's legs.

"You won't be able to scratch with this stuff on," he said. "You'll be like a greased pig." He smiled up at her. She continued to stare into near space.

When he finished covering her reddened legs, now shiny with bacon fat, he wiped his hands on his thighs and sat beside her.

"Albany, you must try to forget what you saw." He put his hand under her chin and gently turned her face toward him. "We need to eat and rest. This seems to be a safe place."

At least until the owners return – who knows then.

He dropped his hand from her chin. "Will you come and help me cook something? I'm hungry and know you must be, too."

Albany looked down at her bare legs. The petticoat was still waded up on her lap. Paxton saw her lift the hem and start to drop the garment over her legs.

"Wait. The grease will get on the petticoat. I'll fetch that bandage material you used on my ankle. We'll wrap your legs in that."

But when he brought the white fabric from the haversack, Albany made no effort to help as he knelt and wrapped the stripes around her legs. He ripped the ends to create ties.

"There, how's that feel? Better?" He stood up. "You can't scratch your legs now."

Meeting his eyes, she wailed, "Haven't you been listening to me?"

"Yes, I've been listening." He sat beside her again. "I know how that sight has affected you, but there is nothing I can do to alter the memory. You just have to think of other things. That's the only way to get through this."

She turned her head away. Putting both hands on her cheeks, Paxton turned her face back toward him and said, "I am not going to let you drift among morbid thoughts, Albany. We have too much else to deal with – such as who this house belongs to and when they might return. Are they friend or foe? When might the enemy burst in that door and take us prisoners? When is a cannon blast going to explode through the wall?"

"Stop it." Albany leaped up.

Paxton stood and grabbed her shoulders. "Are you listening to me?"

"I am. I hear you," she whimpered.

"Then stop thinking only about those burned men," he said in a stern voice. "Think about what we have to do to survive and to get back where we both belong."

Tipping her head to one side, she asked, "Where is that, Paxton?"

"You at home and me with my men."

"I do want to go home."

In a soft tone, he said, "I'll do my best to get you there."

Releasing her shoulders, Paxton took the dress from the bed rail, handed it to her, and said, "Take off your shirt and put this on." He turned his back on her.

What would my company say if they knew I'm in a room with a woman undressing?

"Explain to me again about the yarn?" He crossed his arms and stared at the wall.

81

"I feel like a ball of yarn, all unwound." She unbuttoned the shirt and dropped it on the bed.

"Not in control, you mean."

"I guess that's what I mean." Albany donned the dress. "When I knit, the yarn stays in a ball but now it's fallen and rolled, so everything feels unraveled."

"Yarn can be re-wound." He uncrossed his arms. "My mother and sisters knit. I was often enlisted to hold the skein of yarn while they twisted it into a ball." He paused. "Let me try to help you as I helped them. Together, we can create a new ball of yarn, all tightly rolled together as it should be."

"As it should be..." Albany spoke in a dreamy voice.

"Dressed yet?"

"All dressed."

Paxton turned around and held his breath.

She's lovely. What a truly lovely woman.

* * *

A big, long-haired, reddish-brown dog was lost. The booming guns hurt his ears. He had run from the friendly men. During his flight from the battlefield, he fell into a marsh. His fur was wet and muddy. He could not find his way back to those men who fed and petted him. Hunger, a familiar sensation, gnawed at the four-footed creature. Having been abandoned as a puppy, he was grateful to find a home among the friendly men, but now that home was gone. He sought another place with friendly people.

* * *

In the small kitchen, Paxton found coffee beans and potatoes. He happily prepared coffee while Albany peeled potatoes. With coffee brewing, he continued searching the cupboards.

"Here are some saltine crackers." Setting the tin on the table, he turned back to the pie safe. "Well, look at this." He held up a can and read the label. "Borden's Condensed Milk -- bless Mr. Gail Borden for inventing the way to preserve milk in cans. This will make our potato soup taste like Mother's."

Staring at the items on the table, Albany thought: *Like Mother's. Oh, Mother, I wish I was home with you now.*

She scooped the peelings into a pile. He sat down near her, started cutting the peeled potatoes into chunks, and chatted about army food.

What's he saying? Food the soldiers ate? Is Father eating well in the hospital? When will I see my parents again?

Putting the pan of potatoes and milk on the stove, Paxton was stirring the soup when Albany burst into sobs. She dropped her head onto her arms crossed on the table.

I want to be home. I want to forget what I saw.

Coming to her side, Paxton pulled her out of the chair and embraced her. He felt her soft hair under his chin. With her hands in fists, her knuckles pressed against his collar bone. Her body sagged against his.

"Don't cry, Albany. Please don't cry."

Stroking her back, he kept murmuring comforting words as she wept. When her sobs began to subside, after several long minutes, he asked, "Tell me. What is it?"

"I can't get that sight out of my mind."

"I know." He petted her tangled hair. "It's an awful thing to see."

"Don't soldiers experience …?" Without finishing her question, Albany took a restorative breath, turned her head, and rested her cheek against his broad chest.

I feel his heart beating. He's not dead like those men.

"No, my dear, soldiers do not experience sights like we saw." Paxton rubbed one hand under her hair and across the back of her neck. His other hand splayed across her back. "I've never seen burned men -- so many over such a large area." He shivered. She felt his tremor. "I've seen wounded men, gathered around the hospital tent, awaiting their visit to the doctor or recovering from having seen the doctor, but never … what we saw." He pushed her away to hold her at arms' length. Taking her hands in his, he met her eyes shiny with tears. "We need to pray."

"Can the Lord help?"

"Always." He kept her hands in his as he knelt on the wooden floor, pulling her down beside him. "When we don't know what we need, the Holy Spirit prays for us."

Albany listened to his prayer.

"Heavenly Father, I do not know what to say. You know our plight. Albany cannot get the awful image of burned men out of her mind. She needs to get home where she can seek comfort among familiar things. I need to return to my men. But we are in the house of strangers."

Albany said, "We thank you for the shelter you have provided, Lord."

"Yes, Lord, thank you for provision in our time of need."

"For a barn for Joab, too."

Paxton smiled and concluded. "Now we pray for guidance. Bring us safely through. Hear our prayer, in the name of Jesus. Amen."

* * *

When Albany was recovered enough from her crying, Paxton set her to stirring the soup while he searched the house.

"I want to find out who lives here," he said. "Where have they gone?"

Are we in danger? When might the owners return? Are enemy soldiers nearby?

He opened a drawer in the tall bureau in the central room, took out several letters, and scanned the envelopes.

"Benjamin Pritchett." He called to Albany. "Do you know him?"

She repeated the name before saying, "He's the overseer on Thomas Anderson's place."

"Can you find your way home from here?"

I need to get her home.

"No." Albany shook her head. "The Andersons are not close neighbors."

Returning the letters to the drawer, Paxton came to the kitchen, took the big spoon from her, and scooped up a piece of potato. He blew to cool it before tasting.

"Needs a little longer in the pot." He gave the spoon back to her and looked in the cupboard for bowls. "What do you know about Thomas Anderson?"

"They don't attend my church."

That doesn't help me.

Paxton set the bowls on the table and continued his search.

"Here are some newspapers." He picked up the issue on top and announced, "April – not recent." He set the newspaper down. "I wonder how long they've been gone. Did they leave because they knew the Yankees were invading?"

"Invading," repeated Albany, taking up a piece of potato.

"Yes, this is an invasion of our country." Paxton set spoons on the table. "What else would you call it?"

"I'd call it war." Albany ladled soup into the bowls.

* * *

Grandon Faulconer, having just relieved himself, climbed into the canvas-topped wagon next to Ainsley Bracken.

"Ready?" asked the older man.

"Yah." Grandon tugged his hat down to protect his face from the rain. Glancing behind him into the wagon bed where three wounded soldiers lay, Grandon frowned. "I thought we'd just haul supplies. I never expected to transport wounded."

"Better than hauling the dead," said the older man.

Like the man on our last trip. Paxton's brother shivered as the shocking memory came to mind. He had poked the man to awaken him before realizing that man was dead.

"Fix your badge," Ainsley said.

"What?" Grand looked down at the ambulance badge on his jacket. The wind had blown his lapel over to cover the shiny object.

"You want to be sure the Yankee sharpshooters can see it."

Grandon turned his label back in place so the badge was clearly visible and said, "Do these pieces of tin really guarantee our protection?"

"As good as can be," replied Ainsley.

"In these woods, I'm surprised the snipers can see to hit anything."

Ainsley shook his shaggy head and remarked, "I've never seen battles fought in woods like these. We mostly kill each other on open ground so we can see the enemy."

After a brief silence, Grandon asked, "What do you think the army will do now?"

Letting the reins go loose because of the traffic jam ahead, Ainsley answered, "No telling what Bobby Lee's got up his sleeve. He's never faced this new western general."

Grandon, keeping his eyes on horses ahead, said, "Grant has a good reputation from his battles in the west."

"How do you know?"

"I've read about him in the *Gordonsville Gazette*. The editor reprints stories from Yankee newspapers."

"We shouldn't depend on our news from the Yanks," grumbled Ainsley.

"Do you think this Grant fellow might …" Grandon did not finish his sentence. There was no need. Ainsley easily guessed the question.

"Don't fret none. Our army is like the famous Toledo blade – it can be bent backwards and double over on itself, but then it springs back again into perfect shape."

"Like a Toledo blade," mused Grandon, smiling.

* * *

Although Paxton had no need for a knife as he and Albany sat in the kitchen and ate, he had placed a butcher knife beside his plate.

My gun would be better but it's in the other room.

"Is that to cut the bread?" Albany asked.

"There isn't any bread," said Paxton.

Albany jerked her head from the knife to the door.

"Do you expect to be attacked?"

"I don't know what to expect," said Paxton. "But I want to be prepared. Don't be alarmed, Albany. I'll protect you."

But could I really protect her?

* * *

Paxton's older brother Thornton, having protected General Longstreet on the journey to the Meadow Farm, home of the General's friend Erasmus Taylor, now rested in the parlor. Upstairs, Mrs. Taylor nursed the wounded commander while awaiting the train to Lynchburg. As soon as the Confederate commander of the First Corps was aboard the train going to the hospital, Thornton and his comrades could return to the battlefield.

Looking at the rain splattering the window, Thornton said, "This reminds me how the weather was after Gettysburg."

"Did it rain during the battle?" asked the young soldier across the room.

"Not during but the day following," replied Paxton's brother. "It rained all day July 4th." Staring at the ground, he said softly, "The rain made me think it was the Lord's tears, weeping over what we had done there."

* * *

After their simple meal, Albany and Paxton shared the work of cleaning up the kitchen. Paxton stored the left-over soup in a jar and told her about his life as a lawyer in Gordonsville.

"Help me pick out a book we can read aloud to each other." He hung the damp dish towel over the rod on the cabinet door. "Although the day is gloomy, we can open the curtains to get what light there is. We don't want to waste the Pritchett's candles or oil in the lamps."

In the living room, they browsed the titles on the small bookcase.

Paxton asked, "Have you read any of these?" as he pointed to several novels.

"Not these," Albany said, "but I do read novels. Father disapproves, so I read in my room and don't tell him."

Glancing at her beside him, he smiled and returned to the book search.

"What about this one by Charles Dickens?" Paxton asked.

Albany read the spine. "American Notes for General Circulation."

"I've heard of this book. It's about his trip to our country," said Paxton. "I like Charles Dickens. Do you?"

Albany nodded. "I like travelogues."

This will be a good diversion for her.

He pulled the small book off the shelf. They sat side by side on the horsehair sofa.

"Do you want to read first or should I?" Paxton held the book toward her.

"You read," she said.

They were engrossed in the section about the ocean crossing during a storm. When Albany read about people sliding from one end of a sofa to another, she got the giggles and, unable to read, handed the book to Paxton.

It's good to hear her laugh.

They were ten pages farther in the book. Albany was reading about Charles Dickens' visit to the Perkins Institute where Dr. Samuel Gridley Howe taught blind and deaf children. She stopped reading and looked at Paxton.

"I wonder how Dr. Howe broke through Laura Bridgman's sightless, silent world."

"I cannot imagine being both blind and deaf," Paxton said. "Having been blind myself, albeit for a short time, I can assure you, it is most distressing."

"It would be like living in a silent, dark tomb."

Oh, no, not depressing thoughts again, Albany.

"Miss Bridgman must have been highly intelligent," he said.

"And desperate to connect to others."

"Read more." Paxton pointed to the page. "Let's see how Dr. Howe accomplished this miracle."

So engrossed in the story, they both jerked when a sound came from the door. Albany clutched the book to her chest. Paxton rose and quietly walked toward the pegs on the wall. From his holster, he slipped out his gun.

The brownish-red dog continued scratching on the door.

"Have the Pritchett's come home?" Albany asked.

Is it Yankees?

Paxton aimed the gun and pulled the wooden bar across.

"Who is there?" Paxton spoke through the crack.

"Don't shoot him!" Albany leaped up and rushed toward Paxton.

"Woof!"

Albany froze. Paxton laughed and yanked the door open. The muddy animal bounded into the house.

"Well, do you live here?" Paxton shut and locked the door again.

"He's tracking in mud." Albany knelt and held out her arms to halt the dog. Licking her cheek, the dog wagged his tail rapidly.

Paxton headed for the kitchen as he said, "Let's get his paws wiped off."

Returning with two rags, Paxton handed one to her, knelt, and began drying the dog's paws. The dog bestowed his slobbery licks on Paxton, too.

"I'm glad you didn't bring any Yankees with you, Mr. Dog," said Paxton.

The dog's wet tail hitting Albany in the face caused her to laugh.

She's laughing. Thank you, Lord.

"We can't call him Mr. Dog." Albany pushed the tail away.

"Does he belong to the Pritchett's? Do you know if they have a dog?"

"No, I don't know." Albany petted the dog's head.

"He could be a regiment's mascot," said Paxton.

"Maybe he's just a stray."

"No doubt he's hungry."

Albany's eyes were bright. Her mouth kept its smile. "Can we keep him?" she asked.

Paxton stopped wiping the dog's feet, now as clean as could be, and looked at her.

Lord, is this your answer to the help I requested?

"I don't know why not." Paxton stood, offered his hand to her, helped her up, and led her into the kitchen with the dog at their heels.

"Our left-over soup no doubt will be welcomed," said Paxton.

A few minutes later, they watched the dog lick the bowl clean, noisily scooting it across the floor. They both laughed at the sight. Paxton picked up the empty bowl and pumped water at the sink to fill it.

Albany said, "Do you think he is escaping the war like we are?"

Is that what we're doing?

"The sound of guns might have frightened him."

They washed out the muddy rags while the dog lapped up the water.

"What should we name him?" she asked.

"If he deserted the army, his name could be Deserter."

"Deserter," she repeated.

The dog lifted his head from the water bowl and gave a quick bark.

"That's his name." Paxton smiled.

When they returned to the front room, Paxton said, "I prayed for the Lord to send help. I never expected the answer to my prayer would come in the form of a dog." He chuckled. "That just shows the Lord has a sense of humor."

Albany picked up the Dickens book as Deserter curled up in front of the fire and slept. When Paxton was reading about the visit to the hospital for the insane at South Boston and the success the doctors had with patients, Albany stopped him.

"Do you think their enlightened principles of conciliation and kindness could cure all insane people?" Albany wrinkled her brow. "How do such people know what kindness is when they're insane?"

"My tentmate, my friend, Searcy knew that I was kind to him." Paxton met her gaze. "He often spoke of it. Just because a person is crazy doesn't mean they are dead to emotions."

Albany nodded and returned to reading.

When evening came, Paxton sent Albany to the bedroom while he and Deserter made their bed on the floor by the dying fire. Albany, totally exhausted, fell asleep quickly. The dog, too, despite its long afternoon nap, slept. Paxton, however, could not get comfortable.

What am I doing here? This woman is keeping me from my duty. She has a dog for companionship now and doesn't need me.

Wiggle and roll from one side to the other.

Has the company clerk listed me in the roster as missing? Where is Company C tonight? Are they sleeping beside a fire or did the commander forbid campfires to maintain secrecy?

Turn from side to back. Stare up at the dark beams in the ceiling barely visible in the moonlight.

Listening to Charles Dickens in a warm, dry house -- what's gotten into me? This is not where I should be. I'm shirking my duty.

Too hot. Toss off the blanket.

Lord, why have you brought me to this? Is it to take care of Albany? Or has the devil conspired to keep me from my duty?

After midnight, Paxton awoke from a restless sleep to hear Deserter barking.

* * *

CHAPTER SEVEN

GETTYSBURG REVERSED

Monday, May 9, 1864

Moaning loudly, Albany tossed and struggled amid the bedcovers. She was not fighting a sheet and a quilt. In her nightmare, she battled burned skeletons. Deserter pawed at the closed bedroom door and barked. Paxton, wearing only his drawers, stumbled in the dark toward the dog, found the door, and turned the knob. Deserter pushed the door open, bounded toward the bed, leaped up, and licked Albany's face. She jerked and screamed as her eyes flew open. Paxton pressed his hand over her mouth.

Someone might hear her.

With one knee on the mattress, Paxton kept his other foot on the floor.

"Hush, Albany, you're all right. Get back, Deserter." He elbowed the dog away. "You were having a nightmare."

She must stop screaming.

Paxton climbed on the bed. Using one hand on the back of her head, he pressed her face against his bare chest.

Remember she's a lady. I'm a gentleman.

As Albany gained consciousness, her screams stopped. Slowly, Paxton removed his hand from her mouth. She went limp and made a soft whimpering noise.

She's in my control. I could... No, think of my sisters. She's like Lorella and Eunice. I would not want them harmed.

"It was just a nightmare, Albany." He brushed her tangled hair off her face. "You're safe now with me."

Placing his palm on her cheek, he said, "You're hot as can be. Let's get this quilt off."

First, Paxton shoved the dog off the bed, and then heaved the covering toward the foot of the bed. Albany drew her feet under her borrowed nightgown and shivered, not from cold but from remembering her frightening dream.

"You're safe, Albany. I'm here." Paxton patted her back.

She hugged a pillow and murmured, "Stay."

Like a sister. Keep thinking of that.

"All right, I will." Paxton fumbled with the bedding. "You get under the sheet and I'll lie on top."

There needs to be a barrier between us. Will a single sheet be enough?

Albany slid under the sheet. Deserter jumped onto the bed and settled at the foot. The bed springs squeaked when Paxton stretched out beside her.

This is not Albert. Remember, this is Albany – a lovely young woman.

Paxton tucked his feet beneath the quilt. Deserter moved to make room. Albany turned on her side and reached toward Paxton. When her hand touched his chest, he reached up and held her hand slightly away.

I can't have her touch me. She is entirely too tempting as it is.

"The nightmare is over, dear one. We will talk of other things until you can sleep again."

"You won't leave."

"When you fall asleep, you mean? No, I'll stay all night, if that's what you want."

"I do."

They were silent for a long moment.

Albany asked, "When will it go away?"

"I don't know."

She's talking about the past. I'm thinking about the present.

"I wish I could reach into your brain and pull out the memories." His voice was soft. "I'd blow them out like we extinguish candles. The thoughts of recent events would vanish. Your mind would be like a slate erased clean of all the ugly things."

"The chalk dust would disappear," she whispered.

"Yes." He nodded. "Chalk dust blowing in the wind until nothing is left."

If only my desire for you could vanish so easily.

Paxton asked, "Are you tired?"

"No. Are you?"

"Wide awake."

"Can we talk about something besides the war?" she asked.

"Certainly." Paxton took a firmer hold of their joined hands. "We can't read Dickens in the dark. You said you read novels, didn't you?"

"Yes."

"Tell me the story of one you read recently."

That will be a good escape. We both need to think of something else.

"I recently read <u>The Lady and the Sea Captain</u>."

"Interesting title." He wiggled his toes in Deserter's fur. "Was it set in England?"

"How did you know?"

"My sisters read novels and told me they often have an English background."

And I must think of you as I would my sisters. That will keep our night in a bed together unsullied.

"What's the plot?" Paxton let his body relax.

Albany stared into the darkness and recalled the story.

"The heroine, Sophrona, was a beautiful but impoverished young lady who had a domineering mother."

"Intrigues me already."

"The evil mother insisted she marry a wealthy older man so they could be financially secure."

"Good plan. Was the rich old man kind?"

"Not at all," Albany expressed excitement. "He was a beast."

Her voice is animated. She's forgotten the nightmare.

"In the first scene, they rode in the carriage after attending the opera when his behavior became inappropriate."

"No need to explain. I can guess."

My behavior toward you will never be inappropriate, I hope.

"As Sophrona jumped out of the moving vehicle, he tore the shoulder of her lovely gown. Fortunately, coming right behind the carriage was Captain Kincaid Stashower on his way back to his ship."

"Kincaid Stashower -- an unusual name. The hero, I presume."

"Indeed so." Albany straightened her legs and her toes felt Deserter's fur. "The captain was returning from an orphanage where he had contributed the majority of his prize money. Captains get prize money for capturing other ships. Did you know that?"

"I did," said Paxton. "So this fact tells the reader that Captain Stashower was a good man, unlike the evil old rich fellow."

"That's right. He rescued Sophrona from her predicament, having a brief set-to with her attacker, and whisked her away to his ship."

"Where he behaved like a perfect gentleman." Paxton smiled in the dark.

"In truth, he did," said Albany. "He gave her his jacket until she had proper clothes. He gently rubbed ointment on her injured hands, which resulted when she fell from the carriage."

"I'm familiar with injuries caused by falls." *As well as rubbing ointment on a woman.*

"Oh, yes, you fell from your horse."

"Go on."

"The captain insisted she write a note to her mother. Sophrona did not want to return to her mother because she was a scheming, wicked woman who thought only of herself and money."

"Villains make interesting characters in novels," he said. "They hold the reader's interest."

"The mother was certainly a villain. Although Sophrona wrote a note, she refused to tell her mother where she was or where she was going. The Captain conceded that point. He understood. They sailed from Bristol, England, in his ship, the HMS Bliss."

Paxton chuckled. "Clever writer."

"Why?"

"I assume the captain and his lady found bliss on the ship."

"They did have interesting adventures in faraway places." Albany nodded and Paxton felt her movement on their shared pillow. "Sophrona found her father on a Brazilian plantation where Kincaid became the overseer. He married Sophrona under an arch of swaying palm trees."

"How romantic."

"The father retired to sit on the porch and write his memoirs. It had a very happy ending."

"As all good romance novels should." Paxton drew her hand to his throat. "Who was the author?"

"The author was anonymous." Albany felt his prickly beard on the backs of her fingers. "Mother thought a sailor wrote it because there was so much information about the sea and ships but I think a woman wrote it."

"Why?"

"Because the writing was so accurate about falling in love."

What is it like to fall in love, Albany?

Instead of asking the question in his mind, Paxton said, "Don't you think a man can know about love?"

"Can they?"

I dare not continue this. We need to sleep.

"Are you sleepy yet?" he asked.

She gave a deep sigh. "Yes. I think so."

Before many minutes passed, they were both asleep.

* * *

While Albany, Paxton, and Deserter slept, the Confederates dug ditches, piled up logs or fence rails, and threw dirt forward to cover the timber. The men labored diligently, having learned the value of such barriers. They left openings for the muzzles of their cannons to stick through the embrasures.

Not far away, Federal soldiers were also digging and erecting earthworks facing the enemy. The soldiers of both armies could hear the sounds of trees falling and wood being chopped.

"Keep your head down. Their sharpshooters are good," a Union veteran ordered.

"We've got good marksmen, too. Those Rebs better keep their heads down," said a new recruit.

"Reminds me of Gettysburg last year only reversed," said the veteran.

The younger man looked across the moon-lit ground. "What do you mean?"

"At Gettysburg, we had a fishhook design to our lines," the veteran explained. "That enabled us to send men to any spot where reinforcements were needed."

"What's the fishhook design matter about sending reinforcements?"

"Our interior lines protected the soldiers as they moved from one place to another." The older man spoke slowly as a school teacher might. "They were not exposed to danger as they relocated."

"So the Rebs have a fishhook design?"

"No, but they've got a line enabling them to move men, out of sight and out of danger, from place to place."

"What about that bulge in their line?" The young man pointed to the three-sided shape jutting in front of the defensive line. "Doesn't that make them more vulnerable? We can hit them from multiple directions."

"And they can hit us from more angles." The veteran studied the terrain. "It looks to me like they're trying to hold the nearest high ground. They have pushed their line out in a mule shoe shape. I don't know if that's going to be to their advantage or their detriment."

The salient the Confederates created would be known as the Bloody Angle, another similarity to the Battle of Gettysburg.

* * *

Paxton awoke before Albany, quietly slipped out of bed, motioned for the dog to come, and went to the living room where he dressed. After going to the outhouse, he went to the barn with Deserter trotting at his heels.

What are the men doing this morning? Are they preparing for battle?

"Morning, Joab. Did you sleep well?" He closed the barn door and went to pet the horse's nose. "This is our new companion. Deserter meet Joab, a good horse. Joab, this is Deserter."

The horse lowered his head and sniffed the dog, while the dog raised his head to smell the horse. Taking a pitchfork, Paxton tossed hay into the trough. Deserter explored the barn.

"I slept well in your mistress's bed. Rest easy now, Joab. Don't get riled. I behaved myself."

Would that it could have been otherwise -- no, don't dwell on such a thought.

"Deserter was there to chaperone."

Raising another forkful of hay, he said, "You know your mistress is a pretty young lady. I wonder if you could tell me about her gentlemen callers."

Paxton chuckled.

"Or do you give her rides to the homes of her beaux?"

She must have suitors. She is too pretty not to.

"What is it, big fellow? Do you have secrets you can share with me?"

He petted the horse's mane.

"This is what happened. Your mistress had a nightmare. I went to comfort her."

That was all I did.

"It was perfectly innocent, nothing improper."

The horse munched the hay. Paxton began to clean the stall.

"What do you think, Joab? Should I return to my men? What about your mistress? What can I do about her? There must be a lane from the house to the road. I need to find out where we are. Do you know the way home from here?"

Joab nickered in response to Paxton's words.

"Is that a yes or a no? I need a definitive reply."

Paxton chuckled and continued his work.

Upon returning to the house, Paxton stopped, looked up at the sky, and prayed. *I need your help, Lord. I want to keep Albany safe, to get her home, but you know I belong with my men. You certainly know what is going on with the armies hereabouts. Lead me, Jesus. I pray in your name. Amen.*

In the house, Paxton looked in the bedroom where the bed was empty. He went to the kitchen. Albany was standing by the window and watching the birds in the nearby branches. She wore a red shawl over the white nightgown. Her unbound hair fell in curls onto her shoulders. He stopped in the doorway.

Am I seeing a tableau? She is a silent, motionless beauty. But Albany is not an imaginary artist's model. She is real.

"Good morning," he said, entering the room. "Are you hungry? I need coffee. Will you help me make breakfast?"

* * *

As Albany and Paxton prepared breakfast, Federal troops made adjustments to their line. Union General John Sedgwick, sitting on a cracker box, directed the placement of artillery. Bradby Tucker, drinking coffee, stood at a distance and observed.

"Come away from there," said Sedgwick's chief of staff, Martin T. McMahon. "You're too exposed."

Chuckling, the General replied, "Those Rebels couldn't hit an elephant at this distance."

A Confederate sharpshooter aimed his rifle and fired. The bullet struck General Sedgwick beneath his left eye. He collapsed in the arms of Lieutenant Colonel McMahon. Both men fell to the ground. Bradby dropped his tin cup.

"The General's hit!"

"Get the doctor!"

"Hurry!"

Blood trickled down General Sedgwick's face. He did not move. The stricken group knew their leader was dead.

* * *

Albany took the jar of oatmeal flakes from the pie safe. "Do you like oatmeal?"

I need to keep busy. I don't want to think about things – the bodies, the nightmare.

"Oatmeal sounds good." Paxton started the fire.

"What's on my legs?" Albany pumped water into the kettle.

"Remember – those wool pants and bug bites made your legs itch."

"You put bacon grease on me."

"That's true. You can wash it off after breakfast." He watched the flame catch. "There's a tub in the barn. I'll bring it in. Wear a dress today. You don't need to disguise yourself as a soldier while we're in the house."

It will be nice to wear a dress again.

Albany nodded agreement. "Delivering a map seems so long ago."

They were eating when Albany asked, "Where do you think the Pritchett's went?"

"Maybe to the big house, a safer place than this isolated location." Paxton scooped up a spoonful of oatmeal. "Who did you say he works for?"

"The Andersons – Thomas and Jane," she answered.

"The main road will be easy to find from the Andersons' place."

"I want to stay here."

"The Pritchett's might return and not appreciate our taking up residence in their house."

"But I'm afraid to go out there again." Albany's lip trembled.

I've seen what's out there. It's horrible.
Paxton said, "Don't fret. You're safe."

* * *

After breakfast, Paxton filled the tub with heated water so Albany could wash her legs. She wore a green cotton dress made for a woman twenty pounds heavier and several inches shorter. When she came into the living room, Paxton noticed her ankles showed.

"Are your legs better?" asked Paxton, who wore a well-fitting, clean shirt and his own pants and suspenders. His jacket hung on the wall peg next to his holster and Albany's haversack and canteen.

"Yes. Cotton is so much nicer than wool when the weather is warm."

They settled on the sofa and Paxton took the first turn at reading the Dickens travelogue. When Paxton handed the book to Albany, he went to the window.

"I'm going to open the window," he said. "It's getting hot."
I need to hear if there's gunfire nearby.

Albany took up reading where he had left off. Several times, Paxton's mind wandered as he wondered what might be happening on the battlefield.

I should be scouting.

During his turn, Paxton read about three young women in adjoining cells at the Eastern Penitentiary in Philadelphia.

"In the silence and solitude of their lives, they had grown to be quite beautiful. Their looks were very sad, and might have moved the sternest visitor to tears."

Albany stopped him with a wave of her hand. "That description makes me think of Laura Bridgman again. She was in silence and solitude."

"But those prisoners had the hope of one day being free," Paxton said.

"Hope, yes, that's important."
I hope you take a nap so I can scout.

* * *

At the same time Albany and Paxton read Dickens, Albany's mother, Luciana Trubridge, and her fellow boarder at the Stuart mansion on Grace Street, Eliza Edgerton, were returning to Chimborazo Hospital.

"I hope my husband will be well enough to go home soon," said Luciana.

"And I hope the war ends soon so all the men can go home," Eliza said.

They walked up the sloping hill toward the tent city.

"Have you read the newspapers you're bringing to your husband?" asked Eliza.

"No, I'll read them with him. He wants to know the war news," said Luciana.

Half an hour later, Luciana was seated beside her husband's bed and reading to him.

"A gunboat on the Red River had to be blown up by order of Admiral Porter," she read. "It seems that our forces attacked while they were endeavoring to lighten the cargo. To prevent their ship from falling into our hands, the Federals blew it up."

"Good. That's good," said Shedrick. "See what other war news is published."

Glancing over the front page, his wife said, "Here's a story." She held the paper closer to read the tiny type. "General Grant made a violent and tremendous attack to pierce the enemy's center in hopes of dividing our forces but failed."

"Where was that?"

Luciana scanned the article. "In Spotsylvania County." She lowered the paper and stared at her husband. "Oh, my sakes, Shedrick, that could be near our house."

* * *

In the Pritchett's house, Albany and Paxton took a break from reading to play with Deserter. Paxton knotted a rag into a ball and tossed it across the room. Retrieving the toy, Deserter pranced toward the man but when Paxton tried to pull the ball away, the dog growled and clenched his teeth on the fabric. Albany reached for the ball. Deserter dropped the ball at her feet.

"So you favor the lady, do you?" Paxton watched Albany throw the ball. When Deserter returned with it, Paxton snatched at the ball. Again, Deserter tussled with the toy, not releasing it.

"You take it," Paxton said to Albany.

Once again, Deserter let her have the ball. They both laughed as they played with the dog.

"Did you have dogs growing up?" asked Albany, waiting for Deserter.

"Three boys without a dog." He chuckled. "We always had a dog. What about you?"

"Yes, I've always had a dog, too," Albany said. "I was grateful to them for warning when strangers came."

"Warning you?" He reached toward Deserter. The dog backed away. "Didn't you like having visitors?"

Should I tell him my secret?

"You must be careful about strangers," she said. "When you don't know them and especially when you live on a plantation far from civilization, you have to watch out."

"You call them strangers not visitors."

Does he suspect?

"Well, isn't everyone a stranger until you get to know them?" Albany tossed the ball.

Paxton eyed her askance. "And what does Matthew 25 tell us to do about strangers?"

"Treat them as we would treat Jesus," Albany said.

Deserter sat with the ball in his mouth but neither of his playmates reached for it. "Then they are no longer strangers," he said.

"I've always been afraid of them." Albany pressed her lips firmly together.

There — my secret it out. I've told him.

"You weren't afraid of me." Paxton patted Deserter's head. "I was a stranger under that fallen horse."

Albany petted the dog's back. "I know. That seems odd. I don't know why I came to your aid."

"Could it be that you are overcoming your fear of strangers?" asked Paxton.

"My parents and servants have been hoping for that," Albany said.

Deserter dropped the rag ball.

* * *

At the Trubridge plantation, Susa and Coffer were changing Gerow's bandage while Audine set out writing materials on the little table. At the top of the paper, she wrote: *May 9, 1864, Dear Wife,* and said, "I've dated your letter and addressed it to dear wife. What's her Christian name?"

"Myrta." Gerow spelled the name and Audine wrote.

"Write that I have been wounded and am being cared for by a kind family near Spotsylvania Court House." He waited until Audine stopped writing. "Do not fret about me. There is no need for you to come."

Audine inked her pen and said, "I think that is wise. It's not safe for a lady to travel alone. The trains are full of soldiers and ne'er-do-wells."

Susa thought: *The poor old lady doesn't realize Albany is traveling alone.*

"Where does your wife live?" asked Coffer, dropping the used bandage into a basin.

"Cincinnati," answered Gerow.

"Is that a long way from here?" the servant asked.

"Hundreds of miles," answered Audine. "Too far for you to run off to, so don't think it." She positioned her pen on the paper. "What next?"

"If you write to me, send it to my regiment as usual. I'll get your letter when I return." Gerow was silent as the old woman wrote.

Coffer and Susa wrapped the fresh bandage around Gerow's chest.

"I pray for you as I know you pray for me."

The only sound in the room was Audine's pen scratching on the paper.

"I send all my love, from your loving husband, Gerow Gately."

"Do I have to give your full name?" Audine wrinkled her forehead. "Doesn't she know who you are?"

Audine dipped her pen in the ink bottle. Gerow chuckled and said, "It's my custom."

Audine wrote and then handed him the pen. "You write your name."

The servants halted their bandaging until Gerow had written those two words. Audine made two folds in the letter, poised the pen above the middle third on the unwritten side, and said, "Address, please."

Gerow gave his home address in Cincinnati. Audine finished writing, recapped the bottle of ink, and waited. When Coffer took the letter, Gerow asked, "Can letters get through?"

"Couriers smuggle them," said Coffer.

"Do you know couriers, Coffer?" asked Audine.

"I know some."

"Well, that's taken care of." Audine stood and went to the door. "Susa, I need to find my Bible. I seem to have lost it."

Susa followed her mistress.

Gerow said to Coffer, "When you meet the courier, ask what news he has of the armies."

"Yes, sir, I'll do that." Coffer nodded and departed.

* * *

Albany and Paxton played with Deserter, read Charles Dickens' travelogue, and ate lunch.

"You didn't get much sleep last night," Paxton said. "Why don't you take a nap? I need to tend Joab."

That was easier than I expected, Paxton said to himself, twenty minutes later as he walked down the lane leading from the overseer's house to the Big House. *She made no protest. I just hope she doesn't panic when she finds I've gone.*

He dodged an overhanging branch.

I could have brought the dog -- a good lookout for me, but better to be her companion. She might wake up before I return.

He glimpsed buildings at the end of the lane and slowed his pace.

I wonder if anyone is there.

He reached for his hip and realized that he had forgotten to strap on his gun.

Forgot my gun. What would my company say about such stupidity? I wonder what are they doing now?

* * *

The Thirteenth Virginia, Paxton's regiment, was almost completely broken down. The men were in a vile mood. The Third Corps commander, Ambrose Powell Hill was so ill that he could not mount his horse. General Lee assigned General Jubal Early as a temporary replacement. Lee then gave command of Early's division to General John Brown Gordon as reward for exceptional service in the Wilderness battle.

* * *

Paxton now clearly saw that the buildings ahead were slave quarters.

I'll watch for a bit and see who is around.

Paxton moved cautiously behind a tree at the edge of the clearing that bordered the ramshackle little houses. Not seeing or hearing anyone, he soon ran from the tree to the first house, then to the next one, making his way to the Big House. He just reached the last slave house when he heard hoof beats and halted.

Soldiers! Which side? I see them. They're blue-clad.

Paxton remained where he was, concealed at the corner of a slave shack. Three men on horseback began encircling the house as two men dismounted and went inside.

I'd better hide.

Paxton ducked indoors and hurried to the single window, just a hole in the wall without glass.

What are they doing? Where are the residents?

Before long, a Union soldier appeared at the door of the Big House and announced, "No one home."

"Plenty of space for the wounded," said the second soldier exiting the house.

"See any slaves?" asked a mounted man.

"Don't see a soul."

"Let's report to the doctors."

"They'll like this better than a tent."

The two soldiers from the house mounted. All five men rode away.

Well, no need to go in there now. It will soon be overrun by Yankees.

Paxton started back to the overseer's house. Halfway there, he heard a cannon boom. Halting, he waited until he was certain the sound was far enough away that he was not in danger.

Will Albany be awakened by the cannon? Will she be frightened?

At the Pritchett's house, Paxton found both doors locked.

She's put the bar across.

Deserter barked as the front doorknob rattled.

"Albany! Let me in! It's Paxton!"

He banged on the door. Deserter kept barking.

Are there Yankees nearby to hear me?

"Albany! Open the door!"

Paxton heard a wooden bar slide through a metal sleeve. As soon as the noise stopped, Paxton pushed the door wide. Albany backed away. She aimed his Colt revolver at him.

"It's me, Albany."

If her finger moves, I'm a dead man.

"There's nothing to fear."

Paxton took a small step.

"Put the gun down."

Her hand is shaking.

Paxton held out his hand and took another step.

"I mean you no harm, Albany."

Lord, don't let her finger move.

Paxton reached for the gun as their eyes met.

"Paxton?"

"Yes. It's me." He gently removed the weapon from her hand.

Thank you, Lord.

Albany collapsed against him. He embraced her with one arm while shoving the gun into its holster hanging from the wall peg.

"I am sorry I was away so long." He took a backward step to push the bar in place, locking the door, and then wrapped both arms around her. "I thought you would stay asleep until I returned."

"Where were you?" She raised her hands to his chest.

"I went to the Andersons' house. The Yankees will be using it for a hospital."

* * *

In Washington, Major General Henry Wager Halleck, having been reduced to Chief of Staff since General Grant took command, sat at his desk in the War Department and read the most recent message from General Grant.

The enemy holds our front in very strong force, and evinces a strong determination to interpose between us and Richmond to the last. I shall take no backward step.

* * *

CHAPTER EIGHT

EMORY UPTON'S BOLD PLAN

Tuesday, May 10, 1864

Emory Upton, a handsome young man with well-groomed whiskers, attended Oberlin College in Ohio for two years before attending the U.S. Military Academy at West Point, graduating one month after the first shots of the Civil War were fired. Now, as dawn brought a dim light to the Wilderness, the twenty-four-year-old sipped his coffee and pondered a plan of attack against the enemy.

* * *

Paxton awoke to the sound of scattered gunfire. He cautiously crawled out of bed, glanced at Albany sleeping peacefully, motioned for Deserter, and went into the living room. After dressing, he went to the outhouse and then to the barn. Deserter investigated the barn while he tended to the horse.

"She had another nightmare, Joab. I shared her bed again last night." He petted the big animal's mane. "No need to fuss. Nothing happened. I got her calmed down and had her tell me another story from a novel." He forked hay into the trough. "That gets her mind off her nightmare. She needs to be home. I must get her there."

As he worked, he talked about the men in his company and what they must be thinking about his absence. Going back to the kitchen, Paxton rubbed his face.

I need a shave.

Within a few minutes, Paxton was shaving and singing.

"Let all on earth their voices raise, to sing the great Jehovah's praise."

Deserter howled. Paxton laughed at the dog. His razor slipped. He nicked himself on the jaw. Albany entered, saw the spot of blood amid the white shaving cream, and gasped.

"It's nothing." Paxton dropped the razor in the basin. "I just cut myself a little." He snatched up a towel and blotted the tiny wound.

Albany, wearing the same nightgown and shawl as yesterday morning, came to the sink.

She is so lovely. Her hair curling over her shoulders is beautiful.

"Does it hurt?" Albany moved the towel aside to look.

"No. It's just a minor cut."

How fortunate her husband will be some day.

He covered her hand and a portion of the towel with his own hand. "I am not wounded," he said.

"I don't want to see bleeding men."

"Nor do I." Paxton pulled a chair from under the table. "Sit down and let me finish shaving, then we can make breakfast."

Albany sat and watched him as he completed his shaving ritual. Deserter rested his head on her knee, awaiting her attention. She petted the dog.

"Tell me about your family," Paxton said. "I don't know much about them."

"My family? Why?"

"I need to get you home to your family. I'd like to know about the people I will see when I get there. Tell me."

"Well, there's Grandma Audine Trubridge, the matriarch of our family." Albany watched the razor glide over the white shaving cream. "Grandma will be fretting about me. I've been gone longer than I said I would be. She's getting old and forgetful. Hopefully Coffer and Susa can sooth her."

"Who are they?" Paxton rinsed his razor in the water.

"Our slaves, the only two who are left." She crossed her arms. "The others ran off in '62."

"Susa and Coffer," he repeated. "Are they married?"

"No but they are fond of each other."

"Why don't they wed?"

"Coffer has a wife." Albany unfolded her arms and held her hands in her lap. "She was sold apart from him; his sons, too."

"That is sad when families are separated."

"Father didn't do it. A previous owner parted them."

"I see." Having finished, he wiped the dots of white off his face, hung up the towel, and emptied the basin. "What about your parents?"

"Father has been serving in the Quartermaster Department. He became ill." She whispered the next word: "Dysentery." Raising her voice, she continued, "So Mother went to Chimborazo to tend him and accompany him home as soon as he's well enough to travel."

"So your parents don't know you have left home."

Deserter, seeing Paxton go to the stove, left Albany and followed him. Paxton started the fire. The dog found the empty tin bowl used for his food yesterday, got it from under the pie safe, and carried it to Paxton.

"I think our dog is hungry." Taking the bowl, Paxton set it on the table and said, "You'll get our leftovers soon enough."

"No, my parents don't know I've gone." She got the jar of oatmeal. "I would not have been able to leave if Father were home. He's very protective of me."

"That's understandable." Paxton added wood to the fire. "My father is protective of my two sisters."

"You have sisters." She smiled. "I wish I had sisters."

She is so pretty when she smiles.

"Are you an only child?"

"I am." She started to pump water into an iron pot. "I had two brothers but they died as infants."

"How old?" Paxton took over her job of pumping.

Maybe I should not ask her about her deceased brothers. She's seen enough of death.

"My first brother died the day he was born. I was six years old and remember seeing his tiny, lifeless body." She measured out oatmeal.

"Should we talk about something else?" Paxton carried the pot to the stove.

"No, it's all right. My brothers were not like those soldiers. My second brother died of fever at the age of seven months. They both have neat little, well-tended graves amid a grove of trees. They are mourned and remembered." She stirred the oatmeal. "Will those men have graves?"

"The army grave diggers will bury them." He lightly touched her shoulder and asked, "What other family members?"

No more talk of graves and the dead.

"I have an aunt and uncle in Fredericksburg. They have a big family. I'm an only child. I like visits with my cousins."

As she talked about her relatives, they completed breakfast preparations, sat down, prayed, and began eating.

"What would your family say if they knew you were here?" Paxton asked.

"Perhaps it is best that they not know."

"Can you keep this adventure secret?"

Albany looked up from her bowl. "Is this an adventure?"

"What would you call it?"

"Well, it did begin as an exciting adventure." She held her spoon idle above her bowl. "But the whole thing did not come about as I imagined it would."

"How so?"

She seems better today. The anxiety is easing.

"After I delivered the map to the Yankees, I vomited." She glared at her oatmeal. "At least, I emptied my stomach of what was there, which wasn't much. No heroine would do that."

"Do you think of yourself as one of those heroines in the novels you read?"

Her eyes met his as she said, "I guess I do. That's silly, isn't it?"

"Not at all." He smiled at her. "I imagine myself being raised in rank on the field for doing some heroic deed. Such thoughts seem to be human nature."

Albany returned his smile.

* * *

As Albany and Paxton settled down with the book by Dickens, Colonel Emory Upton called his commanders for a meeting. They stood on the edge of the woods facing Doles' Salient, named thus because the brigade

109

of George Doles was entrenched there. The young New Yorker revealed his bold plan to the twelve regimental leaders while journalist Bradby Tucker stood nearby taking notes.

"We will attack in columns and hit that spot," said Emory, pointing to the location, "without pausing to trade fire."

"No firing?" asked an officer.

"That's right. There must be no delay in reaching the breastworks," Colonel Upton answered. "We want to overwhelm them and achieve a breakthrough before they know what they're about. No one is to aid a wounded man or yell or cheer. Only when they reach the earthworks are the men to fire, spread out, and use their bayonets freely."

"That's not the way we usually attack."

"A massed frontal assault carries the day."

"Not this day," the young colonel responded. "We will not be striking like a wave but like a fist."

Across the top of his paper, Bradby wrote: *Not a wave but a fist.*

The officer beside the reporter saw those six words and whispered, "That should make a good headline."

"Especially if it succeeds," said the *New York Times* correspondent.

* * *

Paxton was reading about Charles Dickens and his party being waited on by slaves for the first time in Baltimore. Albany halted his reading by putting her hand atop the page.

"How well do you think freed slaves will be accepted after the war?" she asked.

"Are you assuming that the North will win?"

"You know the South cannot hold out much longer." She withdrew her hand from the book. "Consider what Mr. Dickens thinks about our country continuing to hold slaves when England abolished slavery fifty years ago. It's barbaric of us."

Paxton nodded. "Perhaps you are right about the North winning, although the changes that will come are hard to imagine. As for former slaves finding their place in a free society, I cannot even speculate."

They temporarily forgot about Charles Dickens as they discussed a future country after the war ended. Although the travelogue was entertaining literature, Albany and Paxton found many narrations in the story resulted in discussion. When they read about the Englishman visiting a prison, Paxton remarked that he hoped never to be caught as a deserter and locked up in a prison. Albany commented that she was grateful for privileges and her desire to make life better for others.

* * *

In the woods, not far from embattled soldiers, Coffer Dunn came upon Statesman Prather, a slave owned by Myers Chesterton, hiding behind a tree. Statesman was coal black and younger than Coffer. The two slaves attended the same outdoor church, fished in the same watering hole, and gathered in secret whenever possible.

"Statesman, that you?"

What's he doing in the woods this time of day?

Statesman motioned for Coffer to come toward him.

"It's me, Coffer."

Coffer joined the younger man. "What you doing hiding, Statesman?

"Watching for blue-coats."

"Why?"

Statesman pressed his back against the tree trunk, making room for Coffer to hide.

I can probably guess the answer.

"I might join them," answered Statesman.

I guessed right.

"What about Liney?"

"She doesn't want to leave the Chesterton's." Statesman peeked around the tree, saw no one, and faced Coffer again. "The missus is bad sick. They haven't got a letter from the master in a long time."

"Your Liney is a good woman," said Coffer.

"What about you? What brings you out?"

"Looking for our mistress, Albany. She went off on her horse a few days back and hasn't come home."

"You think the soldiers done got her?"

Please no, Lord.

"Can't tell." Coffer shook his head. "Sure hope not."

"Have you seen any of those Federal soldiers?" Statesman scanned the landscape.

"No, but you can't leave your wife." Coffer put his hand on Statesman's shoulder.

"I'd come back for her after the war."

The older man tightened his grip and said. "You stay together. If she won't go, you don't go."

"I don't hanker to be a slave when freedom is in sight."

"None of those Union soldiers are in sight." Coffer waved his hand toward the trees. "Your freedom needs to wait a little longer.

"But President Lincoln made us free," said Statesman. "I want to claim what I got."

"It's not Mr. Lincoln that frees you. The blue-coat soldiers make Lincoln's words stick." Coffer turned to go. "You know Lincoln's words aren't worth a piece of straw in Virginia."

"I know." Statesman nodded. "That Chesterton boy, the big one, Forrester, keeps reminding me Jeff Davis is the president here, not Mr. Lincoln."

Coffer shook hands with Statesman and said, "If you see or hear about Miss Albany, come and tell us."

"I'll do that."

"And don't go anywhere without your good woman beside you."

The two slaves parted.

* * *

Albany and Paxton ate lunch while molasses cookies baked in the oven.

"Let's take our cookies to the back yard." Paxton gathered up the dishes and took them to the sink." There's a bench where we can sit and read."

They washed the dishes before going outdoors and sitting side by side on the split-log bench. Deserter sat at their feet. Joab munched on grass nearby. No sounds of gunfire disturbed the peace of the afternoon. Although the day was hot, the bench where they sat was in the shade. Albany wore the same borrowed dress. She had taken the greased bandages off her legs because the bug bites were better. Paxton wore his civilian pants and shirt.

Albany was reading Dickens's description of one pig being startled by his mud-covered brother pig. "He shot off as hard as he could go: his excessively little tail vibrating with speed and terror like a distracted pendulum."

Bursting into giggles, Albany had to stop reading. Paxton chuckled and smiled at her.

What a lovely laugh she has. Thank you, Lord, for Charles Dickens, and his ability to make her happy.

During Paxton's turn reading in chapter fifteen about travels in Canada, he read about a beautiful girl of twenty, captured during the Canadian insurrection, and imprisoned. "She acted as bearer of secret dispatches, sometimes dressed as a girl, and carrying them in her stays; sometimes attiring herself as a boy would, which was nothing to her, for she could govern any horse that any man could ride."

Albany interrupted him, saying, "I found it very freeing to ride Joab while wearing pants." She smoothed the skirt of her green dress.

Deserter perked up his ears, lifted his head, barked, and stood. Three muddy men appeared from the shadowy forest. Swishing his tail, the dog growled.

"Afternoon folks," said the biggest man.

Albany stiffened. Standing, Paxton stepped in front of her.

"Good morning, gentlemen."

These are not gentlemen. I wish I had my gun.

Paxton looked from one disheveled man to the other. Deserter continued to snarl. Paxton reached down and rested his hand on the dog's head.

"Does he bite?" asked the big man.

"He does," said Paxton.

"You two the only ones here?" The second man, with bushy eyebrows, aimed his rifle barrel toward Paxton's stomach.

"That's right," replied Paxton. "I've made a stop home to visit my sister."

Forgive me for lying, Lord.

"Yer sister, huh," said the third man, tall and thin, as he tried to look around Paxton and see Albany.

I don't like this. Can I fight all three of them?

"What are you doing here? We didn't think the Federal Army was so close." Paxton's gaze traveled from one dirty face to the other.

"Our enlistments are up."

The three soldiers laughed.

"Up early."

"Just in time to miss this fight."

"Yah, that's right. We decided."

They're deserters.

"That your horse?"

"It is," said Paxton.

Albany clutched her hands in her lap and stared at the back of Paxton's shirt.

"He's done some hard riding," said Paxton.

"We've done some hard walking; could use a horse."

"Let's get some food first."

"Yah, I'm hungry."

"Got anything to eat?"

"There's food inside." Paxton nodded toward the kitchen door. "You're welcome to it."

Will they eat and go?

"No need for guns, gentlemen," Paxton added. "You can see that we pose no threat to you."

"We might like to get better acquainted with your sister," said the big man.

Suddenly, Albany felt saliva seeping into her mouth. She clasped her hand over her mouth and leaned forward. Paxton glanced behind him.

She's going to vomit.

Growling, Deserter nipped at the big man's pants leg. He kicked at the dog. Deserter yipped, backed away, and barked.

"Get out," Paxton snarled.

Pandemonium ensued. The big man lunged for Paxton. Deserter attacked the man with bushy eyebrows. The tall, thin man headed for Albany.

"Don't tell me to get out."

"Ow. Damn dog bit me. I'm bleeding."

"She's a wild cat." The thin man attempted to hold Albany's arm.

Paxton and his attacker were wrestling on the ground. Deserter's barks and growls drove Bushy Eyebrows toward the woods. Albany freed herself and ran into the house. She tried to shut the door. Her pursuer shoved the door and entered the kitchen. Albany grabbed the iron skillet. With one swing, she slammed it into the side of the Yankee's head. He stumbled backwards. Blood streamed from the wound. He dropped unconscious atop the cellar trap door.

Carrying the skillet, Albany ran outside. Paxton and the big man were fighting over possession of the rifle. Both their hands were on the weapon. Albany raised the heavy pan over her head. She stepped to one side to avoid the brawling men. In the next moment, they separated. She bashed the skillet down as hard as she could. The big man lay motionless. Paxton jumped up.

"Give me that." Paxton grabbed the skillet, went to the dog, and clobbered the third attacker.

"Where's the other one?"

"I hit him in the kitchen."

"Good girl." Paxton ran into the house. Albany and Deserter came right behind him. Seeing the man with the bleeding head wound, Paxton shoved him aside, pulled the metal ring to open the trap door, and lowered the man into the hole.

"We've got to get out of here," said Paxton. "The soldiers are too close."

"There could be more?" Albany twisted her hands at her waist.

"Go and change into your uniform," Paxton told her. "I'll put those other two down there."

Albany tugged the dress over her head as she ran to the bedroom. Paxton hauled the other two men to drop them into the root cellar. Albany returned to the kitchen.

"Did you kill them?" she asked.

"No, they're all breathing." He moved the table to cover the trap door.

Paxton went to the wall peg and strapped on his holster as Albany donned Gerow's hat. They filled the canteen with water. One of the deserters began banging on the underside of the trap door before they fled the house.

* * *

Colonel Upton's twelve regiments moved noiselessly to the edge of the woods as they prepared for their unusual attack while on another part of the battlefield, cannoneers loaded their weapons.

* * *

After an hour's riding, Paxton realized the horse could not get through the tangled brush, so he dismounted, took the reins, and led Joab at a walk. Albany remained in the saddle.

"Will they follow us?" Albany leaned over the pommel to avoid a low branch.

"No," answered Paxton. "They don't know which way we went."

"You see why I've been afraid of strangers. They do bad things."

"Not all strangers."

A shot rang out. Paxton dropped the reins and yanked Albany out of the saddle.

Where'd it come from? Don't see the gunman.

A second bullet zinged past Paxton's shoulder. Deserter barked a quick yip. Paxton pushed Albany under a bush and covered her body with his own.

"Halt there!" shouted a man.

Another bullet zinged through the air. Bushes rustled. Branches snapped. Four skirmishers were coming.

Behind us. Sounds like more than one.

Deserter crawled beside Albany and Paxton as they moved on hands and knees deeper into the thicket. Joab, neighing and attempting to rear, remained where he was, unable to penetrate the dense woods.

Zing! Zing! Two more bullets flew.

"Did you hear a dog?"

"Get that horse!"

Paxton rolled onto his back and drew his gun.

I can't see them. If I fired, I'd give away our position.

Turning toward Albany, he put his finger to his lips. Albany nodded. She hugged the dog close. Deserter kept quiet.

"Where'd they go?"

"Do you see 'em?"

"Take the horse. Forget about the rider."

Deserter licked Albany cheek. With her sleeve, she wiped away the saliva.

They must not catch us.

Paxton barely breathed. Albany closed her eyes. The dog remained motionless. They listened as the men stomped and Joab whinnied.

"I got him."

"Beauty of a horse."

"Who gets to ride?"

"We draw straws."

"Only fair way."

The voices grew fainter as the four men moved away. Paxton holstered his gun. When he no longer heard the men, he stood up, looked around, and extended his hand to help Albany to her feet.

"They took Joab." Albany's lip quivered.

"And our haversack with the molasses cookies," said Paxton.

* * *

Liney Prather and her husband Statesman filled four buckets at the well in the back yard of the Chesterton Plantation. He told his wife about his meeting with Coffer Dunn. Liney, an attractive young woman, with lighter skin than her husband, could have passed for a sun-tanned white woman. She kept her curly black hair in a neat braid encircling her head.

As they carried their filled buckets to the basement door, Liney said, "I don't like you off in the woods with the fighting men so close."

"I was looking for the Union soldier boys." He lifted up the horizontal door. "Coffer was looking for his mistress?"

"Who?"

"Miss Albany." He waited for her to descend the stone steps. "She's gone off."

"What for?" whispered Liney, looking around the basement to see how close anyone was.

Three boys were on their knees playing marbles in the center of the brick floor. In the corner, the mistress and her daughter sat on a mattress almost completely covering an old rug. Statesman lowered the door, went down the steps, and said, "Later" to his wife. Not until the slaves were on the back porch, emptying the used bathwater, did they continue their conversation.

"Why was Coffer looking for Miss Albany?" Liney asked.

"Coffer didn't rightly say."

"I hope she's all right."

"I expect she'll come home directly." Statesman shook the pail and watched the last drops of water fall.

"Did you see any soldiers?" Liney did the same with her pail.

"I did."

"Oh, Statesman, you won't go off and leave me."

"This might be our last chance for freedom," he said.

"No, no, the war will end soon. Mr. Lincoln promised us our freedom. We just have to wait until that wicked Jefferson Davis is gone, so Mr. Lincoln can take charge."

"I can't wait."

Liney set the pail on the porch and wrapped her arms around her husband's waist. "Don't go without me. At least, wait for the master to come home."

"The master might never come home." Statesman embraced her.

"Oh, dear, don't say that."

"He might already be dead," said Statesman. "They haven't had a letter from him for some time. You know that."

"Yes, I do know." Liney rested her head against his chest. "The missus is so poorly. We can't leave the children when their mother's consumption could kill her any day now.

"Young Master Forrester can take charge," Statesman said.

"He's just a boy," Liney protested.

"The boy's fifteen, mostly full grown."

"He is getting tall." Liney nodded. "He looks me straight in the eye now."

"Forrester likes being the master, giving orders." Statesman held her away and looked into her eyes. "He's a smart boy. The children will be all right."

Back in the basement, both Statesman and Liney attended to their work of serving Madelyn Chesterton, suffering from tuberculosis, and her four children. The slaves' chores had increased since the move to the basement a few days ago. Mrs. Chesterton feared bullets piercing the windows or soldiers invading, so had insisted they live in the low-ceiling basement until the armies moved away.

Thirteen-year-old Florence, pretty, with long blonde curls, tucked the sheet under the mattress when the rubber ball her brothers were tossing landed near her. Picking it up, she tossed it to Forrester, who was closest.

"Be careful," she said. "You could hit Mama. Move farther away."

Forrester motioned for his twin brothers, Blake and Drake, aged eleven, to go to the far side of the large room. "Move, boys."

"When can we go upstairs?" Blake asked.

"I wanna look out the windows," said Drake, "and see if soldiers are about."

"Hush." Forrester threw the ball toward his brothers. "We must wait until Mama is napping. Keep your voices down. Let her fall asleep."

Minutes later, Forrester set their ball at the bottom of the interior steps.

"You all be careful," Florence said as her brothers began tip-toeing up the stairs. "Come back before Mama awakens."

Statesman scowled at the boys but they avoided his stare. Liney gathered up the blood-stained hankies from beside the bed and took them to the basin to wash.

"Don't you worry," said Forrester, his blue eyes bright with excitement. "The Yanks don't scare us."

"That's right," added Drake. "We're brave warriors."

Half way up, Blake asked, "How long do soldiers fight in one location, Forrester?"

"For as long as they want to," answered the older boy.

* * *

With wild cheers, the Union soldiers rushed toward the enemy entrenchments at 6:20 p.m. When they gained the parapet, a deadly hand-to-hand conflict ensued. The first Federal units broke a hole in the line, sweeping the Confederates from their works. Emory Upton personally led a charge that captured a Rebel battery firing canister into the Northern ranks. The blue-clad men rolled the line 200 yards back within two minutes.

When Colonel Upton ordered his fourth line forward, he discovered the Vermonters had mingled with the assaulting force so they were no longer available as a reserve. Worse news was the fact that the planned support on his left never materialized. There was confusion among the Union generals. Who was supposed to support Upton's attack? How it was to be done?

Bradby Tucker, pencil in hand, paced while awaiting the returning soldiers.

"How was it?" the New York journalist asked soldier after soldier.

"Should have succeeded."

"The Colonel's tactics were brilliant."

"Corps commanders failed us."

"No support came up."

Bradby scribbled quickly.

"Colonel Upton protested General Grant's order to withdraw. I heard him."

"What else could he do?"

"It's too dark to see the Rebs now."

The Union soldiers continued grumbling as they moved into camp. Bradby could not hear their exact words but he had enough information for an article. He underlined three words on his note pad: *disappointed*, *angry*, and *betrayed*.

* * *

CHAPTER NINE

THE SEVERED HEAD

Wednesday, May 11, 1864

Paxton awoke on Wednesday morning to the motion of the ground shaking.

What's happening? Is it an earthquake?

Sitting up, he looked around. Albany, beside him, rolled over. Deserter stood alert. He reached out and patted the dog.

Was I dreaming? No, Deserter feels it too.

With ears erect, Deserter wagged his tail slowly and surveyed the area. Paxton used his other hand to touch the earth.

That's not wagons or marchers. It's cannons exploding.

"Albany! Wake up." He fumbled for her hand. "Hurry; we must go."

Albany stirred. Paxton took her hand, stood, and pulled her with him.

"What?" she mumbled.

"Cannon fire."

Deserter headed away from the sound. Albany and Paxton were right behind the dog. Not until they were far enough away to hear only a few birds chirping did they halt. They were on the edge of a marsh.

"I need to go," said Albany in a low voice.

"As do I." Paxton pointed. "You go behind those bushes. "I'll turn my back."

Albany obeyed him without a word. After relieving herself, she buttoned her pants and called, "May I come back yet?"

"Yes, it's all right."

She doesn't seem to be embarrassed – how far we have come.

"Keep your voice down," he said as she approached. "We don't know who might be about."

"What should I say if we're caught?"

Caught? Captured you mean. Made prisoners of war.

He took her arm and led her to bushes, held the branches aside for her, and knelt in the midst of the thicket. Albany and Deserter sat close to him.

"If they are Yankees, say I'm your prisoner and you are taking me to the provost marshal," he said in a low tone. "But if we meet up with Confederates, I'll claim you as my prisoner."

"Will they believe that?" She whispered. "You're not wearing a Rebel uniform and you're the one with the gun."

"I'll say I'm on special assignment, a scout, which is what I am. I'll have to give you the gun. Be careful with it." He put his hand on her chin and turned her face toward him. "Can you keep that straight?"

"I think so."

A small animal scurried by. Deserter's tail and ears went up but the dog remained where he was.

"You must be hungry." Paxton dropped his hand. "I certainly am. We can go without food longer than without water. That marsh water is brown but it is liquid."

Taking her hand, he led her to the edge of the marsh, cupped his hands, and scooped water to his mouth.

"It doesn't taste too bad, Albany. See, Deserter is drinking. Come join us."

Albany went down on her knees and drank swamp water for her breakfast.

* * *

Joab, too, was drinking water but not from a bog. Albany's horse drank from a barrel roped to the side of a wagon. The four skirmishers who had stolen the animal yesterday now drew straws to determine today's rider.

"Whoo-ee, I got it!" exclaimed one of the men.

"Better enjoy a ride while you can, before the cavalry boys come and steal the beast from you."

The happy skirmisher attempted to mount Joab. When one boot

slipped into the stirrup, the horse reared. The reins zipped through the startled man's hands. He tumbled hard onto the ground. The watching soldiers laughed.

"Can't hold a good horse; dad burn you."

"Cavalry's gonna get him sooner than later."

"Ha, ha, look at him go."

"You're not catchin' that horse."

"Come join the infantry again."

Joab recognized the Brock Road and knew his way home.

* * *

As Joab's rider was startled by his sudden unseating, Albany too jerked in fright. A snake dropped from a tree at the edge of the swamp. Its tail slithered over her shoulder. She screamed. The snake landed at her feet. Paxton grabbed her and slapped his hand over her mouth. Deserter attacked the snake.

"Hush. You're all right." Paxton spoke close to her ear. "It didn't hurt you."

When he removed his hand, she said, "I h-hate s-s-snakes."

"I know." He petted her back. "I'm not fond of them myself."

Looking over her head, he called, "Come on, Deserter, leave it alone."

I don't want him bitten. I've got enough to contend with.

They skirted the marsh, staying close to the bushes whenever possible.

We must have a quick hiding place if we see anyone.

The day became hot well before noon. Paxton slung his jacket over one shoulder. Albany tied her jacket by the sleeves around her waist. Despite being in the shade most of the time, the air felt steamy and oppressive. Hunger pangs and fear of detection were their consuming thoughts.

"Look there." Paxton pointed.

"What's that?" Albany touched his arm.

The couple approached the object of interest. Deserter went ahead of them. They halted in front of a cannon stuck between two trees.

"Well," said Paxton, "that's not a sight I've ever seen."

"Does it mean the soldiers are nearby?"

Briefly patting the barrel, Paxton said, "It is not hot just warm." He scanned the landscape. "The heat could be from the sun not because of firing. No telling when they abandoned this." He sat with his back to one of the trees bracketing the cannon. Deserter came to one side of him and Albany to the other.

"Let's rest here a spell." He tilted his head against the bark.

How can I escort her home? Danger is all around.

"Tell me one of your stories," he said.

"What stories?"

"From one of the novels you read."

That will take our minds off our dilemma. We can imagine someone's fictional trouble instead of thinking about our own.

Albany said, "I recently read <u>Golden Love at Sutter's Mill</u> about Amendia Carver and Vaughn Bostwick."

"Tell me about them." He closed his eyes.

"They met and fell in love on a trip from New York to California."

"During the Gold Rush?" he murmured.

"How did you know?"

"Sutter's Mill was a give-away." He opened his eyes, took her hand, and held it on his thigh. "Which route did they take -- overland or by ship?"

"They went by way of Panama's Chagres River, where they canoed for three days to Panama City, and then boarded a steamship to San Francisco harbor," Albany said.

"Who is the villain in the story?"

"The leader of the group, a swindler who took their money and left them stranded in the Panamanian jungle."

"Does Mr. Bostwick catch him?"

"He does. Their fight in the jungle, with dangerous animals all around, was exciting to read." She rested her head against his upper arm.

We've got dangerous animals all around us. They're called soldiers.

Albany continued, "Vaughn got their money back before turning the bad man over to the Panamanian police."

"I assume they reached California."

"They did and Vaughn struck it rich in the gold fields." Albany folded her fingers over his hand. "He married Amendia, who had been poor all her life, so she was very happy to be financially secure."

Paxton sat silently for a moment before asking: "Is that what makes a woman happy – riches from a gold mine?"

Albany replied, "Amendia told Vaughn she would be happy with him if he was poor as a church mouse. Being together was all that mattered to her."

Paxton chuckled. "What a good novel writer."

"I thought it was too contrived," Albany said. "I liked the sea captain and the lady's story better."

Paxton said, "Hearing your stories reminds me of my mother telling us children bedtime stories."

* * *

Just as Paxton was remembering his mother, Melora Faulconer was opening a letter from her son which Evandon had just handed her. They sat side by side on the maroon velvet settee in the parlor of their large two-story house on Cox Mill Road in Gordonsville. Melora read:

May 3, 1864

Dear Mother, Father, Brother, and Sisters,

I take my pen in hand to write you a few lines. With the spring weather upon us, we expect the armies to be moving soon. I have my scouting duties so will not be with my regiment on the move. However, I will join them as soon as this work is completed. We have become weary of our winter quarters and are eager to end this war. Hopefully, 1864 will see our victory. We should be a country of our own, free from Northern control, very soon. I pray you are well. Give my regards to Lorella, Eunice, and Grandon. I have not seen Thornton for some weeks now. Write me. I treasure your letters and knowing you are all in good health.

Your loving son and brother, Paxton Faulconer

Clutching the paper to her bosom, Melora said, "What a relief to hear from him."

125

"He's doing well," said Evandon, patting her knee. "You can tell that from his words."

"I should send a reply today." She turned to face her husband. "Should I tell him about Leah?"

Evandon nodded and went to the desk where he got out paper and pen.

Holding out the desk chair for his wife, the white-haired gentleman stood behind her to watch as she wrote.

"I suppose it is better he hears the news from us before he comes home," Melora said.

"Definitely better," her husband said.

"How should I word it?" She inked the pen. "What would be best?"

"Simply set out the facts," said Paxton's father. "His intended, Miss Flighty Dighty, married another man."

Melora could not keep from smiling at her husband's remark.

"I don't think Paxton will be too heartbroken," Evandon said. "He just wanted to have a woman waiting for him when he came home. That's my take on the situation."

"He intended to honor his commitment," she said. "Or did he tell you something I don't know."

"Paxton told me that Leah was keen to wed. It was her idea. He didn't want to make her unhappy. I don't see that Leah marrying someone else is much of a loss."

"Don't you think he loved her?"

"He's a loving man, you know that. He would have kept his promise, no doubt, but I must tell you, Melora, that I'm glad not to have Leah Sibert as my daughter-in-law."

Melora wrote the date at the top of the paper as she said, "That makes me feel better about this entire episode. You should have told me."

She wrote in an elegant cursive: *Dear Paxton, Your letter came to hand…*

Evandon watched as his wife wrote: *Leah was married last Sunday. Before the wedding, she paid a visit and told us that she was sorry she could not wait for you. She has moved to Charlottesville, so you will not see her in town when you return.*

Melora lifted her pen and asked, "Should I write that his boyhood friend was the groom?"

"No," said Evandon, "let's do him a kindness and keep that information for his return home."

* * *

Paxton had not thought about Leah Sibert since he met Albany. In fact, he seldom thought about her unless he received a rare letter. His return letter always went months later because he had little to say to her. But Albany's fright from the falling snake brought his fiancée to mind. Leah had been afraid of snakes, spiders, bugs, and most animals.

How brave Albany is compared to Leah. What other woman would endure what she has been …

Paxton did not finish his thought. Albany stepped in a hole.

"Ah!" She reached for him.

Paxton clutched her arm and steadied her.

I will hold you up. I will never let you fall. Rely on me.

"Are you all right?" He took her other arm and helped her out of the hole. "Did you hurt yourself?"

"My shoe is covered with mud."

As Paxton knelt and rubbed the mud off her shoe with a handful of leaves, he heard the distant sound of gunfire.

How soon before the battle reaches us? Can I protect Albany while firing at the enemy? Or am I like those three scalawags who attacked us at the Pritchett house? Am I shirking my duty like the cowards they were?

"That's clean enough." Albany looked at her shoe. "Thank you."

* * *

Grandon and Ainsley both felt grouchy. Their long wagon train, transporting the wounded, was moving slowly. The bleeding, dying passengers groaned, some swore, others prayed. A few of the passengers were silent, waiting their transport to hospitals.

"Why aren't they going?" Grandon grumbled.

"Who knows?" muttered the older man.

"Why are we carrying wounded men instead of supplies?" Grandon looked up and down the line. "Shouldn't the ambulances be hauling these men instead of us?"

"Freight or bodies -- doesn't make much difference," said Ainsley.

The wagon in front of them came to a sudden standstill. Grandon yanked on the reins and the horses stopped.

I wish I was home. I could hop out of a soft bed. Mama would have a good meal for me.

"What's the holdup?" yelled Ainsley. "Get moving!"

His shouts did no good. The wagon remained motionless. A voice behind them called, "Water, please."

"I'll see to him." Grandon spoke as he climbed over the seat and entered the canvas-topped shelter.

"Who's asking?" Wedged between the stacked bunks, Grandon scanned the dim interior.

"Here." The man in the middle right bunk lifted his hand.

"Sure thing." Grandon uncorked the canteen. "Where are you hit?"

The wounded soldiers had been loaded so quickly that neither Grandon nor Ainsley had time to assess the injuries before they moved out.

"Elbow." The soldier used his good arm to hold the container Grandon offered.

When the injured man quenched his thirst, Paxton's brother asked, "What did the doctor do for you?"

"Cleaned it with turpentine."

Turpentine on an open wound. Grandon shivered.

"So you just need to rest up at a hospital and you'll recover in no time," Grandon said cheerfully.

"Have you heard how the battle goes?"

"No, can't say I have. I hear the guns but don't know who is winning."

The wagon jerked as the horses plodded forward, almost knocking Grandon off his feet.

"I better get up front." He took a quick look at the other men. No one else made a sign of needing anything. "You rest easy now." He patted the man on his shoulder.

I'm sure glad that is not me. I hope it's not my brothers either. I'd hate to think of them wounded like these poor fellows.

* * *

Something unprecedented in the history of warfare was occurring. Here in Spotsylvania County, there were not the usual brief individual battles followed by long periods for maneuvering, studying maps, caring for the wounded, burying the dead, and resupplying ammunition and other necessities. In this wilderness, two large armies faced each other day after day, fighting continuously. The battles went on without let up.

* * *

No sooner was Albany's shoe cleaned of mud than the three of them heard sounds of battle. The cannon fire came closer. Deserter perked up his ears and turned his head in the direction of the booms. Paxton grabbed Albany's hand and ran. But they were not fast enough. A cannon ball roared overhead. Seven soldiers ran out of the smoke toward them. Another cannon ball crashed down, hitting a man directly in front of Albany. The iron ball decapitated him. The severed head flew back and struck Albany, knocking her three steps backwards before she fell. Men shouted.

"Gad!"

"Good Lord!"

"God Almighty!"

"Don't blaspheme!"

"Spare me."

"Who is it?"

"Don't know."

Waving her arms in front of her face, Albany screamed hysterically as she rolled on the ground. Deserter barked. The soldiers kept running. Paxton dropped to his knees and frantically wiped blood and pieces of flesh off her face.

Was she hit? Is this her blood?

Albany flapped her arms, striking Paxton.

"Are you hurt?" He swept bloody gore off her shoulders.

The decapitated head lay in the grass. The dog barked at the face. One of the dead man's eyes was dangling from its socket. The other eye was gone. Albany kept screaming and flailing.

"You're all right, Albany." Paxton pulled her to stand. Parts of the headless body fell off Albany's clothes.

Oh, dear Lord.

"You're not hit."

Brushing blood-wet hair off her cheek, Paxton put an arm around her and covered her mouth with his palm. Deserter sniffed the head and whined.

"Stop that, Deserter," Paxton ordered. "Leave it alone."

The dog backed away.

"Don't scream, Albany." Paxton had trouble keeping his hand over her mouth because she fought him. "Hush, Albany. You must keep quiet."

He felt something between them. Pulling slightly away, he saw a glob of bloody flesh on the bodice of Albany's dress.

Part of the dead man.

Quickly, he brushed the piece away.

"Come over here. Get away from this." He spoke as he moved.

Albany, shaking and crying, stopped resisting him. Paxton lead her into the trees. The dog followed.

"That was a terrible thing to happen." He hugged her against his side. "But you are unhurt." He spoke an inch from her ear.

Albany buried her face hard against his shoulder.

"My poor darling," said Paxton, nuzzling her head under his chin.

Why did this happen to her? Why not me?

"Albany. Albany, you're not hurt. You're all right. You're safe."

Soldiers ran twenty feet away. Paxton, with his arm securely around Albany, ran deeper into the trees and away from the fighting men. Deserter kept close to their heels.

We've got to get out of this maelstrom.

Albany stumbled and would have fallen but for Paxton's firm hold. He practically lifted her off her feet as he ran. They crashed through the bushes. Not until the sounds of fighting became dim did Paxton stop. He dropped. Albany fell against him.

"We're away from it now, Albany." Paxton was out of breath but needed to speak, to reassure her. "No harm has come to you." He stroked her hair, rubbed her back, and breathed heavily. "Try to forget what you saw."

How can we forget such horror? Is this the third bad thing Grandma Faulconer warned about?

Albany began to sob. Deserter licked her face. Paxton pushed the dog away.

"Oh, my dear, you have every reason to weep." Paxton nestled his head over hers. Deserter wedged himself between their legs. Albany's violent sobs turned to exhausted crying. Paxton spoke softly.

"We are away from the war now, Albany. The soldiers are far away." He took a deep breath. "I am so sorry this has happened to you. Please don't cry anymore. Sit up and talk to me."

But Albany did not sit up. She remained huddled against his chest, her head tucked under this chin, and her legs folded beneath her.

I must get her to talk. She cannot end up like Searcy. What can I do for her? Lord, show me how to help her?

Paxton repeated his comforting words. Soon Albany shivered and was still. Paxton pulled her up further so her head rested on his shoulder.

"That was truly horrible, Albany." He tipped his head down intending to look in her eyes but her eyes were closed. "I wish I could take your anguish to myself." Paxton saw blood in her hair.

I need to clean that blood away.

"Will you talk to me, my dear? Tell me what you are thinking."

Paxton lifted her chin. Albany opened her eyes and stared, not seeming to comprehend.

Was Grandma Faulconer wrong? Can there be four bad things happen in a row? Is this the fourth for us? Has Albany lost her mind?

* * *

Torrents of rain descended as Albany, Paxton, and Deserter trudged through the woods seeking shelter.

We must get out of this rain. There has to be a barn or something. Please, Lord, don't let it be occupied by wounded soldiers.

Albany clung to Paxton's hand as she stumbled after him. Deserter kept close. Albany's silence, her altered demeanor, brought a stab of memory to Paxton.

She's like Searcy. He went quiet toward the last, just before the doctor had him sent to the insane asylum. That cannot happen to Albany. Please, no, Lord.

Paxton was remembering his former tentmate when a building appeared before him.

"Look!" Paxton pointed. "A cabin."

Because it was dusk, they saw only one cabin not those beyond. These were the quarters for ten slave families on the Chesterton plantation. Now, however, only one dwelling, the one closest to the Big House, was occupied. Statesman and Liney Prather lived there. The one-room shanty that Albany, Paxton, and Deserter entered was at the far end of the row, closest to the woods.

Paxton pushed open the door held by only one hinge. Deserter entered and sniffed his way around the small room.

"Anyone here?" Paxton tightened his hold on Albany's hand.

Smells rank.

'Come in, Albany." He tried to see the interior but could not until his eyes adjusted.

Rain dripped from several places in the roof.

"No one is here." Paxton left the door ajar to let in the fading light. "Watch out for the rain water." He pulled her away from the stream of water coming down, making a mud puddle.

Paxton lead Albany a few steps across the dirt floor to the center of the room. Deserter went to the far corner and stepped onto the bed, nothing more than a wooden platform six inches off the ground with a straw-filled mattress atop the boards.

Recognizing the sound of the crunching straw, Paxton said, "Found the bed, have you, Deserter? Good boy."

He guided Albany toward the dog.

"Lie down, my dear. You must be exhausted. I am."

They did not see the dust that made them cough as they lay down.

"I should close the door." Paxton started to get up.

Albany grabbed his sleeve. Putting his hand over hers, he said, "I am coming right back. I just need to shut the door. We don't want a forest animal to come in, although I'm sure Deserter would protect us."

And we don't want any soldiers coming in.

Gently releasing her hand, Paxton went to the door. A sudden thought came to him.

I could walk out and leave her. Deserter would stay and be her guard. I could return to my men. Lord, what's wrong with me, to think such a thing? Abandon her – how could I?

Scraping the door across the ground, Paxton felt for a rope or bar to secure the door but found none. Back on the musty mattress, Paxton gathered Albany in his arms as he lay down. Deserter made a low woof and settled at their feet.

"I'm so tired. You must be, too." Paxton stretched and his feet went over the edge. Pulling his feet back, he hugged Albany close.

Albany fell into a deep sleep but Paxton lay awake. His mind filled with strange images.

Yellow-clay faces. Blood smeared over rigid bodies. Blank eyes staring. Lips contracted to reveal teeth. Teeth would never eat again. Eyes would never see again. Blood would never circulate again. Oh, Lord, take these memories from me.

The dog got up, walked in a tight circle, and lay down again as Paxton endeavored to rid his mind of morbid thoughts.

* * *

At the opposite end of the cabin row, Liney and Statesman lay down on a similar straw-filled mattress except no dust flew and no dog joined them. They had no suspicion that, not far away, another of the shacks was occupied but not by fellow slaves.

Snuggling close to her husband, Liney whispered, "I'll go with you when you leave, Statesman."

Statesman stroked her hair as one arm wrapped around her small body.

"I hoped you would," he said. "I could not leave without you."

"But you made me think you would," she whispered.

"I had to change your mind, my dew drop." He kissed her cheek. "You are my life. How could I live without you?"

She turned and kissed him on the lips. They were silent for a long moment before Liney asked, "Should you dig a grave before we go?"

They had no need to speak of the grave's occupant. Both knew Madelyn Chesterton would die soon.

"It would be too much work for the boys," Liney added.

"I'll dig a grave." Statesman stretched out his legs. "How much longer will it be, do you think?"

"Not more than a week or two, I expect," said Liney. "She's coughing up more blood every day."

"Does she have a shroud?"

"I heard her say, not many days back, she wanted to be buried in her wedding dress."

"Does it fit?"

"Won't matter if the buttons don't come together in the back." Liney gave a deep sigh. "No one will see."

After a brief silence, Statesman said, "Little Miss Florence will be brokenhearted. She's been a good nurse to her mama."

"Indeed she has." Liney could not say more because of the catch in her throat.

"The boys will do better than Florence," said her husband. "They have been taught to be manly."

"Young Master Forrester is certainly that, giving orders like he owns the place already," said his wife.

Statesman nodded. "That's a fact, sure enough."

Liney had no answer. The couple fell asleep.

* * *

Paxton could not get comfortable on the thin straw-filled mattress. His clothes were wet and clinging. The straw smelled bad. Frogs croaked close by. Although the rain had stopped, water kept dripping from the roof holes. He was aware that Albany slept. She did not move. A vivid memory pounced into his brain.

When was it that the rolling cannon ball struck the soldier beside me? He died as I watched. Why didn't it hit me?

Opening his eyes, Paxton turned from his side to his back and stared into the darkness at the low ceiling.

Why have I been spared? Why was Albany spared? The ball hit that man and not her. The ball months ago – I can't even remember when it was – hit the man next to me and not me. Why does God protect some and not others?

Paxton turned again and slipped his hand over Albany's waist. He cuddled her close.

Oh, dear lady, I wish you would talk to me. Tell me the plot of one of the novels you read. Banter with me as you did when I thought you were a teenage boy. How could I have thought that?

He gently brushed a tangle of her hair away from his face.

What have these experiences done to you? Will you recover, be normal again, and talk to me as a sane woman does?

Deserter got up and moved toward the head of the bed. Paxton reached out to push the dog away.

"Don't wake her, Deserter," he whispered. "She's sleeping."

Thank you, Lord, for sending us this dog. He's a comfort to her. But why did you have to take away the horse?

* * *

Coffer, having too much work to finish during the day, sat on the back steps of the Trubridge house and, by the light of an oil lamp, repaired a boot eye seam that had torn. When he heard hoof beats, he clutched the leather boot.

Soldiers coming!

Coffer leaped to his feet. Susa, working in the kitchen, rushed outside. The couple saw a horse race around the corner of the Big House.

"Joab!" Coffer shouted.

"Oh, my land!" Susa pressed her hand over her mouth.

Coffer leaped down the steps. The horse halted in front of him. The man grabbed the dangling reins.

"Where have you been?" Coffer stroked the horse's nose.

"Where's Albany?" Susa hurried down the steps.

They both looked in the direction the horse had come as Coffer rubbed Joab's sweaty side. Susa too petted the horse as they waited several long minutes. No one appeared in the dusk.

Susa wailed, "Has evil befallen her?"

Coffer whispered, "No telling."

Susa stifled a sob. Coffer placed his arm around Susa's shoulders and hugged her to his side.

"Help me tend to Joab." Coffer started toward the barn. "Don't fret about Miss Albany. She will come home directly, same as Joab did."

* * *

CHAPTER TEN

THE BLOODY ANGLE

Thursday, May 12, 1864

As there had been a place called the Bloody Angle at the Battle of Gettysburg, so too was there such a place at the Battle of Spotsylvania Court House. At Gettysburg, the site was located at a little clump of trees toward which the Confederates advanced on the third day, in what Virginia reporters called Pickett's Charge. Because two other divisions besides General Pickett's took part, it was really Longstreet's Assault. Hand-to-hand fighting broke out at that little clump of trees in Pennsylvania just as it would almost a year later at the bulge in the line called the Mule Shoe, the salient, and the Bloody Angle in Virginia.

Between midnight and 3:00 a.m., Federal units of the Second Corps assembled on a hill near the Brown House, ready for the attack at dawn. Two divisions from Wright's Sixth Corps moved up for support. Almost 19,000 Union soldiers were prepared to attack. Many of the blue-clad soldiers were close enough to see the Confederates' campfires, glowing bright despite the darkness and heavy rain.

* * *

Paxton, restless, unable to get comfortable, turned this way and that until he almost fell off the edge of the bed to the muddy floor inches below. Getting up, he stumbled to the door with mud oozing between his toes. Deserter followed.

"You've gotta go, too?"

Fog spread a gossamer glow over the landscape as the rising sun attempted to penetrate the mist. Paxton stepped outdoors and led the way to the bushes. Minutes later, as Paxton buttoned his pants, he rotated his head to try and determine which way was east.

"Looks a little bit lighter over that way, don't you think?" he asked the dog.

The flapping of an owl's wings startled both Paxton and Deserter as the nighttime bird flew from a branch. Another noise, at a distance, sounded familiar. Paxton crossed his arms and listened.

"It's cannons, Deserter." Paxton turned back and forth in an effort to determine the location of the gunfire.

In the next minute, he hurried inside.

I should be there. I should be fighting with my regiment.

But instead of fighting, Paxton removed his damp jacket and shirt. He hung the shirt on the back of a chair, the only one in the cabin, and took the jacket to the bed.

How can I leave her like this? What would she do in the morning if I was gone? Lord, you know my dilemma. What is the solution?

Feeling cool air coming between the boards, Paxton shivered. Albany stirred. He lay down and covered himself with the jacket, keeping to the far side of the bed away from Albany.

* * *

Federal soldiers struck the enemy salient almost at the top of its apex. Reaching the abatis, they pulled the branches and logs apart with their bare hands and rushed over the barricades. Thus began the longest sustained hand-to-hand battle in the Civil War. With loud cheers, the Union soldiers rushed the breastworks. When their guns were empty, the men clubbed each other with the butts. They smashed pistols over men's heads. They rammed bayonets and knives into their enemies' flesh. The violence was unprecedented. It was attack fury of the highest order.

* * *

Albany awoke, rolled toward Paxton, and touched the damp skin of his upper arm. She yanked her hand away. Paxton, coming awake, said, "My shirt was wet. I took the dog out. It's still raining."

He got up and put his shirt on but did not button it.

"There's a fight going on." He went to the door. "I heard it earlier when Deserter and I were out." Opening the door, he listened. "I can still hear it."

Albany sat up. She heard the sounds of battle. Deserter cocked his head and whined.

* * *

An officer led 23 enlisted men with their battery into the killing ground. They were able to fire 14 rounds from their cannon. By that time, only two men were standing. The other 22 had been killed.

* * *

As rain drizzled through the roof holes, Paxton searched the cabin, found a piece of rawhide covering a hole in the wall, gave it a shake, and said, "This will do for an umbrella."

Going to the door, he said, "I'll see what I can find for our breakfast, Albany. You cover up. Deserter, stay."

Albany said nothing. Paxton pulled the door closed and hurried to the neighboring cabin. His bare feet squished footprints in the mud.

What awful weather. How can the armies fight in this rain?

Finding the cabin empty, he went to the third dilapidated house.

Slave cabins. Where are the slaves? Did they run off? Where's the Big House?

Walking cautiously along the row of cabins, Paxton scanned the yard, seeing a smoke house, a shed, a well, and then the main house.

There's food in there. Dry clothes. Warmth.

Something caught his eye. He turned toward the motion. A man on a low hill lifted a shovel. Paxton froze.

What's he doing? What are those? Tombstones. He's digging a grave.

Statesman Prather stopped digging when he saw Paxton. The slave slung the shovel over his shoulder and walked slowly toward the white man.

"Morning, sir," Statesman greeted.

"Not a very good morning." Paxton made a quick assessment of the man.

Muscular, steady gaze, denim overalls.

"Are you digging soldier graves?" Paxton raised the piece of rawhide slightly so their eyes met.

"No, sir, not soldier graves." Statesman held down the wide brim of his straw hat. He wore an oilcloth jacket. "That grave be for the mistress."

"Your mistress has died?"

"Not yet but soon." Statesman walked toward the house. "Digging's easier when the ground is wet."

Paxton kept in step with the black man as they headed toward the Big House, passing a half-buried ice house.

"I have a friend and a dog in the far cabin." Paxton motioned toward the row of little shacks. "We could use some food."

* * *

At the Bloody Angle, wild screams and agonizing moans rent the air. Officers could not issue orders because most of them were dead. Amid the chaos, Thornton Faulconer saw three Union soldiers surround him. Having no chance to run, he surrendered his gun now useless without bullets.

"This way, Reb!"

"Get going."

Thornton, along with four fellow soldiers near him, went as ordered by the enemy. He would join the hundreds of Confederate prisoners captured at the slaughter-pen.

* * *

At the Chesterton Plantation, Statesman held open the back door and Paxton entered the anteroom to the kitchen. The slave took a rag off a hook, handed it to Paxton, and said, "Don't track in mud."

Removing his shabby shoes, Statesman thought: *We must keep quiet. Don't want them below to hear us tramping around.*

"Are people living here?" Paxton wiped mud off his feet.

"Hiding in the basement."

"Soldiers?"

"No, sir. The Chesterton family."

Should I be telling him this? I don't know anything about this man.

"Who?" Paxton hung up the muddy rag.

"Four children and Mistress Madelyn, their mama." Statesman led the way into the kitchen. "She has consumption bad."

What difference does it make if he knows? Liney and I will be leaving soon.

"Sorry to hear that." Paxton followed Statesman into the spacious room. "What is there to eat?"

As the two men gathered items to fill a basket, Statesman asked, "Lost your army?"

"Why do you think I'm a soldier?"

"Most strangers hereabouts are soldiers."

"In truth, I am a soldier temporarily separated from my men. My friend is a lady who has helped me. I am trying to escort her home."

"What's her name?"

"Albany Trubridge."

* * *

At the Trubridge Plantation, soldiers carried wounded men into the rooms now converted to a Union hospital. Audine fretted and paced. Susa and Coffer were too busy moving furniture and making space to take time with her.

"Oh, look, they're tracking in mud," Audine wailed.

"I do apologize, Mrs. Trubridge," said Doctor Angus Mintzer. "We can clean the floors after the men are tended."

"Keep them downstairs," the old woman said. "I have my bedroom upstairs."

"We'll do our best." The doctor hurried into the kitchen where Susa was clearing off the table.

"Will this do for surgery?" Susa asked.

Audine, scurrying behind the middle-aged doctor, said, "My son is coming home from Chimborazo. My granddaughter has disappeared. I am all alone. The world is coming to an end."

Ignoring her, Doctor Mintzer said to Susa, "Yes, thank you. Can you assist me? What is your name?"

"I'm Susa." Her dark eyes met the doctor's kind gaze. "I will help all I can."

Coffer, carrying one end of a stretcher, met Susa's eyes and smiled at her. She returned the smile.

"Coffer, stop right there." Audine put her hand on the stretcher. "This man is the enemy."

"There are no enemies here," said the doctor, pointing the stretcher bearers toward the cleared table.

With the old woman continuing to protest, Coffer and the medical assistant moved the wounded man onto the table.

"Take the missus to visit with Mr. Gately," Susa told Coffer.

Coffer nodded, took Audine's arm, and led her into the adjoining sick room where Gerow was sitting up in bed, reading the Bible.

"Can she visit for a spell with you?" Coffer asked. "The house is filling up and…"

"Certainly," Gerow said. "I could use the company. Sit down, Mrs. Trubridge. I've just been reading about the fall of Jericho. Permit me to read aloud to you."

"That would be nice." Audine sat in the chair beside the bed. "There is so much noise in the house."

Coffer quietly shut the door when he left.

* * *

Paxton and Statesman introduced themselves while brewing coffee. Liney had a pot of oatmeal cooking.

"Did you make this?" Paxton lifted the lid.

"My wife Liney – we're the only slaves left here."

The men spoke briefly about the battles and the two armies. Paxton carried a coffee pot while Statesman carried the basket. Skirting the mud puddles, they went to the far cabin.

"Might the family see us?" Paxton looked up at the windows of the Big House. Several were broken.

"They're all in the basement," said Statesman. "But those boys sneak around upstairs sometimes."

"Who broke the windows?"

"Booming guns."

Paxton stepped ahead of the slave to open the cabin door as he said, "Albany, I've brought breakfast."

Seeing her sitting on the edge of the bed, Paxton entered.

"This is Statesman Prather. He and his wife Liney fixed us something to eat."

"Miss Albany." Statesman dipped his head in greeting.

Deserter sniffed Statesman's leg and wagged his tail. Albany made no response. Placing the basket on the bed, Statesman moved a crate close to the bed and sat down.

"Join us in prayer." Paxton sat by Albany, took her hand, and reached his other hand toward Statesman.

Surprised by the gesture, the slave hesitated only a moment before taking the offered white hand.

"Heavenly Father," Paxton prayed, "we thank you for this food and the kindness of Statesman. Bless the food and us. Amen."

Paxton poured a cup of coffee first thing. Statesman fed the dog stale bread flavored with bacon grease. Albany took the toast Paxton handed to her.

"Are there other people nearby, an overseer or anyone?" asked Paxton.

"No, sir, just Liney and me."

Two slaves —they pose no threat.

"Are you all right, Miss Albany?"

"She's had a terrible ordeal." Paxton held her hand up to her mouth so the toast touched her lips. "Yesterday, a soldier was decapitated in front of her."

Albany shivered.

Paxton said in a gentle voice, "You're all right now."

He waited until she took a bite of the toast before removing his hand from hers. Statesman watched her chew and swallow before saying, "Coffer's been looking for you."

Albany's eyes widened and met Statesman's gaze for the first time.

"That's true." Statesman nodded. "I saw him in the woods the other day."

He can help her return home. I can join my men.

"Can you get word to Coffer?" Paxton asked.

"No, sir," Statesman shook his head, "not with the war going on everywhere about."

"But as soon as the armies move out? It shouldn't be long." Paxton sipped his coffee. "I need to get back to my regiment."

Statesman looked from him to her and back to Paxton before saying, "Liney and I plan to go along with you Federal soldiers."

Paxton stared at the muddy floor.

He thinks I'm a Yankee.

Seeing the scowl on Paxton's face, Statesman asked, "What regiment are you in, sir?"

Paxton met the black man's gaze and said, "The 13th Virginia, Company C, from Gordonsville."

It's only fair to tell him. He and his wife won't be going to freedom with me.

"But she's wearing a blue uniform. Isn't it yours?"

"No, it belongs to a wounded man who came to the Trubridge plantation."

Statesman said, "I thought when you took my hand …"

You thought a Rebel would not do that.

"It's understandable you would mistake me for a Yankee. You see, my study of the Bible has taught me that all God's children are valuable and should be treated as such." Paxton took a bowl of oatmeal and began eating. "I was raised to treat our servants with kindness. They were hired out, not owned by my father."

They spoke briefly about the differences between slaves working out on their own and paying their master most of the money they earned, and slaves like Statesman and his wife who earned no wages and were completely dependent on their master. Paxton was impressed that Statesman carried on an intelligent conversation.

Eating a piece of toast, Paxton said, "Perhaps you can get word to Coffer."

"Don't see how I can speak to Coffer until the soldier boys go off." Statesman petted the dog. "I have no pass to leave the plantation."

"I can write you a pass."

"You're not my master."

"What about the Chesterton boys? How old are they?"

"Master Forrester is nearly sixteen, tall as me. He's mighty bossy. The twins Blake and Drake are eleven and full of vinegar."

"Too young to handle such a mission, no doubt." Paxton scowled.

"Forrester could do it if he was of a mind to."

"With his mother on her death bed?"

"Most times, that boy does as he pleases."

"Where's the master?"

"Off to war." Statesman picked up the dog's empty tin dish. "It's been quite a spell since they heard from him."

"So he might be dead."

"I'm thinking that."

Paxton finished his toast before he said, "Wouldn't it be better for you and your wife to remain here until the war is over. That way, you would not be fugitives. Even if you are following the army, slave catchers can still take you. Those soldiers are not responsible for the welfare of slaves tagging after them. Many dangers could befall you. You would be wise to wait until the war ends."

"I'm tired of waiting." Statesman gritted his teeth.

* * *

Bradby Tucker and Greenup Fortier, well back from the fighting, waited for the wounded to give them news. Both journalists were shocked by the descriptions they were hearing and both thought the same question: *Will the readers believe this?*

* * *

The volume of musketry at the Bloody Angle diminished but did not cease, showing the embattled armies that the fight was not over yet. The exhausted soldiers refused to give up the life or death struggle. The bullets, like the rain, continued intermittently.

* * *

Albany vomited into a mud puddle beside the bed.

"We didn't eat yesterday." Paxton wiped her mouth with his hand and rubbed his hand clean on his pants leg. "Her stomach is not accustomed to food yet."

Albany covered her mouth and leaned her head against Paxton's shoulder.

My poor, dear Albany, how will she manage when I go?

"Is there somewhere else we can hide?" Paxton put his arm around Albany's shoulder. "This place isn't fit…"

Statesman did not wait for him to finish. "The attic," he said.

"I'll just put on her shoes and we'll follow you."

Minutes later, Paxton, Albany, and the dog trailed Statesman to the Big House where they removed and hid their shoes while Statesman wiped Deserter's muddy paws.

Another hiding place -- what a coward I am. While my men fight, I hide.

Cautiously, the black man led the couple up the servant's stairway from the kitchen to the second floor. Albany, out of habit, reached down to lift her skirt, forgetting that she wore pants. Paxton, behind her, noticed the gesture.

She's forgotten about her disguise.

In the back hallway on the second floor, with the door to the front hallway shut, Statesman opened the attic door and started up the narrow staircase. Deserter had trouble mounting the steep steps so the slave aided the animal. Paxton put his hands on Albany's waist and gently pushed her. Reaching the cluttered attic, Paxton saw only two circular windows, both broken, letting in sounds of distant gunfire.

"Better over in this part away from the windows." Statesman stepped carefully to a far corner. "There's an old feather mattress here."

Paxton took Albany's hand and followed Statesman to a pile of blankets.

Smells musty but it's better than the cabin.

Statesman moved the blankets. Albany sat and curled her legs under her. Deserter prowled amid the clutter. The men, keeping their heads down due to the slanted roof, moved castoffs from the mattress to stack on nearby boxes. The dim light made it hard to see so far from the windows.

"Could your wife come and tend her?" Paxton stroked Albany's hair. "She needs her hair washed. There's still blood there."

"I'll fetch Liney." Statesman went to the stairs. "You stay quiet."

* * *

At the Mule Shoe, two Southern major generals, George Hume Steuart and Edward "Alleghany" Johnson, were captured and sent back to General Hancock's headquarters near the Brown house.

General Johnson, dressed in a double-breasted gray-blue coat, high riding boots, and a battered hat, allowed a few tears to roll down his face as he greeted his old Army friend with a handshake.

"General Hancock, this is worse than death to me," said Allegheny, coughing to hide his emotion.

With a kind smile, Winfield Hancock replied, "I am sorry for your misfortune, Ned, but if you had to be captured I am pleased that it is my good fortune to entertain you. This is the fate of war, General, and you must not forget that you are a soldier."

When the Union General turned toward George Steuart, however, the confrontation was decidedly different. Winfield extended his hand and intended to give George news of his wife in Washington City where he had recently seen her.

"How are you, George?" Winfield said.

Spurning the proffered hand, General Steuart puffed himself up and replied, "Sir, I am General Steuart of the Confederate Army!"

General Hancock pulled his hand away and replied, "Under any other circumstances, General Steuart, I should not have offered you my hand."

* * *

"You need to give me a hand with something," Statesman whispered to his wife as she stacked dirty dishes in a pail to take upstairs.

"I can't find the basket for dishes," Liney said. "Have you seen it? What do you need a hand with? If those boys have taken that basket for one of their games..."

"I took it." Statesman met Liney's gaze. "We have company."

Snatching the pail, he walked with her to the interior stone steps. Before going upstairs, Statesman looked around the large basement and saw only Madelyn, her eyes closed, and Florence reading poems aloud to her. The doors of the four smaller rooms were closed.

"Where are the boys?" he whispered.

"They snuck upstairs."

As Statesman and Liney went upstairs, she asked him, "What company do we have?"

"A lady in the attic needs her hair washed. There's blood in it."

"Is she bleeding?"

"It's not her blood," he said.

Liney's eyes widened. "Who is he?"

Statesman, helping wash the dirty dishes, told his wife what he knew from his recent encounter with the two white people hiding in the attic.

"She doesn't talk," Statesman said.

"Why not?" Liney handed him a cup.

Drying the cup, Statesman said, "She was hit by a head."

"What?"

"A soldier's head got blown off and hit her."

"Oh, my sakes." Liney gripped the plate half in and half out of the wash water.

"Mr. Faulconer is kind to her."

"Is he from around here?"

"Gordonsville, he said."

"What about her? Who is she?""

"Albany Trubridge."

"The Trubridge girl -- Miss Albany that Coffer is looking for?"

Statesman had told his wife about meeting Coffer in the woods and about his search for the missing Albany.

Nodding his reply, Statesman finished wiping the clean dishes as Liney began gathering up soap, a wash cloth, and a towel.

"Could you find a dress for her?" he asked.

"Why? What's she wearing now?"

"A Yankee uniform."

Liney simply shook her head and said, "I'll get one of Mistress Madelyn's cast offs."

"Be mindful of the boys," he admonished.

* * *

The Chesterton boys hid their shoes under the bed in the front parlor, which had been converted to their mother's bedroom when she became too weak to go upstairs. That was last month. Her health had deteriorated swiftly since then. She had not been strong enough to walk down to the basement. Statesman had to carry her.

With Forrester leading the way, the boys tip-toed single file up the wide front stairway. The three boys could easily be identified as brothers by their ash blond hair, wide-set blue eyes, and similar mouth contours. Forrester was a head taller than his identical twin brothers, who were distinguishable by their voices and mannerisms. Blake spoke rapidly and gestured often, whereas Drake was more reserved and spoke more slowly. Both were devoted to their older brother.

Forrester lead the twins up the curving staircase, looking all around as he went.

"You don't think anyone's in the house, do you?" asked Blake.

"Never know; could be. Keep your eyes peeled." Forrester thought: *What fun it would be if there was an intruder – a soldier from the enemy army.*

Drake whispered, "I wish we had a gun."

"Papa took the guns," Blake said.

Having reached the second floor, Forrester went to the front room on the east corner, formerly his mother's room.

"We'll get a good view of the entrance lane from here. Now, don't stand directly in front of the windows. Remember about sharpshooters."

I'd be a sharpshooter if I was a soldier.

"Why would they shoot at us?" asked Drake.

"Might be a stray bullet," replied Forrester.

I wonder if stray bullets hurt the same as aimed bullets.

With only one front window in the room, all three boys crowded against the window frame. Forrester was on the side where the vanity table was against the wall and easily pushed it several inches away to give him space. The twins, on the other side, were wedged against the heavy oak wardrobe, so Drake knelt while Blake stood above him.

"We will be mindful of the bullets." Blake saluted. "What are your orders, General?"

I am the General. I'm better than Lee or Longstreet or even Stonewall.

Returning the salute, Forrester said, "Survey the terrain, Private. Locate the best site for a battle."

I wish there really was a battle I could fight.

"Might our plantation become a battlefield?" asked Drake.

"With the armies swarming throughout Spotsylvania County, why not?"

* * *

Drake knocked over a tea table. He was going to the side window. Both of his brothers admonished him to keep quiet. Statesman and Liney heard the noise as they reached the back hall and halted.

"Wait here," Statesman whispered.

Liney watched as he went to the connecting door between the front bedrooms and the servants' quarters. Opening the door a crack, he listened and heard the indistinct sounds of boys' voices. Gently, he shut the door, turned, and motioned his wife toward the attic door.

Should we be doing this? But I cannot disobey my husband. What if the missus finds out? Oh, my.

Liney forgot about Madelyn Chesterton's disapproval when she saw Albany with Paxton. The handsome young man was holding Albany's hands as they sat on the mattress from which feathers protruded. He was speaking softly to her.

He has kind eyes. What did Statesman say his name is?

"Hello. I'm Liney."

"Paxton Faulconer." He nodded. "Pleased to meet you. We appreciate your help."

Liney set down the soap, comb, towels, dress, and underclothes. Statesman put the tin basin and pail of warm water on the floor near his wife.

"This is Albany," Paxton said. "I've been trying to get her to talk but without success. I assume your husband told you…"

"He did," Liney said. "I'm so sorry."

What a sad sight she is. I remember her from town but not looking this way.

Deserter brushed against Statesman's leg. He petted the dog and said, "Why don't we take him outdoors? I can get you some clean clothes, sir. Liney can manage."

The men and dog quietly left the attic and Liney tended to Albany.

She's a pretty lady. Once she's washed and clean, with her hair fixed and in a dress, she will be even prettier.

Paxton washed, shaved, and put on clean clothes belonging to Myers Chesterton, who would never wear them again because he was dead. Albany wore an old green dress that Madelyn Chesterton would never wear again because she would soon be dead.

When Deserter climbed the stairs to the attic, helped by Statesman pushing him, Paxton heard Albany emit a low cry.

"Is it proper to come?" Statesman called softly.

"Yes, come," replied Liney.

Paxton saw the cause of Albany's pain. With difficulty, Liney tugged the comb through her long, wet, tangled hair. He noticed Albany's green dress sprinkled with dainty pink flowers.

"Here, give me the comb, Liney." Paxton held his hand out.

Will he scold me for hurting her?

Taking the comb, Paxton said, "I'll do that."

He didn't scold.

Liney moved around him so he could come close to Albany. Statesman joined his wife. The couple sat on a padded bench with a broken leg, held upright by a stack of boxes. Paxton began carefully to comb Albany's hair with short strokes while keeping one hand at the top of her head.

"I never did see that before," said Liney.

"What?" Paxton glanced from Albany to Liney.

"A white man combing a woman's hair," she replied.

"Albany has become very special to me." He held a strand of hair in his palm as he slowly combed the ends. "I intend to court her after the war."

Did she hear what he just said? She doesn't appear to.

"You look very pretty in that dress, Albany." Paxton smiled at her and took another strand to comb. To the couple watching, he said, "How far is this house from town?"

"About an hour's walk," answered Statesman.

"Do you know where the two armies are?"

"I heard the Confederates are in the town."

"What about the Federals?" Paxton asked.

"Couldn't rightly say."

Liney added, "They seem to be everywhere."

As the men talked about the armies, Liney searched amid the clutter for a ribbon to tie back Albany's hair. She handed Paxton a brown ribbon when he finished combing.

"Thank you, Liney." Paxton took the ribbon and tied it at the nape of Albany's neck. Her snarl-free hair came to the middle of her back.

That man surely does care for Miss Albany. I wonder what will become of them.

* * *

"I need to find out where the 13th Virginia is," Paxton said as he followed Liney and Statesman to the bottom of the attic stairs. "At least, I must learn where the Confederates are located."

I wonder what is happening. I hate not knowing.

Albany, curled in a fetal position on the mattress with Deserter, did not hear the whispering voices in the stairwell.

"I'll try to get word to Coffer." Statesman took the door knob but waited to turn it. "We have a way, like a grape vine, to pass messages."

In a whisper, Liney said, "We'll look after her if you go."

Liney thinks I would leave Albany. I told her that I'd protect her. I never said I would leave her with strangers.

Shaking the thought from his mind, Paxton said, "I want to get Albany home."

"She needs to be home," said Statesman.

"You both need rest," Liney said.

"You're right about that. Last night in the cabin was not very pleasant."

I forgot – they have to sleep in a cabin like that every night. Maybe their place is better.

Paxton quietly closed the door after the Prather's. Going back upstairs, he thought: *How would I find my regiment if I left? I don't know this area at all. Yankees could be anywhere. Should I stay or go?*

He sat cross legged on the mattress and pulled Albany from reclining to sit up beside him.

"No naps, my dear. I want you to sleep well tonight."

Should I tell her I'm thinking of leaving? No. How could I desert her?

"Let's look at some of this junk and see what's interesting."

I wish she would talk to me. I want her to recover. She must not go insane.

"Here's an old scrapbook." He blew dust off the large book. "Let's look at this."

* * *

The Chesterton boys left the east bedroom and went across the hall to their father's room on the west side. Forrester stationed himself at the front window overlooking the green lawn and motioned for his brothers to look out the side window.

"Can you see any soldiers?" Forrester peeked around the window frame.

Where are they? Why don't they come and shoot each other on our land?

"I can't," said Blake.

"Me neither." Drake shook his head.

Cavalry could gallop up any minute. Infantry might be hiding behind the trees.

"What about smoke over the trees?" Forrester glanced across the room at his brothers. "Their cannons send up smoke, you know."

"No smoke, no flags, nothing." Blake turned from the window to look at his older brother. "You've got the best look-out. Trade places."

"No, I can't. I'm the commander, remember? If the enemy comes, they'll approach down the lane. I'll give you warning."

"What should we do when they come?" Drake, too, looked toward Forrester.

"Obey my orders. That's paramount."

"What's paramount mean?" The twins spoke the same question at once.

"Of utmost importance."

Forrester left the window and began rummaging in the bureau drawers.

"What are you doing?"

"What are you looking for?"

"Weapons," answered Forrester. "We'll need to protect ourselves."

"Papa took his guns when he left."

"I mean knives, swords, heavy things to bash over the Yankees' heads." Forrester slammed a drawer closed and opened another one.

"You could always get a knife from the kitchen," Blake said.

Drake said, "But Liney would miss it. She'd know you took it."

"Why would she know?" Forrester opened the double doors of the wardrobe.

"Because you're the only one who does stuff like that."

"Yah, we're well-behaved young lads, aren't we?"

The twins giggled.

* * *

Paxton talked softly to Albany about the hodgepodge of items surrounding them. The scrapbook, their first piece of entertainment, was all about a journey taken to London to attend the Grand Exhibition at the Crystal Palace. Paxton was fascinated by the pictures, clippings, and hand-written commentary. Albany paid little attention as he poured through the scrapbook.

When Statesman brought their dinners, Paxton asked him, "This scrapbook is about a famous fair in England in 1851. From the notes, it appears Mr. and Mrs. Chesterton attended. I'm wondering about their children. There is no mention of them."

"Liney and me weren't here in '51, but I've heard the master and mistress say the children were left with cousins in Richmond."

"It seems strange to me that parents would leave their little ones for months at a time to attend a fair in a foreign county." Paxton shook his head.

"Not very good parents," murmured Statesman as he unloaded the food from the basket.

When Statesman headed toward the stairs to leave, he heard hoof beats. Paxton leaped up and rushed to the window, knocking over a stack of *Southern Illustrated News*. Statesman hugged one side while Paxton ducked to the other side of the broken window. They peered out.

"Cavalry," Paxton whispered.

"Which army?"

Paxton gave another peek. "Yankees."

They watched as the soldiers watered their horses at the well. Some of the soldiers went into the ice house and came out chomping on chunks of ice.

Statesman whispered, "Can runaways go with horsemen when they have no horse to ride?"

"No, the cavalry can't accept runaways," Paxton said close to Statesman's ear. "Those men won't offer you safety. Wait for the infantry."

When the riders left, Statesman hurried to the basement where he found the two women and girl fretting but safe. The boys came down the stone steps two at a time and apologized to their mother.

"We had to hold the fort against the invaders," said Forrester. "They didn't come in the house. I saw to that."

Statesman glared at the teenager.

* * *

CHAPTER ELEVEN

IMPRISONMENT IN THE TOWER

Friday, May 13, 1864

An hour before dawn, Paxton awoke suddenly. He felt cool night air waft from the broken windows into the stuffy attic, doing little to dispel the musty odor. He felt Albany's hip against his thigh. Turning on his side to look at her, he saw an image in white. Liney had helped Albany get ready for bed by dressing her in an old nightgown and twisting her hair into a single braid. Paxton touched Albany's hip bone and slowly slipped his hand lower.

Taking her would be so easy. Would she resist? She has not protested anything since that man's severed head hit her.

On Paxton's other side, Deserter moved closer to his feet.

Nothing hinders me. There is only the dog. Who would know?

Snatching his hand away, Paxton wiped beads of sweat off his forehead.

What would things be like for Albany and me tomorrow if I made love to her tonight? Would she even remember? If she did remember, would she hate me?

He sat bolt upright.

How can I be thinking such things?

Paxton climbed off the thin feather mattress and made his way to the window, knocking into several obstacles as we walked. Deserter followed him.

I should be ashamed of myself. What's wrong with me? I've been in her company too long. I need to be with my men. I'm a soldier not an escort for ladies lost in the woods.

He reached down and petted Deserter's head.

I cannot stay safely in the attic while my fellow soldiers are fighting the enemy. I cannot succumb to these immoral thoughts spinning around in my mind.

Paxton glanced toward the dark recesses of the big room.

Easy, so easy, to go back to that bed, to waken her with kisses, and to love her as …

"No. Deserter, come. We're going outside."

Without further thought, Paxton went to the stairwell and quietly descended the steep steps. The dog came close behind. As soon as Paxton was outdoors, he started for the nearest slave cabin. To keep from thinking about Albany, he recalled the conversation he had with Liney.

She told me why they don't use those servants' rooms at the back of the house but sleep in a cabin little better than a chicken coop. What was it she said? Those rooms are for white servants. It was a simple answer. Even with the master gone and the mistress dying, the slave won't disobey protocol and sleep in a better place. Nevertheless, Statesman is planning to run off with the Yankees.

Paxton reached the Prather's cabin and knocked at the door. Deserter barked once. Paxton heard voices. Presently, Statesman opened the door a few inches.

"It's me, Paxton. I must talk to you."

The slave stepped outside.

"I'm leaving. I must return to my men. Will you and Liney look after Albany until Coffer can come for her?"

Statesman ran his hand through his hair and nodded. "Reckon so."

"I have to go. You understand. My place is with the 13th Virginia."

"Yes, sir."

"Keep the dog." Paxton held out his hand. Statesman shook his hand and opened the door wider for Deserter to enter the cabin.

"Have you got an idea which way I should go?"

Statesman pointed and Paxton went in that direction.

* * *

The army leaders discounted the superstition that Friday the thirteenth was unlucky. Nevertheless, neither side was able to organize an assault that day.

A trained engineer, General Lee believed the Confederate line could hold with its left anchor on the Po River and its right held at the town of Spotsylvania Court House. But the Southern commander was wrong. After intense fighting, at two o'clock in the morning on Friday, May 13, Southern soldiers received orders to withdraw and move back twelve hundred yards to a new line which had been dug the previous day.

Meanwhile, General Grant began shifting his army to the left across the Fredericksburg Road. General Lee countered by sidling one of his corps to the right. Some soldiers, too exhausted to fight, gathered spoils on the battlefields. The roads were too muddy to travel. The commanders were undecided. At the hamlet, only a few Southern troops stood guard. However, General Grant was unaware of General Lee's lax vigilance at Spotsylvania Court House.

* * *

As Paxton walked down the Chesterton lane, he recalled Albany's body but not in the blue uniform; in the nightgown outlining her bust, hips, and legs.

Would she have given in to me? Just a single garment covered her. What if I had removed that gown? What if… No, stop it.

He stepped on a twig. The snap startled him. He jerked.

My nerves are on edge. I've left the safety of that house for the unknown of this wilderness. Anything could happen here.

Paxton came to the end of the lane, looked both ways, saw no one, and turned right in the direction Statesman had indicated.

Into his mind flashed a memory from the summer of 1862. A firing squad marched out to face a blindfolded man with hands tied behind him. Twenty guns lifted to eye level. Ten of the guns were loaded with blanks and ten had bullets. No gunman would feel guilty for killing his comrade because no one knew what was in the barrel of his gun.

Why should I remember that firing squad now? Because it could be me if I'm found and court marshaled as a deserter, I could be the blindfolded man.

Hearing a sound, he ducked into the bushes. A raccoon crossed the road. Paxton returned to continue his walk.

No. I'll tell them I don't want a blindfold. I'll be brave. Why? Brave or cowardly, I will be executed.

Shaking his head, Paxton endeavored to clear the memory from his thoughts.

Think of something pleasant. Think of Albany – how sweet she smelled, how her body felt under my hand. What will she do in the morning? Will she call my name? Will she remember me?

"Lord, help me think pure thoughts," he whispered. "Point my mind in the proper way."

No soldiers in sight. No wagons or horses. I don't see the flicker of camp fires. I must stay alert.

How long he walked Paxton did not know. When he saw the glow of a camp fire in a clearing, he crept toward the light.

Lord, watch over me.

At the edge of the camp, Paxton halted and listened. Three soldiers in the shadows beyond the firelight talked in low tones.

Can't see the color of their uniforms. If I could hear their accents, I might know whether they are friend or foe.

Two of the soldiers laughed at something the third soldier said.

When will I hear Albany laugh? Will she cry when she finds me gone?

* * *

Albany was dreaming. Bullets zipped around like bees gone wild. Fog covered the ground, obscuring a mass of bodies. As the fog dissipated, she saw dead and dying soldiers.

How can men do that to each other?

She asked that question as her dream image wandered among the fallen. She saw herself carrying an armful of shrouds, dropping the white fabric atop the dead men as she wandered the burned-over ground.

A shroud for you, one for you, here, take all that I have.

In her dream, Albany found her arms empty.

I've given all the burial wrappings away. There are none left for the rest of you. You must go to your graves all bloody and dirty, just as you are.

In her dream, she saw the dead bodies rise up, like the dry bones in Ezekiel's vision, and hold out their blood-stained hands toward her.

Where is my shroud? What have you done with it? She heard the dead men question her.

Albany heard herself say, "It's not my fault. You did this to yourself?"

But the men surrounded her. Fear filled her mind. Albany awoke in a panic.

"Paxton," she whispered and felt the mattress.

Deserter licked her hand.

* * *

In New York City, readers were pouring over the news item which Bradby Tucker had telegraphed to his employer.

At daylight on the 12th of May, Gen. Hancock attacked with his accustomed impetuosity, forcing the first and then the second line of the enemy's works, capturing the whole of Gen. Edward Johnson's Division and part of Gen. Early's, together with Maj.-Gen. Johnson, Gen. Geo. H. Steuart, and from thirty to forty cannon.

* * *

Finally, after hiding on the edge of the camp site for nearly half an hour, Paxton heard one word to convince him he was near the enemy.

"Grant will get us out of this wilderness," said one of the soldiers by the fire.

Grant. They're Yankees.

As quietly as possible, he retreated to the road. It started to rain. He sought shelter under a dense growth of bushes. Morning light dimly lit the area but the rain continued. Paxton dozed off.

Heavy rain awakened Paxton. He sat up and flexed his shoulder muscles.

My back aches. I'm hungry and thirsty. I need to pee. Why did I leave that attic?

* * *

Albany awoke when Deserter whined at the top of the stairs. She had gone back to sleep after awakening from her dream. Although she did not see Paxton, she assumed he was somewhere close. She got up and stumbled around the attic clutter in her search for Paxton. Deserter watched the stairs. Albany toppled a box over, creating a bang on the wooden floor. A collection of baby rattles and toys spread onto the dusty floor. A few minutes later, Statesman hurried up the stairs. Deserter wagged his tail. The slave saw Albany standing amid the scattered play things.

Does she know he's left her?

"You must be quiet, Miss Albany." He mounted the top step. "Liney's fixing your breakfast. She'll bring it up directly. I'll take the dog out." He motioned for Deserter to come. "Be quiet now. I'll be back and pick up those baby things."

Statesmen crept down the back stairs with the dog at his heels.

When can I get a message to Coffer? What if the missus finds out? Worse yet, what if Forrester finds out? How will Miss Albany be without Paxton here to tend to her?

"She's awake." Statesman said as he passed Liney in the kitchen.

Deserter bounded out the door as Statesman held it open and followed the animal into the yard. The slave soon realized that the dog was looking for Paxton, the same as he had done shortly before dawn when Paxton left and Statesman returned the dog to the attic. Deserter raced from one area of the yard to the other, sniffing at the buildings.

"He's not here, Deserter. You must take care of your missus now. He left you to do that. Come along."

With difficulty, Statesman urged the dog back into the house. As Liney prepared breakfast, Statesman fed the dog.

"Are the folks downstairs awake yet?" he asked.

"Just Miss Florence." Liney poured rolled oats into the boiling water. "She's reading her Bible."

"Can you take Miss Albany's food up to her or do you want me to?"

Without answering him, Liney stirred the porridge and asked, "Why are we helping her? We could get in trouble for this."

"We're showing hospitality." Statesman put a bowl, spoon, and cup on a tray. "Hiding folks in the attic is our good deed."

"But Forrester would punish us for sure if..."

160

"Hush now." Statesman came to her side at the stove. "If he threatens us, we'll run. You need have no fear. I won't let anyone hurt you."

Leaning against her husband, Liney stirred the porridge slowly. "Oh, Statesman, what's to become of us?"

"My dew drop, when this war ends and we are free," Statesman kissed her forehead, "we will open a restaurant in the town of Orange on Main Street. White folks will have their businesses right next door to ours. You will become famous for the delicious meals you cook for travelers and townspeople. We will have more money than we know what to do with."

"Don't be silly." She giggled and stirred the oatmeal.

"That's not silly. It's my plan for our future once we're free."

"Why in Orange?"

"I like the name," he said. "A round, rare, orange-colored fruit that suddenly becomes a town. It kinda makes me think of us slaves suddenly becoming free."

* * *

Paxton came upon a Confederate artillery unit moving their cannon into place. A cannon ball zoomed overhead. Horses pulling the caisson galloped near Paxton.

"You there! Who are you?" yelled a gray-clad soldier.

"Paxton Faulconer, looking for Hoffman's Thirteenth Virginia. Do you know where they are?"

"Heard the 13th was left of Ewell's line."

"You can't get there. Yanks are between us and them."

"Have any experience with artillery?"

"We could use you."

A soldier handed Paxton a bucket of water and a rod with a sponge on the end. He ran with his fellow soldiers to the site where they positioned their cannon.

I could be in bed with Albany, holding her, loving her.

One soldier dropped a bag of gunpowder into the front of the barrel.

We could be snug and dry in that lofty tower.

Another soldier rammed the projectile after the bag of gunpowder.

How warm and soft and willing she would be.

A third soldier, at the back of the cannon, put a friction primer into the breech. The friction primer had two tubes, a large one of gunpowder and a small one of fulminate of mercury.

What might I be doing right now instead of watching these men prepare a weapon to kill people?

Another member of the gun crew yanked a lanyard attached to a wire. The lanyard pulled the wire through the fulminate friction compound, causing a spark that ignited the gun powder in the larger tube.

Lord, watch over us.

The gunpowder exploded, hurling the projective out of the barrel. Paxton covered his ears. Quick as he could, Paxton swabbed the barrel with the wet sponge to get out any smoldering remains. The men loaded a fresh charge.

"Here, use this cotton." A soldier handed Paxton a wad of cotton. He torn it in half and stuffed the balls into his ears.

"What's the range?"

"Looks like five or six hundred yards."

"Get this thing loaded."

The artillerists worked hurriedly as the infantry moved up.

"Aim high enough," a Confederate yelled over his shoulder. "If your shots hit us, we'll turn around and shoot you."

The artillerist next to Paxton shouted back. "We know our job! You just do yours!"

The next yell was, "Well!"

The artillerists stood clear of the recoil path.

"Ready!"

Men clapped their hands over their ears filled with cotton wads.

"Fire!"

A man yanked the lanyard. The cannon, like an enormous musket, blasted its iron ball into the air. Smoke billowed up. The soldiers dropped to the ground in anticipation of the missile from the enemy facing them. As soon as the Yankees' projectile passed over their heads, they leaped up.

"Well!"

The men moved back.

"Ready!"

Hands over ears.

"Fire!"

The mindless routine continued.

Sponge, load, aim, back up, cover your ears, fire, sponge, load, aim...

* * *

In the forenoon, Forrester, avoiding his brothers, climbed the attic stairs with the intent of looking out the highest windows. Upon seeing Albany, dressed in a nightgown and kneeling on an oriental rug in the dark, dusty room, he halted on the top step.

Where did this statue come from?

Albany gasped. Forrester jerked.

"You're real." He took the last step up and stood ramrod straight, staring at her.

"Who are you?"

The soft rays of light coming from the broken window illuminated Albany's face. Her skin appeared ivory, her gown like snow. She held her palm open. With her legs bent on one side of her, he saw her bare feet peeking from the hem.

What's she holding?

"What have you got there in your hand?" Forrester stepped toward her.

They're on the rug, too.

Albany leaned back, closed her hand, and clutched her fist to her chest.

"I won't hurt you." Forrester sat on the far end of the rug and studied the objects.

"Buttons." The teenager smiled. "You've been in Granny's button box."

The rosewood box with lid up sat next to Albany's knees.

"That's my grandma's old button box." He pointed to the polished wooden box. "What are you doing?"

Albany's eyes were wide as she stared at the stranger. Her mouth opened slightly as she drew in her breath. Her single braid was mussed from sleeping. Liney had not been upstairs to tend to her yet.

I've never seen such a beautiful woman. Who is she?

Forrester sat down and crossed his legs. Albany scooted back a few inches.

"How did you get here?"

She brought her other hand up to clutch the hand holding the buttons.

I've seen her in town. I know I have. What's her name? Why doesn't she talk?

"I am Forrester Chesterton. This is my house. Will you tell me your name?" Forrester awaited a reply. When she kept silent, he looked down at the buttons in little piles between him and her. "What are you doing with the buttons?"

No answer. Is she deaf and dumb? Surely not. I would know if we had a deaf mute in the county, especially such a beautiful one.

"My family is living in the basement because of the armies fighting." He reached over and tugged on the hem of her nightgown. "Is that why you're here, to escape the fighting?"

Has she been amid the battles? Is that why she's mute?

"Did someone bring you to our attic? How long have you been here?"

He reached for the button box. She rose on her knees and tried to back away from him.

"Don't be afraid of me. I mean you no harm."

Forrester took a handful of buttons and said, "I see each pile is a different color. I'll help you sort them."

The slaves did this. Statesman and Liney brought her to our attic. Wait 'til I find them.

* * *

At the Union outpost at Todd's Tavern, General Edward Ferrero saw the courier approach and lowered his coffee cup. The messenger handed him a piece of paper from General Meade. After reading quickly, the general gave it to his aide and announced, "We're moving to Piney Branch Church."

Private Wilfred Davies, a black man, read the order and asked, "Does this mean we might see some action soon?"

"Could be," replied the officer.

"About time."

The two untried black regiments of United States Colored Troops lead by General Ferrero were eager to prove themselves. Before long, they would have their opportunity.

* * *

Florence and the twins were playing checkers. The boys acted as a team.

"You forgot to crown our king." Blake pointed to a red checker.

"Oh, sorry." Florence set another checker on top of the new king.

How can I concentrate on this game when my mother is dying?

"When is Forrester coming down to play with us?" Drake looked toward the interior staircase but saw no one there.

"When he's good and ready," said Blake.

"He shouldn't be upstairs." Florence scowled.

If a bullet comes through the window and kills him, it will be my fault for not keeping him in the basement.

"As long as Mama doesn't know."

"What did you tell her?"

Florence looked from one twin to the other. "I didn't tell her anything. She doesn't know what's going on."

Don't they understand?

"You could say he's tending to his personal business."

"In the water closet."

"For hours."

Blake and Drake grinned at each other.

"Oh, boys, don't you realize that our mama is dying?"

* * *

In the attic, Forrester gave no thought to his mother and siblings in the basement. He carefully sorted the buttons, dropping them on the piles Albany had created.

"Should this pale blue one start a new pile or do you want it with the dark blue ones?" Forrester held the tiny button toward her.

He's not Paxton. Who is he?

Albany took the button, being careful not to touch his fingertips, and set in on the rug.

"A new pile, huh? Okay. Light blue and dark blue – fine with me." He smiled at her.

Why is he smiling?

"When I was little, I played with these buttons while Grandma sewed something or other in her lap." Forrester dropped several black buttons on the largest pile. "Did you ever play with buttons when you were a child?"

Albany glanced at him and returned to her sorting.

Where is the dog? Did he take him away? Where are the kind servants?

She studied the buttons in her palm. They were all black. A memory came to her mind.

They're all burned from the fires. They need to be buried.

Slowly, she put the buttons from her hand onto the pile and then started to spread out those buttons, placing them in rows.

"What are you doing? Don't you want the black ones in a pile like all the others?"

Forrester watched her intently spacing out the buttons from that one pile.

"Should I put these green buttons in rows, too?" He pushed flat the pile of green buttons.

Albany reached across the rug and scooped the green ones into a little hillock again.

"Oh, so it's only the black ones." Forrester added a black button to the row she had started.

"They need graves," Albany said in a barely audible voice.

Whose voice is that? I sound strange.

"Who needs graves?" Forrester scowled at her.

Doesn't he know?

"The burned men."

"These aren't burned men." He pointed at the rug. "They're just buttons."

He doesn't understand. Paxton understands. Where is Paxton?

* * *

Paxton reloaded, fired, swabbed the gun barrel, reloaded, and fired, again and again. When one of the artillerists dropped to the ground, blood gushing from a wound, Paxton took up his job. He carried projectiles from the caisson, sponged down the hot barrel, and worked until his back ached and his head buzzed.

"We're out of ammo!"

"Limber up and haul out!"

"Retire by prolonge."

"How?"

"What?"

"Drag the guns backwards." The soldier yelled. He was not the sergeant. That man was dead. He was just a private. "Maintain a rate of fire. The gun's recoil will help move it."

No further explanation was proffered.

The horses are dead. We've got to do this.

Paxton heaved on the bar to pull the gun carriage.

Why are we moving so slow?

Paxton looked around amid the haze of gun smoke.

There are only two others.

His foot tangled in a vine. He stooped to yank the bramble off. A bullet whizzed over his head.

If I were standing, that would have hit me.

He started to haul the cannon again. It did not budge. He searched for the two men. They were gone.

Were they shot? Did they run?

He dropped the wooden bar.

I can't do this alone.

* * *

Together, Albany and Forrester continued sorting buttons. The attic was hot and stuffy. The teenager had removed his jacket, flinging it over a baby cradle.

"Explain to me what you mean about burned men." He dropped an orange button on the pile of red buttons. "Have you been on the battlefield? Did some soldiers get burned?"

Albany plucked up the orange button and started a new pile.

"All right, you decide the pile, but let's not do this." Forrester pushed the row of black buttons back into the heap. "We'll keep them all together."

Albany met his eyes.

"You have very pretty eyes," he said softly.

She's not objecting to her rows becoming a pile again. I wish she would object. I'd like to hear her voice again.

Albany turned to the rosewood box and took out another handful of buttons.

Holding up a mustard colored button, Forrester asked, "Lemon yellow pile or start a new pile?"

Albany took the button from him and put in on the rug near the yellow buttons but not with them.

Her fingers touched mine. They're soft and warm. I wonder if all of her skin is soft and warm.

"I've seen you in town but I can't remember your name. Tell me what you are doing here. Have you seen dead men on the battlefield? Talk to me."

She raised her eyes and met his gaze.

Such a beautiful face – like a princess.

"You're like Rapunzel in the tower. You know – the fairy tale. I'm the handsome prince come to rescue you. You're safe with me." Forrester reached toward her, intending to touch her hair, but she leaned back. "I won't hurt you. You have no reason to fear me."

When Forrester returned to sorting buttons, Albany leaned forward and did the same. They worked in silence. Forrester moved the rosewood box so they could both reach it between them.

"I have a sick mother and three siblings in the basement. We've got two slaves. Did they bring you up here?"

If you won't tell me, I'll get the truth out of them.

"We moved to the basement because it's dangerous upstairs. Bullets can come through the windows. Don't stand up at the windows."

I sure don't want you hit by a bullet.

"I think you're beautiful," the teenager said. "Rapunzel must have been beautiful for the prince to climb up her hair and fight with the wicked witch. Do you know the story I mean?"

Albany scooped up a new handful of buttons and studied them in her palm.

What a perfect wife you would make – sweet and silent. I'd hear no harsh words from a wife like you.

"Want me to call you Rapunzel? If you won't tell me your real name, I have to call you something?" Forrester sorted buttons as he talked. "I forget the ending of the story. Did the prince kill the witch? Do you remember?

168

I haven't read fairy tales in years. I read adult books now. How about you? What do you read?" He dropped a green button on the blue pile.

Albany, moving the green button to its proper pile, said, "Dickens."

* * *

With all the members of the artillery unit dead, wounded, or deserted, Paxton started out, not knowing where he was going. A wounded man, leaning against a tree, waved to him.

"Can you help me?" called the blue-clad soldier.

He doesn't know I'm a Confederate. I'm out of uniform.

"Where's your hospital tent?" Paxton came to his side.

He looks so young. He should be in school not on a battlefield.

"It's that way I think." The young man pointed with his left hand while his right hand covered his bleeding side.

"I'll help you." Paxton lifted the man's left arm around his shoulders. With his other arm, Paxton supported the man around the waist.

"My wounds aren't too bad," the young man said.

"Wounds?" Paxton looked down and saw blood dripping down his pants leg. "Let's stop and put a tourniquet on that."

Since Paxton did not want to give up his gun belt, he searched the nearby dead bodies for a belt to use. Once the tourniquet was applied, they resumed their journey. The battle raged at a distance. Stray bullets and yelling soldiers made Paxton and his companion aware of the maelstrom in the nearby woods.

I don't hear any orders. Where are the officers?

"Is this the way to the doctor?" Paxton asked a man running by.

That man did not answer but the next man he asked did.

"Over there in the barn."

The injured young man was resting his head against Paxton's shoulder when they entered the barn.

Better than a tent. Awfully crowded in here.

"They'll get you bandaged in no time."

But Paxton's optimism vanished when he looked around. Two doctors stood beside improvised operating tables. One doctor had a saw in his hands. The soldiers having their mangled arms and legs amputated were insensible from chloroform. The other doctor was bandaging wounds.

Soldiers acted as nurses. The uniforms were dirty but Paxton saw blue, butternut, and gray.

"Here's a nice straw bed for you." He lowered the man and knelt beside him. "Let me look at your wounds."

Paxton lifted the torn cloth, soaking in blood, on both his chest and his back. "The bullet went through. No need for surgery to remove it. You're fortunate. Let's see about your leg."

Ripping the pants leg, Paxton declared, "It's just a flesh wound. I'll bandage you up. Rest easy now."

Paxton had finished bandaging the young man when a bearded Union soldier slapped his hand on Paxton's shoulder.

Is he taking me prisoner? Am I caught as a deserter?

"Help us bring in the wounded," said the bearded man.

"Sure. Glad to." Breathing a deep sigh of relief, Paxton stood up. "I've been separated from my men."

"So have a great many of us."

Paxton gave his patient a brief handshake. "You'll be all right now, my friend."

"Th-thank you." He nodded and gave a weak smile.

Paxton followed the soldier out of the barn and into the pandemonium.

* * *

Peace reigned in the Chesterton attic. All the buttons were sorted. Forrester picked up the button box and turned it upside down to be sure they had not missed one.

"We got them all," the teenager said. "Now let's get things tidied up a little." He began moving boxes. "This place is a mess. I wish I could bring you to the basement, but …" *But I want to keep you to myself.* "There's too much commotion down there. It's much nicer here. Probably just as safe if you stay away from the windows."

Statesman opened the attic door. Deserter scampered up the stairs, getting better at the new skill.

"What's this? A dog." Forrester went to the stairs.

Statesman!

"Do you know about this?" The teenager motioned toward Albany, hugging Deserter.

"No, Master Forrester." The slave climbed the last steps. "Who is she?"

"I'm asking you that." Forrester glared at the slave. "Where'd you get that animal?"

"Found him wandering in the woods, Master Forrester."

"What were you doing in the woods? We told you not to go farther than your cabin."

"That dog came out of his wandering right up to my cabin door, looking for food."

Turning to look at Albany and Deserter, Forrester said, "She acts like she knows him."

"He's a friendly dog."

Planting his fists on his hips, the teenager faced the slave again. "You didn't just find that dog. It's her dog. You're lying, Statesman. You brought her and the dog to our attic. Tell me the truth."

"The dog was just wandering. I don't know about her, Master Forrester."

"If you're lying I'll whip you. I can. I'm big enough now."

Dropping his arms, Forrester softened his voice as he looked at Albany. "I know her. I've seen her in town. I can't remember her name. She's escaping from the battle."

"Yes, master."

"She doesn't talk."

"Yes, master."

"She must have gotten that old nightgown out of one of these boxes. I wonder what happened to her clothes."

Statesman said nothing.

"I was just starting to straighten stuff up. Help me do that." Forrester moved a box. "Look for her clothes. They must be here somewhere."

The slave stacked up a pile of books.

"Haven't you seen her in town before?" asked the teenager.

"I don't look at white women in town, Master Forrester."

* * *

As soon as he could, Statesman spoke privately to his wife. They were in the butler's pantry, putting away clean dishes.

"Forrester found her," Statesman whispered close to Liney's ear.

Her eyes darted toward his. "What did you do?"

171

"I lied to him, said I didn't know a thing about her."

"He found the dog, too?"

Statesman nodded and said, "The boy says he's seen her in town but can't remember her name."

"Oh, dear, I haven't had time to get upstairs and help her dress."

"That nightgown she's wearing is a might flimsy."

"Forrester should not see a woman dressed in only a nightgown," said Liney.

"I don't think he did anything."

"Land sakes, I hope not."

Statesman took the tea pot from his wife and set it on the high shelf she could not reach. "He wants to tend her himself. We're not to go to the attic."

"Does he know I …?"

"No, I said you didn't know about her."

"What about Mr. Paxton?"

"Forrester knows nothing about him."

Finishing their work in the tiny room, Liney asked one more question before they went back to the kitchen. "Do you think he means her harm?"

* * *

CHAPTER TWELVE

ALL THE HOSTS OF HELL

Saturday, May 14, 1864

Saturday morning, as Liney Prather washed underclothing in a big tub in the kitchen, Statesman added more heated water.

"I need to get Miss Trubridge dressed in proper clothing," Liney said.

"You can't do that." Statesman touched her arm. "I don't want the young master to know you've tended her. I told him you didn't, that you don't know anything about her."

"But for her to be in her nightgown all day with him…"

"It can't be helped. If he finds out I've lied, he can whip me. He said he would. He's big enough."

"Oh, no, don't say that." Liney twisted Florence's pantaloons and dropped them in cold rinse water.

"Have you been able to get word to Coffer?"

"Not yet. No one has stopped by."

"Are you sure Forrester hasn't behaved improperly?"

"I'm sure." Statesman brought the basket from the storage room and set it beside the rinse tub. "I go up there often enough, taking the dog in and out, more than he really needs to go. Forrester was reading to her last time I was there."

Statesman started to ring out the clothes and put them in the basket.

Liney said, "That boy has all the fire in him that a man does."

"But I don't think he will do her mischief."

"We can listen at the bottom of the attic steps, can't we?"

"If he doesn't catch us," Statesman replied.

Liney said, "Oh, I wish that Mr. Paxton would come back."

* * *

Paxton was trying to come back to the Chesterton House. After helping the wounded to the barn, he had joined a South Carolina infantry unit and fought with them for several hours. He used the rifle of a dead man until he ran out of bullets. Using his pistol, he fired at the enemy until all his bullets were gone.

I'm not going to search dead bodies for bullets. I'm going back to Albany. Why did I leave her?

Shoving his pistol into the holster, he said to the man nearest him, "I'm going." Paxton put his hand on the soldier's shoulder. "Don't shoot me."

"Y'all be careful."

Paxton disappeared into the trees. He heard gunfire in the distance and avoided the area. With a full canteen taken from a corpse, he felt fortified for the trek.

Will I find her better or worse than when I left her? Will she talk or is she still traumatized from what's she's experienced?

A deer bounded in front of him. Paxton halted, scanned the surroundings.

There is no one who might have frightened him.

Continuing his journey, Paxton looked for any landmarks he remembered when departing from the Chesterton's lane.

Will she even be there? Maybe Statesman got word to Coffer and he's taken her home. Maybe the Chesterton family has found her. What might they do? Will I ever see Albany again?

* * *

In the attic, Forrester watched Albany organize the envelopes containing the buttons which they had labeled with their color and then placed into the rosewood box.

"How do you want them arranged?" Forrester moved closer to her and looked at what she was doing.

She's not backing away from me like she did yesterday.

Forrester had given in to Statesman's suggestion that Liney tend to the lady in the attic. The teenager consented reluctantly. Due to Liney's care, Albany now wore a raspberry colored dress with a pink ribbon at the nape of her neck. Her hair was brushed neatly with tendrils, too short for the ribbon, curling on her cheeks.

I'd like to take off that ribbon and keep it as a knight of old took a keepsake from his lady fair.

"So you want them in the box alphabetically, do you?" asked Forrester, watching her thoughtful movements as she placed the envelopes. When she closed the lid, Forrester took the box from her.

"We'll put it over here beside Granny's sewing basket." He set the box by the basket.

Albany went to the window, pressed her body against the side frame, and peeked out.

"Are you looking for someone?" Forrester came to the opposite side of the window. "Do you see any soldiers out there?"

If the enemy appears, I must fight them off.

"Don't worry. You are safe here. I will protect you like the prince protected Rapunzel from the wicked witch."

Albany looked at him and said, "Rapunzel."

"It's your name since you won't tell me what it really is."

I will find out when I take you home. I'll meet your family. I'll request the honor of calling on you.

"How can I take you home and introduce myself to your family when I don't even know your name?" Forrester scowled. "You must tell me."

Forrester waited for an answer but Albany remained silent. They were gazing out the window when Statesman returned from taking Deserter out. The dog ran to Albany. She petted him.

"Can't you and Liney find out who she is?" Forrester asked.

"I could ask at church tomorrow?"

"Are you going to have church while the armies are still fighting?"

"If Preacher Eleutheros calls us to worship," said Statesman, gathering up the used dishes and heading for the stairs.

"Yes, you do that. Ask your pastor."

* * *

Eleutheros Supplee, about twenty-five years old, lived alone in a cabin on the edge of town. Although he was a slave, he was allowed to work as a barrel maker, giving most of his earnings to his master. The simple cabin served as his shop. On his desk under the window, his Bible was open and Eleutheros was reading the text he intended to preach tomorrow.

Eleutheros had learned to read when the master's children taught him, thinking it was fun to play school and teach their black playmates. They knew it was against the law and were happy to keep the lessons a secret. For Eleutheros, the secret was more than play. He wanted to read the Bible, and had done so, making the study of Scriptures a daily habit.

Now, he was not only a barrel maker and preacher to the black community, but also a courier, taking messages addressed to northern locations. He had taken the letter to Myrta Gately several miles to the next courier.

Turning the page of the well-worn Bible, Eleutheros thought: *I wonder if the soldiers will stop fighting on the Lord's Day. I hope so. I don't want any of my flock to get shot tomorrow.*

* * *

At least I didn't get shot, thought Thornton Faulconer, captured at the Mule Shoe and now trudging east along the Fredericksburg Road. Thornton listened to the humiliating jeers and taunts as he and his friend Oliver Frankinberry moved amid a crowd of gray-clad soldiers. The Confederate prisoners had camped the previous night in a damp field, where their guards organized them around poles designating their regiments, so today they were marching with men they knew.

"Is that you Thornton?"

Turning toward the greeter, Thornton exclaimed, "Biglor."

Biglor Bibb, the typesetter for the *Gordonsville Gazette,* held out his hand. The two men shook hands.

"Sorry to see you here, Thornton."

"I can say the same to you." Motioning toward his friend, Thornton introduced his fellow townsman to Oliver.

"When did they get you?" asked Biglor.

"Yesterday. You?"

"Yesterday as well."

"Where do you think we're going?"

Oliver entered the conversation, saying, "I hope it's anywhere but Elmira. I heard that's a hell hole."

"Is any prison camp good?"

"Do you think we can get away?"

"Have you got a plan?"

Biglor said, "I don't know about escaping. The Yanks aren't evil. That breakfast this morning was the best I've eaten in some time."

"It wouldn't cause you to swallow the yellow dog, would it?" asked Oliver.

"I might," Biglor whispered. "Changing sides isn't so bad. We're all Americans."

"But just to get better food?" Thornton glared at Biglor.

"Taking an oath of allegiance to the Union might be something we'll all have to do sooner or later," said Biglor. "Their General Grant fights like he means it."

"We've still got our General Lee," said Oliver. "He won't give up."

* * *

General Grant ordered an attack on General Lee's right but by the time this operation was set to begin on that Saturday morning, the Southern commander had detected the maneuver and relocated General Anderson's corps to oppose it. Grant rescinded his order.

* * *

In the basement, Madelyn Chesterton was living her last day on earth. She was so weak she barely moved in the bed she shared with her daughter. Although the children took no notice of their mother's prolonged sleep because she had been having long naps in recent weeks, Liney was aware of the missus's decline.

"She's going to die soon, isn't she, Liney?" Florence asked.

Liney simply nodded her head and wiped the dribble of blood from Madelyn's mouth.

"What will become of us?" The girls gazed with teary eyes at the slave.

"The good Lord watches over us," said the young woman. "We are never out of his watchful care."

"My poor, dear mother," said Florence, taking her mother's limp hand to her cheek. "She has suffered so."

"Why don't you read to her?"

"Do you think she can hear me?"

"I believe she can," said the servant. "You go fetch a book."

Florence left the bedside and went across the room to the box of books Statesman had brought down when they moved to the basement.

Liney leaned over the unconscious woman, straightened the sheet up to her throat, and whispered, "You can go home to heaven any time, Mistress Madelyn. Don't fret about the children. Statesman and I will see to them."

* * *

At Chimborazo Hospital, Albany's mother was reading the newspaper to her father. As she finished the article about the fighting south of the Rapidan River, she said, "Oh, I forgot to tell you what Verity Stuart said about being related to James Ewell Brown Stuart."

"Is she?" asked Shedrick.

"No, she isn't."

A doctor walked up to the bed, introduced himself, and handed a piece of paper to Shedrick.

"What's this?"

"Your discharge." The doctor smiled as Shedrick. "You are better off recovering at home. You should be able to travel without a problem."

"Oh, thank you," said Luciana.

"Yes, thank you, doctor." Shedrick glanced at the script.

Shedrick Trubridge is broken in health and unable to continue serving. Discharge from service.

"The omnibus will take you to the depot."

"I must return to the Stuart house where I'm boarding and get my things."

"We'll stop at the Western Union and send Mother a telegram to let her know to expect us."

"I wish you a safe journey." The doctor shook Shedrick's hand. "I've read about the fighting in your county. There's no telling what you might encounter. Be on the alert."

* * *

Forrester set the tray on a crate and went to Albany, seated on a tufted footstool with two feather fans on her lap. She opened and closed them, first one and then the other. Her eyes were fixed. Her lips pressed tightly.

"Oh, beautiful lady, what's wrong with you?" Forrester reached for a strand of hair dangling in front of her ear.

She pushed his hand away.

Who is he? What am I doing here? This isn't home.

"What shall we do today?" He paused. "Where did you find those fans?" He went to the black wicker basket by her knee. The lid was off. He reached in and took out a balsa wood collapsible fan. "No feathers on this one. What do you say we decorate it?"

Decorate what?

Forrester carefully placed the fan on her lap, saying, "I'll get my paint set. Be right back."

As he clomped down the stairs, Statesman ducked into one of the small bedrooms. Forrester went into his bedroom off the front hall. When he rushed back upstairs with his paint set, the slave went to the attic door, opened it an inch, and listened.

"Let's paint each bar of the fan a different color. Won't that look pretty?"

Nothing is pretty. Nothing.

After listening to Forrester's chatter for ten minutes, Statesman went downstairs. In the basement, he reported to his wife what the couple in the attic was doing.

"We must keep checking on him," she said.

"I will," he said. "You look after the people down here."

* * *

Paxton encountered an artillery unit of four guns in the process of relocating. He hid behind a tree.

I don't want to work those guns again. Oh, they're Yankees. Better lay low.

179

"Don't sponge," yelled the Federal officer. "We haven't time."

"It's dangerous," protested a private.

"War's dangerous."

"Load."

"Get back."

Boom, the cannon belched its contents into the air. Confederate sharpshooters, entwined amid tree branches, fired at the gun crews. A caisson rushed past Paxton, missing him by only a few feet. The horses whinnied and reared up when case shot exploded. Bullets zinged. Men shouted. The atmosphere vibrated with sounds and filled with smoke.

I need to get away from here. The blasts are too close.

Paxton turned and, keeping in a crouch, ran as the earth trembled.

How many times will they fire before giving up? When will this madness end? An hour later, Paxton walked slowly, breathing more normally, calming his rattled nerves from the dueling cannonading, when he came onto a field. From the far perimeter, bullets zipped through the air. His muscles tightened. His eyes widened. He turned.

Run. Run.

* * *

Paxton's sisters, Lorella and Eunice, strolled leisurely along North Main Street in Gordonsville, doing their Saturday afternoon shopping. The pretty brunettes, unmistakably sisters, carried baskets on their arms. Lorella, twenty, had the food basket and Eunice, eighteen, held the notions basket.

"How are the children doing with their lessons?" asked Eunice.

Lorella, who began teaching school when the male schoolteacher entered the army, said, "I have trouble keeping them focused on their lessons. The ones who have relatives in the war are worried when they hear news of battles."

"That's certainly understandable," said Eunice, serving as a nurse. "I often have trouble focusing on my work."

"You're working too many hours. You should be at home more."

"I can't sit at home when there is so much to do at the hospital." Eunice stopped to look in a shop window. "Whenever I hear the train whistle, I think: maybe it's bringing one of our brothers."

"Oh, I hope they are not wounded," said Lorella.

They entered the general mercantile. Lorella went to look at the few books for sale while Eunice browsed among the bolts of cloth on display. When Eunice joined her older sister, she said, "I thought you got new books for the children recently."

"We did." Lorella lowered her voice although the other shoppers were not close. "The new textbooks, published in Richmond, were written to eliminate Yankee ideas."

"What Yankee ideas?" the younger woman whispered as she glanced around the busy store.

Lorella said, "We'll talk outside."

When they were again on the sidewalk, Lorella said, "For one thing, the idea that an all-powerful central government is preferred to our way of self-government by each individual state."

"But the Confederacy has a central government with Jefferson Davis at the head," said Eunice.

"And you see what a difficult time he's having with the strong-willed state governments." Lorella stopped in front of the butcher shop. "I'm having an especially hard time explaining our superior form of republic to some of the older boys. They are always arguing with me. When we read the section that said our Confederate republicanism is superior because we recognize the inferiority of the Negro race, Jake Spencer declared that simply is not true."

"Rather than argue, why don't you give up that job and come to work at the Receiving Hospital with Mother and me?" asked Eunice. "We could certainly use you."

* * *

How Paxton escaped being shot he could not have said. He prayed as he made his way from one battle scene to another, avoiding scouts and skirmishers, gray-clad and blue-clad soldiers, cavalry and wagons. Often, he looked heavenward.

Watch over me, Lord. Keep me safe. Get me back to Albany. She needs me. I need her.

Paxton dropped to the ground and crawled under a bush. His head was pounding from a headache. His legs and back ached.

I can't remember when I was so miserable. Oh, yes, I can. When I first met Albany and was blind. Dear Albany, will I ever see you again?

* * *

The Couse home became a hospital for the Union Second and Fifth corps on May 9. Four doctors and a number of male nurses now cared for the 200 Second Corps wounded and 420 casualties of the Fifth Corps. Suddenly, Brigadier General Thomas Rosser led his horsemen onto the Couse property, removed about eighty Confederate walking wounded, and captured any doctors and nurses not wearing a medical badge. The Confederate general declared that the wounded Yankees would be prisoners of war until exchanged. Then, the Southern cavalry began rummaging around and taking various items that struck their fancy while widow Elizabeth Couse and her three adult daughters, Sarah, Cornelia, and Kate, hid in a bedroom. The only man in the household, Peter, age 43, confronted the Confederates about their thievery but to no avail. They rode away with their stolen goods.

* * *

Grandon Faulconer's wagon, part of a long wagon train conveying wounded to hospitals, moved at a snail's pace in the twilight. When the front axle broke, Grandon and Ainsley slid off their seat and landed on top of each other as the wagon fell on its side. Six wounded men in the wagon screamed and fell in a heap inside the broken wagon. Nearby drivers rushed to aid the trapped men amid the debris.

"Quick! Lift it up!"

"I see two men!"

"Drag 'em out. We'll hold this!"

"I got one."

"Don't injure them worse!"

Dazed, Grandon stumbled to the wreckage. Ainsley lay unconscious. A man unhitched the mules. All was bedlam.

"That one's dead. Leave him there."

"Help me with this fellow. Grab his legs."

"Watch out for his head."

"I got you. You're okay."

"You can load two in my wagon."

"I have space for another one."

Heaving a man from under the pile, Grandon fell backwards with the man landing atop his legs. "I've got this one," said Grandon.

"Let me help you with him."

Ainsley, coming to, asked, "What happened?"

"Axel broke," Grandon told him as he helped the moaning soldier off his legs and into a wagon.

Ainsley held his head and made his way to a wagon where he was helped aboard. When the five surviving wounded men were in wagons, men pushed the disabled vehicle off the road. Grandon hopped up next to a driver he did not know. Someone had covered the dead man with a blanket. He lay where he fell. Grandon never saw Ainsley Bracken again.

* * *

With his jacket providing the only covering over his head and shoulders, Paxton fell into an exhausted sleep before finishing his nighttime prayer.

* * *

Albany, having spent the day with Forrester coming and going, slept with her fingers in Deserter's fur and wondering where Paxton was.

* * *

The soldiers in Spotsylvania County tried to rest. However, Grant ordered continued assaults along Lee's line which he thought were weakened by troop movements. This determination and aggression by the Federal commander kept up the spirits of his men. For the Confederates, their new defensive line gave them assurance that their entrenchments could not be taken. They had held on to their one vulnerable spot, the half-mile-wide projection called the Mule Shoe, when Colonel Upton attacked on May 10 and General Hancock two days later. Now, relocated further back on their new line of defense, the Rebels awaited the next battle.

* * *

CHAPTER THIRTEEN

NOTHING LIKE IT EVER BEFORE

Sunday, May 15, 1864

Dawn brought the sounds of singing. Paxton opened his eyes and listened.

Is that an angelic choir? Am I dead?

Sitting up, he slid his arms into his damp jacket.

"I recognize it." In a low tone, he joined in the hymn, "There is a balm in Gilead."

When the singing stopped, Paxton smiled. *My headache's gone.* He stood up and went into the bushes to relieve himself.

I must be cautious. The soldiers are close.

Paxton began walking but was unsure in which direction the singers were. Then, he heard a song that made him realize these singers were not soldiers.

"Go down, Moses, way down in Egypt's land," the song floated on the morning air. "Tell old Pharaoh to let my people go."

Paxton was in no hurry to reach the clearing where the singers stood. When he saw them through the tree branches, he stopped and observed. The black men, women and children, about twenty in all, which exceeded the number permitted by Virginia law to meet without a white man being present, stood in a circle holding hands. They sang a song unfamiliar to Paxton.

"Way up in that valley, prayin' on my knees, tellin' God about my troubles, and to help me if He please. Now no more weary trav'lin, 'cause my Jesus set me free, an' there's no more auction block for me since He give me liberty."

Paxton took two steps forward. The singers heard him and fell silent. All eyes came to rest on the white man approaching.

"Hello." Paxton lifted his hand in a wave. "Good morning."

They're afraid of me. No wonder. They're breaking the law.

"I won't report you." Paxton scanned their faces. "I didn't realize this was Sunday."

That man has a Bible. He must be the preacher.

"Yes, sir, this is the Lord's Day," said Eleutheros Supplee, stepping toward Paxton with his hand outstretched. "You are welcome."

Shaking his hand, Paxton said, "I seem to be lost."

Eleutheros asked, "Where are you going, sir?"

"To the Chesterton house where Statesman and Liney Prather live."

"Are you kin to the family?"

"No. My name is Paxton Faulconer."

"Eleutheros Supplee." The young man smiled. "I could guide you if I was certain that your motives are honorable."

"Indeed they are. I left a friend in the care of Statesman and Liney. I need to get back."

"Very well." Eleutheros handed his Bible to a man in the circle. "Carry on with the prayer needs. Be sure to bring the soldiers before the throne of grace."

Coffer Dunn nodded as he took the preacher's Bible. Eleutheros did not say Coffer's name.

* * *

Southern journalist, Greenup Fortier, alone in his tent, wrote: *Nothing like this battle has ever occurred. General Lee is facing a formidable foe.*

Northern journalist, Bradby Tucker was not alone. He was with General Winfield Scott Hancock when the commander received the news that part of Gershom Mott's Brigade had broken and run under artillery fire. In shorthand, the reporter wrote the Union leader's words. *The colonels of regiments that give way under a little shelling and a few scattered shots had better be mustered out of service.*

* * *

Paxton wished he was out of the service as he followed the agile young man leading him through the woods. Rain started again. They were both drenched despite their efforts to shelter under branches as much as possible.

How many days has it rained? It's depressing. Being apart from Albany is depressing. If only I was not a soldier, I would have no guilt feelings about what I'm doing – returning to a woman instead of my company. Where is the 13th Virginia this morning? What are they doing? What is Albany doing?

"Which way is the town?" asked Paxton in an effort to focus his thoughts somewhere else.

Eleutheros pointed and said, "The Confederates are camped there."

"Are the Yankees moving out?"

"Not that we can tell," said the preacher. "They still keep up a ruckus."

"I enjoyed hearing your hymn singing. At first, I thought it was angels and I'd gone to heaven."

Eleutheros chuckled and asked, "Have you been amongst the shooting, sir?"

Paxton released a heavy sigh before answering. "Indeed I have. I'm with the 13th Virginia but got separated."

"You're not in uniform."

"That's true." Paxton waited as his guide climbed over a fallen tree trunk. "I've been on a special assignment."

Will he lead me into a trap? If he knows the Confederates are in town, does he also know where the Yankees are? Do all slaves have a loyalty to the Northerners? Does he count me an enemy?

"My friend is resting in the Chesterton's attic." Paxton climbed over the tree trunk. "We saw some horrific sights. I'm sorry to say the experience affected her mind."

"Her?" Eleutheros turned and faced his follower.

"Yes, Albany Trubridge."

Eleutheros' eyes became wider but Paxton, behind him, did not see. "Miss Trubridge?"

"Do you know her?" Paxton touched Eleutheros' arm to stop him.

"Coffer was there."

"Her servant? Where?" His hold on Eleutheros tightened.

"In our worship circle. Susa couldn't come. She had to stay with Widow Trubridge."

186

Paxton released the young man, turned, and stared in the direction they had just come. "We should go back for him. He can take Albany home."

"They will have dismissed by now." Eleutheros pulled away from Paxton's grip and continued on their original route. "Coffer asked us to pray that Miss Albany would be found. Her horse came home but not the missus."

"Joab made it home." Paxton grinned. "We rode that horse together."

How good that felt to hold Albany in my arms as we rode Joab.

"The grandmother is beside herself, Coffer said."

"I shouldn't have left her." Paxton shoved aside a bush. "I should have seen her safely home before going back to the fight."

But I was tempted. Who better to understand temptation than a preacher? Should I tell him?

A horseman appeared in the distance. Both men halted. The rider moved swiftly along a row of crouching infantrymen and shouted: "Don't cheer. Don't cheer."

Paxton and Eleutheros hid behind two trees.

"Don't cheer," the Union cavalryman kept repeating.

In the next instant, General Grant, riding a bay horse, came into sight and rode slowly after the cavalryman. The commander kept his eyes on the breastworks. As soon as the general passed the 61st Pennsylvania, those men broke into a loud cheer. At the same moment, Rebel batteries opened. One of the shells burst over General Grant's head. Debris fell down on him along with the raindrops. The federal leader gave no inclination that he heard either the cheering or the cannonading but continued his ride until out of sight.

"We can't go that way," said Eleutheros, motioning for Paxton to follow him.

The sound of cannon shots exploding in the air did not diminish as they made their way to the Chesterton's house.

We made it! We're here!

Paxton stopped his guide by the smoke house.

"I'll go alone from here." He extended his hand. "Thank you, Pastor Supplee. I appreciate your help."

Eleutheros shook his hand. As quietly as possible, Paxton entered the back door, took off his shoes, and pushed them under the bench.

Albany's shoes are still here. She's upstairs. I'll see her again.

Paxton, wondering where the servants were, was half way up the back stairs when a cannon ball landed so near that the house shook. Paxton grabbed the railing to steady himself.

I've got to get her out of here. The battle is too close.

Taking two steps at a time, Paxton rushed up the remaining stairs.

"Albany!" Paxton jerked the attic door open.

Deserter barked, came to the top of the stairs, and wagged his tail.

"Good boy." Paxton patted the dog's head and looked around.

"Albany, where are you?"

Another cannon ball plowed through the nearby trees, knocking off a branch that landed in the front yard, as Paxton made his way amid the discards. He saw Albany wedged between stacked boxes.

"There you are." Paxton went to her. "Albany, I've come back. It's me."

She gasped and covered her face with her hands. The dog went to her, licked the back of her hands, and slowly swished his tail. Paxton knelt in front of her. Reaching up to pull her hands away, he said "I'm sorry, my darling. I am so sorry I left you."

Albany emitted a whine and gripped her hands into fists.

"We must get out of here." He pulled her fists away from her face. "The house is being shelled."

To escape him, Albany pushed back against the boxes. The top box tottered and fell. A cannon ball exploded close enough to rattle the windows. Paxton put his arms around Albany. She uncurled her fists, spread her palms against his chest, and shoved.

"No, don't push me away." He grabbed her hands. "You must come with me. I'm not leaving without you."

Albany struggled against his hold.

"Forgive me." His voice was raspy. "Please, Albany, forgive me for leaving you."

She refused to look at him.

"I'm so weary. If you won't forgive me…"

He released a sob. Unable to complete his sentence, he lowered his head but kept his hold of her hands. Albany raised her eyes and looked at Paxton.

"Please, dear." Lifting his head, his eyes met hers. His eyes shone with unshed tears. Albany, in one easy motion, fell forward. Paxton enfolded her in his arms.

"Oh, Albany, how I've missed you."

Their long embrace was interrupted when the attic door opened. Deserter barked. Forrester thundered up the steps.

"Who are you?" shouted the teenager.

* * *

While Coffer Dunn had been at the worship service in the woods that morning, the Trubridge house became a makeshift hospital. The rooms on the lower level were filling with moaning, bleeding men. Gerow Gately gave up his bed for a dying soldier.

"Who is this man?" Audine asked Susa in the parlor.

Susa, wiping blood off a man's arm, said, "A wounded soldier, ma'am."

"What's he doing in my house?"

"Remember, the doctor asked your permission to let them use the house and you said yes."

"But he didn't tell me they were Yankees." The old woman stared at the blue uniform on the man Susa was tending.

"Some are Confederates," said Susa. "You know Mr. Gately is a Yankee and we've been caring for him."

"Well, don't bother with that fellow now. I need my tea."

Coffer came to Mrs. Trubridge's side and said, "Let Susa finish the bandaging. You don't want him to bleed on your nice things in the parlor, do you?"

As Albany's grandmother left the room muttering, Coffer knelt beside Susa and helped her bandage the injured man.

"A white man interrupted our worship," Coffer said.

"Who was he? Did you know him?"

"No. He was a stranger."

"A soldier?" Susa glanced at Coffer.

"I think so. He told Brother Eleutheros his name – Paxton Faulconer.

He needed help getting to the Chesterton place where a friend of his was staying."

The couple, of course, had no idea that Paxton's friend was their Miss Albany.

* * *

Forrester stomped forward. Paxton kept his arms around Albany.

"Unhand her, you brigand," Forrester hissed.

Albany pressed her body closer to Paxton. Deserter, his ears up, planted himself between the couple on the floor and the belligerent teenager.

"Get away from her I said." Forrester jammed his hands on his hips. "She's mine."

"W-what?"

Did I hear him right? Who is this kid?

Slowly, Paxton stood, bringing Albany with him, and faced Forrester. He held Albany against his side with his arm around her and his hand on her waist.

"I said to release the lady." Forrester lowered his eyebrows. "I'm here to protect Rapunzel."

Albany turned her head and looked at Forrester.

"Rapunzel?" Paxton repeated. "The damsel in the tower?"

"That's right. I don't know her real name."

"Well, I do and I'm taking her home." Paxton stepped forward.

"You can go but not with her." Forrester spread his feet apart.

Deserter growled at the boy.

"I beg to differ." Paxton kept his voice calm.

"She is my house guest."

"House guest?" Paxton tightened his hold on Albany's waist. "This has not been a social call."

Forrester's eyes blazed. "You get out!" He reached for Albany.

Do I have to fight him?

Deserter barked as the door opened. Statesman came up the stairs two at a time with Eleutheros behind him.

"Get back!" Forrester glared at the black men. "Who are you?" The question was aimed at Eleutheros but Forrester did not wait for a reply.

"This is none of your business. Get out. Both of you." Glancing around, he grabbed a tarnished candlestick, raised it, and started toward Paxton.

Deserter nipped at Forrester's heels. Eleutheros stepped between Forrester and Paxton. Statesman seized the candlestick. Forrester was so startled that he did not maintain a grip on the make-shift weapon.

"Statesman, you let me have that!"

"You're not going to hit the white folks," his servant said.

"I'm rescuing the lady."

"He's rescuing her."

Paxton clutched Albany's hand and, evading the teenager and his servant struggling for possession of the candlestick, followed Eleutheros down the stairs. Deserter bounded after them.

"Come back here!" yelled Forrester.

Statesman continued his struggle with the teenager, something he never imagined doing.

Paxton, Albany, Eleutheros, and Deserter were out of the house when Forrester, having lost possession of the candlestick, grabbed an ornamental inkwell and slammed the heavy metal object against the side of Statesman's head. Dazed, Statesman released his hold on the teenager.

Forrester raced down the steps. "I'm going to sell you down the river, Statesman Prather. You're going to pay for this. I'll hire a slave breaker to beat you senseless."

Statesman did not hear the teenager's last sentence because he was too far away. Going to the window, the slave saw the three fleeing people and the dog disappear into the woods. Right behind them ran Forrester.

* * *

Thornton Faulconer and Oliver Frankinberry were trudging toward Belle Plain, where they would be taken by boat to Washington City and then north to various prisons. As they saw soldiers marching toward them, their federal guards ushered their prisoners to the side of the road. The oncoming troops belonged to the United States Colored Troops.

"Who is that?"

"I don't believe my eyes."

Adding to the comments, Oliver said, "Negroes in uniform."

191

"So the damn Yankees have done it," grumbled a Southerner at his elbow.

"Why are you surprised?" Thornton asked Oliver. "The Northern newspapers reported they were going to arm their blacks."

"Drawers of water and hewers of wood," one of the prisoners called to the marching men.

"Bet they're all runaways," said Oliver.

"If they are runaway slaves," said Thornton, "the Yanks have weakened us and strengthened themselves." He paused before adding, "Look how they hold their heads up."

"Proud as peacocks." Using his finger as though it was a gun, Oliver aimed at the black soldiers and said, "I'd like to shoot off their feathers."

As he pushed Oliver's hand down, Thornton said, "Be careful. I dare say those white officers would not like to see that."

"They're probably just used for digging latrines and burying the dead."

"They march well. I don't see any stragglers." Thornton's eyes followed the black men. "What if we enlisted our slaves?"

"We might as well enlist Indians and arm them with tomahawks and scalping knives. That compares with giving guns to Negroes." Oliver spit. "Besides, if we did that, who would pick the cotton?"

"The sacrifice might be worth the price," said Thornton. "They're talking about it in Richmond. We would give them freedom if they would fight for the Confederacy."

"We can't give guns to our slaves," snarled Oliver. "They could shoot us in our beds."

"There might not be a choice," said Thornton. "Our recruitment is drying up, while Yanks enlist their recruits right off the ships from Europe."

"And we have no ships from Europe because of the damn blockade."

Thornton added, "And we have no prisoner exchange because of the damn General Grant."

* * *

Paxton, Albany, Eleutheros, and Deserter ran through the woods as Blake and Drake pounded up the basement stairs. Statesman, holding a cloth to his bleeding head, met the twins in the back staircase.

"What happened to you?" Blake asked.

"Why are you bleeding?" Drake, behind his brother, turned around, went to the basement stairs, and called, "Liney, come quickly. Statesman's hurt."

In the next minute, Liney was wiping the blood off her husband's face as he sat at the kitchen table. The twins circled the big room and shot questions at their servant.

"Where's Forrester?"

"What's been going on?"

"We heard noises. Were other people in the house?"

"What have you been up to, Statesman?"

The slave remained silent.

Drake looked at his twin, crossed his arms, and said, "Maybe he's planning an insurrection like Nat Turner did. Maybe we'll all be killed in our beds."

Blake stepped close to Statesman's chair. "You wouldn't kill us in our beds nor anyplace else, would you?"

"Statesman, speak up." Drake planted himself at his brother's side.

"What's been going on?" Blake demanded.

Liney took the cloth away and waited to see if the bleeding had stopped. Statesman said nothing.

"Liney, what do you know about this?" asked Blake.

"There have been some white folks hiding in the attic," she said.

"Did they kidnap Forrester?"

"Yah, where's Forrester?"

* * *

They had not gone far when Albany's skirt snagged on a branch. She stumbled and would have fallen if Paxton had not caught her. She put her hands on his shoulders as she regained her balance.

She's not afraid of him. He certainly has genuine concern for her.

"We're heading in the wrong direction." Eleutheros caught his breath.

"The Trubridge place isn't this way?" Paxton leaned against a tree. Albany rested against his chest.

"That way." Eleutheros pointed to the west.

"I'm completely turned around in these woods," said Paxton.

Forrester appeared and shouted, "You foolish men!"

Gunfire blasted through the wilderness.

"Why have you taken her out of my safe haven?" Forrester stomped toward Albany and Paxton. "You've brought her into the midst of danger."

Eleutheros blocked the boy.

"I'm escorting her home," said Paxton.

"My house is close and safe."

"No place is safe," said the preacher.

What is it with this boy? Why did he follow us?

"Who are you anyway?" Forrester tried to reach around Eleutheros. "Come with me, Rapunzel."

Albany pressed her body more firmly against Paxton. Forrester pounded his fist into Eleutheros, knocking him to the side, and grabbed Albany's elbow. Paxton struggled with the teenager. Soldiers appeared. Guns blazed. Deserter barked. Forrester saw a rifle pointed toward Albany. He shoved her. The bullet that would have hit her instead struck him.

"Forrester," said Albany.

Like a window blind suddenly snapping up on its roller, Albany's mind became clear, letting in the reality of the present moment.

She spoke. He's shot.

Eleutheros knelt, tore Forrester's shirt, and gazed at the wound. The soldiers with blazing guns moved their fight away. Deserter barked at the running men.

This is bad.

"We must stop the bleeding," said Paxton.

"Use my petticoat." Albany pulled up the hem of her dress. Paxton ripped the white undergarment. Albany scooted Forrester's head onto her lap.

"Looks like the bullet went through," said Eleutheros, helping Paxton bandage the wound.

Sounds of gunfire faded. Deserter stopped barking as the fighters disappeared.

"You'll be all right," said Albany, smoothing Forrester's hair off his forehead.

Forrester writhed in pain as the two men wrapped the white fabric around his middle.

Gut shot. No hope.

Eleutheros and Paxton made eye contact as they finished the frantic bandaging.

"D-don't … leave … me," Forrester muttered.

"I won't," Albany said.

Statesman appeared. He came to the wounded boy's side.

"We need to take him back," said Eleutheros. "Is there a cart to carry him?"

"Yes. Come with me."

The two men raced back to the Chesterton barn while Paxton, with his hands under Forrester's shoulders, moved him off Albany's lap to the nearby bushes where they could hide. Forrester moaned in pain. Once again, Albany scooted close so she could rest the teenager's head on her lap.

Statesman and Eleutheros were not gone long, but the time seemed to drag for Albany and Paxton comforting Forrester.

When the two slaves, pulling the cart behind them, returned to the site of the shooting, Deserter barked to announce their approach. As carefully as possible, the men lifted Forrester into the cart. Each slave grabbed a handlebar and pulled. Paxton took Albany's hand and followed. The dog led the way.

* * *

Upon reaching the Chesterton house, Statesman carried Forrester into the parlor and laid him on the ivory satin settee near the fireplace.

"Am I … going to … die?"

No one answered his question. Deserter licked Forrester's hand dangling on the green and gold rug. Albany lifted his hand and gently placed it by his side. The boy writhed in pain.

"I'll fetch Liney." Statesman hurried to the basement.

"He needs a doctor," said Albany.

"We're not likely to get a doctor to come here," Paxton said. "They're busy treating soldiers."

"But he's in such pain." Albany's chin trembled.

In the basement, when Statesman rushed across the big room to grab his wife's hand and lead her upstairs, the three children followed. Seeing their brother wrapped in a bloody bandage brought the siblings to hysterics. All was bedlam.

Liney said, "Statesman, fetch the master's whiskey."

Paxton said, "He needs morphine."

Eleutheros faced Paxton and said, "I can get some from a doctor."

"If not morphine," said Paxton, "ask him for something to ease the pain."

Without another word, the black preacher headed out the door.

"He's bled through this bandage," said Liney. "He needs a new bandage. Florence, bring me that old bed sheet. You know the one."

Florence, with tears streaming down her face, obeyed. Statesman brought the bottle of whiskey and gave Forrester a sip. He spit and coughed, unable to swallow.

"What happened to him, Statesman?" asked Drake.

"Did you shoot him?" Blake looked up at the slave.

"Soldiers shot him by mistake," said Paxton.

"Who are you?"

"Are you the people Liney told us about – the people hiding in the attic?"

Paxton confirmed the twin's statement as Florence arrived with the bed sheet. They tore the fabric and re-bandaged Forrester's stomach wound while Paxton explained what had happened.

"This is all your fault," said Blake.

"If you hadn't been here, my brother would not get shot," said Drake. "He'd be safe in the basement with us."

The twins burst into tears. Florence hugged her brothers and wept with them. With the re-bandaging complete, Liney took Florence into her arms to comfort her. The twins went to Statesman whose strong arms went around them. Paxton picked up the old bandage, using it to wipe blood off the floor. Albany held Forrester's hand. The dog licked the boy's face before curling up by the low settee.

So began the vigil waiting for Eleutheros to return with morphine and waiting for Forrester to die.

* * *

Despite Forrester's difficulty in swallowing his father's whiskey, Paxton and Statesman continued giving it to him until he was in a stupor.

"Rapunzel… where…"

"I'm here," said Albany, lifting his hand to touch her cheek.

"You're ... talking."

"Yes, I can talk again."

"Buttons…"

Forrester closed his eyes and was silent.

"He's not?" Albany sought Paxton's gaze.

"No, just sleeping. That's good." Paxton touched her sleeve. "What did he mean about buttons?"

"We sorted them together. He was kind to me when you were gone." She paused before asking, "Where did you go?"

"Back to the war."

"Why?"

"I felt guilty. I felt like those three scoundrels who attacked us. Remember -- the deserters."

"I do remember." Albany nodded.

They were kneeling by the settee but Paxton took her hand and led her to the Duncan Phyfe mahogany bench where they sat close together.

"Forrester talked to me." She drew his hand onto her skirt puffing above her thigh. "It felt like a tunnel, all dark and hollow, but I heard him. I just couldn't answer back. He was kind."

"He loves you."

"Does he?"

"You can tell by the way he looks at you."

"I recall his saying that he would marry me when he got a few years older." She tightened her grip. "But he won't get older, will he?"

Paxton simply shook his head.

* * *

With Forrester in an alcoholic haze, Liney returned to the basement to check on the missus. Madelyn Chesterton still breathed but barely. Her eyes were closed. A trickle of blood flowed from the corner of her mouth. The slave wiped the blood away with a strained handkerchief, sat down, and took the limp white hand in her own dark one.

"Your boy is home." The slave's voice was low. She did not expect to be heard. "You will see each other soon."

Statesman came to find his wife. Her face was wet with tears. He lovingly pulled her up from her chair and hugged her.

"She doesn't waken." Liney embraced him.

"It won't be long for either of them," said Statesman.

* * *

At the intersection to the west of Piney Branch Church, Bradby Tucker interviewed some of the United States Colored Troops in camp. The black soldiers rested, napped, ate, cleaned their guns, and chatted.

"How do you like army life?" asked Bradby, holding his pencil ready above his notebook.

"Better than slave life."

"Food is sure better."

"Do you feel that your training has been adequate?" Bradby wrote as he spoke.

Gunfire shattered the peace.

"What's that?"

"Someone's gun misfired."

The yip-yip-yip of the Rebel yell dispelled any question regarding the gunfire.

"It's Rebs!"

The Federal soldiers grabbed their guns. Bradby, unarmed, hit the ground. Brigadier General Edward Ferrero instructed his men who battled the Army of Northern Virginia for the first time in a directed combat action. The brief skirmish was a Federal success. The black soldiers fought bravely. After the encounter, the New York journalist sent his story to the *Times,* but it was ignored. Other news took priority over an article about black soldiers.

* * *

CHAPTER FOURTEEN

VERY DISCOURAGING NEWS

Monday, May 16, 1864

News of fighting on other fronts reached the soldiers in Spotsylvania County on Monday, May 16. For the Union soldiers, the news was very discouraging.

General Franz Sigel was badly defeated at New Market, having faced cadets from the Virginia Military Institute on Sunday. Former Vice-President John C. Breckinridge led the victorious Confederate troops.

General Benjamin Butler was driven from Drury's Bluff on the James River but was still in possession of the Petersburg Road. The Southerners in Richmond rejoiced at this news of their stronghold on the river remaining safe.

Because General Nathaniel P. Banks was defeated in Louisiana, he was replaced by General Edward Richard Sprigg Canby, a native of Indiana, who was one of the most well-read army commanders and highly respected in the military.

* * *

In the Chesterton house, as morning dawned, Albany came awake and took a full minute to acclimate herself to her surroundings.

What is this room? I haven't been here before.

She lay atop a flowered bedspread. A matching canopy hung among the four walnut bed posts. Florence slept beside her. A blue blanket covered them.

Oh, yes, I recall now. This is the guest bedroom. Paxton insisted we get some rest.

Memories of yesterday filled her mind as she gazed at the flowered fabric overhead.

The children cried and carried on so much. What would I have done if left to manage them alone? Thank goodness for Paxton and the servants. They hugged the children and did all they could to comfort them.

Albany reached over and moved a lock of Florence's hair from her cheek to behind her ear.

The poor girl – she was beside herself. How often did she and her brothers go to the icehouse and bring ice to Forrester? He didn't want whiskey. He wanted ice.

Sitting up, Albany looked around the room. She had slept in one of Madelyn Chesterton's nightgowns. The raspberry-colored dress hung in the wardrobe. She climbed off the high bed and dressed, wearing Gerow Gately's shoes with paper stuffed in the toes.

I wonder if Forrester is still alive. I hope Paxton did not leave.

Before going downstairs, Albany stepped in front of the oval mirror above the wash stand.

My eyes look so puffy. I can't remember when I cried so much. What does it matter how I look?

She hurried down the stairs.

* * *

Paxton smiled at Albany when she entered the kitchen. Without a word, he left the stove where he was heating grease in a skillet, embraced her, and kissed her forehead.

"Good morning, my dear," he whispered.

Looking up at him, she asked, "Is Forrester…"

"He's still alive." With his arm around her, Paxton led her to the stove. "Liney made this batter and left me to cook my own pancake."

"Where is everyone?"

"Liney is tending the missus in the basement. She doesn't expect her to live much longer." He released her so he could pour the batter into the hot skillet. "Statesman and Deserter went out to look for Eleutheros. I admonished him not to go far."

"And the boys?"

"Taking turns watching their brother."

"Did Forrester sleep?"

Paxton shook his head. "He's in a great deal of pain."

"Did you sleep?"

"Dozed a little." Paxton tipped up the edge of the pancake to see how it was cooking. "What about Florence? Is she still asleep?"

Albany nodded and asked, "Could you get Forrester to take the whiskey?"

"Only sips." He flipped up the edge of the pancake to see if it was brown. "He just wanted ice."

"Maybe we can dip the ice chunks in the whiskey," suggested Albany.

"We can try that after we eat."

Half an hour later, Albany was feeding a whiskey-soaked ice chip to Forrester when Florence entered the parlor. The twins greeted her with silent hugs.

"Did Mr. Supplee bring the morphine?" Florence asked.

"Not yet," said Statesman.

"What is causing his delay?" She twisted her hands at her waist.

"Today is Monday, Miss Florence. Our Sunday free day ended at midnight. Slaves out on Monday without a pass can be arrested."

"Would anyone arrest a slave on a mission of mercy?" asked Drake.

"How would they know," said Blake. "He might be lying."

"The sheriff could arrest him as a runaway," said their sister.

"Or the soldiers might snatch him."

"Why should he help us at all? He's not our slave."

Statesman hushed the children. "Don't worry about Brother Eleutheros. If he can get morphine, he will."

* * *

Confederate soldiers had captured Eleutheros and put him to work hauling dead bodies to shallow graves. Having failed to find a hospital before dark on Sunday, Eleutheros had slept in the woods. Soon after dawn, Monday morning, the young preacher met gray-clad soldiers who put him to work.

As Eleutheros dragged a body to a shallow mass grave, he felt a twitch from the man's right hand. Eleutheros halted. Dropping the body, Eleutheros knelt, put his palm inches from the man's nose, and felt warm breath blow against his skin.

"This man's alive!" Eleutheros waved to the passing officer.

Upon confirming Eleutheros' statement, the officer ordered, "Take him to the doctor over that way."

In the hospital tent, Eleutheros did what he could for the soldier.

"Do you have morphine?" Eleutheros asked the doctor, working over a profusely-bleeding man.

"The brown bottle there." The doctor tilted his head to indicate his medical bag.

Eleutheros read the labels on the brown bottles, several of which were morphine. He took one and exited the tent. No one attempted to stop him.

* * *

Albany tried to entice Forrester to eat a piece of toast.

"Ice... ice ... please," Forrester said.

"Here is a piece of ice," said Paxton, slipping the frozen sliver of water between the boy's lips.

Albany put the toast on the saucer. Forrester gazed with blood-shot eyes at Albany. The ice melted slowly in his mouth.

"I'll get more." Paxton took the bowl and left the parlor.

"I said ... we would ... marry."

"Yes, I remember," said Albany. "You said that after we sorted all the buttons."

"You're so ... beautiful."

"You said we had to wait a few years until you were older."

"I won't ... get ... older."

The twins came into the room, having finished the pancakes that Liney insisted they eat. Florence, the slowest eater, still sat at the kitchen table, playing with the pancake pieces on her plate. The boys had not heard their brother's statement. As they had done yesterday, Blake and Drake tried to cheer up Forrester.

"You'll be better soon."

"That hole in your stomach will mend itself in no time."

"We need you to play a game of marbles with us. You're the best player."

"Yah, I bet I can beat you, even with a hole in you."

The front door banged open. Eleutheros had arrived.

* * *

An hour later, with Forrester no longer moaning in agony, the others were not so tense. Everyone in the house except Madelyn was in the parlor. Forrester motioned for Albany to come close. When she knelt at the edge of the settee, Forrester reached for her hand.

"The Bible says ... Jesus said ... in heaven ... no marriage."

"That's right," said Albany.

"I'm going ... to heaven."

Albany felt a wave of anguish sweep through her. She leaned over and touched her cheek to his. Close to his ear, she whispered, "I'm so very sorry. This is all because of me."

"Sweet... heart..." Forrester closed his eyes.

Albany pulled back, saw his eyes shut, and looked at his chest. He was still breathing. She burst into sobs. "It's m-my fault."

Paxton pulled her up and embraced her. Eleutheros came to take her place.

"Do you know Jesus as your personal savior, Forrester?" the preacher asked.

As Paxton moved Albany to the far corner, they heard Forrester's weak voice. "I do ... know Him."

Sobbing softly, Albany buried her face against Paxton's chest. Paxton stroked her back as he listened to the black preacher speak comforting words to the dying white boy.

The rain pounding on the windows was the only other sound.

* * *

When Albany, exhausted from crying, went limp in Paxton's arms, he escorted her to the kitchen where a kettle of hot water sat on the stove.

"I'll make us some tea."

Having helped Statesman earlier, Paxton knew where things were. Albany watched him.

"If Forrester had not followed us, if he had not protected me from the bullet, he would not be dying now." She clutched her hands atop the table. "This is my fault, my fault."

"Forrester made his own choice." Paxton set a tea cup in front of her. "You are not responsible."

"But why is he so smitten with me? I hardly remember our time together. I dwelt in my own dark despair. You know that."

"How well I know."

"Is that why you left me?"

Paxton sat close to her and took a sip of tea. She drank her tea and awaited his reply.

"I will tell you the truth about why I left." He set his cup on the saucer. "Do you know the English poet John Donne?"

"Didn't he write the poem about no man is an island entire of himself?"

"Yes, that's right." Paxton studied her expression. "He was the pastor of St. Paul's Cathedral in London later in life, but as a young man he wrote erotic poetry."

"What kind of poetry?"

"Love poetry but what our mothers would consider improper."

"Oh."

"Mr. Donne believed that Joseph's resistance of the advances by his master's wife, in the Book of Genesis, was a greater miracle than Lazarus being raised from the dead in the Gospels."

"Why are you telling me this?"

"Because I was tempted by you as David was tempted by Bathsheba." Paxton drank his tea.

In a low voice, Albany asked, "Did I do something wrong?"

"No, not at all; it was nothing you did."

"You left me to avoid temptation."

"That's right."

"What happened while you were gone? What did you do?"

"I fought the enemy, all the while wishing I was back here with you." Paxton finished his tea. "I felt guilty. I didn't want to be shot as a deserter. I knew you would be safe. Statesman said he'd get you home, that he would contact Coffer."

"Statesman knows Coffer?"

"Yes. Eleutheros told me that Coffer and Susa, Statesman and Liney, are all in their church that meets in the woods."

"Then I can go home as soon as the soldiers stop fighting."

"Yes, that's right."

"And what will you do?"

Paxton did not answer. Albany saw the dismay on his face.

* * *

Having helped wounded soldiers from the wagon into the Trubridge house, Coffer was leading the animals to the water trough when a Western Union Telegraph Company courier rode into the yard on a mule.

"I got a wire for the mistress," said the teenager, holding up a piece of paper.

"You- hoo, I'm up here!" called Audine from the balcony above the front door. "What do you have there? Do I know you?"

"You have a telegram, ma'am," said the Western Union man.

Coffer stopped what he was doing.

"A telegram? Has someone died?"

"No, ma'am. It's good news."

"Well, I don't have my glasses. I can't see it."

Coffer chuckled at the old woman's remark.

"You read it to me."

The man read slowly. "Mother, Doctors released me. Coming home with Luciana. Your son Shedrick."

"That's good. No one died," Audine said.

Coffer left the horses at the water trough and went to the courier. "I'll take it up to her."

Placing the paper in Coffer's hand, the man said, "I always like to deliver good news. I assume there is no reply, ma'am. They're probably on the road by now."

"Who's on the road?" Audine leaned over the railing to look down on the two men. "Is Albany on the road?"

"She's a little forgetful" Coffer said to the courier before raising his voice toward the balcony. "Not Miss Albany, your son Shedrick."

The courier tipped his hat and turned his mule.

"Wait." Coffer grabbed the harness. "We need to send a telegram."

"Who to?"

"Mrs. Gerow Gately in Cincinnati."

* * *

Finishing the noon meal, Grandon Faulconer wadded up the newspaper he had been reading and tossed it into the mud

"That's the last time I'll read a Yankee rag," snapped Grandon.

"Don't do that." Greenup Fortier grabbed up the newspaper before it became soaked. "Our couriers face danger to bring us this. I want to know how the enemy is reporting."

"It's a bunch of lies," said Paxton's brother.

Greenup unfolded the damp paper and read aloud. "The veteran army of Robert E. Lee is breaking up, or rather it is being defeated, demolished, crushed and annihilated by the courage of our soldiers and the masterly generalship of their Commander."

"What falsehoods!" Grandon exclaimed. "Where do reporters get that nonsense? We're not breaking up. We're whipping them."

The Southern correspondent carefully folded the single sheet and tucked it into his pocket.

"Why are you keeping that?" Grandon scowled. "Are you going to cite the liar? Does it have a byline? I didn't notice."

"Byline or not," said Greenup. "I plan to keep this as a souvenir showing the kind of propaganda that our soldiers come across while they're fighting for their lives."

"Propaganda – that's for sure. Why do they write such falsehoods? Do they think we'll surrender based on their lies?"

The *Richmond Examiner* reporter made no response to the question but said, "I read that Mr. Lincoln proclaimed a day of thanksgiving for their victories south of the Rapidan."

"Their victories? What does Billy Yank consider a victory?"

"I don't know," said Greenup, "but I do know that we can thank the

Lord for our superior commanders. That General Grant doesn't compare to our General Lee."

* * *

Grant received dispatches, one of which said General Sherman had compelled Confederate General Johnston to evacuate Dalton, Georgia, and was chasing him. Another message informed the Union commander that General Sheridan had destroyed portions of the Virginia Central and Fredericksburg railroads, had killed General J.E.B. Stuart, and completely routed the Rebel cavalry.

* * *

At the supply depot of the Union Army called White House, located in New Kent County, on the south shore of the Pamunkey River, Confederate prisoners waited for transportation to their northern prison.

Thornton Faulconer, sitting on the ground and sipping coffee, gazed around the busy area.

This is the best coffee I've tasted in three years.

Oliver Frankinberry, joining him, said, "I heard this was once the home of Martha Custis before she married George Washington."

"That's right. We're getting a tour of historic places on our way to the northern dungeons," said Biglor Bibb. "Guess we should enjoy it while we can."

"I'm sure enjoying this coffee," said Thornton.

"Where's the house?" Biglor looked around the clearing.

"The Yankees burned the house," said Thornton, "when they retreated from here in '62."

"It appears the Yanks own it again," said Oliver. "They've certainly made themselves to home with all the stuff they've got stacked up here."

"Wish we had half as much," said Biglor.

"All their stuff might be what wins them the war." Thornton scowled. *I've never seen so many supplies all in one place.*

"What do you mean?" Biglor inquired. "Supplies don't kill the enemy."

"But the guns and bullets in those boxes do," replied Thornton, scanning the area. "The food and shoes and clothes keep the soldiers going."

"We have supplies," said Biglor.

"If we do, those supplies don't often make it down the line to the common soldier," said Thornton.

"He's right," chimed in Oliver. "Without being better provisioned, how can we stay in the field? Our days are numbered."

"We can steal from dead Yanks on the battlefield," said Biglor

"Not a very good long-term strategy," said Thornton. "The Federals have greater resources with their factories turning out weapons and their farms producing food."

The men continued making comparisons concerning agriculture and manufacturing in the two sections of the United States.

* * *

The Chesterton house was covered in mourning before any death occurred. The residents spoke in hushed tones as they went about their activities. Everyone's eyes were red from crying and lack of sleep.

Florence looked for black fabric to cover the hall mirror. The twins read Psalms to Forrester who was resting now that the morphine had taken effect. Paxton and Statesman had taken turns by Forrester's side during the night, so both men snatched cat naps that day. When the men were with Forrester, they quoted reassuring Bible verses. Paxton read the verses, but Statesman, who could not read, spoke memorized Scriptures. Liney kept busy going up and down stairs, caring for the dying mother and son.

Whenever Albany and Paxton passed each other, they touched. The touch would be brief – fingers across an arm, a palm on a shoulder. Their eyes always met. Sometimes, they gave a brief smile.

Eleutheros had gone home after delivering the morphine but said he would return if he could. Deserter stayed beside the settee. Forrester rested his hand in the dog's fur.

Madelyn Chesterton knew nothing of her son's impending death. She was seldom conscious, and then for only brief moments. When the children were not with their brother, they were with their mother. The adults kept close watch over the children.

Although they all knew death was near, they were stunned when it came. Forrester stopped breathing in the evening just as darkness began to fall.

"He's not suffering anymore," said Florence before sobbing into her handkerchief.

"He doesn't need any more ice." Blake cried.

"Nor morphine," wailed Drake.

Albany hugged Florence. Statesman wrapped his arms around Drake who was near him, while Paxton embraced Blake. Liney pulled the cover over Forrester's face. Time seemed to plod as they wept.

* * *

CHAPTER FIFTEEN

THESE BUTCHER'S SHAMBLES

Tuesday, May 17, 1864

Tuesday, May 17, dawned bright and clear. After days of almost constant rain, today no rain clouds were in sight. The day would be hot, and the muddy roads would have a chance to dry.

In Washington, Major-General Halleck read the most recent telegram from General Grant informing him that the army was in the best of spirits and just waiting for the weather to clear up so their offensive operations could start again.

In Spotsylvania County, General Grant drafted orders for Generals Hancock and Wright to march back to their old positions during the night and prepare for a dawn attack. Since most of the enemy had moved to its right in order to match the Union's movement, General Grant thought an attack on Lee's line, which was established after the assault on the Mule Shoe, might be the best way to catch the Confederates off guard.

* * *

Albany and Paxton slept side by side atop the bedspread in the master's front bedroom where she had collapsed, exhausted and too tired to do more than remove her shoes. Florence had wanted to sleep near the twins, so the children had all cuddled together in her big bed.

Sometime around three a.m., Paxton had crossed the hallway from the mistress's room to check on Albany. She stirred, reached for him, and said, "Don't go."

Paxton needed no further word. He had climbed onto the bed and lay beside her. With his arm over her waist, he easily fell asleep.

In the parlor below, Forrester's body lay on the sofa, covered with a satin cloth intended for a table. His facial expression attested to peace.

Awakening, Paxton heard birds chirping. He stretched and moved his hand off Albany's stomach. She felt his movement, opened her eyes, and smiled at him.

"I thought I was dreaming that you were here with me," she said softly.

"I just came to see if you were all right." He smiled. "You asked me to stay."

Albany wrinkled her forehead. "Did Forrester really die?"

"Yes." Paxton took her hand, pulled it toward his mouth, and kissed the back of her hand. "Forrester died."

"What's to be done now?"

"Statesman and I will dig a grave." Paxton recalled the family graveyard. "Statesman was preparing a grave for their mother. The rain probably filled it with mud by now." He looked toward the window. "Perhaps we should have the twins help us. The work might do them good."

Scooting closer to him, Albany asked, "What's to become of the children? Their mother will be gone soon. Their father is probably dead already. Liney told me there's been no word from him in months."

"We must watch over them." He looked intently into her eyes. "Can they stay at your house?"

"Certainly, we have plenty of room."

"Then I will get you and the children home."

"The servants, too," she said.

"Statesman said he and Liney plan to go with the Union army."

"Why?"

"For freedom."

"Oh, but they couldn't leave the children at such a time as this." Albany curled her fingers around Paxton's hand. "Surely, they wouldn't do that."

"We'll see."

* * *

211

When Albany and Paxton went looking for the slaves, they found them in the parlor. Statesman was brushing Forrester's hair. Liney was tying his shoes. Deserter wagged his tail in greeting. Blake and Drake were asleep on the floor. Florence had gone to the basement and crawled into bed with her mother.

"The dog spent the night with him," Statesman said in a lowered voice.

Liney added, "He must have felt the need. Dogs are smart."

Paxton motioned to Statesman. "Can we go look at the gravesite?"

The slave stood. Albany took the hairbrush from him and knelt beside the settee to finish brushing the dead boy's hair.

Walking to the family burying ground, Paxton asked Statesman his plans.

"Are you still set on leaving with the Federal army?"

"Liney wants to stick with the children," said Statesman, "just until they are settled somewhere."

"Albany says they can come to her house. It would be a comfort to the children if you and Liney were there with them."

"They have cousins in Richmond. If you could write to them…"

"Yes, of course, I will," said Paxton. "If they cannot take them, we will find some suitable place for them."

Having reached the grave, the men saw that mud had almost completely filled the two foot-deep space Statesman had dug previously.

"Reckon I need to dig this out again."

"Should we get the twins to help us?"

Statesman nodded and went to the barn for the shovel. Paxton waited and read the barely-legible names on the few stone markers.

* * *

In Cincinnati, Ohio, in a brick house on a hillside, Myrta Gately was busy packing a carpet bag open on her bed while her mother watched.

"I might as well give up trying to talk you out of this foolishness," the older woman said. "You don't seem a bit concerned about the impropriety of a lady traveling alone, as well as the danger of such an undertaking."

"Women must travel alone when there is no man available to escort her." Myrta folded a nightgown and dropped it atop pantaloons in the bag.

Myrta's mother picked up the telegram from the bureau where her daughter had tossed it. "The wire says Gerow is receiving good care. There's no reason for you to go."

"If Father was wounded, you would go." Myrta tucked a handkerchief in the small side pocket of the valise.

"Wait for your father to get home from work? Perhaps he will go with you."

"Papa's too busy at Procter and Gamble." She got a dress out of the wardrobe. "They can't do without him."

"But you don't even know where to go. Where is Spotsylvania County?"

"I'll ask at the train station." Myrta packed the dress and went to the bureau to get undergarments. "I can't stay put when my husband needs me. You would do the same, Mama. You know you would."

The distraught mother plopped onto the bed as her daughter finished packing. "But it's in Rebel territory. The papers say Grant is fighting in Virginia."

Myrta put her cape over her shoulders, looped the drawstring of her reticule over her wrist, closed her carpetbag, and went to the door.

Following, her mother asked, "But what will you do when you get there? How will you know where to go? What's the name of these people?"

"Trubridge," answered Myrta.

* * *

Bradby Tucker carried the front end of a stretcher from an ambulance into the Trubridge house. The journalist had been helping move the injured to whatever available building or tent was designated as a hospital.

Gerow Gately, wearing a sling, held the door open for the recent arrivals.

"Where do you want him?" Bradby asked.

"In there," replied Gerow, nodding toward the sick room he had recently occupied.

After placing the injured soldier on the bed, the newspaper man left his care to the medical attendant carrying the rear of the stretcher. Coming into the kitchen, Bradby got a cup of water.

Gerow asked, "Are the armies moving on yet?"

"Don't appear to be," said Bradby, going to the window and watching the activity in the yard. "Do you live here?" The reporter glanced at Gerow's civilian clothes.

"No. These clothes belong to Mr. Trubridge, who has been at Chimborazo. He and his wife will be home soon."

"Who are you?"

Offering his hand, he said, "Lieutenant Gerow Gately, Third Ohio."

"Bradby Tucker, reporter for the *New York Times.*"

They shook hands.

"A pen-pusher hauling litters -- that's a rare sight," said Gerow.

"I didn't expect to be doing this but can't very well refuse. They're short-handed," said Bradby, sipping his water. "What about you? What's your story?"

"I was wounded and they took me in."

Gerow waited for Bradby to finish drinking before he asked, "Have you gotten some good stories from this battle?"

"Do battles ever make good stories?" Bradby set the empty tin cup on the counter. "I think readers are getting tired of heroism and nobility. What does it all mean, anyway?"

Gerow scowled. "It means an empty chair at the table, a field unplowed, and a lonely branch on the family tree."

After a brief silence, the reporter said, "There must be something redemptive in all this chaos." He crossed his arms. "I want to write a human interest story, something that will touch the reader. American soldiers killing each other in one location and then in a different location, with one commander and then a different commander -- what's the purpose?"

"To win the war, of course." Gerow leaned forward. "To free the slaves."

"Yes, certainly, there is that noble purpose – freeing enslaved people -- but couldn't we provide freedom for the black people in a peaceable way?"

"If there was such a way, our politicians should have found it before now," said the Ohio soldier.

The men had to end their conversation in the kitchen. The doctor needed the table for an arm amputation. Gerow and Bradby went outdoors and continued talking.

* * *

214

Paxton's parents finished their morning devotions in the parlor of their house in Gordonsville. Melora and Evandon Faulconer took turns reading the verses of Isaiah chapter 42. Paxton's father placed the black ribbon to mark the place and closed the Bible on the book stand.

"Do you see us like those Israelites of old?" asked Melora on the settee beside her husband.

"How so?" Evandon asked.

"We just read about how the exiles were punished for disobeying God's covenant. He called them to be a blessing to all nations, a light to the Gentiles."

"So how does that compare with us?"

"We have failed God just as they did," she answered.

"Because we have kept black people in bondage." His voice was low.

"Yes." She twisted her hands in her lap. "I am so convicted that slavery is wrong, but what can I, a mere woman, do about it?"

"There is nothing any of us citizens can do," Evandon said. "This war will be the deciding factor as to what is done about slavery." He stood and offered his hand to help her rise.

They went to the door but, when he opened it, she hesitated to go into the hall.

"Listen to how quiet the house is." Melora glanced around at the hallway, the umbrella stand, and the bureau. "I miss the boys. This hallway was always so busy when they were home."

Putting his arm around his wife's shoulders, Evandon said, "The boys will return before long."

"Will all three of them return?"

"We must pray that they do."

Melora stepped from the carpet of the parlor to the painted linoleum of the hall. "So many men are dying. Will our girls ever marry? Who will be left for them to marry?"

"You are imagining problems that have not yet arrived," he said and smiled down at her as they walked on the decorative pattern. "The good Lord will provide husbands for our girls and wives for our sons if it is his will, and someday grandchildren will be running back and forth in this hallway."

"I wish I was as certain as you are." Melora stopped at the bureau to see if any mail had been placed in the tray. There was no letter. "Perhaps it's because I see so many men dying at the Receiving Hospital."

"Should you stop working there?" He opened the front door for her. "There are other things you can do for the soldiers."

"Yes, I know, but caring for them at their bedside gives me the greatest satisfaction. I think of them as my sons, and imagine some kind woman sitting by their beds, tending them as they get well."

He took her hand and tucked it into the crook of his arm as they descended the steps to begin their daily walk in Gordonsville.

* * *

An Associated Press reporter, not Bradby Tucker, sent an erroneous story to the newspapers which stated that the Rebels were in full retreat to the North Anna River and that fresh Union troops were in hot pursuit. No such thing was happening. General Lee and his Confederates were holding their ground. There was no rout. There was no hot pursuit.

* * *

Besides newspaper reporters following the armies, a new breed of men – photographers -- came in the wake of the battling warriors. Timothy H. O'Sullivan, the chief photographer for Alexander Gardner, a Scotsman who had a studio in Washington City, was traveling in Spotsylvania County. His covered wagon, which crossed the Rapidan with the army, not only carried supplies but also served as a darkroom. Sam Worth, his teenaged assistant, handled the reigns as Timothy looked for favorable spots to take photos.

"So glad the rain has finally stopped," said Timothy.

"It would have been a wasted trip if the sun never shone," said Sam.

"The rain wasn't the only thing that kept us from getting any pictures."

"What else?"

"We haven't had a rest stop long enough for the exposures."

"Yes, there is that."

"Too many trees have been another hindrance." Mr. O'Sullivan scanned the landscape. "We need to find an open area as soon as the bullets stop flying."

"An open area where Confederates lie," said the assistant.

"Most assuredly; we're not photographing any Union bodies. Those won't sell to our northern customers."

"Could we take their jackets off so no one will know?"

"Someone might recognize the face."

"We can turn the face away from the camera."

The photographers would find their spot for recording the dead soon enough.

* * *

In the forenoon, the sun shone upon the small group gathered around Forrester Chesterton's grave. Everyone was there except Forrester's mother. Madelyn Chesterton would not have understood the information. Her mind was adrift as tuberculosis consumed her. Paxton had read Scripture and prayed before encouraging the children to talk.

"Mama will be surprised to see Forrester waiting for her at the pearly gates," said Florence, dabbing at her eyes with her soggy handkerchief.

"Will Saint Peter let him in?" Blake scanned the faces of the adults around him.

"Yes, he will." Paxton patted the boy's shoulder. "Your brother declared Jesus as his savior."

"Jesus forgives us of all our sins," Statesman added.

Deserter barked. Riders galloped into the yard. The mourners jerked in surprise.

Sergeant Ramscar Coleman led his four men up the slope and demanded, "Who is that you're burying?"

"Forrester Chesterton," said Paxton, noting the Confederate uniforms of the five horsemen.

"A soldier?"

"Only a boy," Paxton scanned the faces of the riders. "A soldier's bullet killed him."

Florence emitted a loud sob. The twins remained stoical, standing like sentinels on each side of Florence.

"Who are you?" asked Paxton. "What do you want here?"

"We're with the Provost Marshal looking for deserters. Seen any?"

Is this the moment I'm taken prisoner? Has the time finally come?

217

"There are no deserters here," said Blake, "except the dog."

"What?" Ramscar glared at the animal.

Deserter had stopped barking but his ears and tail were up.

"That's the dog's name, Deserter," said Drake. "Watch out. He will bite you."

Turning from the twin to look at Albany and Paxton, Ramscar asked, "Are you their parents."

"We are friends of the deceased," said Paxton.

"Neighbors," added Albany.

Ignoring her, Ramscar glared at Paxton. "Why aren't you in the army?"

"I am," said Paxton. "I lost my horse and came to buy another one. Soon as I get mounted, I'll be back with Stuart's cavalry." *That's a plausible story.*

"Stuart's been killed. Haven't you heard?"

"No." *Is it true?* "I have not heard that."

Sergeant Coleman nodded toward the shovel on the ground and pointed at Statesman. "Fill in the grave later. Come and water our horses now." He pointed at Liney. "You get us something to eat."

He doesn't suspect me. I'm safe.

In the house, when Paxton asked about the fighting, Ramscar and his men proceeded to tell him about the Federals' dawn attack.

"By nine this morning, the battle was done. What a butcher's shambles they left. We saw some gruesome sights."

"Bodies blown apart."

"Some crushed into pulp."

"Hush." Paxton put up his hand to stop the men. "The children don't need to hear that."

"It was a grand day for our Second Corps artillery," said Ramscar, ignoring Paxton's admonition.

Florence fled to the basement and sought solace in her mother's bed. Blake and Drake crossed their arms, pressed their backs against the wall, and listened as the Provost men ranted.

"I shook hands with the gunners and patted the warm tubes of their guns."

"They're a talented bunch of artillerymen."

"I swear we blew five hundred of those Yanks to pieces."

218

Statesman went to the twins, said in a low voice, "Downstairs," and ushered them to the interior stairway leading to the basement.

Before the boys could go down the stairs, a boom followed by a crash startled them.

"It came from the dining room." Drake ran into the central hallway.

Right behind his brother, Blake called, "There! Look!"

The twins stopped in the dining room doorway and stared. A foot-thick oak tree protruded through the broken window. Paxton moved the boys out of the way. The men hurried to the window to examine the downed tree.

"Artillery did this."

"Got it clean through."

"Imagine if that hit a man."

Liney wailed, "The good dishes."

The military policemen made no offer to clean up the mess. They left Paxton and Statesman to hammer a board over the window opening, and then, taking turns with the broom, sweep the pieces of china and crystal, twigs and leaves, and window glass into the dust pan. Statesman brought a log hopper to carry the debris to the backyard and dump it behind the barn. Liney, scowling as she did so, prepared food for the strangers. Albany went to the children in the basement.

Well fed and eager to be off, the Provost men mounted up. Cannon booms sounded through the trees as they rode away.

"That's the last we'll see of them," Paxton muttered to Statesman.

But he was wrong.

* * *

Madelyn Chesterton died in the late afternoon during Drake's spell of sitting by her bed. The boy, reading a book, did not know until Florence came to take his place that their mother was not breathing. Florence let out a wail.

Liney, in the kitchen, dropped a tin basin. Reddish wash water from Madelyn's blood-stained handkerchiefs, splashed on her bare feet.

Statesman came in the back door, saw the expression on his wife's face, heard Florence screaming, and knew that death had entered the Big

House. Slowly, he put his arm around Liney's shivering shoulders and hugged her.

* * *

At the same time, Generals Humphreys and Wright were discussing the possibility of moving their troops.

"Lee has probably weakened his left at the rear of the salient so he can counter our buildup east of the Fredericksburg Road," said Andrew Humphreys.

"If my command can attack the Rebel position at first light," said Horatio Wright, "I think the prospects for success are very good."

"I agree." General Humphreys put on his hat. "Let's go see Grant and Meade, and tell them what we think."

Both Generals Meade and Grant agreed with the idea, so, at 7:00 p.m., General Meade ordered General Hancock to move his Second Corps back to the area of the Landrum house. He was directed to prepare for a vigorous attack at dawn.

* * *

By seven o'clock in the Chesterton house, with Madelyn laid out in the parlor where her son had been just hours before, the adults had calmed the children enough to eat something.

"Sit down in the dining room," said Liney. "I'll have your supper ready soon."

What can I cook that they will like?

When Liney brought a plate stacked with pancakes into the elegantly-furnished room, Blake declared, "We can't eat pancakes for supper."

Drake said, "Mama's rule is pancakes only for breakfast."

"Does this mean we don't have to follow rules anymore?" asked Florence.

"I know you like pancakes." Liney forked a pancake onto each plate. "Master Paxton, does the Bible say God created all good things for us?"

Brother Eleutheros says so.

"God did indeed."

Liney smiled at Paxton and asked, "Then will you please say a blessing on this good food the Lord provided?"

Paxton prayed but, before sitting down, he went into the kitchen.

Where's he going? Did I forget something?

A moment later, Statesman and Paxton came into the dining room and set two more places at the long table which seated twenty.

What are those men doing? Land sakes, he's sitting down.

Liney stared at her husband. Paxton came to the empty chair nearest Liney and held it out for her.

"Please join us," Paxton said as he took the serving plate from her.

This white man is holding a chair for me.

In amazement, Liney sat. Paxton forked a pancake on her plate and then went to his own place beside Albany.

"They never eat with us," muttered Blake.

"Things are different now," said Paxton.

Florence swallowed, looked across the table at Paxton, and asked, "What's to become of my brothers and me?"

"After we bury your mother tomorrow," said Paxton, "we want you children to come to Miss Albany's house."

"Will we live there?"

"What about our house?"

"Where are Liney and Statesman going?"

"We will come with you," said Statesman.

What did he say? He hasn't told me.

Liney stared at her husband. He returned her stare with a smile.

Paxton said, "I will contact Army headquarters in Richmond to find out any news about your father."

He's dead, I'm sure. His letters were regular until they weren't.

"We must tell him about Mama and Forrester," said Florence.

Albany rubbed her hand down Florence's back. "We will."

Blake said, "If Papa's dead, we're orphans now."

"Will someone adopt us?" asked Drake.

"I don't want strangers to adopt us," said Florence.

"Would anyone take all of us?"

"We can't be split up. We belong together."

Of course you belong together. Oh, I hope they can stay with one family.

Florence looked at Albany and asked, "Can you adopt us?"

"I don't know if that's possible. I'm unwed." Albany faced Paxton. "Does the law allow maiden ladies to adopt children?"

"I don't know." Paxton touched her hand under the table. "The issue has never come up at my legal practice."

"But you need not worry." Albany scanned the children's faces. "I will see that you are cared for."

Emphasizing the first word in his statement, Paxton said, "We will see that you are cared for."

Lord, Lord, thank you for these white folks that drifted into our lives. What would Statesman and I do if they weren't here?

* * *

CHAPTER SIXTEEN

WITH GREAT GALLANTRY

Wednesday, May 18, 1864

Starting at four in the morning of Wednesday, May 18, two Union divisions marched toward the ground on which they had fought so heroically six days earlier. The blue-clad troops trod the ground covered with discolored, bloated corpses exuding a stench that caused some soldiers to vomit. Flags fluttered but no bands played. The Federals held their muskets on their shoulders as they advanced over the dead bodies. Not until eight o'clock were the northern troops in line of battle and ready to attack with great gallantry.

But the Federals did not know that the Confederates had strengthened their earthworks, using bayonets and tin cups to dig barricades. The gray-clad men hunkered down behind broken tree branches, and, seeing the blue-clad enemy like fish in a barrel, they began to shoot.

* * *

Not knowing that a battle raged, the small group consisting of a young white couple, a black couple, a girl, and twin boys prepared to leave the Chesterton house. They had buried Madelyn Chesterton. They planned to walk through the woods, avoiding the roads, to Albany's house.

"I'll change back into Mr. Gately's uniform before we go," Albany said to Paxton in the downstairs hall.

"Why? You look so pretty in a dress."

"I need to return it to him." She started up the stairs. "Liney said she cleaned it as best she could. I won't be long."

When Albany came downstairs, the others were waiting by the door.

"Why are you wearing that?" Florence asked.

Albany gave a brief explanation.

Paxton said, "Before we go, let's pray." He took Albany's and Drake's hands. The others held hands. After Paxton spoke a few sentences, Statesman also prayed, asking for travel mercy. Liney said, "Guide us through the wilderness, Lord, as you did Isaiah the prophet." Albany and the children each spoke a sentence. Paxton said, "Amen."

Statesman led the way with the twins and dog close to him. Florence and Liney walked in the middle of the group while Paxton and Albany came last. At the edge of the big yard, Florence turned around to get one last look at her house.

"Will we ever come back?" asked the girl.

"Of course we will," said Drake. "It is our house."

"If it survives the war," Blake said, "if cannon balls don't blow it up."

What brave children they are. Would I have been so brave if I had to leave my home in Gordonsville?

Liney put her hand on Florence's shoulder and urged her forward.

"But I hate leaving Mama and Forrester." Florence, her chin trembling, stared at the ground.

Liney said, "Your mama and brother aren't back there. They're with you – right here." She gently tapped the center of Florence's chest.

Dabbing at the tears trickling down her cheeks, Florence said softly, "I know. I just miss them."

I would miss my mother and Thornton and Grandon. I know how you feel, little girl.

There was no opportunity for conversation as they plunged into the thick woods. The men and boys held branches away for the females to pass. Deserter ran back and forth, checking on everyone. Statesman stopped frequently to listen for the sound of battle. When that sound came, they stopped abruptly.

"Solid shot through the woods!" shouted a man. "Shells through the cleared openings!"

Paxton yelled, "Get down!" and shoved Albany to the ground.

It's Federals moving at the double quick.

The blue-clad men ran past. The children and slaves scrambled under the bushes with Albany and Paxton.

Cannons began tearing gaps in the ranks of the Federals. They kept coming.

The cannon aren't stopping them.

Flashes of flame zoomed up. A crash sounded. A hissing noise followed.

"Get your feet under here" Statesman yanked on Blake's legs until they were beneath the bushes.

"Ugh," groaned Florence. "A branch stuck me."

"Move over." Drake shoved his brother.

The children and adults covered their ears. Deserter whined. Thud, thud, thud came the sound of lead striking bodies. Soldiers fell. Smoke obscured the color of uniforms.

I can't get them out of danger. Men are dropping too close.

Three soldiers collapsed within a foot of Paxton. He moved back further into the bushes. One of the three stood up and ran.

How can I get us out of this safely? Will we survive?

"This way," said Statesman, pulling on Paxton's sleeve.

The soldiers continued their race. The small group of adults and children crawled under the bushes until they reached an area where they could sit up, still enclosed by trees and undergrowth. "Keep your heads down," Statesman admonished.

"Come here, Flo, and sit close to me," said Liney, and the girl moved toward the woman.

The twins sat on each side of Statesman, with his strong arms hugging them to his side.

They could not see the battle raging behind them but they heard.

"Here they come!"

"Like Gettysburg!"

"Except this time they're getting mowed down not us."

The voices of the Confederates were lost amid the sounds of gunfire. When the Union's front columns came within canister range and were hit by both canister and case shot, they broke in confusion. The blue-clad soldiers could not stand. In disorder, they left the field.

"Cease firing!" shouted an artillery officer.

"Cease firing!"

"Cease firing!"

The battle of Spotsylvania Court House had lasted for two hours. Throughout the battle, Albany, Paxton, the slaves, children, and dog remained hunkered down beneath bushes, easily within firing range. As soon as the guns stopped blasting projectiles into the air, Drake asked, "Is it over?"

"Let's wait a spell to be certain," said Paxton.

* * *

As Paxton waited to be sure it was safe to move, his sisters were walking toward the Exchange Hotel in Gordonsville, used as a hospital since June 1862.

Lorella and Eunice lifted their skirts a few inches as they climbed the hill above the Gordonsville train depot. Lorella had given up her teaching job so she could help the overworked nurses. Eunice had explained to her sister how the former hotel was organized as a hospital. When patients arrived on the Orange & Alexandria or the Virginia Central, they were brought up the hill by wagon and placed on one of the three floors according to whether they were sick or wounded and also based on what kind of a wound they had.

"Hello, there," called Amelia Lebby, wife of Dr. Brewerton Lebby, administrator of the Receiving Hospital, as she joined the sisters. "Did you see the newspaper this morning?"

When they both shook their heads, the doctor's wife said, "A front page article gave an estimate of how many wounded are expected in the Washington hospitals?"

"How many?"

"I hate to hear the number."

"Six to eight thousand," said Mrs. Lebby. "Just imagine, if the Federals expect that many, what should we expect?"

Lorella frowned and lifted her skirt another inch higher.

"How can we continue with so many deaths?" Lorella switched her bread basket to her left hand so she could hold up her skirt.

"Are your brothers still fighting?" asked Amelia.

"Grandon is not fighting," said Eunice. "He's just driving a wagon for Longstreet's Corp."

"He could still get shot." The doctor's wife touched her fingers to Eunice's arm. "Oh, forgive me. I don't mean to distress you. What about the other two?"

"We have no news," said Lorella.

"I am praying for all three of them," said Eunice. "I trust the Lord will watch over them."

In a low voice, Lorella said, "All the women folk are praying for that."

Together, the sisters and doctor's wife entered the hospital. Wounded men on stretchers filled the first floor hallway as Dr. Lebby decided where to place each patient. Eunice recognized a man on one of the stretchers.

"Trusten, is that you?"

"It's me, Eunice," murmured Trusten Hite, who had gone to school with Eunice.

"Are you badly hurt?"

Trusten smiled. "I feel better already for seeing your pretty face."

Eunice followed the stretcher bearers and spent the next hour tending to Trusten.

* * *

Albany, Paxton, and the others had been walking for an hour or more when Ramscar Coleman rode from between two trees and shouted, "Halt there!"

The Confederate Provost Marshal's detail, still searching for deserters, was now reduced to three men instead of five. The group stopped and waited for the horsemen.

"It's them again," Albany whispered as Paxton stepped in front of her to shield her from the men riding up. She touched her cheek to his shoulder blade.

What do they want? Will they keep me from getting home?

"We've seen you before," Ramscar snarled. "What are you doing out here?" He rode closer. "Who is that in the Yankee uniform you've got hiding behind you?"

"My prisoner." Paxton put his hand behind him and touched Albany's arm to keep her from moving. "You're not taking him."

"Why not?" Ramscar dismounted.

What will I do if he …

But Albany did not finish her thought. Ramscar reached behind Paxton and yanked off her hat. Her hair tumbled down.

"It's the woman!" Ramscar tried to grab Albany.

"Don't touch her." Paxton shoved Ramscar.

Ramscar punched Paxton in the stomach. Albany stumbled back against a tree. Liney ushered the children away from the brawling men. The other two Provost Marshals remained on their horses.

"Hit him a good one."

"Knock him out."

"We need that woman."

"Some prisoner, huh?"

"You got him a blow that time."

Paxton and Ramscar grappled with each other. Deserter, barking, circled the fighters. Liney picked up Albany's hat. Statesman searched the ground for a sturdy stick. None of the marshals noticed the slave pick up a thick branch. When the wrestling men came near enough, Statesman, being careful not to hit Paxton, slammed the piece of wood down hard on Ramscar's head. The Confederate fell unconscious.

"Go! Now! Run! Into the bushes!" Paxton snatched Albany's hand and headed through the woods. Liney and Florence ran together. Statesman took a twin by each hand. They ignored branches that scraped their faces. The two horses could not follow through the thick tangle of foliage.

"We gotta go back for Coleman."

"You go back. I'll get 'em."

But the marshal who wanted to pursue did not get far before he too turned back. As soon as they were no longer followed, Albany, Paxton, the slaves, and children collapsed and caught their breath.

"What would happen if they caught us?" asked Drake.

"Would they shoot us?" Blake's lower lip trembled.

"No, they don't shoot children," said Paxton as he felt of his bleeding lip.

Albany pulled the cuff of her shirt to wipe away the blood.

"Are you hurt anywhere else?" she asked.

"My stomach – it's nothing." Paxton took her hand and held it as he faced Statesman. "Thank you for striking the disabling blow." Paxton smiled and the slave returned the smile with a nod.

Liney handed Albany her hat. "I'll help you with your hair."

* * *

In Fredericksburg, Albany's father removed his hat as he knocked at the door of his brother's house. Joram answered the door.

"Sarah! We have company," Joram called before hugging his brother.

"So good to see you." Shedrick returned the hug.

"Oh, Sarah dear, we are so sorry to call without notice." Luciana took her sister-in-law's extended hand. "We arrived just this morning and learned no stage will go to Spotsylvania Court House."

"Fighting in the area," said Shedrick.

Joram escorted the newcomers into the parlor.

"Do sit down." Sarah moved her knitting basket from the settee to the table. "You must be hungry. What can I get you?"

"Are you well, Shedrick?" asked his brother. "We knew you were at Chimborazo."

"Well enough to travel. I've been given a medical discharge so I'm out of the army."

"Thank goodness," said his wife as she sat where the knitting basket had been.

"We have so many wounded men here in town." Sarah started for the kitchen but stopped to add, "They've turned the churches into hospitals – our own Baptist church has 72 and St. George's Episcopal has more. They're larger."

Sarah called the maid, a slave they hired by the day, and told her what food to serve.

Joram said, "The Yankees have even forced private homes to take in their soldiers."

"That's not right," said Shedrick, sitting in an overstuffed chair.

"They send them to Washington City as soon as they can travel." Joram sat down near his brother. "That woman from Massachusetts, you know, the one with all the news stories about her, is even caring for the wounded right here in our town."

"Who?" asked Shedrick.

"Clara Barton," said Sarah. "Have you read about her? She's in all the Yankee newspapers. Just think of it -- bleeding men in the Lord's houses. The blood on the floors will probably stain permanently. We'll have to buy carpet."

"Tell us about the fighting in Spotsylvania County," said Shedrick. "How bad is it?"

* * *

On the outskirts of the town of Spotsylvania Court House, Statesman said to Paxton, "Eleutheros' house is not far from here. We need food and rest."

"Lead the way," Paxton said.

Soon, they arrived at the cabin where Eleutheros Supplee lived.

"Why does he have his own place?" Paxton looked around and saw a small, recently-plowed garden next to the log building.

"His master hires him out and lets him pay rent to live here." Statesman knocked on the door. "His house is also his barrel-making shop."

When no one answered, Statesman pushed open the door. "Eleutheros, are you here?" He entered and looked around. "He's not home. Come in."

The travelers entered the neat little cabin filled with building materials. A ladder on the far wall led to a half loft which served as a bedroom.

"There is a bed up the ladder," said Statesman. "Ladies, you may rest up there."

Albany led the way, having no trouble with the ladder rungs, while Liney and Florence held up their skirts and climbed with difficulty. The boys sat on the bench used by customers and leaned against each other, completely exhausted. Paxton and Statesman, having the same thought, eyed each other.

Statesman closed his eyes, lowered his head, and said, "Thank you, Lord, for bringing us safely here."

"Keep us in your care," Paxton said. "Amen."

When the men were stretched out on the wooden floor, their heads on a rolled-up blanket, Paxton asked Statesman, "Where do you think Eleutheros is?"

"He might be doctoring. He does that for folks."

"We should eat something."

"He won't mind."

"I don't feel like moving."

"We can wait a spell."

When they were rested, the men went to the crate nailed to the wall as a cupboard. They found saltines and cheese, and called the others to join them.

"I wish Forrester was here," said Drake, taking the food Statesman handed him.

"I miss him." Blake stepped to his brother's side. "He would make this trip into an adventure."

"Do we dare light a candle?" asked Florence.

"Better not," said Paxton.

"What are we going to do?"

"There's nothing to play with – no games or books."

Paxton said, "Albany can tell a story from a book she has read."

"Oh, I can't think of any right now," Albany protested.

"Then we can make up a story together." Paxton sat cross-legged on the floor with the twins, Statesman and Deserter. Albany, Liney, and Florence sat on the bench and chair. The children popped out questions.

"How do we go about it?"

"What kind of story?"

"Who starts?"

Paxton held up his hand. "First we must decide on the setting -- mountain top, ocean vessel, English castle, what?"

Albany murmured, "Not a battlefield."

"Certainly not," said Paxton. "Florence, you choose."

"A stately home."

"In what location?"

"In a peaceful land," the girl said.

"Very good." Paxton nodded. "Once upon a time in a peaceful land in a faraway kingdom, there lived ... who?"

The children quickly participated in the story creation. Florence encouraged Liney and Statesman to take part. The slaves had never interacted with white people in this way before, but Statesman accepted the girl's invitation.

"When our hero is weary from his travels, searching for the heroine," said Statesman, "he stops at a busy restaurant, where the cook is a lovely lady, in a town called Apple."

Liney giggled and covered her mouth with her hand.

"What's funny?" Albany asked.

"The town's not Apple," said Liney. "It's Orange." The simple statement made her laugh more.

The others laughed with her.

Statesman's eyes twinkled as he explained, "That's my dream for our future, once we're free. I want to run a restaurant in the town of Orange."

"You can't do that," said Blake. "You belong to us."

Drake said, "Maybe orphans can't own slaves."

"Maybe we're not orphans." Florence turned from her brother to face the adults and asked, "Does owning slaves matter if both our parents are dead?"

Blake asked, "Can children own slaves on their own?"

Paxton started to answer but Albany intervened, saying, "Slave ownership is determined by Union soldiers winning battles. They are really the ones who free the slaves."

Drake said, "I thought it was Mr. Lincoln signing that piece of paper."

"No," said Albany. "Southerners don't recognize President Lincoln's authority." Scanning the faces around her, Albany added, "I was raised by a loving mammy and played with black children. I read northern newspapers and the novel, Uncle Tom's Cabin. Thus, I've come to believe that slavery is wrong."

Liney asked, "What is Uncle Tom's Cabin?"

Albany gave her a brief explanation.

Florence said, "We were not allowed to read it. Mama was very firm about that. Remember, boys?"

The twins both nodded.

"Don't you see slavery as a positive good?" Paxton focused on Albany. "It's believed to be the best thing for black people until they can manage on their own."

Looking intensely into his eyes, Albany asked, "Do you know William Cowper's poem, The Negro's Complaint?"

"I've heard of it." He nodded. "Do you want to recite some of it?"

Before Albany could speak, Florence asked, "Are we allowed to hear this?"

"It won't hurt you," said Paxton.

Albany delivered from memory a verse from the eighteenth-century poem. "By our blood in Africa wasted, ere our necks received the chain; by the miseries that we tasted, crossing in your barks the main; by our sufferings, since ye brought us to the man-degrading mart; all sustained by patience taught us only by a broken heart."

Paxton said, "For some of the people coming from Africa, they have a better future." He lowered his eyebrows. "I know that's not always true. Some have cruel masters but we have laws to punish them."

"We never used a chain on Statesman," said Drake.

"What are barks the main?" asked Blake.

"Ships crossing the ocean," answered Paxton.

"Do you have a broken heart, Liney?" Florence looked across the shadowy room at the slave.

"Yes, miss, I do." Liney said softly.

Blake asked Statesman, "Would you rather be a factory worker in the north where your boss puts you out when you're sick or too old to work, or a slave in the south where you're cared for all your life, sick or well?"

Without hesitation, Statesman said, "I'd rather order my own life." He paused before asking, "Wouldn't you?"

The children did not answer.

"Let's get back to our story," said Paxton. "What will be the ending?"

"It must be a happy ending, of course," said Albany. "That's the only way to end a novel."

When they concluded their storytelling, Statesman asked Paxton, "Do you sing?"

Paxton nodded, smiled, and asked, "What songs do you know?"

In answer, Statesman began singing in a low, rich baritone, "Lord, unto us draw nearer, and reveal yourself still clearer. Where we are, near or far, let us see your power, every day and hour."

Paxton joined Statesman as he sang the song a second time. Their melodious voices blended beautifully. They were careful to sing softly in case anyone was near.

"You pick the next one," said Statesman.

Paxton, after a moment's thought, sang, "If in this darkness wild I stray, be thou my light, be thou my way. No foes, no evils need I fear, no harm, while thou, my God, art near."

The men went back and forth selecting songs from their memories, singing first alone, and a second time with both of them. When they sang a song the children knew, they joined in. Albany and Liney reluctantly sang two songs with the others. Fortunately, Eleutheros' cabin was solidly built so sound did not penetrate.

As the soldiers beyond Eleutheros Supplee's cabin went about their duties, the people inside the cabin recovered from their recent traumas. They talked about Mrs. Chesterton and Forrester. Albany spoke about the short time she and Forrester spent together. The children were surprised to hear some of the things Liney and Statesman said.

"I didn't know Papa bought you in Richmond," said Blake. "When was that?"

Statesman said, "When you were just learning to walk."

"Did you come from the slave auction in Richmond, too?" Florence asked Liney.

"No, Miss, I was inherited when your grandpa died."

Some of the remembrances brought laughter but others brought tears.

"Let's play some parlor games," said Paxton. "That will cheer us up. What games do you know?"

"Teapot."

"Earth, Air, Fire and Water."

"The feather game."

"Well, it seems everyone has a favorite." Paxton smiled at the children. "We can probably play them all before bed time, although I confess I don't know the teapot game."

Drake quickly explained. "The person who is it – I'll be it first – leaves the room while you all decide on a word."

"It has to be a word with many meanings," interrupted his twin.

"I'm telling this. The word chosen must have more than one meaning," continued Drake. "When I come back in the room, you talk but substitute the real word for the word teapot. Got it?"

"I think so." Paxton watched Drake go to the door and added, "Don't go far. Stay close to the door."

When Blake brought his brother into the cabin again, Drake listened carefully to the conversation.

"Do you think it will teapot tonight?"

"We've had so much teapot."

"Queen Victoria has had a glorious teapot."

"I don't like teapot. It's depressing."

Drake shouted, "Rain!"

"Correct," said Paxton, "but not so loud. We don't want anyone outside to hear us."

After everyone had a turn, they played Earth, Air, Fire and Water. The adults knew this game, Albany and Paxton having played it as children and the slaves from having watched their master's family play.

Florence tossed a knotted rag onto Albany's lap and said, "Water."

Albany said, "Dolphin," and tossed it to Paxton with the word, "Air."

"Albatross." Paxton smiled. Albany giggled.

"What's an albatross?" asked Statesman.

"I large web-footed seabird," said Paxton, "as well as anything that causes anxiety."

"The Union Army is an albatross," said Blake.

Albany said, "Slavery is an albatross."

Not waiting for more comments, Paxton tossed the rag to Albany. "Earth."

"Humans," she said and tossed it to Liney.

The games brought much-needed diversion as the story creation and singing had done. They could not play the feather game, blowing a feather to keep it from landing on the floor, because the cabin was too dark to see. Albany and Florence climbed the ladder again, but Liney said she would sleep with Statesman in one corner of the cabin. The twins slept in another corner. Paxton curled up with the dog in the corner nearest the door.

* * *

When Eleutheros came home, shortly before midnight, only Paxton awoke.

"Don't be startled," said Paxton, recognizing the young man by the

235

moonlight on his face as he stood in the doorway. "You have house guests. It's me, Paxton Faulconer." He named the other people in the cabin and finished with a question. "Where have you been?"

"The Trubridge house," answered the black preacher.

CHAPTER SEVENTEEN

BATTLE OF HARRIS' FARM

Thursday, May 19, 1864

General Grant promoted Horatio G. Wright to replace John Sedgwick. Doling out various other promotions, Grant made the structural changes needed for the Union Army to continue the fight. The next battle was about to take place.

Just arriving on the field were General Robert O. Tyler's heavy artillerists. These Federal soldiers had been manning their guns in the forts around Washington City, but were now called into action. They tromped into place in front of Lee's battle-hardened, entrenched veterans and prepared for their first battle.

The sun shone brightly on this Thursday morning, the first time in weeks that no rain clouds concealed the sunshine. Despite the soldiers' exhaustion from continual fighting, they felt more hopeful upon seeing the sun.

* * *

Sam Worth turned the photography wagon into the lane to the Trubridge Big House. "Horses need watering."

"Of course; I would like something to drink, too," said Timothy O'Sullivan.

"We should get some good photos on a day like this."

"Indeed we should. All we need is dead bodies."

Sam halted the wagon near the watering tough. Two wagons were parked near the door and men were unloading stretchers. Bradby Tucker was filling a bucket at the trough and greeted the two newcomers.

"Good morning," said the journalist. "Have you got wounded?"

"No. I'm a photographer – Timothy O'Sullivan." He offered his hand.

Bradby introduced himself, gave the name of his employer, and shook hands with Timothy and Sam.

"What is happening here?" asked Timothy. "Is this a hospital?"

"It is now." Bradby set his full bucket on the ground. "I'm bedding down in the barn with some more of the wounded. The house is full."

Timothy asked, "Who lives here?"

"The Trubridge family but only one of them is present now. That's the old lady, Audine Trubridge, a bit daft." Bradby grinned. "Do you want a photograph of her?"

Timothy chuckled. "No, thank you. We want pictures of the Confederate dead. That's what sells."

Sam said, "Our photos of the dead Rebels at Gettysburg sold like hot cakes."

"Too bad you can't photograph the young missus," said Bradby.

"Who is that?"

"Why can't we?"

"Miss Albany, a pretty young lady, judging by the painting of her in the parlor, ran off a few days ago to take a map to Grant."

"To Grant, you say?" Timothy's eyes widened. "A Virginia girl helping the Yankees?"

"That's right," said the reporter. "I've written a brief story about her, but I really hope she comes home so I can interview her."

"Can we see the painting in the parlor?"

"You'll have to step carefully." Bradby led them toward the door. "The wounded are close together on the floor but there's a path among them."

Bradby told the two young men about Gerow Gately, finishing his narrative with: "So brave Miss Albany, nothing more than a slip of a girl, leaped upon her trusty steed Joab and rode off into the wilderness."

* * *

Two divisions of General Ewell's corps created a large arc and moved undetected to the north, then to the east, thus coming within three quarters of a mile of the Fredericksburg Road. Because the Confederates knew this road was the main supply route for the Union Army, and now seeing it deserted, Lee realized the enemy had shifted to the right. Located along this vital roadway were the green troops of General Robert Tyler. The woods were dotted with crouching soldiers. Both sides awaited the coming onslaught.

* * *

The eight people crowded into Eleutheros Supplee's cabin slept late. Paxton let Deserter out about dawn and returned to his corner to drift back to sleep. When he woke up again, he smelled coffee, opened his eyes, and saw Eleutheros crouched at the fireplace.

"Good morning," Paxton whispered as he joined Eleutheros.

"I hope it is a good morning."

"Tell me what you saw at Albany's house."

The slave poured a cup of coffee and handed it to Paxton. "It's being used as a hospital. I spoke to Coffer. He said a doctor from Philadelphia, Angus Mintzer, is in charge."

"A Yankee hospital," murmured Paxton.

"Coffer says the doctor treats any man who comes, no matter which army."

"Well, that's good to know, but the Federals are still in charge and could arrest me if they wanted." Paxton took a sip of the hot liquid. "I've had enough trouble with their Provost Marshals."

"I told Coffer that Miss Albany is safe." Eleutheros poured himself a cup of coffee.

"Is her family well?" Paxton asked.

"Only her grandma is there. Her parents are expected any time. The house is full, upstairs and down. Some of the wounded are in the slave cabins. Gives them a chance to see how we black folks live."

Paxton met Eleutheros' gaze, nodded, and drank his coffee. Eleutheros opened a cloth bag and said, "Have a biscuit. You might have to dunk it. They're not fresh."

After Paxton took one, Eleutheros gave a biscuit to Deserter.

"Statesman thought you might be doctoring." Paxton dunked his biscuit in his coffee.

"I helped for awhile but I wanted to get back and report to Miss Albany and you."

"I appreciate that." Paxton took a bite.

"How have the children been?"

"They're grieving. We've done our best to take their minds off the deaths."

"Deaths?"

"The boy and then his mother."

"That's a lot to suffer in so short a time."

After a moment of silence, Paxton asked, "Did you see any regiments?"

"I avoided the soldiers. I heard them several times. I didn't want to be caught again and forced to dig graves."

Albany awoke and joined the men at the fireplace. Since there were only two cups, Paxton gave his cup to her. Eleutheros poured her coffee, held out the biscuit bag for her to take one, and told her what he had seen at her house.

* * *

Evandon Faulconer came to the Gordonsville Receiving Hospital to escort his wife and daughters home from their all-night vigil. The three women had worked in the big building throughout the night, taking only brief naps, because so many wounded had recently arrived. The stately gentleman carried an armful of newspapers to pass around to the soldiers who were well enough to read.

Lorella greeted her father in the first floor hallway with the news, "The Corby's oldest boy died."

"You were with him?" asked Evandon.

She could only nod. Her mother, having overhead, joined them and said, "I hope he had a good death."

"What is a good death, Mother?" Lorella wiped away a tear.

"The dying man must be conscious and indicate his willingness to accept his fate," said Melora. "He must show signs of his belief and trust in the Lord. If possible, he can leave messages to his loved ones."

"Did young Corby do those things?" Evandon looked down at his daughter's sad face.

"He said… "Lorella swallowed hard, "to tell his folks … he was safe in the arms of Jesus."

Her sister Eunice joined them and, having heard the last few remarks, said, "I am sure that whoever you're talking about would have preferred to live in the arms of his family."

Taking several of the newspapers from her husband, Melora said, "We'll help you distribute these."

As Eunice took several of the papers, her father asked, "How is young Trusten Hite?"

"He's recovering well, Father." Eunice blushed. "Thank you for asking."

Her parents noticed Eunice's reddened cheeks and smiled at each other.

* * *

Before Albany, Paxton and the others set out from the slave cabin that morning, Eleutheros prayed aloud for safety and then took the lead. He knew a way through this section of the woods which was unfamiliar to Statesman. Deserter trotted beside Eleutheros. The children walked with their slaves, followed by Albany and Paxton.

"Does this wilderness look familiar to you?" Paxton asked her.

"Not at all." Albany reached for his hand as she stepped over a fallen log. "When I went riding, I stayed on the road. I never came into the wilderness. It can be dangerous."

She intended to release his hand but Paxton held her hand firmly in his, so she curled her fingers around his hand again.

"Especially when men are fighting each other," said Paxton.

"I'm glad you're not fighting."

"I will have to go back."

"Why?" Albany stopped and faced him.

How can I answer her? What should I say?

"I don't want to be a coward."

"Is it cowardly to recognize when a cause is hopeless?" She started walking again.

"I'm not sure it is hopeless," he said in a low voice. "That's not the only reason, Albany. I don't want to be disloyal to my state, to Virginia, to my hometown, Gordonsville, to the people I know and love, my family, neighbors."

Florence tripped over a skeleton and fell in front of them. When she saw what caused her fall, she screamed in fright.

"It's … it's a …?" She pointed at the whitened scull at her feet.

"How did a dead man turn into a skeleton so fast?" Blake asked.

"Doesn't flesh take longer to rot off a body?" questioned Drake.

The twins looked at the scattered bones as Liney hugged Florence, shivering in her arms.

"Those aren't bones from this battle." Paxton covered the bones with dried leaves. "That skeleton has been here since last year when we fought in these woods."

Statesman said, "The rain must have washed him out of his shallow grave."

Blake came to Paxton's side. "What battle was that, last year in these woods?"

"Chancellorsville," answered Paxton.

"Where Stonewall died," said Drake.

"Stonewall Jackson didn't die at the battle," said Paxton. "He died a week later at Guiney Station. He had been recovering well. It was a shock to learn of his death."

I should not be talking about death to the children. They're experienced enough of that.

"Come, Florence, did you hurt yourself when you fell?" Paxton motioned for the group to continue walking.

Florence brushed dirt off her skirt and fell into step with Liney. "No. I'm all right." She turned around to look at Paxton and asked, "How will their families know they died?"

Liney answered. "They won't come home."

* * *

The Battle of Harris' Farm began about 2:00 p.m. and covered three properties: on the Union right at the Peyton Farm, at the Union center at the Alsop Farm, and at the Union left at the Clement Harris Farm. When General Hancock heard the sounds of battle, he spurred his horse across the fields to take command. The vicious battles had men firing at point-blank range.

* * *

Resting with her head against Paxton's shoulder, Albany scanned the people sitting around her. They huddled against tree trunks at the edge of a clearing, tired from their long walk.

I will be so glad to get home. I wonder if Mother and Father are there yet. Grandma will be so glad to see me. She will love the children.

"I'll see if it's safe to cross this clearing," said Eleutheros, leaving Blake and going to the edge of the tree line.

Without a word, Statesman joined him. The two slaves searched the trees in all directions.

It's so peaceful and pleasant here. I wish we could stay.

"How much farther is it, Eleutheros?" Albany called.

"I can't tell you in miles, Miss Albany, but you will be home before dark."

Home before dark — what a lovely notion.

Suddenly, horses burst from the trees at the far end of the clearing. Pulling caissons and cannons, they sped through the tall grass. The ground shook from the thundering hooves and heavy guns. The peaceful moment was shattered.

"Get up!" Paxton leaped to his feet and yanked on Albany's hand.

What is it?

Albany caught a glimpse of the cannons speeding by.

"We must go!"

The others responded to Paxton's demand. Scrambling up, they headed away from the clearing. The slaves held the children's hands. Deserter barked as he ran. They rushed deeper into the woods, not stopping until the earth no longer shook.

* * *

Thornton Faulconer felt the gentle swaying of the steamship heading for Washington City.

Well, I'm out of the fighting. That's for certain. But what now? Where are they taking us? What will be the name of the prison? When will I be able to write home?

Leaning over the railing, he watched the water swirl away from the ship and trail off until the white foam disappeared.

I hate the thought of being locked up. I wonder what we'll do all day. I can't stand idleness. Even digging ditches is better than being idle.

"Move back from the railing, fellow," said a blue-clad soldier. "We don't want you jumping over."

Thornton moved back.

He was polite. For being the enemy, you wouldn't know it. Why am I fighting them? Why not swallow the yellow dog and join them. What could be the harm? Well, I couldn't live in Gordonsville after the war. That's for certain.

"Nice boat ride, isn't it?" Biglor came to Thornton's side.

Coming to his other side, Oliver said, "Wonder if there's good fishing here."

"Listen, friends, I've made a decision." Thornton looked from Oliver to Biglor.

"What's that?"

"Have you got a plan to escape?"

"No, I've decided to swallow the yellow dog." Thornton crossed his arms.

"You're crazy," snapped Biglor.

"You can't do that," Oliver protested.

"I've thought a lot about it," said Thornton. "I think the cause is hopeless."

"That's not true."

"You've been reading those northern papers."

"You can't trust those newspapers."

"They just print a bunch of lies."

"It is not lies." Thornton shook his head. "Sherman has forced Johnston out of Resaca. Our boys evacuated during the night. That doesn't bode well for us."

"Sherman probably outnumbered Johnston," said Oliver. "He probably had no choice."

"Well, I have a choice," Thornton said. "The news is too dire. I don't think Lee can pull us out of this. We are outnumbered. That fighting in the wilderness was like nothing I've ever seen.'"

"Shut up." Biglor turned his back.

"Go and do it," said Oliver, "but don't speak to me again."

Oliver and Biglor walked away.

* * *

Albany, Paxton, and the others resumed walking but not far. Bullets like hailstones zinged through the trees. Shells hissed overhead. Paxton dropped to the ground, pulling Albany down with him. He covered her back and head with his chest, being sure her head was turned so she could breathe and not pressing heavily on her. The slaves protected the children with their own bodies. The rush and roar of battle surrounded them.

Trying to see better, Albany raised her head a few inches but Paxton pushed her down. She saw Drake, closest to her, and tried to force a smile to reassure the boy, but her facial muscles were frozen. Instead, she breathed in the sweaty familiar smell of Paxton and went limp.

Paxton, aware of her stiffness draining away, cuddled her more closely. *Get us out of this, Lord. Protect us from harm.*

Voices penetrated the trees.

"Load up those guns! Move to the right!"

"Hogan, support that infantry going forward!"

"We'll smash them now!"

As quickly as the soldiers appeared they were gone.

Florence wailed, "I want to go home."

Eleutheros said, "Miss Albany's house is closer than yours."

"But we could get killed." Florence turned to Liney.

Hugging the girl, Liney said, "Those fighting folks have high tailed it out of here; time for us to go now."

With that said, Statesman took Drake's hand and Eleutheros took Blake's. Albany struggled to rise. Paxton helped her.

I could not do this without the help of these slaves. Maybe Albany is right and I'm wrong. Maybe slaves should have their freedom. At least these three should.

Blake, after his nerves settled, turned to look at Paxton and asked,

"Is is always like this for a soldier – fighters coming out of nowhere and disappearing fast as lightning?"

"Sometimes," said Paxton. "But in truth I've never witnessed battles like these."

"What do you mean?" asked Drake.

"We usually stop fighting after a single battle," said Paxton. "We rest and reconnoiter, tend our wounded, and bury our dead."

"Why is this different?" Statesman's eyes locked onto Paxton's for a moment.

"This doesn't stop," answered Paxton. "I served briefly with some artillerists and with South Carolina infantry. They filled me in on what I've missed since being with Albany."

Eleutheros said, "I've heard there has been fighting every day since the Federals crossed the Rapidan."

"That's unprecedented," said Paxton.

"What's unprecedented mean?" asked Drake.

"Never happened before," answered Paxton.

"The things Paxton and I have seen is unprecedented for me," said Albany. "I don't know how I would have survived it without him." She gave his hand a gentle squeeze.

Eleutheros, quoting Isaiah, said, "Those who wait upon the Lord shall renew their strength; they shall mount up with wings as eagles; they shall run and not be weary; they shall walk, and not faint."

"That's what we're doing, all right," said Drake, "walking but not fainting."

"Tell us a Bible verse, Drake," Eleutheros said.

Drake smiled and said, "Jesus wept."

Blake patted his brother on his back and said, "Abraham laughed."

Eleutheros said, "That verse in Genesis 17 says Abraham fell upon his face and laughed."

For the rest of the way to the Trubridge house, the adults and children recited verses they had memorized. If they had trouble remembering exactly how the wording went, Eleutheros helped.

* * *

By six p.m., Union reinforcements drove General Ewell's gray-clad men from the field, leaving about nine hundred casualties, thus ended the fighting at Spotsylvania Court House. The Battle at Harris' Farm was the last engagement of the two armies in the Spotsylvania Campaign.

* * *

Darkness began to bathe the landscape as Eleutheros led the small group of tired wanderers along the lane leading to the Trubridge house. Audine was sitting in a wicker chair on the balcony above the front porch, as she often did just before going to bed.

"Come home, Albany. Come home now. It's getting dark; time for bed."

Susa opened the door from the upstairs hall and said, "You come inside, Mrs. Trubridge. Albany will be right along."

"I see her coming." The old woman pointed to the shadowy figures moving down the lane.

"That's just the night wind blowing the tree branches." Susa took Audine's arm to help her up.

"Look." Audine stepped to the wrought iron railing. "Don't you see her?"

Susa looked where the grandmother pointed. She caught her breath. In the next instant, she fell into the hall.

"Coffer! Coffer! Come quick!"

Coffer ran from the kitchen and met Susa at the bottom of the front stairs.

"She's home." Susa grabbed Coffer's arm. "She's coming."

They ran out the front door.

"Wait for me," said Audine, clutching the railing and slowly stepping down the wide stairs. "I'll be there in a minute."

Susa and Albany squealed with delight and crushed each other with a hug. Three white men came onto the front porch and watched. They were Dr. Mintzer, wiping his hands on a towel, Gerow Gately, smiling, and Bradby Tucker, pulling out his note pad as he watched the scene.

"You must be Coffer." Paxton shook hands with the black man.

Eleutheros said, "Coffer, this is Mr. Paxton Faulconer from Gordonsville. He's been watching over Miss Albany while she's been gone."

Coffer, his eyes moist with tears, shook Paxton's hand longer than usual.

Albany and Susa parted. Both young women brushed away tears on their cheeks. Coffer and Paxton released hands. Albany's eyes met Coffer's. She rushed to him and, in a quick movement, wrapped her arms around him for a brief hug.

"Joab came home safe," said Coffer, looking down at Albany.

"So did I."

Gerow came down the steps. Albany turned to him and said, "I've come to return your uniform, Mr. Gately.

"Is that you, old boy?" Bradby extended his hand to Paxton. "I last saw you on the other side of the Rapidan, when the army was starting to cross. Remember? They were burning their winter huts."

Paxton smiled and shook the journalist's hand. "A lot has happened since then, Mr. Tucker. But before I tell you, I must confess I was working as a spy among the Yankees."

"Well, now, isn't that an interesting story." Bradby pulled out his note pad. "Tell me all about that."

* * *

CHAPTER EIGHTEEN

SPIRITS RISE WONDERFULLY

Friday, May 20, 1864

The Army of the Potomac made preparations to depart from Spotsylvania County. They would move out in the night. General Grant issued orders for his army to proceed south. Excitement raced through the ranks when the blue-clad soldiers heard the news.

"We're not retreating."

"We are going in the right direction, by golly."

"About time we got a commander who fights."

Listening to the soldiers talk as they prepared to move, Horace Porter said to Adam Badeau, "Their spirits rise wonderfully."

"Most assuredly they do," said Adam, smiling.

Grant's staff officers saddled their horses and discussed the orders they would be carrying to the generals.

"The roads are still in bad condition," Horace said to his friend.

"But the men are eager to finish the business."

"I'm glad to see we're marching toward Richmond."

"Grant doesn't want Richmond. He wants Lee's army."

As Friday dawned, the clinking of canteens against gun barrels gave evidence of marching men.

* * *

The new arrivals at the Trubridge house slept late. Susa and Coffer had seen that the newcomers were washed, fed, and put to bed; Paxton and the twins shared the master bedroom with Dr. Mintzer, the New York reporter, and Gerow Gately; Albany and Florence slept in Grandma Audine's room. For the first time since they had known each other, Coffer went to Susa's bed, held her as she wept tears of relief, and slept soundly, fully clothed. Eleutheros slept on the parlor floor with five wounded men, for whom he fetched drinks of water in the night for two of them. Liney and Statesman went to one of the vacant slave cabins. Deserter slept between Blake and Drake.

* * *

Timothy O'Sullivan and Sam Worth were finishing with the development of photographs they had taken after the Battle of Harris' Farm. They moved carefully amid the tight space inside the covered wagon.

"This one of the fellow we leaned against that broken-down fence came out well," said Timothy, holding up the photograph.

"Falling fence rails symbolizes the falling Confederacy," Sam said.

"And his having an open mouth like that makes it really morbid."

"Makes him look more dead."

"More dead?"

"Deader."

The two men looked at each other and smirked.

"Have we been doing this too long?" Timothy shook his head in disbelief over their callousness.

"Could be." Sam set a photo on the pile of completed ones. "I'd rather be taking pictures of wiggling children, telling them they're going to be just a blur if they don't sit still."

"We'll get back to that cheerful business before too long," said Timothy. "These should bring us a good profit."

"Susa ought to have breakfast ready." Sam wiped his wet hands on his thighs. "Can we go indoors, Tim?"

The photography wagon was parked near the barn where Coffer was tending to Joab. Neither Timothy nor Sam knew about last evening's arrivals. They would soon be pleasantly surprised with an opportunity to photograph wiggling children.

* * *

The big kitchen in the Trubridge house was a busy place. Male nurses came and went. Two soldiers, one using a cane and the other with a bandage encircling his head, helped Susa with breakfast preparations. The children and Albany sat at the table and ate. Grandma was still asleep. The men ate while standing.

"Coffer showed me your portrait in the parlor, Miss Trubridge," said Bradby. "He told me about your mission. I'd like to write a story about your adventures. Would you allow me that privilege?"

"I think I'll write my own story, Mr. Tucker."

"Well, I don't want to wait for printed words," said Susa. "Can't you tell us in words from your mouth?"

Albany took a spoonful of oatmeal, swallowed, and said, "I can give you a summary."

"Should you tell it all?" asked Paxton, scowling.

Susa's head snapped around to look at him. "Did you do anything improper?"

Smiling, Albany answered for Paxton. "Mr. Faulconer has been a gentleman, Susa. I don't know how I would have survived without him."

"I might not have survived when my horse was shot and fell on me." Paxton took a sip of the best coffee he had had in some time. "That's how we met."

Turning from Susa to Paxton, Albany smiled at him. "That seems like ages ago. So much has happened since then."

Timothy and Sam entered the kitchen and were introduced to the new arrivals.

"We saw your portrait in the parlor," said Timothy. "Mr. Gately told us about your borrowing his uniform, which I understand you wore in order to deliver a map to General Grant."

"Why do you want such a photograph, Mr. O'Sullivan?" Albany asked.

"I have no picture of a woman," he replied. "I think the public would like to know how a young Virginia woman aided the Federal army."

Sam added, "We would also like to photograph the poor, little, orphaned children."

Florence and the twins exchanged glances.

Bradby said, "I could have an engraving made from the photograph to include with an article." He pulled up a stool and sat beside Albany. "You can write the book about what you did. My article would be a shorter version. In fact, at the end, I will tell the reader to look for a more complete version in book form by the adventuress herself."

Albany faced Paxton and asked, "What do you think? Should I give him our story?"

For the next hour, amid the clatter of pots and pans, Albany and Paxton shared their story as Bradby took notes. When anyone came into the kitchen, they spoke in hushed voices so as not disturb the narrative being recorded for *The New York Times*.

With the journalist's notebook almost full, he asked, "What was that like, the blue-blacks as they call it, when you were not speaking?"

"Like being in a pool of nothingness; like a ball of yarn all unraveled; like nothing I've ever experienced." Albany twisted her hands in her lap.

"And the dark curtain over your mind lifted when Forrester was shot." Bradby let his pencil rest on the notepad.

"It snapped up quick as a gunshot."

"How did you handle this time, Paxton?" Bradby turned from Albany to look at Paxton.

"I had a tent mate, Searcy Ryals, who went through something similar. It is not so uncommon."

Bradby asked, "Where is Mr. Ryals now? I'd like to know more about how war affects the mind. Perhaps I can interview him."

"He was committed to an insane asylum."

* * *

While the Federal army marched out of Spotsylvania County, the Confederate army remained secure in their mud-pie works, as they called the entrenchments they had constructed with bayonets and tin cups. Out of necessity, the Southern men had connected the trenches, giving them room to move about. They would remain in their defensive ditches until the night of Saturday, May 21, when they would reluctantly climb out.

* * *

After the prolonged breakfast, while the photographers set up their camera and equipment on the front lawn, Albany went to see Joab. Paxton accompanied her to the barn where Statesman was helping Coffer with the chores. The twins had tagged along with Statesman and were playing in the loft. Deserter sniffed around the barn stalls.

Before Albany spoke, Joab raised his big head from the manger where he had been rending a knot of hay, whinnied loudly, and turned toward her.

"Oh, Joab, I'm so glad you made it home." Albany reached for the animal's nose. "Were those Rebel soldiers cruel to you? I hope not." She petted Joab's nose. "We really missed you. My feet are sore from walking."

"They might be sore from those army shoes you wore," said Paxton.

"It is nice to be in my own dress again."

"You look lovely." Paxton smiled and gazed over her slender figure, wearing a well-fitting white gown with pink flowers and ruffled scoop neckline.

Rubbing Joab's back, Paxton said, "We need to make plans, Albany."

"Plans for what?"

"Us."

"Oh."

He stepped away from the horse and took her hand. "Come and sit on the bench under the maple tree."

Minutes later, as they sat on the sturdy bench, their hands remained entwined.

"Eleutheros and I had a good conversation this morning, before the others were up," said Paxton. "He's a smart young man. He knows the Bible well."

"What did you talk about?"

"Paul's letter to the Corinthians, in the chapter about eating meat offered to idols and making your brother to stumble."

"Does this have something to do with our plans?"

"It does indeed." Paxton brought her hand to his mouth and kissed the back and then the palm. "Do you know how much I love you?"

"How could I know?" Albany said. "You have never told me."

"Well, I am now." He leaned toward her and kissed her cheek, lightly and briefly. "I love you with all my heart."

Smiling at him, Albany said, "And I love you." Her eyes danced with happiness. "I cannot imagine loving any other man." As Paxton embraced her, she rested her head against his shoulder. "My heart reposes in your love."

After a long, silent, peaceful moment, Paxton spoke again.

"Let me tell you what Eleutheros and I discussed." Paxton tipped his head to rub his cheek against her hair. "You know the problem with which the Apostle Paul was dealing in the Corinthian church – whether or not it was lawful for the new Christians to eat meat offered to pagan gods, idols."

"Yes, I've read that in First Corinthians," said Albany. "Go on."

"I came to realize, in talking it over with Brother Eleutheros, I believe I've made the Confederacy an idol, something to worship, like the pagans worshiped false gods." Paxton took a deep breath. "My loyalty, my patriotism to the Confederate States of America, has become idolatrous. I'm guilty of idol worship because my ideas have taken priority over people."

"What people?"

"You must know." He tipped his head to smile down at her. "Eleutheros, Statesman, Liney."

"Slaves, you mean."

"Yes, slaves, who have helped me in ways that I never imagined." Paxton gazed into the distance. "I could not have managed without them. Their helped with the children facing the two deaths in their family, Eleutheros getting the morphine and guiding us here, all the big and small ways they have worked for our welfare." He held her away from him and met her eyes. "There is no reason they should be enslaved and I should be free."

"I agree," said Albany, leaning up to kiss his smooth, recently-shaved cheek. "I am so glad that we can agree on that." She settled back to her place in his embrace. "Since you have told me about the change in your attitude, I must tell you about the change in mine."

"How have you changed?" he asked.

"Remember how I told you that I was always afraid of strangers?"

"Yes, I remember."

"Well, I'm not anymore."

"Just like that the fear has vanished?"

"Not just like that," she said. "The change has been coming gradually but these past few days have brought it suddenly to completion. I have no reason to fear people after all that we have endured. I've met so many strangers and now see the results. Three children have come to live at my house. I am certain my parents, when they get home, will welcome them. Mother and Father have always regretted that I was an only child."

"Then we have both benefited from our recent experiences together," he said.

"Benefited, I should say." Albany moved her arm to a more comfortable position against his side. "I cannot imagine my life without you."

"Nor can I think of going through life if you are not beside me."

Albany wrapped her arms around Paxton. For a long moment, they were silent.

"How does all this affect our plans?" asked Albany.

"I cannot continue fighting for the Confederacy," replied Paxton. "I have decided to swallow the yellow dog."

"What?" Albany jerked away from him and stared into his eyes.

Pulling her back into his arms, he said, "It's an expression we use – not a very nice concept for my fellow Virginians. It means changing sides."

"You intend to become a Yankee?"

"I've despised that word for four years." Paxton shook his head. "Yes, my dear one, that is what I intend to do."

"Will they put you in prison?"

"I've heard they are sending Southerners, who join their army, out to Indian Territory where General John Pope is fighting the Sioux. I would still be a prisoner of war, but I would not be locked up in a cell."

"But you could be killed fighting Indians the same as you could be killed in the war."

"We will pray for the good Lord to preserve my life so I can marry you."

With those words, Paxton lowered his head, closed his eyes, and touched his lips to hers. Albany shut her eyes. Their first kiss was soft and tender, lasting for a long moment.

* * *

Timothy O'Sullivan gathered the children and grandma to be photographed, telling Statesman and Coffer to bring two chairs for Audine and Albany.

"Should we bring one for Miss Florence?" asked Statesman.

"I thought she could stand. How tall is she?"

"She's a lady, too," said Liney.

"All right, yes, that will make it even – three ladies sitting and Paxton with the twins standing behind," said the photographer.

Sam said, "I'll get another chair."

"Can Deserter be in the picture?" asked Drake.

"He can sit in front," said Blake.

"Absolutely not," declared Timothy. "Dogs can't sit still. He would just be a big blur. Where are Miss Albany and Paxton? Has anyone seen them?"

"In the back yard by the barn," said Susa.

Timothy sent Sam to fetch them while he arranged the chairs. Sam saw the couple in the shadow of the tree and, unaware they were kissing, called their names. With two more steps, he recognized two heads move apart and blushed at his blunder.

"I apologize," said Sam. "I didn't know you were... I mean... well, I'm sorry. Mr. O'Sullivan wants you in the front yard where the light is best. He's set up his camera there."

Taking Albany's hand and helping her up, Paxton said, "No apology needed." He smiled down at Albany. "That was the best first kiss."

Albany returned his smile and gave a slight nod. Sam led the way around the Big House to the front yard.

"We've got three chairs," said Timothy, "for the grandmother, Miss Albany, and Miss Florence. The twins and you, Paxton, stand in back."

"We need two more chairs," said Paxton.

"What for?" asked the photographer.

"Liney and Susa."

Mr. O'Sullivan's mouth dropped open. "I've never photographed black people with white people before."

"Well, this will be a first for you," said Paxton. "Statesman and Coffer, please bring two more chairs. You will both be in the picture, too. Where is Eleutheros?"

As the two slaves went into the house, Sam asked, "How will everyone be arranged?"

Paxton answered while pointing to the chairs. "Liney, Florence, Grandma, Albany, and Susa, seated, with Statesman standing behind Liney, Eleutheros behind Florence, no one behind Mrs. Trubridge, I'll be behind Albany, and Coffer behind Susa. The twins will sit on the ground in front of Grandma Trubridge."

Susa went to fetch Audine. The men arranged the five dining room chairs in front of the porch.

"The pillars make a nice frame," said Timothy, gazing at the group.

Sam whispered to him, "Do you expect such a picture to sell?"

"Paxton is paying me."

With that said, Timothy began the tedious work of photographing slaves, children, an old woman, and a young couple in front of the impressive Big House. The twins were getting fidgety when they heard a carriage coming up the lane.

"Boys! Boys!" Timothy yelled. "You will just be a blur if you don't remain still."

"I hear a carriage," said Drake.

"Who is coming?" asked Blake.

As the vehicle came closer, Albany hopped up and exclaimed, "It's my parents!"

"That's good," said Paxton, taking her hand. "I look forward to meeting them, especially your father."

"Father," said Albany, looking up at him. "Why?"

"Because I have an important question I need to ask him."

* * *

EPILOGUE

The Civil War ended in Spotsylvania County when the two armies moved on to Hanover County, Virginia. There, the one battle General Grant regretted fighting took place on June 3, 1864. The Battle of Cold Harbor was General Lee's last great battle in the field. During the previous month of campaigning incessantly, the Union lost 50,000 soldiers, amounting to 41% of General Grant's original army, whereas the Confederates lost 32,000 or 46% of General Lee's men. The Federals were able to replace their losses within a few weeks, but the Rebels could not do the same. The gray-clad men dwindled in numbers, especially after the devastating Battle of Sayler's Creek, until only 26,765 Southern soldiers were present at Appomattox Courthouse on April 9, 1865, to lay down their weapons, accept their paroles, and go home.

When Shedrick heard Paxton's important question, he called Albany into the parlor to hear what she had to say on the matter. Albany confirmed that she wanted, with all her heart, to marry Paxton. Therefore, her father consented. They agreed to wait until the war ended. But Paxton was not with the Confederates when they surrendered at Appomattox. Instead, having talked it over with Albany, Paxton crossed the picket line at the North Anna River and surrendered to the Federal Army.

Like other Confederates who changed sides, Paxton was sent to Minnesota to serve under General John Pope fighting the Sioux. Although Paxton was still a prisoner of war, he served ably with the U.S. troops, proving himself trustworthy and loyal. General Pope gave him the job of company clerk because of his excellent penmanship.

In March, when Thornton arrived at the fort in Minnesota, he was surprised to see his brother. Thornton had taken the oath of allegiance to the United States before he reached Elmira Prison. The brothers bunked together for the few months remaining in the Civil War. As soon as the Confederate armies surrendered, Paxton and Thornton traveled to Spotsylvania Court House, a peaceful town again.

Albany was sewing lace on the collar of her wedding dress when the Faulconer brothers rode up to the Trubridge house. They waited for the arrival of the groom's family from Gordonsville before having Albany and Paxton's wedding in the parlor of her house. Following their honeymoon in Niagara Falls and Canada, the newlyweds made their home in the Walnut Hills neighborhood in Cincinnati where Gerow and Myrta Gately welcomed them.

On December 6, 1865, the day on which the required number of states ratified the Thirteenth Amendment to the Constitution abolishing slavery, Thornton Faulconer and his bride, Matilda, a widow with two children, arrived in the Queen City, bought a house in Walnut Hills, not far from Paxton and Albany. Thornton began working in a general mercantile store. Within two years, he purchased the busy store when the original owner retired. Matilda and Thornton had four children together. When Thornton introduced his children, he always said, "Two of them are not mine, but I forget which ones."

After driving a supply wagon in the wilderness, Grandon Faulconer signed up with the Army of Northern Virginia, lying about his age, and fought with General Lee to the end of the war. He received a minor wound at the Battle of Sayler's Creek but, with his forearm bandaged, was at Appomattox for the mass surrender. Like many Southern men at that event, he wept when he laid down his weapon. He worked at the *Gordonsville Gazette,* becoming editor at twenty-one. He married Florence Chesterton the week after she turned eighteen. They fell in love during family gatherings when the Trubridge and Faulconer families got together every summer. Florence and Grandon had three children. Grandon often spoke at meetings of the Confederate veterans, telling of his experiences as an underage soldier.

The Chesterton children never knew where their father died. Like many soldiers, his grave was unmarked. He was listed as missing and presumably dead. Their cousins in Richmond were too impoverished to give them a home, so Shedrick and Lucinda Trubridge took the orphans into their home. Florence, Blake, and Drake were legally adopted by Mr.

and Mrs. Trubridge in 1866. Deserter lived many years with the enlarged Trubridge family, giving comfort and joy to the children.

When the Chesterton plantation was sold, Shedrick invested the money in railroads and property, both of which proved to be financially successful. Blake and Drake used their inheritance to attend the University of Virginia. They both became successful businessmen. Florence used her money for a Grand Tour of Europe on her honeymoon and to set up housekeeping in Gordonsville.

Paxton and Albany's first child, a boy named Forrester Trubridge Faulconer, was born on April 9, 1866. He became a lawyer like his father.

Their first daughter, Virginia Audine, was born in 1867, just two months after her great-grandmother, for whom she was named, died peacefully in her sleep. They called her Ginny.

Ginny was a chubby toddler when Albany gave birth to Alberta Suzanne in 1869. But tiny Alberta was, the doctor said, very low on life, and remained on earth only three weeks and two days before departing for heaven.

Their next daughter, Luciana Melora was born in 1873. They called her Lucy.

The last child, a boy named Evandon Shedrick, called Evan, joined the family in 1877. He studied at the University of Edinburgh and became a doctor.

Gerow and Myrta Gately became good friends of the Faulconer brothers and their families. The oldest Gately son, Welden, married Ginny Faulconer.

Liney and Statesman Prather moved to Orange, Virginia, adopted five orphans, and ran a profitable restaurant on Main Street. They visited the Chesterton children, in May every year, to gather at the family graveyard and remember Madelyn and Forrester, as well as Master Myers, whose grave was unknown.

Coffer Dunn went to Richmond and searched for his family. He found his sons and learned that his wife had died within a year after being sold at the slave auction. Coffer brought Moses, age 15, and Aaron, age 12, back to Spotsylvania County where he married Susa and bought a small farm, purchased with a bank loan guaranteed by Shedrick Trubridge. Moses, too, became a farmer. Aaron attended Oberlin College and became a teacher.

Eleutheros Supplee expanded his barrel-making business and crafted well-made furniture, becoming a successful merchant with an expanding work force. His first wife died in childbirth and he married a second time. They had five children.

Paxton's sister Eunice married Trusten Hite, had four children, and a happy marriage. Lorella never married because her sweetheart died at Petersburg. Instead, she continued teaching school and doted on her many nieces and nephews. During her parents' declining years, Lorella cared for them.

While Albany and Paxton were separated, from May 1864 to August 1865, they wrote letters to each other every few days, thus coming to know one another in a deeper way than their few weeks in May had enabled them to do. Albany also wrote a novel, loosely based on her own adventures during the war in her county. The difference from reality was that she made the hero to be a scoundrel who turned out to be good because he fell in love with the heroine, who had dressed in male attire. She mailed each chapter to Paxton who commented with neatly-written notes in the margins. Albany's novel was published and sold well. Paxton encouraged her to continue writing. She devoted an hour each morning before the family awoke, and published a novel every year or two. The love letters they had exchanged while separated the last year of the war were never published. They were treasured by their descendants and are still read by them today.

THE END

* * *

AFTERWORD

This is a story I was not eager to write. How do you tell a love story in the midst of two major battles? The Battles of the Wilderness and Spotsylvania Court House changed warfare. Previously, Civil War armies would fight, separate, pause, recruit, replenish, devise a new strategy, and strike again. This time, there was no retreat. Following the two-day Battle of the Wilderness, the killing went on day and night for thirteen days during the Battle of Spotsylvania Court House.

According to Confederate General Alexander, from May 5 [1864] to April 9 [1865], "the two armies were under each other's fire every day." [Page 346, <u>Fighting for the Confederacy, the Personal Recollections of General Edward Porter Alexander</u>, edited by Gary W. Gallagher.]

Because I wanted to write a story about a woman disguised as a soldier, I selected these two battles fought in May 1864 as the time for my heroine to wear men's attire and go onto the battlefield. Research has shown that at least four hundred women did this. Undoubtedly, there were many more about whom we do not know.

Some women went with their husbands. Single women joined alone. Their motivations varied from better pay to patriotism to adventure. Some women were envious of the freedom men enjoyed and merely wanted to escape their hum-drum lives. Because the Civil War brought a social revolution in freeing slaves, the gender traditions also changed dramatically. No longer were women confined to the kitchen, parlor, nursery, and bedroom. Now they could enter into a man's sphere. Now they could take part in the fiery furnace of war which would change our country forever.

As a re-enactor, I know what it feels like to wear Civil War clothing with the cumbersome hoop skirt, long sleeves with muslin under-sleeves

263

(even in the summer), pantalettes, camisole, gloves, hairnet, and bonnet. When I am in costume, I must remember to pick up my skirt so I don't step on the hem; to be careful when I eat so I don't soil my fingerless gloves; and to be mindful of my wig so my real hair doesn't show. Freedom comes when I change into blue jeans and tee shirt. The contrast is remarkable. With this knowledge of how important clothing is to a person's self-image, I could identify with my heroine.

The heroine's name came from my granddaughter Abigail, who said she thought Albany was such a pretty name. I chose Albany's male name because of the similarity to Albert Cashier, nee Jennie Hodgers, who enlisted in the 95th Illinois Volunteer Infantry on August 3, 1862, and continued to live after the war disguised as a man, even receiving a military pension.

Having two people fall in love during those May 1864 days of slaughter in Spotsylvania County seemed like a daunting plot to create. Nevertheless, I resolved to write Albany and Paxton's story, making the narrative as realistic as possible. Having the heroine suffer from post traumatic stress disorder seemed natural, especially considering the sheltered lifestyle of young, elite women in Victorian times. Having the hero suffer from survivor's guilt as well as feeling guilty about deserting his men, was an understandable consequence of the events described in the story.

In my draft of the first three chapters, I had the story begin on Tuesday, May 3, when the advance elements of the Union Army crossed the Rapidan River. However, I soon realized that the real story starts on Wednesday, May 4, when the entire Army of the Potomac made that crossing thus beginning the Overland Campaign. Therefore, I did some rewriting so my characters would experience those memorable events straightaway.

My readers and friends Tom and Nancy Roza in Campbell, California, suggested that I eliminate the mini table-of-contents at the beginning of each chapter as I have written in previous novels. Therefore, I have done so. My purpose for this chapter preview feature was to make the novel appear more like books published in the 19th century. I have replaced that italicized summary with the date of the events occurring in the chapter that follows.

The term xenophobia was unknown at the time period of this novel, but the symptoms were known. Xenophobia, the fear and hatred of strangers or foreigners, is usually outgrown as children come in contact with others. However, my heroine lives on a Virginia plantation which isolates her from the world, until suddenly the world comes to her county.

Dr. Philippe Pinel unchaining the insane in Paris is a story I learned from my service as a docent at the Indiana Medical History Museum. On the wall in the library of that museum there is a large reproduction of the famous painting of Dr. Pinel performing the merciful act of releasing the chained women. From seeing this painting and learning about moral therapy, I researched the York Retreat operated by the Quakers in the English county of my ancestors, Yorkshire.

Two articles from *Reader's Digest* helped me with the plot. Kim Porter's article "She Lifted a Finger" in the May 2018 issue confirmed my idea that Albany could suddenly overcome her post-traumatic stress and completely forget to be depressed as she helped Paxton. Also, Michaela Hass wrote "Fighting Trauma the Military Way" published in the June 2019 issue. This story told me that people who have a crisis, such as a near-death experience, post-traumatic stress, or feelings of utter helplessness, can become better by focusing on good things. My heroine Albany is an example of the wisdom in these two articles.

Although four major battles were fought in Spotsylvania County, my story takes place during only the last two of them. The other two battles were Fredericksburg in December 1862 and Chancellorsville in May 1863. In 1966, the National Park Service published a booklet about these four battles. I became intrigued by the title, Where A Hundred Thousand Fell. That astounding number of casualties in Spotsylvania County inspired me to use this county for my novel's title.

My younger son Gaven and I toured the Wilderness Battlefield in 1988. We planned to stop along the way and get something to eat. However, we did not find anywhere to stop, not a gas station, not a convenience store, nothing. When we returned to the Visitors' Center and told the Park Ranger, he replied: "It was a wilderness then and it's a wilderness now."

* * *

ACKNOWLEDGEMENTS

During my March 2017 research trip to Spotsylvania and Orange counties, Virginia, I received valuable help from Ms. Angel May, Administrator, The Exchange Hotel Museum in Gordonsville, Virginia. With the logo "Where History Lives On," this unique museum offers displays of the building's previous uses as a railroad depot hotel, a Civil War hospital, and a school for the Freedman's Bureau. Ms. May's interesting discussion about Gordonsville gave me the idea of this being the hometown of the hero.

As always, the National Park Rangers at the two visitors' centers were helpful and knowledgeable. I toured the Fredericksburg Battlefield on a chilly Sunday afternoon. At the Chancellorsville Battlefield, I saw displays about the Battle of the Wilderness and the Battle of Spotsylvania.

My bed and breakfast hosts, Marty and Victoria Tourville, at the Inn at Poplar Hill, Orange, Virginia, were gracious and hospitable. They went out of their way to provide Civil War information about their area to aid me in my research. I recommend their lovely hilltop inn.

I want to thank my granddaughter Gabrielle who shared her knowledge about horses when I texted her questions. My optometrist, Dr. Kimberly Forniss, gave me advice about temporary blindness. Renee Bennett, my friend in Macon, Georgia, gave me the Southern perspective, plus her wisdom regarding human behavior based on her years in the family services field.

When I became bogged down in writing this novel, I signed up for "Writing Great Fiction: Storytelling Tips and Techniques" by Professor James Hynes, and produced by Great Courses of Chantilly, Virginia. This excellent course of 24 lectures helped me overcome writer's block and spur me on to finish this story.

Once again, I say thank you to the valuable service provided by my proofreaders. As with my previous six novels, my longtime friend, Martha McDonald, provided not only typo corrections but also her ideas regarding the characters and plot. I always appreciate her insights.

Four people at my church shared their wisdom as they proofread this novel. John Gilmore, also a fellow Indianapolis Civil War Round Table member, is a long-time history buff who told me that he sometimes becomes so caught up in the story that he forgets to look for errors. The late Mary Donahue and Velma Dobbins were vigilant in proofing this novel. I appreciate their efforts to make this a better story.

The fourth person from my church who read this book in draft form is my pastor, to whom I dedicate this book. Despite his busy schedule, Rev. Mark McClintock took time not to just read but to critique this story as an editor would do. An author himself, Mark understands what is involved in this lonely work of writing and offered wise words about how to make Spotsylvania County a better novel. This is the first book he has edited for me and I tender my grateful thanks to him.

Another new proofreader, whose knowledge I admire, is Tony Trimble. Tony has been president of the Indianapolis Civil War Round Table several times and is related to General Isaac Ridgeway Trimble of Gettysburg fame. He is a professor of American history at Ivy Tech College in Indianapolis. When I emailed questions, Tony gave me quick and accurate replies.

After extensive revisions, based on suggestions by Rev. McClintock, three more people read and commented on the final draft. Nancy Niblack Baxter, author of Gallant Fourteenth: The Story of an Indiana Civil War Regiment, Cabinet of Curiosities from the Civil War in Indiana, and The Heartland Chronicles, commended the story.

Steve Magnusen, author of My Best Girl - Courage, Honor, and Love in the Civil War: The Inspiring Life Stories of Rufus Dawes and Mary Gates, is a member of the Indianapolis, Hamilton County (IN), Milwaukee, and Mid-Ohio Valley Civil War Round Tables. His knowledge of the war and his skill as an author were invaluable to me as he made suggestions to improve this novel.

My final reader was my daughter-in-law, Vicki Schofield, wife of my oldest son Rob. Having been a proofreader in the past, she did an excellent job of finding the tiny typos that are so easy to miss. Her proofreading skills are very much appreciated.

I appreciate these readers for critiquing <u>Spotsylvania County</u> and thus enabling me to make changes which improved the book. If any mistakes remain, I am responsible.

* * *

ABOUT THE AUTHOR

Nikki Lynne Stoddard Schofield, born during World War II, became seriously interested in the Civil War when she attended her first meeting of the Indianapolis Civil War Round Table and heard Alan Nolan, author of The Iron Brigade, present the program. She has remained an active member of that club of scholars ever since. Serving in various offices, Nikki has been president four times. She organized and led the annual week-long bus tour for several years.

Stoddard Schofield began writing Civil War romances shortly before her retirement as law librarian at Bingham Greenbaum Doll, a large law firm in downtown Indianapolis where she worked for 37 years. Her motivation for writing her first novel was reading a bad romance novel and thinking: "I can do better." Nikki set several criteria for her novel. Most important, the heroine and hero must be kind to each other and always together. Two common plot twists in romance novels which Nikki dislikes are the heroine and hero disliking each other at the beginning and having extensive separations. She resolved to avoid these devices in her story-telling.

Being a born-again Christian, Ms. Schofield always brings Christianity into her stories. She writes about people during the Civil War such as you might meet in any era, struggling to resolve the problems they confront.

At Speedway Baptist Church, Nikki serves as a deacon, adult Sunday school teacher, business meeting moderator, and assistant treasurer. She is active in the Cooperative Baptist Fellowship, affiliated with her church.

As a tour guide at Crown Hill Cemetery since 1993, she has developed Civil War tours including "Treason in Indianapolis" based on her third book, Treason Afoot. Many of the characters in that novel are buried at Crown Hill. Other tours she has created are "Drama and Disaster" and "Tombstones and Trees." One day a week, Nikki works as the staff genealogist at Crown Hill, the third largest private cemetery in the country.

Stoddard-Schofield is a docent at the Indiana Medical History Museum on the grounds of the former Central State Hospital for the mentally ill. For many years, she volunteered in the Manuscripts and Rare Books Division of the Indiana State Library, creating finding aids for the collection.

Nikki portrays several Civil War women for various events and meetings. Annually at Crown Hill, she tells Mary Logan's story of General John Logan establishing Memorial Day and portrays the second wife of Frederick Douglass for Spirit of Freedom honoring the black soldiers who fought for the Union in the Civil War. Her most recent portrayal is Clara Barton, known as the Angel of the Battlefield.

A member of the Buster Keaton International Fan Club, she attends the annual convention in Muskegon, Michigan, during the first week-end of October, which is close to the silent screen comedian's birthday.

Her other interests are reading, gardening, stamp collecting, old movies (especially film noir), and genealogy.

Nikki is the mother of two sons, Rob and Gaven, six grandchildren (Bridget, Stephanie, Nicholas, Abigail, Gabrielle, and Lily), and five great-grandchildren (Gee, Bella, Elias, Sebastian, and Aria). Born in Michigan, she has lived most of her life in Indianapolis.

* * *

BOOK CLUB DISCUSSION QUESTIONS

1. Are you surprised to learn that at least four hundred women dressed as men and served in the Civil War?
2. If you had lived at this time, would you have voluntarily joined the army?
3. Who is the character you most identify with and why?
4. What did you learn about the medical care during the Civil War?
5. How did knowledge of the blackened clearing affect you?
6. Did you find the Historic Notes of value?
7. Would you recommend this book to others?

* * *

CLASSROOM DISCUSSION QUESTIONS

1. What new fact did you learn about the Civil War?
2. If you had lived during the Civil War, on which side would you fight and why?
3. Does this story inspire you to read more about the Civil War?
4. Name a method of medical care during the Civil War that differs from today.
5. How does post traumatic stress disorder of today compare with what the heroine experienced in this story?
6. In what ways would you have behaved differently than Albany and Paxton did?
7. What aspects of the Civil War interest you the most?

* * *

APPENDIX OF HISTORIC NOTES

BATTLE OF THE WILDERNESS: The Battle of the Wilderness ended when night fell on May 7th. Union casualties were 15,387 killed, wounded, and missing. The Confederates lost 11,400. Those burned bodies in the blackened clearing remained unidentified. As for who won the Battle of the Wilderness, each army held substantially the same ground that they had when the two-day fight began. On the night of May 7-8, the two armies rushed toward Spotsylvania Court House to hold that vital crossroads.

* * *

BLOODY ANGLE: Two locations were named the Bloody Angle, one at Gettysburg on July 3 and one at Spotsylvania, where it was also called the Mule Shoe and the salient. When 20,000 Federal soldiers poured through the gaps they made in the line and controlled the cannon at the Bloody Angle in the Battle of Spotsylvania Court House on May 12, they turned those guns on their previous owners and fired at close range. The Confederates could not afford to leave their enemy in possession of the ground and made a strenuous effort to regain the position. Southern soldiers swarmed from the left to the broken point of their line and attacked the foe furiously. General Hancock fell back slowly. General Lee sent his men charging in attack five different times. The lines of combatants sometimes stood only a few feet apart. Federals captured several thousand prisoners. Acres of woodland were destroyed. Soldiers were under fire for twenty four hours.

* * *

CANNONS: Cannons were the basic artillery pieces on both sides during the war. They are metal tubes made of iron, bronze and steel, placed on

277

a mount, thus becoming artillery. The most popular was the Napoleon, a smooth-bore, muzzle-loading, 12-pound howitzer. According to Mark Mayo Boatner III, in The Civil War Dictionary, "the Napoleon probably inflicted more casualties than all the others combined." Besides cannon balls exploding out of the metal tubes, various other kinds of killing projectiles were used. Ammunition came in many descriptions. Smoothbores could hit a target 1,500 yards away, while rifled guns could reach 2,500 yards. Gatling guns, invented by Dr. Richard Gordon Gatling, were used by the Navy, but the Quartermaster for the Army did not want to spend the $1,000 which each one cost. General Benjamin Butler purchased six Gatling guns with his own money.

* * *

CHARLES DICKENS: Three years after the end of the Civil War, on April 18, 1868, Charles Dickens spoke at a public dinner held in New York City attended by 200 newspaper reporters. He said how astounded he was by the amazing changes he had seen on every side since his visit 26 years earlier. These changes were moral and physical, pertaining to the rise of vast new cities and the growth of older cities, and changes in the amenities and graces of life. Charles Dickens wrote about the United States both before and after the Civil War. He dedicated his book, American Notes for General Circulation to his friends in America who welcomed him and left his judgment free to write about the country they love, bearing the truth "when it is told good-humouredly and in a kind spirit."

* * *

CONSTANT RAIN: At 8 A.M. on Monday, May 16, 1864, General Grant sat at his field desk and wrote to Major-General Halleck in Washington, D.C. "We have had five days almost constant rain without any prospect yet of it clearing up. The roads have now become so impassable that ambulances with wounded men can no longer run between here and Fredericksburg. All offensive operations necessarily cease until we can have twenty-four hours of dry weather. The army is in the best of spirits, and feels the greatest confidence of ultimate success."

* * *

EMORY UPTON'S BOLD PLAN: Colonel Upton's daring plan on May 10, worked to perfection. During his hour or so of fighting, he learned that Lee's line could be broken. The salient was the weak spot. The Northern army captured 913 enlisted men and 37 officers. But Upton was angry that the Federal high command failed to send reinforcements and properly support the breakthrough. With their interior lines, the Southerners had a great advantage because they could move soldiers quickly to needed locations. After Upton's attack was over, the armies rested until the next fight along the Confederate line, a fight that was larger and the bloodshed greater. Its location was just a quarter of a mile east of Doles' Salient where Colonel Upton broke through.

* * *

GENERAL GRANT AND MAPS: General Grant seldom consulted maps, in comparison to most commanders during the Civil War. The reason for this was that once he saw a map, Ulysses seemed to photographically imprint the details in his brain. The General could follow the features without referring to the map again. Besides this ability, General Grant had an almost intuitive understanding of topography. He never got confused about the points of a compass. In fact, he lost his bearings only once, in Cairo, Illinois, where the looping configuration of the Mississippi River bewildered him. Concerning that occasion, he said, "The effect of that curious bend in the river turned me completely around, and when the sun came up the first morning after I got there, it seemed to be that it rose directly in the west." Now, in Spotsylvania County, there was no such confusion. General Grant knew where he was going – south; and he knew why – to annihilate the Confederate Army.

* * *

J.E.B. STUART'S DEATH: At the Battle of Yellow Tavern, on Wednesday, May 11, the beloved commander of the Confederate cavalry, James Ewell Brown Stuart, defended the city of Richmond from a Union raid led by General Phillip Sheridan. General Stuart emptied his pistol on withdrawing Michigan cavalry. Private John A. Huff, an expert marksman, aimed his 44-caliber pistol and shot Stuart in the right side of his abdomen. Soldiers transported J.E.B. to the home of his brother-in-law, Dr. Charles Brewer, in Richmond, where he died the next day. When General Lee received the news,

279

he told his staff that General Stuart never delivered a piece of false information to him. The Confederate commander was clearly shaken by the death of his flamboyant cavalry leader.

* * *

MEDICAL CARE: Medical care during the Civil War experienced major changes in the way the sick and injured received treatment. These changes were due to the skillful doctors who made life-and-death decisions. In the North, Surgeon General William Hammond had the foresight to recognize the value of wartime experiences in learning from the wounded, and established the Army Medical Museum to which doctors donated specimens and reports for education and study. In the South, Major Hunter Holmes McGuire, while only in his 20s, served as the medical director of the Stonewall Brigade and organized the lifesaving ambulance corps. Whether in a field hospital or a city hospital, soldiers were getting better care as the war progressed and doctors utilized newly-acquired knowledge to benefit the wounded.

* * *

MENTAL ILLNESS: Mental illness during the Victorian Era gained no benefit from psychiatry. Most doctors equated any deviation from social and moral standards as insanity. Mentally ill people were called lepers, moral refuse, tainted persons, and demon-possessed. Some said that insane people were less capable of recovering than a savage was able to depart from barbarism. Soldiers with mental health problems were seen as malingerers, weak-willed, and cowards. The distortion of reality which raged in the minds of mentally ill people found no cure from the various methods of quackery. The great crusader for better treatment of the insane, Dorothea Dix, said that insanity could reasonably be treated as curable as a cold or a fever.

* * *

NIGHT OF MAY 8-9: Because General Grant wanted to break the deadlock at Spotsylvania Court House, now held by the Confederates, he consulted with his commanders throughout the night of May 8-9. He ordered a portion of Major General Winfield Hancock's Second Corps to cross the Po, a branch of the Mattaponi River, and find General Lee's left flank. But the

Rebel spies saw Hancock's move. Therefore, Confederates shifted divisions to counter the plan. Throughout the night, gray-clad soldiers used their bayonets and tin cups to dig trenches, stack fence rails and logs, thus constructing abatis as an obstacle to protect them against the bullets to come. They were unaware that the salient they created would become famous as the Bloody Angle.

* * *

PROVOST MARSHALS: Provost Marshals were the military police of the army. During the American Revolution, General George Washington requested that a provost marshal position be created to handle disciplinary problems. William Maroney, appointed in 1776, was the first Provost Marshal of the Continental Army. The Office of the Provost Marshal General was established in the middle of the Civil War, in 1863. They oversaw the Veterans Reserve Corps, the group which maintained law and order at the garrison locations. Other provost guards served on the front lines. They carried the Harper's Ferry Pistol, manufactured at the Harper's Ferry Arsenal. When the Civil War ended, they were no longer needed.

* * *

UNIQUE FIGHTING: There had never been fighting like that which existed in Spotsylvania County in the month of May 1864. In military operations, the usual way of combat was for the opposing armies to come together, fight one battle, and then separate. The strain of battle would last only a few days, such as the three-day Battle of Gettysburg. When there was a siege, only a small portion of the opposing forces are close together. However, the warfare in the spring of 1864 when Grant first faced Lee was different. As Confederate General Edward Porter Alexander wrote in <u>Fighting for the Confederacy</u>, page 386, quoting Union General Andrew Humphreys, "From the 5th of May 1864 to the 9th of April 1865, they were in constant close contact, with rare intervals of brief comparative repose."

* * *

XENOPHOBIA: Xenophobia, the fear and hatred of strangers or foreigners, goes back a long way in history. Ancient Greeks called foreigners "barbarians," and believed themselves superior. This idea justified their enslaving foreigners *whom they conquered. Ancient Romans also considered themselves better than other people, whom they called worthless and born for slavery. Although not a recognized medical phobia, xenophobia nevertheless manifests itself in many ways similar to a physical fear. As an anxiety disorder, xenophobia can cause the sufferer to experience significant emotional distress. Specific phobias can be treated with exposure therapy, where the affected person confronts the object or situation causing the stress until that fear is resolved. During the Civil War, the word xenophobia was unknown.*

* * *

RESOURCES

The author consulted these books and recommends them for further reading about this important story in our country's Civil War history.

Alexander, Edward Porter, <u>Fighting for the Confederacy, The Personal Recollections of General Edward Porter Alexander</u>, Edited by Gary W. Gallagher, University of North Carolina Press, 1989

Aubrecht, Michael, <u>The Civil War in Spotsylvania County, Confederate Campfires at the Crossroads</u>, The History Press, 2009

Bierce, Ambrose, <u>Ambrose Bierce's Civil War</u>, edited and with an introduction by William McCann, Warbler Classics, 2019

Boatner, Mark Mayo, III, <u>The Civil War Dictionary</u>, David McKay Company, Inc., 1959

Charles River Editors, <u>The Overland Campaign, The Battles of The Wilderness, Spotsylvania Court House, North Anna, and Cold Harbor</u>, Charles River Editions, 2020

Cutshaw, Wilfred Emory, <u>The Battle Near Spotsylvania Courthouse on May 18, 1864</u>, An Address delivered January 20, 1905, Forgotten Books, 2015

Dame, William Meade, <u>From the Rapidan to Richmond</u>, Owens Publishing Company, 1987

Dickens, Charles, <u>American Notes For General Circulation</u>, Made in the USA, Lexington, KY, 14 December 2017; originally published 1842

Dunkerly, Robert M., Donald C. Pfanz, and David R. Ruth, <u>No Turning Back, A Guide to the 1864 Overland Campaign from the Wilderness to Cold Harbor, May 4-June 13, 1864</u>, Savas Beatie, 2014

Faust, Drew Gilpin, <u>This Republic of Suffering, Death and the American Civil War</u>, Random House, Inc., 2008

Fitzpatrick, David J., <u>Emory Upton, Misunderstood Reformer</u>, University of Oklahoma Press, 2017

Frassanito, William A., <u>Grant and Lee, The Virginia Campaigns, 1864-1865</u>, Charles Scribner's Sons, 1983

Gallagher, Gary W., editor, <u>The Spotsylvania Campaign</u>, University of North Carolina Press, 1998

Garrison, Webb, with Cheryl Garrison, <u>The Encyclopedia of Civil War Usage</u>, Cumberland House Publishing, Inc., 2001

Gottfried, Bradley M., <u>The Maps of the Wilderness</u>, Savas Beatie LLC, 2016

Grant, Ulysses S., <u>Memoirs and Selected Letters, 1839-1865</u>, Penguin Books, 1990

Haas, Michaela, "Fighting Trauma the Military Way," Reader's Digest, June 2019

Holzer, Harold, & Craig L. Symonds, editors, <u>The New York Times Complete Civil War, 1861-1865</u>, Black Dog & Leventhal Publishers, 2010

Jaynes, Gregory and the Editors of Time-Life Books, <u>The Killing Ground, Wilderness to Cold Harbor</u>, Time-Life Books, 1986

Jordan, David M., <u>Winfield Scott Hancock, A Soldier's Life</u>, Indiana University Press, 1988

Kernek, Clyde B., M.D. <u>Field Surgeon at Gettysburg</u>, Guild Press of Indiana, 1993

Longstreet, James, <u>From Manassas to Appomattox, Memoirs of the Civil War</u>, First Rate Publishers, unknown date

Mackowski, Chris, <u>Hell Itself, The Battle of the Wilderness, May 5-7, 1864</u>, Savas Beatie, 2016

Mackowski, Chris, and Kristopher D. White, <u>A Season of Slaughter, The Battle of Spotsylvania Court House, May 8-21, 1864</u>, Beatie Savas, 2013

Matter, William D., <u>If It Takes All Summer, The Battle of Spotsylvania</u>, University of North Carolina Press, 1988

McElfresh, Earl B., <u>Maps and Mapmakers of the Civil War</u>, Harry N. Abrams, Inc., Publishers, 1999

Porter, Horace, <u>Campaigning with Grant</u>, 1906, Big Byte Books, reprint 2016

Porter, Kim, "She Lifted a Finger," Reader's Digest, May 2018

Rable, George C., <u>The Confederate Republic, A Revolution Against Politics</u>, University of North Carolina Press, 1994

Rhea, Gordon C., <u>The Battles for Spotsylvania Court House and the Road to Yellow Tavern, May 7-12, 1864</u>, Louisiana State University Press, 1997

Rhea, Gordon C., <u>The Battles of Wilderness & Spotsylvania</u>, Eastern National, 2014

Sheehan-Dean, Aaron, editor, <u>The Civil War, The Final Year Told By Those Who Lived It</u>, Literary Classics, 2014

Shenk, Joshua Wolf, <u>Lincoln's Melancholy</u>, Houghton Mifflin Company, 2005

Silber, Irwin, compiler and editor, <u>Songs of the Civil War</u>, Dover Publications, Inc., 1995

Sorrell, G. Moxley, <u>Recollections of a Confederate Staff Officer</u>, G. Moxley Sorrell, 1905

Straubing, Harold Elk, <u>In Hospital and Camp, The Civil War through the Eyes of Its Doctors and Nurses</u>, Stackpole Books, 1993

Thomas, Benjamin P. and Harold M. Hyman, <u>Stanton, The Life and Times of Lincoln's Secretary of War</u>, Alfred A. Knopf, 1962

Thomas, William H. B., <u>Gordonsville, Virginia, Historic Crossroads Town</u>, Green Publishers, Inc., 1980

Trudeau, Noah Andre, <u>Bloody Roads South, The Wilderness to Cold Harbor, May-June 1864</u>, Little Brown and Company, 1989

Tsouras, Peter G., <u>Major General George H. Sharpe and the Creation of American Military Intelligence in the Civil War</u>, Casemate Publishers, 2018

Tsouras, Peter G., Editor, <u>Scouting for Grant and Meade, The Reminiscences of Judson Knight, Chief of Scouts, Army of the Potomac</u>, Skyhorse Publishing, 2014

Various Authors of Articles in <u>Battles and Leaders of the Civil War</u>, Volume IV, The Century Co., 1888

Walker, Frank S., Jr., <u>Echoes of Orange</u>, Orange County Historical Society, 2013

Wright, John D., <u>The Timeline of the Civil War, The Ultimate Guide To The War That Defined America</u>, Thunder Bay Press, 2007

* * *